"You, sir," Sarah said, lifting her chin, "are a self-absorbed country gentleman with very little to recommend himself to a lady."

"Am I?" Geoffrey asked, stalking toward her.

"A tyrant and a boor," Sarah continued. "You should be kissing Melanie's feet; she is so kind and good. But then, perhaps I shouldn't suggest that. No doubt, your kisses are as ungallant as the rest of you and Melanie is glad to escape them."

"My kisses are none of your concern," Geoffrey snapped.

"A sweet mercy," Sarah said. "I was merely pitying poor Melanie."

"Pity her, do you?" Geoffrey said, reaching out and jerking her to him. Sarah had not a moment to object, for his lips captured hers swiftly. Sarah froze, struck by a sensual lightning. She'd been kissed before—chaste salutes, begged honors, worshipful offerings. Geoffrey's kiss did not worship, it demanded equal desire.

Sarah, held tightly against a body with a strength even greater than hers, met that desire with a new, unknown passion of her own. She became fluid heat as Geoffrey bent her, his hands learning her curves, even as she learned the taste and scent and power of the man. Yet their kiss changed. No longer did it hold demand, but gentled to one of breathless need and shared wonderment . . .

Books by Cindy Holbrook

A SUITABLE CONNECTION

LADY MEGAN'S MASQUERADE

A DARING DECEPTION

COVINGTON'S FOLLY

A RAKE'S REFORM

LORD SAYER'S GHOST

THE ACTRESS AND THE MARQUIS

THE COUNTRY GENTLEMAN

Published by Zebra Books

The Country Gentleman

Cindy Holbrook

Zebra Books
Kensington Publishing Corp.
http://www.zebrabooks.com

ZEBRA BOOKS are published by

Kensington Publishing Corp.
850 Third Avenue
New York, NY 10022

First Printing: December, 1997
10 9 8 7 6 5 4 3 2 1

Printed in the United States of America

One

"You shall not have me," Sarah said. She lifted the bronze statue clutched in her hand and brought it down with a resounding clank upon Ravenwich's head.

Ravenwich stiffened. His strangling hands slid from her throat. Surprise, and then outrage, flared in his dark eyes as he stared at the statue in her hand. "Damn you!" he whispered, and toppled over.

Sarah, stunned, looked at the statue. It was Ravenwich's prized one of the god Pan. The frolicsome god was decidedly bent, as if doubled over in pain; very much like his owner, no doubt. Sarah's gaze turned to Ravenwich and froze.

He lay sprawled, his head at an odd angle, a footstool toppled close to him.

"Ravenwich?" Sarah asked. She dropped the statue to move swiftly to him. Her hand shook as she reached out to feel for a pulse at his throat. It shook even more when she could not divine one. She jerked her hand back and stood.

He was surely dead. If not, it did not matter. She was at his isolated estate and the only residents within were his relatives. Clearly, they would not applaud or support her mayhem, even if it was in defense of her virtue. She could envision herself stepping outside the room and saying to Ravenwich's kith and kin, "I'm so sorry to interrupt the engagement party, but I am not going to marry Ravenwich and I have killed him. I hope you do not object."

She shook her head. She doubted if even *she* could manage to pull that one off and she didn't intend to try. In this god-forsaken place they could have her tried and hanged before anyone knew. She moved quickly to grab her shawl from the floor and wrap it around her bruised throat and torn bodice. Quietly, she slipped out the door and hastened through the house. She gained a strange look from the butler when she crossed the foyer and made directly toward the door. His expression turned to surprise when she said in haughty tones, "I believe I shall take a turn in the gardens."

It showed the man's training that he did not question her, even though the hour was late, she was in a disheveled state, and it looked to rain soon. It only strengthened her resolve not to marry Ravenwich, that was, if he had been alive and not dead. Servants took their behavior from their masters and it was clear Ravenwich's butler did not concern himself with the proprieties and would tolerate any kind of havy-cavy behavior.

Sarah struck out across the yard and slipped into the stables. She could hear the grooms in the back tack room, their discussion about whose turn it was to deal the cards a loud and fractious one. Quietly, steadily, she saddled the nearest horse, whose snorts and whinnies could not compete with the men's disagreement.

Sarah mounted the horse. The animal fretted and objected, but received no quarter from her as she goaded it out of the stable door and whipped him into a gallop. She did not know the direction she took, nor did she care.

Three hours later, the threatening rain came unleashed, pouring down in torrents. Thunder rumbled. A brilliant streak of lightning rent the night sky. Sarah's horse screamed and reared. The slick reins slipped through her numb grasp. She flew from the horse's back.

She hit the ground, rolled, and then scrambled up as the beast disappeared into the darkness. Sarah stared after it one dazed, angry moment. She shouldn't have expected more from a horse out of Ravenwich's stables.

Turning, Sarah lunged from the road, diving into the woods. A branch snagged at her shawl and she ripped it from her, deserting it as she crashed through the underbrush. The ground beneath her suddenly disappeared and she fell, rolling down the steep incline of a ravine. She splashed into a cold, stagnant pond at the bottom of that abyss. Surfacing, she waded forward and fell upon the muddy bank. Her fingers dug into the sludge.

"Disgraceful," she said, and laid her head down.

Her hands relaxed and the tension drained from her body.

Geoffrey, the Earl of Grey, moved silently through the woods carrying his gun, his eyes alert. Dawn tinged the trees pink, and the woods, washed from the night's storm, offered up its finest scents. This was the time he liked to hunt most.

He topped the ravine and halted as his gaze caught a flash of white upon the bank of the pond below. Eyes narrowed, he realized the huddled shape which had drawn his attention was human. Cursing, he swiftly traversed the incline and came to stand over the still body.

He knelt and turned it over. He pushed back sodden, muddy hair to discover the even muddier face of a woman.

"Madame," he said, and patted her cheek.

The woman did not stir. Her skin was cold to his touch. He slid his fingers to the base of her throat. The slightest pulse fluttered there. Without hesitation, he picked up the wet, grimy woman. She was of a sturdy size and weight and Geoffrey thought it was fortunate he had discovered her and not some other man of lesser stature.

He hefted her up over his shoulder and without any more consideration began to walk.

* * *

Geoffrey shifted his heavy burden and opened the door to Grey Manor. He entered into the gleaming foyer and shouted, "Mrs. Biddington, come here!" He paused but a moment and then strode across the foyer toward the side stairs.

"My lord!" a high, quivering voice called out.

Geoffrey turned to discover Mrs. Biddington, his house-keeper, standing in the door across from the foyer. Mrs. Biddington was a small, birdlike woman with nervous movements. She twitched uncontrollably now and her faded blue eyes bulged from her head. "What . . . what is it?"

"*It* is a woman, I believe," Geoffrey said.

"A . . . a woman?" Mrs. Biddington gasped. Her gaze fell to the marble floor. A definite trail of mud and water betrayed his path. "Oh, dear."

Geoffrey shrugged. "I am sorry, it could not be helped. I found her down at the pond well nigh drowned."

"But . . . but who is she?" Mrs. Biddington asked.

The weight of his burden was growing heavier by the moment. "I do not know, she has not deigned to speak. Most likely because she is unconscious. Be pleased to send Thomas for a doctor, and set to heating some water so that we may give her a bath."

"My lord!" squeaked Mrs. Biddington.

"I meant you," Geoffrey said, gritting his teeth. "I myself will be in need of one as well."

"Y-yes, my lord," Mrs. Biddington said in a strangled voice.

Geoffrey turned toward the stairs once more. "I shall put her in the blue room."

"Should I also send a message to Mrs. Devon and Miss Melanie?" Mrs. Biddington asked.

Geoffrey halted and turned. "Why should you send for them?"

"W-we do not know who she is," Mrs. Biddington said, "and . . . and this is a bachelor's establishment."

Geoffrey frowned. "Mrs. Biddington, do you actually

imagine this muddy baggage I carry is in any danger from me, or I from her?"

Mrs. Biddington drew herself up to her full short height. "I was only thinking of the proprieties."

"The proprieties will not be necessary if she dies on us," Geoffrey said. "Now, do what I order."

He turned sharply and took the stairs, fully irritated. Mrs. Biddington was an excellent female, and knew exactly how to order his establishment to his liking, but her slips into feminine vapors and excessive sensibilities did not please him one whit. He strode into the blue room and gave it a cursory glance. Debating which piece of furniture to soil with his sodden charge, he decided upon the brocade chair set next to the fire. Patterned with full-blooming roses, it was a piece he did not favor.

He walked toward the chair, but suddenly tripped over the fringe of a throw rug. He lost his balance and toppled directly forward. His fall was cushioned by the body he carried, his curse muffled against a muddy, full chest.

"Good Lord . . . what . . . ?" a low female voice said. The woman beneath him stirred. Geoffrey was just able to raise his head far enough over her chest to catch the woman's gaze as she peered at him. He saw her eyes widen. Then her mouth opened just as wide.

"Don't scream," Geoffrey said, realizing the significance. "I'm not . . ."

She screamed. Then she erupted into a squirming, slapping fury. She boxed his ears resoundingly. "No, you shall not!"

"Stop it!" Geoffrey commanded, and strove to untangle himself. "I'm not going to hurt you." He received a well-placed fist to the jaw for that. Cursing, he finally broke free. He sprung to his feet. The woman sat up quickly, two green or perhaps blue eyes, blazing from a face of mud. "Damn," he said, nursing his jaw. "I told you I wasn't going to hurt you."

"Just what were you doing then?" she asked, breathing heavily.

"I fell," Geoffrey said.

She blinked. "You fell?"

"Yes," Geoffrey said. "I was carrying you and I fell. I assure you, I harbored no base intentions."

Her eyes narrowed. "Why were you carrying me?"

Geoffrey stiffened. "I am not certain anymore. I found you unconscious down at the pond. I made the mistake of not leaving you there."

"I—I see," she said. She studied him a moment. It seemed she smiled, or at least the caked mud around her lips cracked. "You actually carried me?"

"Yes," Geoffrey said. " 'Twas no easy task."

" 'Tis ungallant of you to admit it," she said. Groaning, she crawled from the floor to her feet. She immediately swayed. Geoffrey, muttering a curse, went to support her.

She slapped at him. "Unhand me, sir! Unhand me, I say!"

"With pleasure," Geoffrey said, and drew back.

"Heavens," the lady said, and lurched drunkenly. Geoffrey reached once more for her, but she waved him away. "I shall do fine, sir, if you will desist in manhandling me."

"Manhandling you?" Geoffrey asked, his arms falling to his side. "Faith, I far preferred you when you were unconscious."

"My exact sentiments," she said. Her gaze traveled about the room and then returned to appraise him. "You are quite dirty, you know?"

"If I am dirty it is because of you," Geoffrey said, looking pointedly at her.

The woman looked down at herself. "Yes, so I see." Her tone was displeased. She took a cautious step and pulled in a breath. "Lud, you have certainly bruised me."

"I did not," Geoffrey said. "I have no doubt you arrived that way."

"Did I?" she murmured. "Faith, I am weak as a kitten. If I could rest a moment?"

"Sit over there." Geoffrey pointed at the rose chair.

"But I shall soil it," she said.

" 'Tis of no moment," Geoffrey said. "I dislike the chair."

The woman chuckled. "In that case I shall oblige you." She tottered over and Geoffrey clenched his hands in determination not to assist her. She fell into the chair in a heap. She straightened, and even with the muck and mud, she appeared regal. "Who are you, sir?"

"Who am *I?*" Geoffrey asked, stiffening. "Rather, who are *you?*"

She did not answer him direct, but studied him a moment. Then she smiled and said, "I did ask you first."

"Very well. I am Geoffrey Vincent, the Earl of Grey."

"And most definitely not at my service," the lady said in a dry tone. Considering Geoffrey had carried her all the way from the pond and then received a good cuffing for it, he thought her comment went beyond the mark. She cocked her head to one side. "The Earl of Grey . . . I do not remember the name. Do you know me, sir?"

Geoffrey exhaled a breath of impatience. "I would not have asked who you were if I already knew, would I?"

"No, I suppose not," she said. "But please think, are you positive you do not know me?"

"Madame," Geoffrey said with gritted teeth. "I am positive I do not."

"I see," she said, and then sighed. " 'Tis a pity."

"Madame, I doubt that," Geoffrey said.

She looked at him and laughed, a deep, rich laugh. "No, Mister Ungallant, I would agree with you upon that head. However, if you did know me, it would at least be a convenience, not a pleasure to be sure, but a convenience."

"Why would it be convenient?" Geoffrey asked.

She smiled. "Because you could tell me my name."

"What?"

"My name," the woman said. "Then you could tell me . . ."

"I heard that," Geoffrey said. "But what do you mean by it?"

"It is quite mortifying really," she said. "But I fear my name appears to have slipped my memory. As well as any other thought of who I am, where I am, or how I came to be here."

"What?" Geoffrey roared.

She lifted her chin. "My lord, I may not remember my name, but I distinctly remember you asking that only moments ago. Can you not ask me something else?"

Geoffrey stiffened. "I do not care about anything else, I just want to know your name."

"I assure you," the woman said. "I would like to as well."

"Good God," Geoffrey said. "Just what kind of foolery is this?"

"The foolery of one who cannot seem to remember her name," the woman answered. "I have no doubt, if given time, I shall remember."

"Madness," Geoffrey muttered, and paced across the room. "Sheer madness."

"So it would seem," the lady said, watching him. "But I do not feel exactly deranged. I have no desire whatsoever to rant or rave. Unlike some people."

Geoffrey halted and glared at her. "Madame, I am not ranting or raving, but I cannot believe you do not know your name."

"Yes, it does seem rather silly," she admitted. "And quite confusing. I seem to remember to speak, with words and everything, but when I try to say my name, it eludes me. And when I try to think of memories, they seem to be hidden from me. Very disconcerting, not to have memories, I assure you."

"Amnesia," Geoffrey said.

"Is that my name?" the woman asked, smiling. "I thought you said you didn't know . . ."

"No." Geoffrey waved an impatient hand. "It is a sickness or condition rather. Brought upon by either one being hit in the head . . . or suffering a trauma one does not wish to remember."

"Oh, are you a doctor?" the woman said. "How fortunate."

"I am not a doctor," Geoffrey said. " 'Tis merely that I read extensively."

"I see," she said, and frowned. "It appears that is what I have, or as you said, I am mad." She laughed then. "Or merely a want-wit. I seem to *think* I am intelligent, though I cannot be certain, of course."

"Perhaps too intelligent," Geoffrey said, with narrowed eyes.

The woman looked up at him and he saw her stiffen. She stood slowly. "Well, I cannot say it was a pleasure to meet you, Lord Grey, for I doubt you would permit me that polite lie. But I can thank you for dragging me from the pond." She walked toward him and held out her hand. "I shall take my leave now. I am sorry I am unable to return the favor of a name, but there you have it." Geoffrey merely stared down at her muddy hand. She pulled it back. "Forgive me. I have shared enough of my mud with you, have I not?" She walked past him toward the door.

Geoffrey spun. "Just where do you think you are going?"

She turned, her hand upon the door. "I do not know, but I can see I have trespassed upon your 'charity' long enough."

"You intend to go wandering the roads looking like that and without a memory of your name?" Geoffrey asked.

"What is in a name?" she said, waving a grimy hand. "But if you would be so kind as to tell me where I am?"

"You are at Grey Manor," Geoffrey answered curtly. "The next residence is ten miles from here, and the village twenty miles."

"Which village is that?" she asked.

"Thomasonville," Geoffrey said.

"Thomasonville?" she said.

"You'll have a long walk," Geoffrey said implacably.

She looked at him, and suddenly she swayed. Muttering an oath, Geoffrey swiftly crossed the room and caught her up. This time she did not fight. Her fingers clutched his jacket and she sagged heavily against him. "Oh, dear."

"Damn!" Geoffrey said, and picked her up in his arms. He carried her to the bed, but as he bent to lay her upon it, she clutched him around the shoulders.

"No," she said. "I shall soil the bed."

"I do not care," he said, lowering her down.

"Do you not like anything in this room?" she asked, still clutching to him.

"Madame," Geoffrey said, discovering himself in the awkward position of being gripped by a woman supine upon a bed, "now 'tis you who manhandle me."

"Yes," she murmured, and slowly drew her arms from him. "Th-there is nothing more tiresome th-than being mauled, is there not?"

Geoffrey stood and stared down at the grimy woman, nonplussed. Her head was turned away from him and he saw her body shake. Unaccountably, Geoffrey picked up her hand. She would not look at him, but she clutched it tightly.

"I am sorry," she said. "Now I am being truly foolish. And here I thought I was . . . was acting so well."

"You were," Geoffrey said.

She turned to look at him, tears swelling in her eyes. "Thank you."

"Madame," Geoffrey's voice was strained. "Do anything but cry."

"Odious, is it not?" she said, sniffing. "I rarely resort to it. It is so useless, and it makes one's eyes so unbecomingly red."

Geoffrey stared at her, not certain if she were serious or not. "Indeed. Now rest. I have sent for the doctor and he should arrive soon."

"The doctor? Do you think he'll know me?"

"No," Geoffrey said. "But I wish to ascertain that you are not hurt in any other manner."

"Of course." The woman's chuckle was a cross between a laugh and sniff. "I was not thinking."

"I have also ordered a bath to be brought up," Geoffrey said.

"A bath! How wonderful," the woman said, her eyes lighting. "And here I castigated you upon your lack of gallantry. Forgive me."

Geoffrey pulled his hand away and stepped back. "Of course. I shall leave you so that you may rest, madame."

"Do not call me madame," she said upon a sigh. "It makes me think of a headmistress."

"Then what should I call you?" Geoffrey asked.

She smiled slightly. "Amnesia?"

He shook his head. "No, it will not serve."

"Then let us shorten it," she said. "How about Ami?"

Geoffrey started. "No! No, that is not a proper name."

"Really?" the woman said. She turned her head away. "Then Amy shall have to do for now."

"Yes," Geoffrey said. "That will do."

She did not look back at him and Geoffrey silently left the room.

Lady Sarah sat upon a clean bed. She was mercifully clean, her hair washed and drying. She was dressed in Lord Grey's nightshirt. Lord Grey's tiny housekeeper, Mrs. Biddington, had been in a regular fluster over what to put Sarah in, informing her it was a bachelor's establishment and there was not a female employee who came near to matching Sarah's grander lines. Fortunately, the housekeeper, once calmed, had bethought herself of Lord Grey's nightshirt. That having been settled, Sarah was finally left to herself to await Dr. Hobbs, who apparently could not come to her until he had delivered a certain Lucy Tillington of child.

Sarah drew her knees up and hugged them. Oddly enough, she finally felt safe. She had searched her memory, and seemed to remember a man in passing who had talked about a distant cousin, a Lord Grey, who was a queer fellow, a recluse who spurned London and his peers and resided somewhere in the wilds of Devon. She could not ascertain how far she had ridden last night, but perhaps she had succeeded in finding that "wilds of Devon," and hopefully it was that Lord Grey in whose house she resided and whose nightshirt she wore.

She knew well she had never seen the tall, blond man with the impatient gray eyes before. She was wont to remember any man who could top her five feet and nine inches by a goodly five more. Also, his unfashionably direct personality could not have been missed or forgotten.

She laid her head upon her knees and closed her eyes tightly. She wondered how long she could possibly deceive the gentleman. She knew she had offset him when she had stated she could not remember her name. It was fortunate he was knowledgeable enough to know of the condition, else the ruse would not have worked. It almost had not worked, she thought with a frown. He indeed had almost let her walk out the door.

Her notion to faint was masterful, yet the fact that she had well nigh done the actual deed when he had held her worried her. That she had clung to him so and started crying was beyond everything foolish. She could not afford to lose control, nor become a weak, silly woman if she were to deceive the gentleman.

She shook herself sternly, bracing her confidence. She was not called the Incomparable Lady Sarah for nothing. Surely if she had all of London at her feet, she could manage to wrap one country gentleman around her finger, no matter how unusual and brisk he was. And wrap him around her finger she would, for she could not have him discover her true identity or that she had killed her fiancé.

Sarah snapped her eyes open quickly, and scrabbled from the bed. She walked swiftly to the fire that had been lit on her behalf. She stretched out shaking hands to the flames, feeling cold, cold to her marrow. She had been such a fool. She should never have accepted Ravenwich's proposal of marriage in the first place. She knew Ravenwich was considered a dangerous man, knew his reputation as a rake and libertine. But at the time, those were the very things that had drawn her to him. She had become so weary of her endless social rounds and the fawning men, that when Ravenwich entered her life she had enjoyed the excitement and challenge.

Her father had warned her she was playing with danger out of boredom and he had said it would be better for her to join him in his hunts in Africa to dispel it, rather than to marry Ravenwich. Sarah remembered laughing, saying he did not know what he was talking about and then promising not to become wed until after his sojourn there.

Then she had discovered Ravenwich had bedded a young maid servant and gotten her with child and had cast the poor girl off with shocking cruelty. Sarah had been so enraged, she had not considered her tenuous position when she had confronted him in private and broken their engagement. Of course, never in her wildest imagination would she have dreamed he would try to force her into marriage by raping her. Or that she would accidentally kill him.

She drew her hands from the fire and hugged herself tightly. It was useless to repine. Her father always said there was no good in regret, or fighting what one could not change. She could not change the past, but she could try and control her future. She was safe for a moment within this household, if she could only maintain her pose. She knew she would have to return to the world sometime, and face whatever charges would be leveled against her. She would wait, however, until her father returned, and she had not only her own money and position to support her, but his as well. She was no fool. It was still a man's world, and that was one thing she was not.

A knock at the door distracted Sarah and she turned. "Come in."

The door opened and Mrs. Biddington entered. She stopped abruptly. "Oh, oh, my dear."

Sarah lifted a brow. "What is it, Mrs. Biddington?"

"I—I did not know you were up," Mrs. Biddington said. "D-doctor Hobbs has arrived."

Sarah sighed. "Very well, please show him in."

Mrs. Biddington retreated and then returned with a blustery older man. When he saw Lady Sarah he started and exclaimed, "Gadzooks."

Sarah smiled. "How do you do, Doctor Hobbs?"

The man stared. "Fine. Fine. I am here to see how you are instead, Miss . . ."

"Call me Amy," Sarah said. "And I am well, I believe, except for an unfortunate lapse of memory."

"I am sorry Mother was unable to come," Melanie said as she sat upon the settee. "But she has gone to visit Aunt Mary, who is sick. Indeed, I received a missive from her just before yours arrived, asking for me to follow her."

Geoffrey looked up from where he stood at the fire. " 'Tis of no moment. It was Mrs. Biddington's notion after all. She seemed to think it scandalous to have a strange woman in my household without a proper chaperone."

Melanie laughed. "Indeed, that is Mrs. Biddington's way."

Geoffrey laughed. "I don't know who she thought needed the chaperone. If she worried about the woman, she knows very well I am no ladies' man. And if she worried about me, I fear her attics are to let, for a more unappealing, nettlesome woman I have yet to meet."

"She really does not remember who she is?" Melanie asked. She shook her head. "How very dreadful. She must be so frightened."

"Frightened? Not she," Geoffrey said. "Women who are frightened do not cuff you and then tax you on your lack of gallantry."

Melanie's eyes widened. "She did that?"

"She did that," Geoffrey confirmed, his tone grim. "Faith, the woman told me she would leave, and I was fool enough to stop her."

"Oh, no," Melanie said. "You could not have let her leave, not in her condition."

"I know," Geoffrey said. "But, faith, I have no desire to host any woman, let alone one like her. I am far too busy to be playing nursemaid."

Melany frowned. "If you wish, I will remain and we can have her come and stay with me, until she remembers who she is, that is."

"God forbid," Geoffrey said. "I would not dare fob her off upon you or your family. No, I was the one foolish enough to fish her out of the pond and 'tis I who will suffer the consequences. I will go to the Squire and put it about we have found a missing person and inquire if anyone knows of her."

At that moment a knock on the door interrupted them and Dr. Hobbs entered.

"Joseph," Geoffrey said. "How is the patient?"

Joseph, frowning, walked over to a chair and lowered himself into it. "Odd case, very odd case. The gal doesn't remember her own name, or anything else. I know when one gets a knock on the head one can go daffy, but strange, very strange."

"Amnesia," Geoffrey said, nodding.

"Heh? What?" Joseph looked up.

"That's the name for it," Geoffrey said.

Joseph waved his hand. "If you say so. Never cared to worry over long names. But the gal's got it, that's for sure."

"What can we do for her, Doctor Hobbs?" Melanie asked.

"Do for her?" the doctor asked. "Ain't nothing you can do. The gal either remembers or she don't. If it's from a knock on the head, it will come back naturally, or it won't. If the gal's been shocked and she's afraid to remember, then she won't. Mind's a queer thing. Even with her best will, she ain't going to remember until her bone box says she can."

"Oh, my," Melanie whispered.

"How is she otherwise?" Geoffrey said.

Joseph shook his head. "She's cut and bruised all over. A woman with a lesser constitution wouldn't be moving. But the gal's got a fine constitution on her." He flushed and said, "Hmm, yes, fine constitution."

"Then it won't require much to take care of her," Geoffrey said.

Joseph looked up and then he started laughing. "Geoffrey, my boy, I'm wondering if you ain't blind. With a woman like that under your roof . . ." He halted suddenly, casting a quick look to Melanie. "Well, no matter. One thing I wanted to tell you and almost forgot. As I said, the gal's bruised all over, but the most notable bruises are around her throat."

"Her throat!" Geoffrey exclaimed.

"Oh, no," Melanie said.

"Yes," Joseph said. "Looks suspiciously like handprints, but we can only speculate since the gal can't tell us. Since she's bruised all over, it may be part and parcel with the rest."

"I see," Geoffrey said, frowning.

"Take a look yourself and see what you think," Joseph said, and rose. "Well, I'd best be going. Left instructions with Mrs. Biddington about what to feed the gal and all. Rest will heal her the most."

"Yes, of course," Geoffrey said. He frowned. "Joseph, perhaps we should not mention our patient to anyone for the nonce."

Joseph's eyes were sharp upon Geoffrey. "I didn't intend

to. The rest will be your choice." Then he laughed. "It won't require much to take care of her. That's a good one." He shook his head as he walked from the room.

Geoffrey watched the doctor's departure, frowning. Then he looked at Melanie. "I fear I have a house guest for an indeterminate time."

Melanie's eyes showed concern. "What do you think happened to her?"

I don't know," Geoffrey said. "But I believe I won't go to the Squire until I talk to the woman." He crossed and sat down. "But let us have our tea before you leave, and stop worrying over her. You go and help your mother and I will attempt to be an exemplary host to the invalid."

"Indeed," Melanie said, smiling. "I shall be gone only two days."

Geoffrey laughed. "I doubt anything can happen in two days, so do not worry."

Geoffrey knocked upon the door of the blue room. He heard a call to enter and he opened the door. He stepped into the room to discover his visitor standing at the window, looking out to the now-darkening sky. She turned to him.

Geoffrey exhaled quickly, feeling as if some unknown force had punched him in the stomach. The woman who stood before him was no longer the muddy creature he had hauled home, but the most beautiful woman he had ever seen. He had gathered, despite the mud, that her hair was dark, but he had never imagined it to be a glossy, raven black. The mask of mud had also hidden a beautifully shaped face of the purest alabaster, with delicate, flaring brows and full, sensuous lips. Her eyes, which had commanded even from a filthy face, were the most intriguing sea foam color, not green and not blue.

"Good Lord," Geoffrey breathed, now understanding the doctor's amusement at his expense.

"I am sorry." Amy smiled, and plucked at a fold of what Geoffrey recognized as his own nightshirt. "Mrs. Biddington lent me a nightshirt of yours."

"It's of no moment," Geoffrey said, still staring.

"I am glad to know," she said. "Mrs. Biddington was quite overset. It seems my clothes were quite past repair, and she did not know what to dress me in. We determined your night-shirt would fit far better than trying to squeeze me into one of her nightgowns."

"Good lord, yes," Geoffrey said. " 'Tis remarkable you fill my nightshirt out as well as you do."

Amy flushed, and Geoffrey cursed himself. He was gawking at her like a schoolboy. She turned from the window and walked toward the glowing fire. "Did you speak with Doctor Hobbs?"

"Yes," Geoffrey said, frowning. He stepped farther into the room. " 'Tis why I came to talk to you."

She did not look up from the fire. "Indeed?"

"He says you suffer many bruises," Geoffrey said.

"Yes," Amy said with a slight laugh. "I do feel rather pulled."

"Do you have no notion how you came to be in such a state?" Geoffrey asked.

He saw her stiffen, and she turned to him. "Must we go through all the questions again? I told you I do not know." She waved her hand. "However, if you wish, I shall make up a story for you."

"No," Geoffrey said, "there is no need."

"Let's see," she continued. "Perhaps I was trampled by wild horses. Or I'm just the clumsy sort, took a tumble down the stairs, lost my memory, and took off wandering."

"You do not seem like the clumsy type," Geoffrey said, walking slowly toward her. She did not back away, but her chin lifted. She looked him unwaveringly in the eye, a new experience since he did not have to look very far down. "Doctor Hobbs says you are bruised about the neck."

Something flickered in her eyes, but she only asked, "Am I?"

"I would like to see the bruises," Geoffrey said.

"I beg your pardon?" she asked.

"I assure you," Geoffrey said, "it is clearly a medical matter. Doctor Hobbs asked that I look at them to see what I thought. I do not ask for any lascivious intent, so do not feel you need to cuff me again."

"No," she said. "I was quite mistaken. Yours is not of the amorous nature at all."

"Just so," Geoffrey said. "Now if you please."

"If you insist," she said, and turned her head away from him. She did not move, nor indicate she would help.

Geoffrey, after the slightest hesitation, reached out and parted the nightshirt's collar. At the base of her neck, on both sides, were dark bruises, almost formed in the shape of handprints. Slowly, he placed both his hands over the marks. She gasped, and he felt her shake. He looked swiftly up to her. Her eyes were aquamarine, and for the first time showed fear, and something else—a hidden dread. His instinct was to remove his hands, but he held them there with gentle determination. "You do not have to be afraid of me."

He saw her swallow hard. "I—I am not afraid of you, but could you kindly remove your hands now?"

Geoffrey slowly withdrew them, still feeling the warmth of her skin against his palms. He meticulously returned the shirt collar back to cover those bruises. He did not need to see them. He did not need to feel the strange anger rising within him at the sight of them. "It looks as if someone tried to strangle you."

Amy's eyes widened, and then she brushed past him, putting the room's length between them. She turned and looked at him with raised brow. "How very dramatic."

"No," Geoffrey said in a level tone. "Only logical. Since you have no memory, we must go upon logic."

"And logic says someone tried to strangle me," she said.

A lost look entered her eyes, and then she made an impatient gesture. "What kind of logic is that? It sounds more like a story from some cheap play. Me, the poor heroine running away from the villain who tried to strangle me." She halted, her face drawn but her eyes defiant. "Or do you think I am the villainess of the piece?"

Geoffrey thought of the bruises, remembered the fear he had seen in her eyes. "No, I do not think that."

"But I could be," she said. "Perhaps it is I who is evil. I may very well have escaped a well-deserved death. You should be frightened of me."

"I am afraid of no female," Geoffrey said.

"No, you wouldn't be." Her tone was not complimentary.

Surprisingly, it made Geoffrey laugh. "Let us not start that again. Doctor Hobbs says the best thing for you is rest."

She looked down. "And when did he say my memory should return?"

"He does not know," Geoffrey said. "Therefore, madame, I offer you my home." Her gaze lifted to him, and for a moment they both stared at each other. Geoffrey looked away first and walked swiftly toward the door. He halted, and without glancing at her, said, "Dramatic or not, I will not bring your presence here to anyone's attention unless you wish it. If you do, I shall make inquiries for you." Finally, he looked at her.

Her head was bowed and she shook it. "No, no I do not wish it. If you will but suffer my presence, I—I would be grateful."

Geoffrey looked again at the most beautiful woman he had ever seen. The most beautiful woman who had no memory, bruises upon her neck, and was wearing his nightshirt. The word "suffer" whirled about in his head as he walked silently from her room.

Two

Sarah was frustrated and moving post haste into angry. Her stomach growled. Oh, yes, and she was hungry, very hungry. She paced the room in her nightshirt, frowning severely. It had been a frightful day.

She had slept late that morning, which was understandable. Therefore, she had not caviled when Mrs. Biddington had arrived with simple toast and tea and nothing else. Feeling much better, and knowing full well if she were left alone with her thoughts she would only turn demented, she had informed Mrs. Biddington she would take luncheon with his lordship at the appointed hour, and if the housekeeper would be so kind as to find her something to wear she would appreciate it.

Mrs. Biddington had jumped like a startled rabbit. "Y-you, you wish to take luncheon w-with Lord Grey?"

"But of course," Sarah had said, surprised at the aghast look upon the housekeeper's face. "I believe the company shall do me good."

"B-but, b-but . . ." Mrs. Biddington had trailed off when Sarah lifted a brow. "I—I will ask his lordship."

Mrs. Biddington had departed hastily. Sarah had thought no more of it, except to look forward to a luncheon with better fare than toast and tea. Thus, it had shocked her mightily when the luncheon hour had come and gone and she had neither been called for nor attended.

Indeed, it had been much later when Mrs. Biddington had entered with but a bowl of broth. When Sarah had asked the meaning of it, she had been told by a quivering Mrs. Biddington that his lordship had already taken luncheon.

"Did you not inform him of my wishes?" Sarah had asked, quite stunned.

"Y-yes, Miss Amy," Mrs. Biddington had said. "But his lordship said you should rest and follow the doctor's orders."

Sarah had glanced at the bowl of broth. "And was it the doctor's orders that I should be starved to death?"

"Miss Amy," Mrs. Biddington had stammered. "It is the proper food for an invalid."

"Broth is not a proper food," Sarah had said. "However, since you have brought it, I shall eat it. But please find me some clothes and notify me for tea."

Now, even when it must surely be past tea time, she had still not seen Mrs. Biddington, nor the clothes she had requested. Sarah paced to the bell pull, only to remember there was not one within the room. She knew this full well. She'd had all day to look for it.

She heard a tap on the door and spun when it opened. Mrs. Biddington entered with a tray. Sarah immediately focused upon the tray. It held a single bowl upon it and it didn't require a strong intelligence to guess what was in that bowl.

She frowned. "What is the meaning of this? I have been waiting for tea."

Mrs. Biddington's face turned red. "My lordship was occupied and did not come in for tea."

"And since he did not wish for tea, I was not to have any?" Lady Sarah asked.

Mrs. Biddington looked confused. "No, Miss Amy."

Sarah looked at the bowl with a sickening premonition. "Why have you brought me broth again?"

"Th-this is your dinner," Mrs. Biddington stammered.

"At five!" Sarah exclaimed.

"Yes," the housekeeper said simply.

Sarah's eyes narrowed. "And is his lordship eating now?"

"No, miss," Mrs. Biddington said. "He is delayed and will take dinner at six."

"I doubt he will eat broth," Sarah said.

"Of course not!" Mrs. Biddington gasped.

"Very well," Sarah said through clinched teeth. "That will be all."

Mrs. Biddington stood a moment, her mouth working. Then she departed, which was fortunate, for Sarah did not wish to lose her temper with a servant. It was not her way nor was it Mrs. Biddington's fault. It was clear Lord Grey's wish was the only one which mattered within the household, and obviously he intended to starve her and keep her confined to her room with naught but a nightshirt to wear.

She paced across the bedroom in aggravation. The man had offered her his home last night, but clearly he had neglected to extend his hospitality as well. She would not support it. The country gentleman obviously needed lessons on how a lady guest should be treated, whether her presence was wanted or not.

Her stomach growled at that moment and she walked over to the cooling bowl of broth. She picked up the spoon, hesitated, and then splashed it back into the bowl. Enough was enough. If her host did not stand upon ceremony or regard the proper conventions, then she did not need to follow their restraints either. What she did need was food other than broth, and clothes other than a nightshirt. She smiled suddenly. My Lord Ungallant was about to learn a lesson in etiquette . . . or the lack thereof, as it were.

Sarah could not help but make a notable entrance into the dining room, since the boots she had purloined from Lord Grey's room were far too large and clunked noisily upon the floor. She stopped when Geoffrey Vincent looked up from his plate. She remained posed, permitting him to garner an eyeful, a thunderous eyeful at that, of her britches, overly large shirt, and mistied cravat. Actually, they were his britches, overly large shirt, and mistied cravat, but she chose to ignore such details.

"Good God!" Geoffrey exclaimed.

Mrs. Biddington, who was just then standing over him with a china pot of tea, was not so verbal, but far more emphatic. She dropped the tea pot. It clattered to the table, cracked in two, and gushed hot tea into Geoffrey's dinner plate and over the table onto his lap.

"Blast and damn!" he roared, springing up.

"Tsk, tsk," Sarah said. "Do control yourself, my lord. I am sure it was a mere accident, was it not, Mrs. Biddington?" Geoffrey grabbed for a napkin and blotted his unmentionables while Mrs. Biddington chirped and twittered, wringing her hands. Sarah clunked to the table, and leaning over, picked up the sodden plate and forced it into Mrs. Biddington's hands. "Be pleased to take this and bring a fresh place setting for his lordship, as well as one for me."

"What?" Mrs. Biddington squeaked, and promptly dropped the plate.

"What?" Geoffrey asked, stopping to stare at her.

"Mrs. Biddington, this is clearly not your day," Sarah said, shaking her head in sympathy. "I have no doubt the plate was slippery from the tea. Do clean that up. And, my lord," Sarah said, glancing at him and then lowering her gaze, "please move that napkin a tad from whence it is placed. I am blushing, positively blushing."

Geoffrey looked down, cursed, and sent the napkin sailing. "Bedamn!"

"We shall need more napkins," Sarah said with a sigh and took up the chair to the right. "My, I am hungry. Do hurry with my place setting, Mrs. Biddington."

"My lord?" Mrs. Biddington quivered, her face blanching to almond.

"I assure you," Sarah said to him with a pleasant smile,

"you do wish her to bring a plate for me. Else I shall tease you to serve me from yours. Or I might even dive into the bowls of food with my fingers, which would be the greatest breach of etiquette imaginable. However, in this household, it may very well go unnoticed."

"My lord?" Mrs. Biddington repeated.

Geoffrey raked Sarah with a stern eye. Sarah merely raised her brows and said, "You are looking at a woman fed upon toast and broth for an entire day. It would not be wise to pull caps with me. Indeed, I might wrestle you for that roast I see."

Something flickered in Geoffrey's eyes, whether it was of understanding or not, Sarah could not tell. "Mrs. Biddington," he said. "Please clean this up and bring two place settings."

"Very well," Mrs. Biddington said, and scurried from the room.

Geoffrey sat down and studied Sarah, his gaze assessing. She lifted a cuff, which flapped open, one link dangling from it. "Do you think you could assist me with this? I do not seem to have the knack for it yet."

"I most certainly shall not," Geoffrey said, leaning back. "You should not be wearing men's clothing and I most certainly will not help you to become accustomed to it."

"Indeed?" Sarah asked. Then she frowned. "I shall strive to remember the next time. But I do seem to recollect that one should not come to the table in one's nightshirt."

He brow rose. "You were not supposed to come to the table at all."

Sarah smiled sweetly at him. "I know, I was supposed to starve. I have no doubt the doctor was well meaning, but he does not know my constitution is such that I require more than toast, tea, and broth to sustain it. As for why you supported my starvation, I haven't a clue. I know I am not fashionably slim, but to force a diet upon me at this time seems quite cruel."

Geoffrey stiffened. "I have no care for whether you are fashionably slim or not, I assure you."

Sarah fluttered her lashes. "Then you do not consider my figure disgusting?"

"No, of course not," Geoffrey said.

"Truly?" Sarah said with a gush. "Some men think me far too tall and . . . fullsome."

"Ridiculous. I think that . . ." He halted. "What I think does not matter."

"But I am a guest in your house," Sarah said in innocent tones. "And as such, it does matter. As should my comfort be a consideration with a host."

Geoffrey looked at her. Only in his eyes did he acknowledge her hit. "In that case I shall thank you not to wear my clothes."

"My lord," Sarah said with a gasp. "If I did not wear your clothes I would be quite undone. I assure you, I am not a woman who will parade around unclad. I realize this is a bachelor's establishment, and you may very well be accustomed to the kind of females who do . . ."

"I am not," Geoffrey said, his eyes flashing, "accustomed to that kind of females."

"Ah, I see," Sarah said, nodding. "Then you meant for me to wear perhaps . . . the curtain . . . or the tablecloth?"

"I did not mean . . ." Geoffrey began, but halted swiftly as Mrs. Biddington entered. He remained silent as the housekeeper nervously placed the plates upon the table.

"Thank you, Mrs. Biddington," Sarah said, though her gaze remained riveted on the food.

"I did not mean that," Geoffrey began again as Mrs. Biddington left.

"Mean what?" Sarah asked, suddenly and totally distracted. Faith, she was more starved than she had imagined. She grabbed up a bowl of potatoes, her sleeve dragging through the gravy tureen beside it.

"Watch out," Geoffrey said.

"Hmm?" Sarah said, spooning out a mess upon her plate. She then set the bowl down and reached for the roast beef. This time her sleeve dipped into the green beans.

"Enough!" Geoffrey snapped.

Sarah stopped and looked up. "No. It is not near enough, I assure you. I am famished."

"I refuse to have my sleeve in every bowl," Geoffrey said, and stood. He stalked over and grabbed up her extended arm. "Ridiculous," he muttered, and very efficiently did up her sleeve and slipped the link through. It was still too large and he shoved the material back all the way to her elbow.

"Thank you," Sarah said, still eyeing the roast beef.

"Now the other one," he commanded.

Without thought, Sarah raised up her wrist to him. He performed the same duty. The minute he released her, she reached out.

"No," he said, his tone curt. "Do not move." He swiftly flipped the end piece of his cravat out of her plate. "I shall serve." He efficiently reached over and skewered a slab of roast beef and thunked it upon her plate.

"Oh, yes," Sarah said. "Another piece, please."

"Another?" Geoffrey asked, his voice disbelieving.

"Do I look like a bird?" Sarah asked.

"Most certainly not," he said, and performed the task.

"And the beans," Sarah instructed.

"Of course," Geoffrey said, and picked up the bowl to spoon them upon her plate.

At that moment Mrs. Biddington entered with another bowl in hand. She halted abruptly at viewing Geoffrey spooning the beans onto Sarah's plate. "My lord . . . what are you doing?"

"Serving Amy," Geoffrey said.

Mrs. Biddington squeaked and promptly dropped the dish.

"Oh, no!" Sarah cried, springing up. "What did you just drop?"

Geoffrey placed a firm hand upon her shoulder. "Sit down.

You shall not eat off the floor!" He slammed her into her chair. Sarah whooshed a gasp.

"Of course not," she said, regaining her dignity.

"Bring some more of whatever it was, Mrs. Biddington," Geoffrey said.

"Yes, my lord," Mrs. Biddington said, backing from the room, her face still horror stricken.

"I have no doubt she'll quit my employ," he muttered, picking up a napkin and tucking it into Sarah's cravat. "There!"

Sarah looked up and said with sincere gratitude, "Thank you, my lord."

Their gazes met and held a moment. Sarah almost thought she saw amusement in his eyes, but then he looked away and his face stiffened.

" 'Twas nothing," he said, and resumed his chair. "That happens to be one of my favorite shirts."

"Is it?" Sarah quickly picked up her knife and fork and attacked her food. At the taste of roast beef, she expelled a sigh of pleasure. It was not cooked very well, but it did not matter. "Forgive me. I had no way of knowing."

"You might have asked," he said, picking up his own fork.

"No," Sarah said, casting him a teasing look as she took another bite. "I have no doubt if I had asked, you would have put a spoke in my wheel, and I did not intend to be thwarted."

"Thwarted?" he asked with raised brow. "Impossible."

"No, no," Sarah said, swallowing quickly and diving into her potatoes. " 'Tis clear your household runs only upon your command. Since you did not come in for tea, no one had tea."

"I was occupied."

"And I was left dreaming of cakes and biscuits," Sarah said. "Do you know there is no bell pull in my room? No way to notify the servants?"

"There are bell pulls in all the necessary rooms of the house," Geoffrey said.

"I would lay odds there is one in your bedroom," Sarah said.

"Of course," Geoffrey said.

"Excellent. Then I shall use that one. I will attempt to be very quiet if I must use it at night. I hope you are not a light sleeper?"

Geoffrey cast her a stern look. "You shall not enter my bedroom, madame, and most definitely not at night."

"Oh, yes. I forgot," Sarah said. "You are not accustomed to women slipping into your room, are you?"

His gray eyes narrowed. "For a woman who has no memory, you are acting amazingly demanding. Quite autocratic, in fact."

"Oh, I have no doubt I am nothing but a scullery maid." Sarah cut off another piece of beef. "But since I do not know for certain, I see no reason not to be whomever I wish. Indulge myself in a flight of fancy, as it were."

"I am sorry, but you will not indulge yourself in anything," Geoffrey said. "This is not a household which will tolerate your 'flights of fancy,' I assure you."

Sarah swallowed a bite and smiled. "A household is merely the mirror of its master."

"Exactly," Geoffrey said, nodding. "And I do not care to pander to airs and whims. We are a simple household and everyone works here."

"My," Sarah said. "I hope you never intend to marry."

"I most certainly do," Geoffrey said. "In fact, I am promised."

"You are engaged?" Sarah's tone held surprise.

"Not officially," Geoffrey said. "But I have an understanding."

"And who is the fortunate lady?" Sarah asked. "Not that I would know her, of course, but since I have this great void in my head, I do not mind filling it with inconsequential information."

"She is a neighbor of mine," Geoffrey said, stiffening.

"Indeed? Childhood sweethearts, no doubt."

"Yes."

"How charming. So when does this 'understanding' become official?"

"I do not know," Geoffrey said. "I would imagine in a year or so."

Sarah's brows rose. "So long? Faith, what a burning passion it must be. But 'tis good you wait. It will take a year or so for you to make this establishment habitable for a woman."

"I beg your pardon?" Geoffrey asked.

"Well, it is clearly, as you said, a bachelor household," Sarah said. "I mean, no bell pulls in the rooms and the servants ignoring everyone's wishes except your own? Your fiancée, or 'promised,' that is, could not like it."

"She will have no problem," Geoffrey said. "Melanie is not a pampered, spoilt, society lady. She is a level-headed woman, a country girl, who knows how to work and does not laze about as the ladies of London do."

"I see," Sarah said, her fork suspended for a moment in surprise. "It sounds as if you do not care for London ladies."

"I do not," Geoffrey said.

"Have you had that much experience with them then?"

"No," Geoffrey said. "And I do not care to do so. I visited London once or twice in my youth before my parents passed away. I found the men mostly wastrels with no direction in life, while the women were worse. They were frivolous, illogical creatures without one thought in their collective minds past their balls and teas."

"Heavens," Sarah said, shaking her head. "To be able to form such a weighty decision when so young. I see you are quite an intelligent man." His gaze narrowed upon her and Sarah quickly reached for her glass and took a sip. She set it down and said in a pleasant tone, " 'Tis fortunate this Melanie is not such one of those . . . dreadful creatures. I see you have her well trained already. How delightful for you. And what a shame for her."

"Melanie does not see it that way," Geoffrey said, a muscle clearly jumping along his jaw.

"Of course not," Sarah said. "She has not seen anything else, why should she?"

Geoffrey stood quickly, his face thunderous. "Madame, you go too far."

"I do?" Sarah asked, and turned her gaze back to her roast beef.

"Indeed," Geoffrey said, and threw the napkin down. He started away from the table.

"Where are you going?"

"I find I am finished dining," Geoffrey said.

"Will you tell the servants I want dessert?" Sarah asked quickly as he reached the door. He turned and glared. "I don't wish it to be like tea time. They won't serve it if you are not having any."

"I shall tell them," he said, his jaw clearly clenched. He turned to leave.

"One moment, please," Sarah called. "Which outfit of yours should I wear tomorrow? I have a partiality for the brown jacket myself."

Geoffrey turned slowly toward her. "Madame, if you dare to wear it I swear I shall complete the job someone else attempted and wring your neck."

"Oh, dear," Sarah said. "I had better finish this, since it will be my last meal."

He glared at her and stalked from the room.

Sarah ate another bite. "Hmm, I must talk to the cook," she announced to herself. "This fare is far too bland."

"My Lord Grey," Mrs. Wraxton, the village's seamstress said, her heart fluttering as Geoffrey Vincent walked into her small establishment. She had always desired to meet Geoffrey, for she found him an extremely handsome nobleman, but since his was a bachelor's establishment, he had never stepped foot within her circle. "H-how pleasant to see you."

"Yes, Mrs. Wraxton," Geoffrey said. His gray eyes scanned the shop with a wary look. He said nothing more.

"May I help you in any way?" Mrs. Wraxton said quickly and smiled as disarmingly as she could. He had the decided look of a male wishing to be anywhere but in a woman's dress shop.

"Yes, you may," he said, frowning. "I need a dress . . . or dresses."

"You do?" Mrs. Wraxton said with encouragement.

"Yes, a dress," he nodded. "Can you supply one?"

"Certainly."

"Good," Geoffrey said. "Just wrap it up."

Mrs. Wraxton started. "But . . . but what kind of dress?"

"Does it matter?" Geoffrey asked, his brows snapping down. "Anything shall be better than her wearing my clothes."

"What?" Mrs. Wraxton exclaimed.

"I meant . . ." Geoffrey paused a moment. "I meant, the clothes that I gave her. Yes, that is what I meant."

Mrs. Wraxton's heart leapt. The earl had bought clothes for a woman. She had never guessed he was so dashing. There might be hope for a widowed seamstress after all. "And who might 'she' be?"

"She is . . ." Once again he hesitated. "She is my cousin."

"I see," Mrs. Wraxton said, smiling coyly. "And what size is your cousin?"

"I would say she is approximately half a head shorter than me."

"Oh," Mrs. Wraxton said, her excitement fading. Perhaps the female he talked about was his cousin after all, for such height most likely was a family trait. "And is she . . . ?" She hesitated a moment, for the man glowered at her, as if daring her to ask any questions. "Do . . . do you know her size?"

"I just told you . . ."

"No," Mrs. Wraxton said, "I mean, is she thin?"

"Faith, no," Geoffrey said. "She is certainly no feather-weight."

"I see." Mrs. Wraxton frowned. "Can you not give me more specifications?"

"Very well," Geoffrey said, his face darkening. "She is full." His hands spanned to a bountiful size. "Her waist . . . she has a decided waist." His hands curved in. "And her hips . . . er, lower half . . ." His hands moved out. "Full again."

"I see," Mrs. Wraxton said again. If his lordship did not exaggerate she knew she would dislike his cousin excessively. "Well, then. Let me get some patterns. Such a figure requires certain fashions."

"Pattern book?" Geoffrey frowned. "No, I need a dress for her now. This very instant. The day is half over and God only knows what she is wearing."

"Oh . . . I see." Mrs. Wraxton blinked, then she shook her head, "I am sorry, my lord, I do not think I would have any readymade dresses for your cousin."

He glared at her. "You must, I refuse to have her take my . . . You must have one."

"But my lord," Mrs. Wraxton objected. "The size you describe, it is uncommon."

"I do not care if it is uncommon," Geoffrey said. "This is a dress shop and you should have a dress for her."

Mrs. Wraxton stiffened. "My lord!"

"Mrs. Wraxton," he said with a glowering face.

The wind went out of the seamstress. "I shall see what I can do."

Sarah dragged up the cuffs of Geoffrey Vincent's shirt and stepped back to look at the winged chair she had arranged by the fireplace. She nodded. It would do nicely there.

After receiving breakfast, with Mrs. Biddington striving not to glance at her while she served, Sarah had found herself at loose ends, until she had entered the parlor. It was a good-size room, and the furnishings quite adequate, but it was arranged so haphazardly as to hurt the eye.

Therefore, Sarah had set to arranging the furniture to a much better design, feeling quite proud of herself. Not once had she employed a servant in her endeavors. Geoffrey had stated that this was a working household, and thus Sarah had worked, all by herself. She had to admit it had been entertaining, and rather invigorating, to be able to place the pieces completely under her own direction and powers. It would have been far more difficult, she owned, if she had been dressed in anything other than britches and shirt. In truth, she was beginning to enjoy this disregard for convention. She frowned. The angle of the chair was not as fine as she had at first thought. Going over, she bent, and pulled it further right.

"What the devil is going on here?" Geoffrey's voice boomed from behind.

Sarah stopped, and glanced back, to discover the master of the house standing within the doorway, a large package in his hand, and an odd look upon his face. She suddenly realized she was presenting an inelegant view of her backside to him. She straightened quickly and, smiling, said, "Hello, my lord. Do you like it?"

"Like it?" Geoffrey asked. "No, I do not like it!"

Sarah frowned. "I beg your pardon? I have worked at it all this morning and to good effect I thought."

"You have worked . . . ?" Geoffrey appeared to clamp his mouth shut. "In the future, I wish you would not busy yourself with arranging my parlor."

"But it needed arranging," Sarah said. "The furniture is beautiful, yet the way you had it set was unnatural and not conducive to civilized intercourse."

"Perhaps I do not like civilized intercourse," Geoffrey said, stalking into the room.

"Now, that I can well believe," Sarah said. "Indeed, I wonder if you care for any social intercourse, for the settee was upon the one wall, and the other chairs upon the other. Do your visitors engage in shouting matches, or do they merely resort to hand signals? And as for your servants being forced to serve tea, they must suffer many steps. I know you said last night this was a working household, and now I see why. You've arranged the furniture to be an absolute maze."

"Bedamn, woman," he growled. "I do not care. It was arranged in the fashion I liked and I cannot believe you dared to change it!"

Sarah stiffened, but Geoffrey looked so murderous, and merely because she had shoved a few items about, that her sense of humor came to the forefront. She laughed. "You need not become so wroth, my lord. You act as if I had entered your library or study and arranged it."

"Good God!" Geoffrey roared. "If you did such a thing . . ."

"I did not!" Sarah protested. "I know very well not to touch the sanctity of a man's library or study. Just as I also know better than to ever think of driving your cattle. That would be going beyond the mark, and I assure you, I know the distinction."

"I doubt it," Geoffrey said, rather viciously. "I doubt it very much."

"Now, now," Sarah said in a soothing tone, while attempting to hide her amusement. "You are merely overset because I changed something, and I see I should have thought before doing so. You are clearly the typical man, and I know you men cannot abide swift changes. 'Tis interesting. Men run the world, but let one thing be changed in their environment without their prior knowledge and they become positively unhinged."

"I am not unhinged," Geoffrey said through clenched teeth. "But I see no reason, why you . . ."

"Now, Geoffrey . . ." Sarah said in a reasoning tone.

Geoffrey stiffened and his brow rose. "I beg your pardon?"

"Certainly," Sarah said, smiling. "Do. I have a fondness for men begging of me."

"I did not give you leave to call me by my name," Geoffrey said, his tone arctic.

"No, you didn't. But if we are going to have a good dust up, it works much better to speak in the familiar. It quite loses something with you teasing me on a matter so domestic as arranging furniture and me 'my lording' you, don't you think? It takes all the fun out of it."

"This is not fun," he growled.

"Now, Geoffrey," Sarah said once again. "Do come and sit in the chair by the fire, and I shall sit upon the settee, which is now conveniently close, and we shall engage in this argument comfortably." She wafted over to the settee and sat. Geoffrey glared at her but stalked over and lowered himself into the chair. "What have you been doing this morning that has put you out of sorts?"

"I am not out of sorts," Geoffrey said. "Or I wasn't, until I came home to discover you moving things about in my house without my permission."

"How you do stay mired upon one subject," Sarah said, laughing. "You know, you should be grateful to me."

"Grateful?"

"Yes." Sarah nodded. "Else your intended will be. You must learn to allow changes. They happen, you know, when more than one person is living in a household."

Geoffrey's eyes narrowed. "But you are not living in this household. You are only here . . ." He stopped abruptly.

"I know," Sarah said. "I am only here upon sufferance."

"I did not say that," Geoffrey said, his tone stiff.

"But you thought it."

Geoffrey glared at her a moment and then he stood. Walking over, he dropped the package he was carrying down upon her lap. "Here, this is for you."

"For me?" Sarah asked, looking down at it in surprise. "How nice. A present."

"It is a dress," Geoffrey said and stalked back to lower himself in the chair.

"Tsk, you ruined the surprise," Sarah laughed, and tore open the package. Her eager fingers froze, however, and she stared. The color which met her gaze was the ugliest mud green she had ever seen and the fabric beneath her touch the roughest of material. Cautiously, she unfurled the dress. It was the oddest creation, plain and ill cut in the front, and rows and rows of hooks and tabs in the back. "Faith!" she exclaimed.

"It was the only dress Mrs. Wraxton had available," Geoffrey said. "She said your size is uncommon."

"Not as uncommon as this dress."

"It shall have to do," Geoffrey said.

"For rags, most definitely," Sarah said, dropping the dress. "I cannot wear this."

"Yes, you can," Geoffrey insisted. "And you shall."

"No," Sarah said, her good humor evaporating. "I will wear your clothes until we find something more suitable. At least they are of a decent design and material."

"You will not," Geoffrey said, his face set. "You will dress in that. I refuse to have you running about the house in my clothes."

"But . . ."

"You look like a hoyden or a camp Gypsy," he said.

"What?" Sarah asked, stunned. No one had ever mistaken The Incomparable for such!

"And while you are at it," he added, "attempt to do something with your hair."

"My hair?" Sarah gasped, her hand flying up to it.

"Yes, it is as wild as a horse's mane," Geoffrey said. " 'Tis clear when you lost your memory you lost your modesty. But I have not. You shall wear that dress and fix yourself to look like a lady."

"To *look* like a lady?" Sarah asked heatedly.

"Yes," Geoffrey said. "Look like a lady!"

"You, sir," Sarah said, enraged, "clearly do not know what a lady should look like. For no lady would ever be caught dead in that dress."

"Nor my clothes," he returned. "Now, you will either wear that dress or you shall not receive one more meal under this roof! I will make sure of that. And unlike you, madame, my servants listen to me."

Sarah's mouth fell open. "You wouldn't!"

"I most certainly would," Geoffrey said. "You can wear the dress or starve yourself."

"Impossible!" Sarah cried, and sprung to her feet.

"No," Geoffrey said, standing. "Not impossible. Very simple, in fact."

Sarah choked. "I refuse."

"Refuse," Geoffrey said, shrugging. "But then you shall not eat!"

"I shall not tolerate this," Sarah said. "You are overbearing and officious."

"If you do not like it," he said with narrowed eyes, "you may leave."

"I most certainly shall," Sarah said. "I refuse to live with such a tyrant as you."

"And I refuse to have you parading about in my clothes and arranging my house as if it were yours."

Sarah glared at him, even as fear swelled up within her. If she left, she would not know where to go. Geoffrey must have read her thoughts, for he said, with an unkind smile, "Better the evil you know than the evil you don't."

Sarah detested him at that moment, but she drew herself up and said with all the dignity that was within her power, "Very well. I shall wear the dress. If you would be so kind as to send a maid to me, I shall see if I cannot do something with it."

"No." Geoffrey's tone was firm.

"No?" Sarah asked, her eyes widening.

"I do not have an extra maid for your disposal," Geoffrey said. "I have two girls who come into assist Mrs. Biddington. And they are to assist her, not you."

Sarah clenched her hands. "I believe then, I shall starve."

"Be my guest," Geoffrey said.

"Guest?" Sarah replied. "Captive, perhaps. Or lackey, even. But guest? Never!"

Geoffrey but walked over, picked up the dress, and held it out to her. Sarah snatched it from him. "Thank you. As I said, it will make excellent dust rags."

"Or your dinner dress," he said.

Sarah cast him the most withering look in her repertoire and left the parlor. She stalked through the house and took the stairs to her room. She entered her room with the full intent of packing her bags and departing. She halted abruptly. She had no bags and nothing to put in them even if she had.

She looked down to the clothes she wore and the dress in her hand. What famous choices. She could not travel in men's clothes. She wasn't that insane. Which meant she'd end up wearing the abominable dress no matter what she did. She threw it down in disgust.

The fiend was right. Better the evil she knew than the evil she didn't. Or, in truth, better the evil of remaining than sallying forth into the world in that atrocious dress. The earl merely wanted her to sink herself by donning a fashion monstrosity, but the world she feared just might want to sink her into the very ground in an unadorned casket.

She walked slowly over to the chair and sat down, frowning at the dress on the floor. Wanted for murder, living under the roof of a tyrant whom she seemed unable to bring to heel, commanded to wear a dress surely crafted in Hades, and bereft of any maid to assist her. How had she come to such an end?

Three

Geoffrey sat at the dinner table and Mrs. Biddington served him quietly. Indeed, it had been very quiet. Sarah had not appeared at lunch or tea, even though Geoffrey had ordered cakes and biscuits to be prepared for her. He had expected she would not miss the tea, and had intended to reward her for her efforts. She had not appeared, however, and the cakes had sat upon the plate in what seemed reproach.

"Thank you, Mrs. Biddington," Geoffrey said. "Has Amy come to you for anything today?"

"No, my lord," Mrs. Biddington said. "She has not. And . . . and I did as you said. I—I have not served her anything."

"She has not left, has she?" Geoffrey asked.

"No," Mrs. Biddington assured him. "W-we have watched."

"I see," Geoffrey said. "Thank you, Mrs. Biddington."

Mrs. Biddington nodded and left the room. Geoffrey surveyed the large dinner laid out before him and the empty chair before the second place setting. Anger turned his stomach and jaded his appetite. Fiend seize the woman! She had riled him to such a degree he had thrown down his ultimatum without consideration. A foolish move, he was forced to admit. She might castigate him as ungallant and autocratic, but he was not a monster. He wasn't one to starve a woman either. Yet, here he was, staring at an empty plate ncxt to him.

He stifled a curse. He could not back down. She had been in the wrong, and if he didn't stop her now, he had no doubt she would turn his house upside down within a trice, let alone the parlor. Nor could he permit her to parade about in his clothes. That old devil, Dr. Hobbs, had divined the situation all too correctly. It was difficult enough to have such a beautiful woman under his roof, but when she wore his clothes, where both limb and shape were so clearly defined, it was sheer hell.

No, if she were to remain in his household she simply must become properly attired, for her own sake as well as his. She also must, without debate, learn who was master. It was a fight he dare not lose, but his choice of battle had been asinine and he knew it. If the woman was not so damn abnormal and stubborn, it would not have even come to this.

Geoffrey heard a sound and looked up. Sarah stood in the doorway to the dining hall, wearing "the dress." He started as a flood of relief washed over him. It should have been undiluted triumph, but in truth, it was nothing more than pure and simple relief.

She said not a word as she walked slowly up to the table. The ugly, mud-green dress hung on her in an odd manner, the neckline loose and awry, the sleeves bagging, while the skirt fell unevenly, giving her the look of being shorter in one leg than the other. Her hair was pulled back, caught up in what appeared a white cotton ribbon. Glossy black strands escaped it every which way.

"Good evening, my lord," Sarah said in a cool tone as she drew close. She said it with far greater aplomb than a woman wearing such a dress could rightfully employ.

"Good evening," Geoffrey responded. He stood politely. She started back and then maneuvered to face him full front. If it were to give him a broader view of the dress, he didn't think he needed one.

"Please, you may sit," Sarah said, nodding her head.

Geoffrey's brow rose. "After you, madame."

"Very well," Sarah said. She sidled up to her chair and slid awkwardly into it. Her movements were so unnatural that Geoffrey frowned. He also noticed that as she sat, the stiff material at the neckline poked up. He suddenly divined the cause and stepped closer to her.

"My lord," she said, pressing back into the chair. "What are you doing?"

"Could you please stand up, Amy?" Geoffrey said.

"No. I see no reason to do so. I believe I have been kept from my dinner long enough."

"If you do not let me fix it," Geoffrey said, attempting the mildest tone he could muster, "the dress will fall off while you eat."

Sarah's eyes turned frigid. "I beg your pardon?"

"Do stand up," Geoffrey said. "Yesterday it was your sleeves in the food; it won't do to have your entire front in it today. The point was modesty, was it not?" Sarah leveled a narrow, loathing gaze upon him. Having seen the dress clearly now, he couldn't fault her. "I doubt, considering our lack of . . . affection for each other, you will wish to reveal so much of yourself to me."

The softest of rose flushed her cheeks. "Very well," she said, and stood. Her back was ramrod straight as she turned it to him. Geoffrey discovered himself biting his lip. It was clear she had attempted to do her tabs, but had started off incorrectly and ran out of the proper ones by the middle.

"Call me Geoffrey," he said, smiling. "Since I am going to do up your dress, there is no need for such formality. It would quite ruin the fun."

Sarah, with a sound of exasperation, stepped abruptly away from him, but Geoffrey clamped his hands upon her shoulders. "Just wait a moment," he ordered.

He bent his attention to the tabs and hooks, striving to ignore the intimacy of the moment. His worry over the intimacy of the act faded rapidly, however, as frustration replaced it. Sarah had hooked and tabbed herself into such a tangle that he found himself well nigh unequal to the task. He knew he was unaccustomed to doing up ladies' dresses, but that he was so fiddle-fingered he would not accept. Seconds ticked by and still he could not gain ground.

"Just what are you doing that it takes so long?" Sarah finally said.

"I'm almost done," Geoffrey muttered, bending closer to peer at his work. "But you have . . ."

A loud shriek and crash from across the room interrupted him. Straightening, in no little irritation, he looked over Sarah's shoulder toward the noise. Mrs. Biddington stood in the doorway, a stricken look upon her face and broken crockery festooning the floor about her. He frowned. His housekeeper was becoming positively clumsy. "Yes, Mrs. Biddington?"

Mrs. Biddington paled. "M-my lord! What are you doing?"

"The very thing I was asking," Sarah said. "He is taking a day and an age at it."

"I will have the damn deed done," Geoffrey said, "if everyone would stop interrupting me!"

"H-have it done . . . ?" Mrs. Biddington gasped. Her face colored to bright red. "Oh, my!"

"Stop interrupting me." Geoffrey bent back down and returned to his work. "This dress has too many infernal tabs. It's about to drive me mad."

"My lord!" Mrs. Biddington gurgled, her tone horrified.

"Yes," Sarah said. "The dress is dreadful, isn't it? I can quite understand your stupefaction, Mrs. Biddington, but if it doesn't turn Geoffrey's stomach, I refuse to let it turn mine. Perhaps you could bring us another dish of whatever you dropped. I am hungry."

"Yes, Mrs. Biddington," Geoffrey said. "Do as she requests. We must reward Amy after I'm through with her."

"You need not hurry," Sarah said, her tone dulcet. "At the pace Geoffrey is setting it might take all night."

"Merciful heavens!" Mrs. Biddington said.

"At last," Geoffrey said. "I've got it!"

"No," Mrs. Biddington said, covering her eyes and backing away. "No."

Geoffrey straightened and frowned as Mrs. Biddington turned and ran. "Whatever is the matter with her?"

"I don't know," Sarah said, laughing. "But I doubt we'll see her for a while."

"She is becoming flightier by the moment," he said, turning Sarah about to study his handiwork. The dress, alas, even done up correctly, looked no better. Geoffrey's attention was drawn to Sarah's hair and its disheveled appearance. He reached out and swiped the wild strands back. They were silk to the touch, and every time he placed them, they'd slip out again. And her eyes, which had been cold aquamarine, lightened to a sea green.

"I tried," she said. "I truly did."

"So I see," Geoffrey said. He realized he was enjoying playing with her hair far more than that of confining it, and he swiftly drew his hand back. "Enough." He spun her about and reached to untie the white cotton ribbon. That was when he noticed that the white cotton ribbon was nothing more than a strip of white sheet. "I am not going to ask where you got this," he muttered, applying himself to the knot in it.

"You said I could not ask Mrs. Biddington for assistance," Sarah said in a muffled tone. "And I could not find a pin anywhere about."

"You have knotted it," Geoffrey said.

"Ouch," Sarah said as Geoffrey tore it open, catching strands within it. The mass of confined hair fell, a dark cloud about his hands. With its freedom, it released the soft scent of Sarah herself. Geoffrey breathed in, and his hands automatically twined themselves within the silken web. He stood a moment, enveloped in sensations.

"My lord?" Sarah's voice sounded soft, hesitant.

Reality jolted Geoffrey. He drew his hands from her hair and stepped back. "It will have to remain down; you look like a scullery maid otherwise."

A chuckle came from her. "First a camp Gypsy, and now a scullery maid. Your compliments overwhelm me."

"We have already ascertained I have no gallantry," Geoffrey said, and walked over to sit in his chair.

"Indeed," Amy said and sat down herself. "But perhaps I am a Gypsy in reality and that is the problem."

"No." It seemed as if Geoffrey could still smell Amy's scent and feel her hair upon his hands. He picked up his fork quickly. "You are too well spoken for that."

"But I seem to remember I can read tea leaves," Sarah said. "Would you like me to read yours?"

"No! You would only read trouble in them."

Sarah's brow shot up. "Meaning me, I presume?"

Geoffrey looked directly at her. "Meaning you."

Their gazes held a taut moment. Then Sarah laughed, her voice light. "For shame. Here I consented to wear this atrocity for you and you say I am trouble."

Geoffrey smiled, despite himself. "I know very well you are not wearing that dress for me, but for your supper."

Sarah's eyes teased him, but she waved a hand. "A mere technicality. And you are wrong about my intentions. I plan to become quite the country lady, I'll have you know. In this dress, I doubt I can do anything else but that."

Geoffrey started and then laughed. "You? A country lady?"

"Yes," Sarah said. "Meek, mild, and all civility. I'll not touch one stick of your furniture again."

Stunned, Geoffrey leaned back in his chair, studying her. "You won't?"

"No," Sarah said, reaching for a bowl of potatoes and spooning them on her plate. "Potatoes again, I see. Do we have them in the country at every meal?"

"Yes, *we* do," Geoffrey said.

"I see."

Geoffrey watched her a moment as she filled her plate with corn and lamb. "Do you really intend to try and become a lady?"

Sarah lifted her brow. "I said a country lady, my lord."

He grinned. "A country lady then, if there is a distinction."

"I assure you there is," she said. Something flickered in her eyes. "After all, you talked of London ladies as if they are different from country ladies."

"They are," Geoffrey said.

"Well, then," Sarah said, smiling. "I may not know my name, or my past life, but I do know I am in the country, and therefore I shall become a lady of the country. Who knows, perhaps I have always been one and just cannot remember."

"I doubt it," Geoffrey said, his lips twitching.

"I could be," Sarah said.

"No," Geoffrey said. "Nor do I think you ever will be."

Sarah frowned. "Why not? I am deficient in memory, not intelligence. Only define a country lady and I am sure I can become one."

"Well, for the first thing," Geoffrey said, chuckling, "a country lady knows how to dress by herself."

Sarah lifted a brow. "I am sure I will learn. Besides, you yourself saw how difficult it is."

"And she knows how to mend and darn," Geoffrey said quickly. "Do you know how to do that?"

A flush tinged Sarah's face. "I am sure it has merely slipped my memory."

"She knows how to cook."

"Potatoes," Sarah nodded.

"And put up preserves," Geoffrey added.

"Another thing I have forgotten," Sarah said. "It will return."

"And she knows the running of her household," Geoffrey said.

Sarah's eyes lighted. "I am sure I know that!"

"She knows her tenants," Geoffrey said. "And the care of them."

"Now you are hoaxing me," Sarah said, eyes narrowed.

"No, I am not," Geoffrey said, rather smugly he had to admit. "Do you think you can learn those things?"

"I told you," Sarah said. "I most likely already know them and have simply forgotten them."

"Then you must relearn them," Geoffrey said. An evil impulse prompted him to add, "For I assure you, those are the talents a man will look for in a wife."

Sarah dropped her fork. "A wife? Whatever does being a wife have to do with this?"

Geoffrey shrugged, enjoying himself immensely. "If you do not come to remember your identity, it only stands to reason you will have to start a new life. Finding a husband who can take care of you would certainly be a benefit to you, and the men here about will expect you to have a modicum of skills and talents."

"I assure you," Sarah said, "I will regain my memory long before I am forced to such a dire circumstance."

"Will you?" Geoffrey asked. "Doctor Hobbs says there is no telling."

"Well, I am telling you I will," Sarah said, her tone sharp. Then she looked away. When she turned her gaze back it was cool. "I assure you I can find a husband anytime I wish. Indeed, I have but to snap my fingers and I can have a husband, even a country one."

Geoffrey started. "Your modesty is stunning."

"I tailor my modesty to your gallantry, sirrah."

Geoffrey lost his good humor. "No doubt you believe you can behave this way because you are beautiful."

"Beautiful?" Sarah said. "I'm surprised you would even credit me with that much."

"No," Geoffrey said. "You are beautiful. But a country man wants more in a wife than a pretty face."

"Yes. They want a drudge."

"No," Geoffrey said. "But a man does not wish for a woman who turns his house around every time he goes out to the fields, or demands maids to dress her, or sets herself against her husband's will at every juncture."

Sarah's gaze narrowed. "Even when they give a woman a dress like this?"

"Even then," Geoffrey said.

"If that is the case," Sarah said. "I pray to God my memory returns soon."

"You'd best." Geoffrey's voice was sharp as the sudden anger pierced him. "Because 'tis clear by your manner you'll not succeed with the men around here."

Sarah's mouth twisted. "You mean I will not succeed with you, do you not?"

"Precisely."

"Then I am so glad," Sarah said, her voice smooth silk, "that I do not *wish* to succeed with you." She rose abruptly. "I believe I am not hungry anymore."

"Fine," Geoffrey said, with a curt nod. "It will be less strain upon the larder."

"Another concern, I make no doubt, when a country man seeks a wife," Sarah said. She turned and stalked toward the door.

Geoffrey realized she was indeed leaving. It fueled his anger. "Amy, come back here and sit down. You haven't eaten."

She turned, her eyes aglitter. "No. You yourself said I'll never be a country lady and I see no reason to try and become one. So do forgive me if I do not bow and scrape at your command, my lord. As for the thought of having a country gentleman to husband, I'd rather be drawn and quartered." She whipped around and walked out the door.

Geoffrey stared after her. Damn and blast the woman! She had actually walked out on him. His gaze took in her untouched plate. And she hadn't eaten again. So be it. Let her starve. He lifted his fork, then slammed it down again.

What the devil was wrong with him? He couldn't let her starve. He wasn't a beast. His anger faded and reason painfully asserted itself. He *had* been churlish. She'd said she would try to become what he wished, and instead of encouraging her, he had taunted her, driven her in the exact opposite direction. Why, only God knew. He didn't.

Geoffrey expelled an exasperated breath and stood. He strode from the dining hall and went to the kitchen, where he discovered Mrs. Biddington piling pots and pans upon the cook table, tears streaming down her face. He frowned. "Mrs. Biddington, what is the matter?"

"I am leaving, my lord," Mrs. Biddington said, her voice watery. "I-I am but taking the pans that are mine."

"Leaving?" Geoffrey exclaimed. "Why?"

"I will not," she sobbed, "remain in a house wh-where there are s-such goings on."

"What goings on?" Geoffrey asked, confused.

"Y-you and . . . and th-that woman," Mrs. Biddington said, with a fresh bout of tears.

"You mean Amy?" Geoffrey asked.

"Y-yes. And you, my lord," Mrs. Biddington said. "I never thought to s-see the day wh-when you would openly and shamelessly, you know what."

"No." Geoffrey shook his head. "I don't know what."

Mrs. Biddington's face turned even redder. "My mother always warned me of the dangers of—of working in a bachelor household. That . . . that you would undress a woman right in the d-dining room. 'Tis scandalous."

Geoffrey's eyes widened. "Good Lord, Mrs. Biddington. I was not undressing her. I was merely doing up her tabs. She had not been able to do so."

"You were?" Mrs. Biddington asked. She sniffed and then said, " 'Tis still improper and indecent."

Geoffrey flushed. "It would have been worse if I hadn't.

However, I understand how you could have misconstrued the situation. It was my fault. I ordered Amy not to request any assistance from you, and she didn't. The only thing is, she evidently doesn't know how to dress by herself."

Mrs. Biddington twitched. "I—I cannot believe that, my lord. Every woman knows how to dress herself."

"So I thought," Geoffrey said. He frowned. "But Amy doesn't. It may be because she has lost her memory."

"That or something else," Mrs. Biddington said, refusing to look at him.

Geoffrey stared and then laughed. "If you mean she did so to try and seduce me, 'tis a far cry from it."

Mrs. Biddington gasped and paled. "My lord, this conversation is . . . is quite improper."

"Indeed, it is," Geoffrey said. "But I fear with Amy in the household, everything becomes so."

"She should not be here," Mrs. Biddington whispered.

Geoffrey stiffened. "She has no other place to go, Mrs. Biddington. I'll not turn out a woman who cannot even dress herself, let alone fend for herself. Now, be pleased to take up a tray of food to her. She . . . she did not wish to dine with me after all."

"Y-yes, my lord," Mrs. Biddington said, her voice weak.

Geoffrey hesitated, and then expelled a breath. "And tell her I shall take her shopping early in the morning."

"My lord?"

"I am taking her shopping tomorrow," Geoffrey repeated. "I've had enough of that damn dress, I assure you. And also, you best double your wages."

"D-double my wages?" Mrs. Biddington gasped.

"Yes," Geoffrey said, clenching his jaw. "I fear your tasks will become more onerous with Amy in the house. She clearly needs assistance. But I'll be damned if I hire another servant." He turned to leave and then halted, looking sternly at his housekeeper. "Be certain to make it sound like an order when

you tell Amy she is to go shopping tomorrow, Mrs. Bid
dington."

"B-but of course, my lord."

"There is no of course with Amy," Geoffrey muttered, and
turned to depart as quickly as possible.

Sarah permitted Geoffrey to help her down from the
wagon, determined not to show her pleasure or triumph. She
had gained a favor from him, and a lady never gloated. Besides, Geoffrey displayed such a forbidding face that gloating
would not only be unladylike, but highly unwise.

She quickly perused the small dress establishment before
her. It was unprepossessing, but then so was the village they
had driven through. It eased Sarah's mind greatly, for in such
a small burgh she doubted anyone would ever recognize her.
Of course, in the atrocity she wore, no one would recognize
Lady Sarah, The Incomparable, in any way or in any manner.

She focused upon the establishment with undaunted determination. Unprepossessing or not, she would manage to
create a suitable wardrobe. Fashion was one of her greatest
talents and she did not even fear a small-town seamstress.

"Remember," Geoffrey said in a low voice. "You are my
cousin."

Sarah flashed him her most winning smile. "Yes, Cousin
Geoffrey." He appeared to stiffen and his gaze grew wary.
Sarah laughed merrily. "Forsooth, you look as if you are
going to a hanging."

"I have no care for feminine frippery and such," Geoffrey
said. "I have had a busy day planned."

Sarah merely laughed again. "Do come out of the mopes,
cousin."

Geoffrey looked quickly about and nodded to a man who
passed. "Keep your voice down, you are attracting attention."

Lady Sarah looked to the man, who turned to gawk at them. " 'Tis not I, 'tis this frightful dress of yours."

Geoffrey muttered something she could not hear and took up her arm. "Come."

Sarah bit back a swift retort. She knew full well one caught more flies with honey than vinegar, and there was one large, tyrannical fly who definitely needed his wings tweaked.

They entered the shop, and within a glance, Sarah knew she had her work cut out for her. The dresses and hats displayed were dreadfully out of fashion, and made of common stuff. A small, plump woman approached them, an ingratiating smile upon her lips.

"My Lord Grey," she said. "It is such a pleasure to see you again." Sarah observed the seamstress neither took note of her nor included her in greeting. Apparently, Geoffrey could attract feminine attention, regardless of his ungallant ways.

"Yes, Mrs. Wraxton," Geoffrey said. "I brought my—er, cousin. She will need . . . more dresses."

Only then did the woman deign to turn her gaze upon Sarah. Her eyes widened, and a muscle twitched at the corner of her mouth. Sarah was quite accustomed to it. Rarely did females take to her the first time they met. Nevertheless, she presented a disarming smile and said, "How do you do, Mrs. Wraxton? I hope you can help me. Although Cousin Geoffrey was kind enough to buy this dress for me, I do not believe it is to my style."

A slight flush painted Mrs. Wraxton's face. "Of course. However, he wished a ready-made dress, and I had no other . . . of your size."

"Yes," Sarah said. "But if we put our heads together, I am sure we will be able to create something more de rigueur."

Mrs. Wraxton started back, and then her eyes fell. "Certainly, Miss . . ."

"Amy," Sarah supplied smoothly. "Could I perhaps see your patterns?"

"Yes, yes, of course." Mrs. Wraxton hurried over to a table with books upon it. Sarah crossed over to the books as well. She quickly leafed through one. It must have been a year old. She studied the other books, swiftly calculating their advanced age. "Do you not have any more patterns?"

"I—I only have some older ones," Mrs. Wraxton said.

Sarah thought a moment. "Very well, bring those out."

Mrs. Wraxton, her face stiff, nodded and went into the back to fetch them.

Sarah once again flipped through the book, and stopped to study one pattern. It would require work, but with alterations it would be acceptable.

"Why did you ask her for more patterns?" Geoffrey asked. "There are plenty here."

"None of them are to date," Sarah said, frowning. "However, we shall contrive."

"Just be certain you do not spend overmuch," Geoffrey said.

Sarah tore her gaze from the pattern. "Why, cannot you afford a few dresses?"

Geoffrey definitely glowered at her. "I can afford a *few* dresses."

"Thank heaven," Sarah said, smiling sweetly. "Since I have naught to offer but a pretty face, it is important I make the best of it. Do not fret, 'Cousin.' I may not know how to cook, or sew, or any of that, but I assure you, I remember how to dress suitably."

Geoffrey frowned. "Your choice of memory leaves something to be desired."

Sarah stiffened a little, but said, "Do be still, Geoffrey, I will require all my thoughts." She noticed a chair and waved at it. "Have a seat and stop fidgeting. I won't outrun the constable."

Geoffrey frowned at her, but stalked over to the chair and sat.

Sarah returned her attention back to the pattern, her mind churning furiously until she heard Mrs. Wraxton's voice.

"Here are the others," the seamstress said, coming out with an armful of patterns and thumping them upon the table.

"Excellent," Sarah said. "What do you think of this, Mrs. Wraxton? If we were to alter the neckline, and make the skirt less full?"

Mrs. Wraxton came to look. "You mean . . . Why, yes, yes, I do believe it would look delightful."

Sarah glanced up to see the woman's eyes lighting. There was hope for her after all. "And in Indian silk, I should think."

"Indian silk?" Mrs. Wraxton asked. "Such as that I would have to order from London."

"Yes," Sarah said. "Please do." She flipped to the next pattern. "And I believe this dress would be perfect, without the sleeves, of course."

"No sleeves?" Mrs. Wraxton asked, her eyes widening.

"No sleeves?" Geoffrey echoed from his chair.

" 'Tis not in fashion anymore," Sarah said. "And a figured muslin would suffice."

"I have just the thing," Mrs. Wraxton said, her face showing excitement. She spun and bustled to the back.

"You must have sleeves," Geoffrey said from his chair.

"No I mustn't," Sarah said.

"And what is this about ordering from London?" Geoffrey asked. He halted abruptly as the store door opened and two ladies entered. They stopped as they spotted Geoffrey.

"Why, Geoffrey," the shorter, plumper one exclaimed, her eyes widening. "What are you doing here?"

It was clear by the way Geoffrey shifted, he was uncomfortable. "I—I am here to—to help Amy buy some dresses, Mrs. Pendleton."

"Amy?" Mrs. Pendleton asked. She looked around, and Sarah smiled, nodding to her. "Oh, my!"

"Yes," Geoffrey said. "She is my—my cousin."

"Your cousin?" the taller, raw-boned woman boomed as her gaze appraised Sarah. "Didn't know you had one, Geoffrey."

"Well, he does," Sarah said, smiling.

"Can see that," the woman said gruffly. "You come from the Vincent side of the family, don't ye?"

"I do," Sarah smiled. "How did you guess?"

"Can't miss the height," the woman said.

Sarah laughed. "No, you can't, can you?"

The woman cracked a smile. "Bet you hate being saddled with it, don't ye? Yer even taller than me, and I'm usually the one standing over the crowd."

"Amy," Geoffrey said. "This is Mrs. Donovan, the Squire's wife."

"I am pleased to meet you, Mrs. Donovan."

At that moment, Mrs. Wraxton bustled from the back room. "Here it is, it took a moment for me to find." She clasped a beautiful blue bolt of cloth to her bosom. She halted a moment. "Mrs. Donovan and Mrs. Pendleton, what a pleasure to see you."

"Yes," Mrs. Donovan said, and waved a hand. "Don't let us interrupt you."

Mrs. Wraxton smiled. "I will be with you in a moment." She bustled over to the table and set the bolt down upon it. "Do you like it, Miss Amy?"

"Oh, she must," Mrs. Pendleton exclaimed. "It is quite lovely."

"Indeed, it is," Sarah said, fingering the cloth.

Mrs. Wraxton nodded. "And when you remove the sleeves . . ."

"What? What is this about removing sleeves?" Mrs. Pendleton asked. She all but sprinted to the table, her eyes alight.

"Do look," Mrs. Wraxton said in eager tones and shoved the cloth aside to point at the pattern.

"Oh, my," Mrs. Pendleton's eyes widened. "How . . . how dashing."

"And also," Sarah said, "the neckline needs altering."

"What?" Mrs. Donovan said, and trod over to look as well.

"Like this," Sarah said, swiftly sketching a lower neckline.

"Oh, my," Mrs. Pendleton said, giggling.

"Humph," Mrs. Donovan said.

" 'Tis the fashion now in London," Sarah said. "Or so I have heard."

"It is?" Mrs. Pendleton said, her blue eyes sparkling. "If that is the case . . . do you mind if I have one made up like it?"

Sarah looked to the tiny plump lady whose dimpled face was impressed with eagerness. "Of course not, but I think *this* would look far more lovely upon you." She swiftly flipped to another pattern. "I have always admired this fashion, but needless to say, it would not do since I am such a maypole."

"Know what you mean," Mrs. Donovan said.

"Yes, it is pretty," Mrs. Pendleton said, nodding. "But without the sleeves, right? And we change the neckline? 'Tis the fashion, after all!"

Sarah smiled and quickly drew a different line. "I think this would be fetching."

Mrs. Pendleton clasped her hands together. "Oh, yes, yes, wait until my Herman sees me in this."

"And Mrs. Wraxton is sending for some Indian silk from London," Sarah said. "Perhaps she could also order another bolt, in rose I would say."

"Indian silk," Mrs. Pendleton breathed, all but gaining three more inches of importance. "Indeed, yes."

"Mrs. Pendleton," Geoffrey said from his chair. "That will be an expensive dress."

"Oh, I shall steal it from my egg money," Mrs. Pendleton said, giggling. "I simply must have it."

"But . . ." Geoffrey started. At that moment, the door

opened again, and two other ladies entered. Mrs. Pendleton looked up. "Elvira and Tandy, do look at what I am going to order."

The two ladies came over and immediately oohed and ah-hed.

"Yes," Mrs. Donovan said, "And I am going to have one made up like this." She flipped the pages back to the one Sarah had worked for herself. "Looks good on us taller women, don't it, Amy?"

"It will be lovely," Elvira said.

"Miss Amy knows the London fashions," Mrs. Pendleton said.

"And I want it in Indian silk as well," Mrs. Donovan said, nodding emphatically.

"Mrs. Donovan, think of the expense," Geoffrey pointed out, once again from his corner. "Bert may not approve."

"Don't worry, Geoffrey," Mrs. Donovan said. "I shall bake him his favorite roast and parsley potatoes."

"She clearly knows how to cook," Sarah said, smiling sweetly to the grim-faced Geoffrey.

"Miss Amy," Elvira exclaimed. "What are they wearing for hats? I came for a hat."

Sarah's gaze was drawn from the frowning Geoffrey. She immediately forgot him and studied the rather round-faced woman before her. She looked to the hats Mrs. Wraxton had upon display. "Well, this one would be nice, I should think. But not with the fruit upon it. Fruit has become passé. Ostrich plumes are the newest fashion and would be just the thing for you. Not in profusion, of course, but one perhaps which would curl softly about your cheek."

The ladies immediately fell upon all the hats, holding them up and asking questions. Sarah laughed, but immediately went to discuss the merits of each. She dearly loved design and enjoyed advising the fashion-starved women. A pleasant hour passed, with the ladies plucking at hats, rolling out bolts of cloth, and scribbling upon patterns. Sarah was hard pressed to tender her own orders as the others placed theirs in a frenzy. They all wanted a riding habit à la Hussar like she had drafted. They all, even Mrs. Donovan, wanted hats with ostrich plumes. They had just taken to discussing petticoats and the proper laces for them when they were interrupted by Geoffrey who said loudly, "Amy, it is time to go home."

Sarah started. She had become so involved in counseling the women, she had completely forgotten his presence. She looked over to him, as did all the other women. "Oh, dear," she said, a laugh escaping her before she could stifle it. Geoffrey sat, his face grim, holding a hat in one hand, a reticule in the other, while a bolt of material lay sprawled at his feet. Titters and coughs rippled through the women.

Geoffrey stood, casting the women a stern look. The ladies fell silent, though they did glance at each other with reddening faces. Geoffrey, standing at his imposing height, with hat and reticule in hand, was a sight. He stepped over the bolt of cloth and walked to Mrs. Donovan. "Your hat, madame."

"Thank you, Geoffrey," Mrs. Donovan's voice for once was low and weak. "Thank you for holding it for me. I forgot."

"You want two red ostrich plumes to be put upon it," he said, his gaze narrowed.

"Yes, yes I do," she said.

Geoffrey turned and walked over to the petite Mrs. Pendleton, who cowered back slightly. "Your reticule, Mrs. Pendleton. The one you want to have dyed to match the Indian silk you've ordered from London. Rose, mind you."

"Oh, yes," Mrs. Pendleton gasped. "Thank you, my lord."

Geoffrey turned and glared at Sarah. "Now we are going home. I am sorry to interrupt the discussion on Belgian lace for petticoats, but I fear I have a pressing engagement."

Sarah quickly dropped the lace in her hands. "Er, yes, Geoffrey."

The ladies all murmured their consents and goodbyes. Geoffrey did not look at any one of them as he turned and walked, stiff lipped and stiff shouldered, from the store.

"Excuse me ladies," Sarah said, "I believe I should leave."

"Yes, yes, do go," Mrs. Wraxton said. "I am sure I have your orders."

"Make him roast and parsley potatoes," Mrs. Donovan whispered as she shooed Sarah toward the door.

Sarah, stifling another laugh, exited. Geoffrey was already seated upon the wagon, reins in hand and staring straight ahead. It was clear he did not intend to assist her. Sarah clambered up to sit next to him.

"That was very kind of you, Geoffrey," Sarah said, biting her lip. "T-to assist the ladies."

He said not a word, but snapped the reins. The horses surged off and it took a moment for him to bring them in line. Sarah held on and said once he had drawn them to a slower pace, "Really Geoffrey, you need not take it out on the horses."

"Madame, if I did not take it out upon the horses," Geoffrey said, his voice low and angry. "I believe I would take it out upon you."

"What?" Sarah said, striving for an innocent look.

"They all were laughing at me," Geoffrey said.

"Oh, no," Sarah said. "They refrained quite well, I thought. Rather manfully, in fact."

He cast her a killing look. "And you, talking those ladies into such ridiculous things. As if it is not enough you wish to flaunt yourself in such a manner, now you'll have half the ladies of town doing the same birdwitted thing. No sleeves and low necklines!"

"It is the fashion," Sarah murmured. "I assure you."

"They'll catch their death from colds," Geoffrey said with a growl. "I never thought to see sane, sensible country women act so stupidly."

"Every woman needs to feel fashionable," Sarah said.

"Even farm women. And why should they not? They work very hard it seems to me, and should be permitted to indulge themselves once in a while."

"Mrs. Pendleton is using her egg money!" Geoffrey said, his voice condemning. "And for what? So she can parade around half naked?"

"Oh, no," Sarah said. "I assure you, I made certain there was enough material to cover her. And if you noticed, I did not suggest once that any of them should dampen their petticoats! 'Tis a fashion I do not hold with. It reeks of the demimonde, in my estimation."

Geoffrey eyes blazed. "It could not be a fashion!"

"Indeed, I assure you, it has been," Sarah said, and laughed. "But do not fear. I would not suggest it."

"No," Geoffrey said. "You just suggest ostrich plumes, and Indian silk from London, and damn riding habits; à la Hussar. Whatever the hell that is!"

"À la Hussar," Sarah said, "is a habit cut in severe lines." She peeked at him. "Very much like a man's garb, in truth."

"What!" Geoffrey said.

Sarah smiled. " 'Twill be the next best thing, since you won't permit me to wear your clothes anymore."

He barked an angry laugh. "I wish to God now I had allowed. What you have ordered will be no more decent. It also cost me a king's ransom."

Sarah widened her eyes. "No, I am sure it did not."

"It did," he countered.

"I only wanted to look my best," Sarah said, lowering her lashes. "After all, I have nothing to offer but my looks, and I thought it important to do all I could to make the most of them. But if you cannot afford the clothes we shall send word to Mrs. Wraxton to cancel the orders."

"I can afford them," Geoffrey said, and Sarah swore she could hear his teeth grinding. "I can afford anything which will assist you in leaving my house."

Sarah studied him and then shook her head. "You tell me

I must learn to cook and sew and put up preserves to be pleasing. If that is what a woman is supposed to learn for the sake of a man, should not the man also learn the things that would please the lady?"

Geoffrey glared at her. "I just saw what pleases ladies and it is asinine."

"Politeness also pleases a lady," Sarah said, ignoring his comment.

"Forgive me," Geoffrey said. "I believe I've already shot my bent, being used as a hat rack and butler."

Sarah knew better than to laugh. "And also, when a man shows he is not niggardly, but will spend some money upon a lady."

"Some money!" Geoffrey exclaimed. "That was not some money, but a fortune."

Sarah looked at him. Suddenly she began to laugh. "Oh, dear!"

He glared at her. "What are you laughing at now?"

"My lord," she said. "I've just realized it. You *have* pleased me."

Geoffrey's hands jerked up, dragging the reins with them. The horses came to a jolting halt, and Sarah was forced to clutch to the seat to save her balance. Geoffrey looked at her, his face showing rage. "Madame, if you ever say that again, I do believe I shall kill you."

Sarah bit her lip. "Indeed, my lord. I—I will not."

Geoffrey nodded and started up the horses again. Sarah cast a hasty look at the tall, angry man beside her. The slightest smile tipped her lips. The day was most definitely hers. She'd have her fly by the wings yet.

Four

"Surely she cannot be as bad as all that," Melanie said, sipping from her tea as she sat upon the settee, which was now arranged close to the fire.

"No, she is worse," Geoffrey said, standing before the fireplace. "You should have seen her today. She ordered clothes as if they cost nothing. And she had all the women in town ordering the same."

"You did not stop her?" Melanie asked, her eyes widening.

"No." Geoffrey clenched his hands. Once again he saw Sarah, towering over all the ladies, looking like a queen but with her odd sea-foam eyes shining as she talked frills and lace and silks. She had looked so delighted, he found he could not stop her. "Those woman were so excited, I thought they'd lynch me if I had taken her from them." He laughed bitterly. "It's the only blasted thing she knows, forsooth."

"She has lost her memory," Melanie said gently. "She cannot be expected to remember everything."

He shook his head. "She remembers things like à la Hussar, but she cannot remember how to dress. She does not know how to cook or sew or mend, but she has the brass to find me lacking in everything. She never misses a chance to tell me I am ungallant."

"Indeed?" Melanie frowned. "How odd. I wonder why she believes that?"

"Because . . ." Geoffrey halted. There was no reason to

discuss the details. "She apparently believes I should pamper her, offer fulsome compliments, and permit her to buy an exorbitant wardrobe. Faith, I should have left her where I found her that day."

"You couldn't have done that," Melanie said. "You know you couldn't have."

"I suppose not," Geoffrey said. "But I wish she were out of this house."

" 'Twould be cruel. She is alone in the world with no memory. She is utterly defenseless."

"Defenseless!" Geoffrey exclaimed. "Not she."

Melanie's eyes studied him intently and Geoffrey found he could not meet them. She finally said, "You are allowing yourself to be far too overset by her. Do come and sit down and have your tea. You will feel better directly."

"I doubt it," Geoffrey said, but walked over to the chair, placed cozily across from Melanie. He picked up his deserted tea and sipped it a few moments, deep in brooding thoughts.

Melanie broke the silence. "Geoffrey, why not have her come to me? We are now at home and it would be no problem."

Geoffrey snorted. "I doubt your mother would see it that way. No, she will remain here. You have enough people to care for in your household without Amy. Besides, I have no doubt she'd be counting how many bell pulls you owned and in which rooms they were."

"I beg your pardon?"

"It is of no significance." Geoffrey sighed. "No, I shall not foist her upon you."

"I see," Melanie said, and sighed as well. "I wish I could help you in this matter."

Geoffrey smiled at her. "You cannot, unless you can magically change her."

Melanie frowned a moment. "Perhaps I can."

"Impossible," Geoffrey said. "Whatever memory she lacks, she makes up for in sheer perversity and obstinacy."

"But I could teach her," Melanie said. "I could teach her the feminine arts, how to cook and sew and such. Perhaps all she needs is to remember that, and she will become the woman she should be."

Geoffrey stared at Melanie. A deep instinct told him otherwise, but he nodded. He'd clutch at any straw. "Do you really think you could?"

Melanie smiled. "Of course. Indeed, perhaps 'tis what she needs. If she learns the things that are important, surely it will prompt her to remember them."

"Yes." Hope rose within Geoffrey. He smiled at Melanie. "If you could teach her, I would be forever grateful."

Melanie's cheeks showed a charming blush. "Then I will certainly try."

"That is all I ask," Geoffrey said. "If you would simply try."

"Certainly I shall," Melanie said. "Now, do have your tea and do not worry so."

Geoffrey sighed and lifted his cup to his lips. He drank the warming brew, while Melanie remained companionably silent. For the first time in days, Geoffrey felt at peace.

Sarah stood outside the parlor door, suffused in anger. How dare the man talk to his fiancée, or promised, or whatever, about her in that manner. She had foolishly thought she had gained ground, yet now he spoke to another woman about her as if she were naught but a frivolous, trite nothing. She was the Incomparable Lady Sarah who led London and did not follow, and he wanted her to learn silly things like cooking and sewing and whatnot. The feminine arts, indeed!

Worse, he now sat in comfortable silence with that meek and mild paragon, after having figuratively tossed Sarah into the girl's lap, as if she, the toast of town, were nothing more than three-day-old wash to be passed off. A tight smile curved Sarah's lips. Geoffrey thought to have his poor fiancée teach her the lessons but it would be he who learned them.

Sarah straightened her shoulders, widened her smile to affability, and entered the parlor. She feigned a pause and widened her eyes as she looked at Melanie. She was a short thing, with golden-brown hair and dark-brown eyes. "Oh, hello. Do forgive me, I did not know Geoffrey had company. I hope I am not interrupting anything?"

"No, no, of course not," Melanie said with a smile, a truly sweet smile. "Geoffrey and I were just taking tea." Sarah looked at Geoffrey, who sighed loudly and set his cup down. He merely lifted a brow. She imitated it. "My lord, are you not going to introduce us?"

"Of course," Geoffrey said, without rising. "Melanie, I would like you to meet Amy, Amy, this is my neighbor and friend, Melanie."

Sarah's eyes narrowed. If she were Melanie, she would surely take the man to task for his cavalier introduction. Seething, she looked to Melanie and said with a forced smile, "Melanie, I have heard so much about you."

"And I you," Melanie said, rising.

Sarah cast a narrowed glance at Geoffrey. "No doubt."

"I am sorry for your plight," Melanie said. "It must be dreadful to have no memory."

Sarah started at the warmth and sincerity of the woman's words. Flushing, she walked over to her. "I am trying to grow accustomed. Do let us have a seat and be comfortable." She sat down upon the settee and Melanie settled next to her.

"I am sorry I could not greet you earlier," Melanie said. "Mother was visiting a sick sister and needed my attendance."

Sarah reached to lift the teapot from the table beside them. "I hope her sister is better now."

"Indeed, yes." Melanie took up her cup. "Aunt Maria is

on the mend, and I returned, for neither Mother nor I were comfortable with leaving the children so long."

"The children?" Sarah frowned as she poured tea into a cup.

"My brothers and sisters," Melanie said.

"How many brothers and sisters are there?" Sarah asked, setting the pot down and lifting her cup.

"Eight," Melanie said, sipping her tea.

"Eight!" Sarah exclaimed, her cup suspended in mid-air. "My goodness. What a large family."

"Yes," Melanie said, laughing. "They are a handful."

Sarah sighed and shook her head. "I wish I could remember if I had any brothers or sisters."

"Don't," Geoffrey said. "You were an only child."

Sarah stiffened and looked at him. "How would you know?"

" 'Tis clear," Geoffrey said. "You had to be the only child, pampered and cosseted."

Sarah felt the sting, but laughed. "Perhaps I was the last one, and beloved by my parents and siblings."

"Indeed," Melanie nodded, looking at Geoffrey with clear reproach. He shrugged and picked up a farm journal upon the table beside him. Melanie turned her gaze back to Sarah. "Do not let Geoffrey tease you. It is just his way."

"Is it?" Sarah said, finally taking a sip of tea.

"Yes," Melanie said, smiling back almost conspiratorially.

Surprise filled Sarah. She liked Melanie, actually liked her. She settled back into the cushion and said, "Do tell me of your brothers and sisters."

"As I said, they are a handful," Melanie laughed and proceeded upon a list of names and ages of her siblings which sent Sarah's head reeling. She knew to a nicety the peerage and every connection of the nobility in the realm, but she doubted if she ever met Tommy or Josh, Beth, Becky and Susan, Jacob, or the two babies Andrew and Mark, she would ever be able to keep them all straight.

Sarah heard about Jacob breaking his arm from falling out of a tree when trying to steal farmer Nash's apples, and Andrew and Mark's teething problems, and Beth's difficult stage now that she had reached thirteen and thought herself to be a woman who needn't listen to her mother or elder sister. Fascinated, Sarah let Melanie describe to her a life both odd and warm. She would have completely enjoyed herself if she wasn't forced to keep her irritation and outrage with Geoffrey in check. Not once did the clod lift his head from his journal, or deign to enter the conversation.

The clock chimed the hour and Melanie said, standing, "Oh, my. I did not notice the time. I fear I must be going home. Cook will need help with the dinner."

"I enjoyed meeting you, Melanie," Sarah said, standing as well. "I hope to see you again."

Melanie started, and her eyes widened to those of a doe caught by lantern light. Her gaze shied to Geoffrey, who still had his head in the journal, apparently quite absorbed. "Oh, yes. Perhaps we c-could meet tomorrow morning."

Geoffrey did not look up. Sarah's lips tightened as she studied poor Melanie who was clearly floundering. "That would be pleasant, but won't you be too busy?"

"Indeed no," Melanie said. "Beth can watch the children for an hour or so."

Melanie looked so uncomfortable, Sarah took pity upon her. "I would like that. Perhaps you could show me some of the things I seem to have forgotten. Like sewing?"

Relief flooded Melanie's face. "Yes, yes, it would be a pleasure. Now I must be going. Good-bye, Geoffrey."

"Permit me to walk you to the door," Sarah said, and prompted Melanie toward that portal. They made their good-byes at the outer door, and Sarah waved broadly to Melanie as she left. Then Sarah turned smartly on her heel and strode back into the parlor. She walked directly up to Geoffrey and jerked the journal from his hands.

Geoffrey looked up. "What are you doing?"

Sarah took the journal and walked to the settee and sat, leaning back in a negligent manner. She opened it and peered at the pages. "Excuse me, but I simply must see for myself what is so enthralling you must ignore your fiancée during tea."

"I was not ignoring my fiancée during tea," Geoffrey said.

"I see," Sarah said, not lifting her gaze from the paper. "Then it was me you meant to ignore. How unkind to Melanie."

"She did not mind," Geoffrey said, his tone curt. "And I was not ignoring you. 'Tis simply that you two ladies appeared to be enjoying your conversation and I did not wish to interrupt."

"Oh, look," Sarah said. "A plow! And what a fancy one at that." She peered closer. "My, I didn't know plows were so expensive. No wonder you were wroth I spent such a sum upon clothes. What are clothes on a frivolous woman's back compared to a plow?"

"I was not thinking about a plow," Geoffrey said.

"I see." Sarah flipped the page without looking up. "Ah, a wise decision. This cart looks to be a far better choice. Why, you can buy two for one plow."

"I wasn't looking at the cart," Geoffrey said.

"Hmm?" Sarah said. "Excuse me, but I am simply riveted. Here I was being so silly as to converse with company upon subjects that mattered to them, and missed the fact that I could buy two carts for the price of one plow."

"Put the damn journal away," Geoffrey said. "I want to talk to you."

"I am sorry," Sarah said, and flipped yet another page. "Tea time is over. Oh, look, whatever are those things?" She held the journal close to her face. "Ah, they are sheep shears. How divine."

Sarah heard a low growl and the journal was ripped from her hands. She looked up, to a towering, enraged Geoffrey.

"My lord, that is my journal. Surely you have another one to read."

"Enough!" Geoffrey shouted, and flung the journal down.

"Yes, enough," Sarah said through clenched teeth. "I cannot believe you dared to ask your fiancée to teach me to cook and sew and learn the womanly arts, and then had the audacity to leave her to present the issue by herself."

Geoffrey reared back. Knowledge entered his eyes. "You overheard us?"

"I did," Sarah said, springing up. "If you were going to shove the onerous task of teaching me off on to her, you at least could have had the decency to listen to us during tea. Why, if I hadn't helped Melanie with it, she would have sunk."

"That was what I intended to talk to you about," Geoffrey said, his body rigid.

"I see," Sarah said. "Well, there is no need to do so now, is there? I've heard more than enough and Melanie has already done the dirty work for you. And before you pop the question, I will give you the answer. Yes, I will learn everything Melanie chooses to teach me." She spun away and stalked to the fireplace. "Not for you, of course. But for Melanie. You know, you don't deserve Melanie. She is much too good."

"And I am not?" Geoffrey asked.

"You, sir," Sarah said, lifting her chin, "are a self-absorbed country gentleman with very little to recommend himself to a lady."

"Am I?" Geoffrey asked, stalking toward her.

"A tyrant and a boor," Sarah said. "You should be kissing Melanie's feet; she is so kind and good. But then, perhaps I shouldn't suggest that. No doubt, your kisses are as ungallant as the rest of you and Melanie is glad to escape them."

"My kisses are none of your damn business," Geoffrey said.

"A sweet mercy," Sarah said. "I was merely pitying poor Melanie."

"Pity her, do you?"

Geoffrey reached out and jerked her to him. Sarah had not a moment to object, for his lips captured hers so swiftly. Sarah froze, struck by a sudden, sensual lightning. She'd been kissed before: chaste salutes, begged honors, worshipful offerings. Geoffrey's kiss did not worship, it demanded equal desire.

Sarah, held tightly against a body with a strength even greater than hers, met that desire with a new, unknown passion of her own. She became fluid heat as Geoffrey bent her, his hands learning her curves, even as she learned the taste and scent and power of the man. Yet their kiss changed. No longer did it hold demand, but gentled to one of breathless need, shared wonderment.

Geoffrey suddenly jerked his head from hers. For a moment they stood entwined, gazing at each other. Sarah's heart rose to her throat, desire clouding her mind and leaving her dazed. Geoffrey's eyes were dark, traced with passion . . . and confusion. Slowly, he removed his arms from her, as if any sudden movement might bring disaster. Sarah just as cautiously withdrew hers, uncertain that it might not be the case. Then he stepped back, drawing in a deep breath. Sarah found she was holding hers.

He lowered his gaze and said in a rough, uneven voice, "Pity Melanie all you want."

He spun and walked from the room. Sarah stood staring after him one entranced, befuddled moment. Then, weak-kneed, she tottered to the settee and fell upon its cushion. Pity for Melanie was not what she felt.

Sarah looked down at the shirt in her lap, a rent a goodly few inches in the sleeve of it. She was considered an excellent sewer, of pettipoint that is. She knew exactly which stitch was required for a rose or leaf, but running through all her stitches, she was not sure which one would merely mend fabric back to fabric.

"Now what do I do?" Sarah asked.

" 'Tis simple," Melanie said. "Let me show you." Melanie's needle slid through the fabric with ease, and soon the rent disappeared.

"Yes, yes, I see," Sarah said, watching one more moment before plying her own needle. The ladies fell silent for a moment. Once Sarah felt comfortable with the stitch, her mind roved back to a question which had buzzed around like a crazed fly within her head ever since the night before. "Melanie, I hope you do not consider me forward, but Geoffrey told me you and he are promised to each other."

"Yes." Melanie nodded, her shining head still bent over her stitching.

Sarah studied the girl. She had said it almost absentmindedly. "But the date is not certain?"

"No." Melanie looked up, a slight frown marring her brow. "I simply cannot consider marriage yet. When Beth is older and able to help Mother more, then it will be time. But at present she is too young, and with eight children to take care of, I cannot desert Mother."

Sarah frowned. "But . . . but to wait so long to marry Geoffrey? Could not your mother find other help?"

"No," Melanie said, shaking her head. She laughed. "Even if we could afford such help, I doubt they would remain long. I fear my family is a rather rambunctious one. Even the curate declares he'll have naught to do with the teaching of them."

"I see," Sarah said, smiling. "I believe I should enjoy meeting them."

"You would?" Melanie's brow rose and then she laughed. "Yes, perhaps you would."

Sarah cocked her head. "But if you married Geoffrey, would not that be beneficial? I am sure he could assist you."

"Geoffrey?" Melanie giggled. "No, I wouldn't think so.

Geoffrey has been a bachelor far too long. He likes his life settled, and children rarely permit that."

"Lud," Sarah said. "I hadn't thought. He was in the boughs merely because I rearranged the furniture."

"I heard," Melanie said, a smile peeking out. Then she shook her head. "No, Geoffrey has many fine points, but tolerating my family is not one of them. Besides, he is a very busy man." She smiled and returned to her sewing. "Very much like my father."

"I have no doubt," Sarah said.

"Poor Papa," Melanie sighed. "He has so many responsibilities."

"Indeed," Sarah said, feeling not one jot of sympathy. If poor Papa had not busied himself so with the begetting of children, he'd not have so many responsibilities, nine of them to be exact. "And you say Geoffrey is like him?"

Melanie looked up, concern in her eyes. "I know you do not rub along well with Geoffrey, and he . . . he does not always act as he should toward you, but he is a good man."

"A good tyrant," Sarah laughed.

Melanie frowned. "I believe it is because he took the reins of the estate when he was only seventeen. He lost both his mother and father to the fever that year."

"I see," Sarah said, frowning as she drew the needle through the material. "He had no one about to ensure he would not become overly set in his ways. Men by nature will become tyrants if they are permitted to do so. It can quite ruin them."

"Ruin them?" Melanie asked, her eyes wide. "Surely a man should be master in his own house?"

"Should he?" Sarah asked. Melanie looked quite shocked and Sarah said, "You must forgive me. With my lack of memory, I fear I may have forgotten common known facts."

Melanie's smile showed relief. "Indeed. It may very well be." She frowned. "I believe Geoffrey sometimes forgets your situation. It is only you appear so . . ."

"So what?" Sarah asked.

"So self-possessed and assured," Melanie said.

Sarah looked down. "I believe I am, in a manner of speaking. It is an interesting question: If one does not have their complete memory, does their natural nature show through or not." Then she laughed. "Or perhaps I have an inborn belief that when one is unsure, it is best to act positive, else others will take advantage of one's weakness or grow weary of it."

"But as a woman," Melanie said gently, "it should not be held against one. We are the weaker sex after all."

Sarah looked at Melanie. She was a woman who denied her own future and carried the weight of a very large family upon her slim shoulders, yet she professed to be the weaker sex. Sarah did not speak her thoughts, but returned her attention to her sewing, merely saying, "Perhaps I should remind Geoffrey of that."

Melanie blushed and resumed her own sewing. "I—I know he appears overbearing at times . . ."

"All the time," Sarah said, jabbing the needle through the material.

"And he does not offer compliments or do the pretty . . ."

"Assuredly not," Sarah said, drawing the needle through.

"And he is brisk often . . ."

"To the point of rudeness," Sarah said, diving the needle into the material again.

"Nor is he demonstrative by nature . . ."

"What?" Sarah asked, her needle ramming right into her hand. "Ouch!"

Melanie looked up. "Are you all right?"

"Hmm, yes." Sarah raised her hand to her mouth, more to keep it from falling open than to nurture her wound. "Go on. He is not demonstrative?"

"No," Melanie said, returning to her sewing. "Surely you have seen that."

"Er, yes," Sarah looked down hastily. If that kiss last night had not been demonstrative, she did not know what demonstrative was. "But . . . but I am sure he is demonstrative with you, is he not?"

"Ouch," Melanie said.

"I'm sorry." Sarah looked up quickly. "That was a forward question."

"No." Melanie raised her thumb to her lips. "I merely pricked myself."

"Oh," Sarah said. "Then he is demonstrative with you?"

Melanie looked down. "I lost my needle. No, Geoffrey is not overly demonstrative with me either. As I said, it is his nature. It always has been as long as I have known him."

Sarah cocked her head to one side. "How long have you known Geoffrey?"

"Since we were children," Melanie said. "Here is the needle."

Sarah didn't even try to find hers. "When did you become promised to each other?"

"Quite some time ago," Melanie said, once again plying her needle. "Either two or three years ago."

"That long ago?" Sarah asked. She bit her tongue not to ask how Melanie could forget the exact time.

"Yes," Melanie said, nodding. "We were very young and realized it. Also, Geoffrey understood that because of my family obligations I would not be able to marry him for some time. There are many men who would not have understood, I assure you, but Geoffrey did."

"I see," Sarah said. And she did. They were friends. A marriage between them would be a sure security. Neither need worry over their future if they wedded each other. No wonder neither cared about exactly when they would marry. Indeed, she wondered if marrying would not be the most onerous task within their entire friendship.

At that moment Mrs. Biddington entered. Sarah was glad. She had an arsenal of questions for Melanie, all of them quite improper.

"Excuse me," Mrs. Biddington said. "But a message has

arrived for you, Miss Melanie. Your mother has need of you. Young Beth is missing."

"Oh, dear, Mother must be beside herself," Melanie said, rising. She turned to Sarah. "I am sorry. I must go."

"Most certainly," Sarah said, rising herself. "I do hope you find your sister."

"I believe I shall." Melanie's voice was calm. "She has taken to doing this, and she doesn't stray very far. In fact, I have no doubt she is at her favorite cove. But it frightens Mother every time she does it."

"No doubt," Sarah said. "Go and do not worry over me." She looked at the pile of sewing. "I think I have the knack of it now and will try my hand at this stack."

"Very well," Melanie said. "I shall return for tea, I promise."

"Good," Sarah said. "It will be a pleasant break."

Melanie smiled and departed, Mrs. Biddington twittering in her wake. Sarah returned to look at the pile. Determination entered her. If Melanie claimed to be of the weaker sex and could manage to mend all this, so then could she.

Geoffrey walked toward his bedroom, hot and tired. The hay would be ready to take in within the next few weeks and there was much to be done. Now Mrs. Biddington had informed him that both Melanie and Sarah were already at tea and awaiting him. The thought of seeing Sarah after last evening did not appeal to him. He would have to apologize and he was not one to enjoy doing so.

It had been unforgivable to kiss her. Regardless of how angry she had made him, he should not have kissed her. She was a lone woman under his roof and should not be forced to suffer such advances. A sudden heat flashed through him at the memory of their kiss, a heat that made him taut with unwanted desire. Damn, no doubt it was he who suffered the most from his advances.

He walked into his room and halted as his gaze settled upon the bed. A stack of clothes, all neatly folded, towered upon it. Geoffrey walked over, frowning. A note lay on top. He picked it up. All it said was "Surprise, Amy."

Geoffrey laid down the note and, still frowning, lifted up a shirt, studying it. "Damn," he muttered. He dropped it quickly and picked up the britches beside it. He drew the legs out to their full-length. "Blast!" He threw them upon the bed, glaring at the pile. Then his eye fell upon a stack of white handkerchiefs beside it. Stunned, he reached over and lifted one up. Something like a growl emitted from his throat. "That's it!"

Grim-faced, he scooped up the entire armload and stalked out of the room, down the stairs and to the parlor.

"Amy!" Geoffrey bellowed, unable to contain himself when he came in sight of the parlor door. His arms laden, he kicked the door open and entered. Sarah and Melanie sat upon the settee, both with steaming cups of tea in their hands. "What the hell do you mean by this?"

Sarah looked up and her blue-green eyes flared with pleasure. "You found my surprise."

"Your surprise!" Geoffrey gritted. "You she-devil!"

"She-devil?" The pleasure faded from Sarah's eyes. "How can you say that? I worked all day upon them and I have the pricks and blood to prove it!"

"Indeed, Geoffrey," Melanie said. "You should not call her such. Amy worked very hard."

"Oh, very hard," Geoffrey gritted. He stalked over and dumped the clothes upon a chair. "Just look what she has done." He lifted up his shirt, his favorite shirt. Half the arm was sewn to its side.

Melanie's eyes widened and she set her teacup down quickly. "Oh, dear."

Sarah's own eyes widened, but she only said, "Hmm, I fear I was not watching what I was doing there. It was an awfully large hole, you see."

"Indeed," Geoffrey said. He threw the shirt down and grabbed up his britches. "And what about these?"

Sarah flushed slightly. "Geoffrey, please, I may mend your britches, but surely you should not be waving them about in public and at tea time."

"They are no longer britches," he said, unfurling them and holding them up. One leg was a goodly two feet shorter than the other. "Unless for a one-legged man!"

Melanie cocked her head to one side. Her brown eyes lit and her lips twitched. "How on earth did you manage that?"

Sarah frowned. "Well, I was afraid that my first mending was not enough, so I set another seam beneath that one. I had no notion it took up so much material."

"They are ruined," Geoffrey exclaimed, throwing them down in disgust. "Ruined!"

"Perhaps you . . . you could tuck them into your boots," Melanie said, biting her lip.

"Yes," Sarah said, her own voice quivering. "Then it would not be so noticeable."

"Not noticeable!" Geoffrey exclaimed. "And do you believe, madame, that this is not noticeable?" He pulled up a handkerchief which held a large scripted GV upon it, entwined with a rose.

"Heavens!" Melanie exclaimed.

"Yes, take a good look." Geoffrey walked over to throw it into Melanie's lap.

"I thought it would add some grace," Sarah said, her chin lifting. "Plain handkerchiefs are so dull."

"Amy," Melanie said. "This is beautiful work."

"Beautiful?" Geoffrey exclaimed. "There's a damn flower upon it!"

"Wherever did you learn such a stitch?" Melanie asked, peering close at it.

"I don't know," Sarah said. "But it suddenly came back to me. I may not know how to mend er . . . clothes, but I am good at pettipoint, I believe."

"Could you teach me?" Melanie asked, eagerness in her voice.

Geoffrey stared a moment, rage exploding within him. "No! She cannot teach you! There will be no more flowers upon my handkerchiefs."

"Yes, I do think the flower is too much," Melanie said. "Really, Amy, a rose for Geoffrey?"

The two ladies looked at each other and began to giggle.

"I fear it was the only thing I could remember," Sarah said. "Perhaps some ducks or . . . or plows the next time!"

"Plows?" Melanie cried, and the two ladies broke into outright laughter.

Geoffrey stiffened. " 'Tis nothing to laugh about." He snatched the handkerchief from Melanie and shook it. "Worse, she did every one of them. Every one!"

"I—I had plenty of time on my hands," Sarah said, still giggling. "And . . . and I wanted t-to show you that I had learned how to sew."

"Sew!" Geoffrey exclaimed. " 'Tis not sewing, 'tis wanton destruction."

"Geoffrey," Melanie said. "It takes time to learn, indeed it does."

"And until then, I am to have no clothes?" Geoffrey said, glaring at Sarah.

"You . . . you could borrow some of mine," Sarah said, biting her lip. "When they come, that is."

"Damn it!" Geoffrey said, totally frustrated.

"Geoffrey," Melanie said. "You should apologize to Amy."

"I'll not apologize," Geoffrey said. He turned a glaring look to Sarah "I'll not apologize for anything."

Sarah stiffened, and the knowledge of what he meant showed in her eyes. "There is no need, I assure you. I have learned not to expect any gallantry from you."

"Geoffrey," Melanie said, now frowning. "I fear you are

too hard upon Amy. You forget she has lost her memory. It takes time to learn things."

"Not with her," Geoffrey said. "I fear she learns very fast . . . or perhaps she's always known them."

Sarah stiffened. "I believe I have listened to enough. I did not ask for an apology, but I will not suffer any more insults." She rose swiftly. "If you will excuse me."

Knowing he was being churlish, Geoffrey remained stiff-lipped as Sarah strode from the room.

Melanie cried after her, then turned accusing eyes upon Geoffrey. "That was unkind, Geoffrey."

"Was it?" Geoffrey said, and walked over to the chair. With one swipe he dumped the clothes from the chair and sat. "At least she won't be borrowing my shirts anymore."

"What do you mean?" Melanie asked.

"Nothing," he said. "Nothing at all."

"Well," Melanie said, standing. "I believe I must be going home."

Geoffrey looked up to see reproach in Melanie's eyes. "You too?"

"Me too. You ask too much of Amy. It seems to me she is trying very hard to please and you are not giving her a chance."

Geoffrey said nothing and Melanie left the room as well. Frowning, he glared at the pile of clothes upon the floor. On top a handkerchief with initials and flower emblazoned upon it, lay a white flag. He leaned over and picked it up, fingering the tiny stitches. Flag of war or flag of truce? That was the question. He tucked it into his jacket and reached for his tea.

Five

"I never knew there was so much entailed in country living," Sarah confessed as she sat next to Melanie on the cart. Melanie had saved her from a day of boredom and brooding by arriving early that morning and inviting her to accompany her while she visited Geoffrey's tenants. "I mean, I do not have a memory of it."

"Yes," Melanie said as she drove the cart. "All of Geoffrey's tenants, as a whole, are hard-working and good people."

"Not that Mrs. Waltham," Sarah murmured, her eyes narrowing. She had been shocked when she had walked into the first little farm. The common room had been filthy, as were the four children who raced and fought throughout the little house.

"Millicent has never been a housekeeper," Melanie admitted. "And her husband, Jacob, is no better. The villagers joke that when the wind sits in the wrong corner from their house, the entire town holds its nose."

Sarah looked out across the landscape "Perhaps that will change."

"I doubt it," Melanie said with a sigh.

Sarah remained silent. She was not about to confess what she had done. She had noted a putrid bowl of milk set out in front of the door. When she asked the slovenly Millicent if it were for a cat or dog, Millicent had burred it was for the fairies. It seemed Millicent held a strong respect for the wee people, and since three of her children suffered runny noses and rashes, which she claimed the fell fairies had caused, she had left out the milk to appease them. Sarah never doubted the runny noses came from the dirty condition of the children and the rashes from lice. Therefore, when Melanie and she had gone to the cart, Sarah pretended to have left something behind and returned to talk to Millicent.

Sarah told Millicent she had heard from an old crone, who was considered knowledgeable about the wee folk, that such foul fairies did not care for clean habitats. Therefore, the surest way to guard against them was to keep everything clean and smelling of lye. Fairies detested lye. Millicent looked flabbergasted, but Sarah could tell the woman was mulling it over when she left her.

Sarah drew her attention back and said, "The last family, the Talbots, seemed very nice."

"Yes, they are. But I worry over young Jeremy," Melanie said, frowning. "His leg is not mending as it should."

"He dwells upon it too much," Sarah said.

"It seemed you were able to cheer him," Melanie said.

Sarah glanced quickly over, but discerned no sarcasm in Melanie's face. Indeed, she had tried mightily to cheer Jeremy. The seventeen-year-old lad with a broken leg had been clearly in the mopes. Sarah, fully knowing how to bring a man out of despair, had set about teasing and flirting with him. Geoffrey would not claim it a talent, but she knew she had succeeded in giving the lad a better turn of mind when he had asked her with worshipful eyes if once he got better would she dance with him at the next social. Sarah, doubting she would ever attend any of the local dances, blithely promised him one, even a waltz if he so desired. Jeremy had turned a bright red, muttered he didn't know the dance, but by Jupiter he'd sure as check learn it.

"Who are we seeing here?" Sarah asked as Melanie drew up in front of another small cottage.

"Joy Simpson," Melanie said, and her face became set.

"What is the matter?" Sarah asked. "Do you not like Joy?"

"No, I like her very much. She is the sweetest of all creatures. But her husband is the town drunkard. He makes a fair income, but Joy rarely ever sees it. It goes to whisky and . . ." She halted.

"And what?" Sarah asked.

"And low women," Melanie finished. "I fear he is not faithful."

"I see," Sarah said, frowning.

"I should not have mentioned it," Melanie said as she secured the reins and alighted from the cart. "But it angers me so."

"I would imagine," Sarah said as she clambered down from the cart.

They both went to the door, and when Melanie knocked, a fair, diminutive woman answered. Her face was pale and her eyes haunted. They entered to an amazingly tidy cottage, and the two children, though dressed in clearly old and ofttimes mended clothes, were clean and well behaved. Sarah remained quiet as Melanie talked to Joy, asking if there was anything Joy needed.

Joy, in the meekest voice, responded that the family did well and required nothing. Sarah could tell the woman possessed her own pride and dignity. They talked more upon simple matters, both ladies skirting any mention of Joy's husband.

Anger grew within Sarah. In truth, she had always known the life of the common woman was not easy, but this woman's plight seemed shockingly unfair. Thoughts of what her own life would have been if she had married Ravenwich, or if he had succeeded in raping her and forcing her into the union, churned the dark bitterness within her even more. She could easily be Joy and Joy could easily be she.

Melanie and she made their good-byes. Sarah struggled

with her rage until she reached the cart. Then she halted, and said, "Melanie, please forgive me, but I fear I left my handkerchief. I am such a featherwit today."

Melanie's brow shot up, but she spoke not a word when Sarah returned to the cottage. Nor did she say anything when Sarah emerged from it again a goodly twenty minutes later. They merely proceeded to discuss the next tenant they would visit.

Sarah rested upon the bed, a book she had pilfered from the library on her lap. Her stomach growled a complaint. Faith, she was hungry. She and Melanie had arrived back at the hall just before tea time, yet Melanie said she could not remain for tea. Sarah made a quick decision. She would not take tea with Geoffrey alone. Neither would she dine with him alone. Any discussion between them would only be difficult, uncomfortable, and certainly not conducive to healthy digestion. Therefore, she had forgone tea and informed Mrs. Biddington she would take her dinner in her room as well.

A knock sounded at the door and Sarah set her book down in anticipation of her food. "Come in."

The door opened. Alas, not to display Mrs. Biddington with a tray, but Geoffrey. "Hello," Geoffrey said and stepped into the room.

Sarah stiffened. "Hello, Geoffrey."

"Mrs. Biddington said you intend to take your meal here instead of downstairs."

"Yes, that is correct," Sarah said warily. "Or are you going to forbid it?"

"I am," he said in a calm tone, and walked directly up to her. Unaccountably, he reached into his vest pocket and pulled out a handkerchief. He dropped it upon her lap.

Sarah stared down at it a moment, her sewn flower clear upon it. She looked up to Geoffrey with narrowed eyes. "What is this?"

"A flag of truce," Geoffrey said, his gaze direct.

"I see," Sarah said. Her stomach growled loudly.

"One, I believe, you should accept quickly," Geoffrey said with the slightest of smiles.

Sarah glared at him, even as her stomach growled again. "Indeed."

He frowned. "I can fully understand why you do not wish to take dinner with me. My behavior has been . . . unforgivable."

Sarah stared at Geoffrey. She had not expected him to apologize. It must have cost him dearly. She herself did not like to make apologies, and receiving them was just as discomfiting. She looked down at the handkerchief. Smiling, she lifted it up. "I suppose the flower *was* a bit much."

Geoffrey shook his head. "That is not what I am talking about. Though I am sorry for losing my temper over that as well."

Sarah flushed. He was apologizing for the kiss. "I said things that were not . . . not proper either."

His laugh was rueful. "But my behavior far surpassed yours. I should never have kissed you in that manner." He flushed. "I mean, I should never have kissed you at all." He turned and walked over to the window. "I took advantage of you, and I can see why you do not wish to remain in my company, or even in my house. But I would not have you frightened I will repeat the offense."

"I am not frightened," Sarah said. He turned to her, his face stunned. Sarah smiled despite herself. "The kiss wasn't that dreadful." His eyes widened, and Sarah hastily looked down. She should not have said that. It sounded far more brazen than she had intended. Forcing a smile, she looked up. "Besides, I have complete faith you will not repeat . . . the offense."

"You do?" he asked, his brows raising.

"Yes," Sarah said, and waved the handkerchief. "Because

I'll retaliate by embroidering pansies upon this the next time."

Geoffrey laughed, his eyes showing both relief and amusement. "Fair enough."

"Now I believe I will accept your invitation to dinner, my lord." Sarah rose and walked over to him, holding out the handkerchief. "Under the flag of truce, of course."

Geoffrey took it, and Sarah felt an odd flush as he returned it to his pocket. He smiled, and Sarah, for the first time, realized how truly attractive his smile was. No doubt because she rarely saw it when he was in her vicinity. He nodded his head. "Under the flag of truce then."

Geoffrey sat back with his brandy snifter and watched as Sarah studied the chess pieces on the board, her beautiful face set in deep concentration. He could not deny he enjoyed their truce. Dinner had been pleasant, very much so in fact. She had bombarded him with questions about his tenants. He found she had a lively mind and realized perhaps his thoughts of her as nothing but a frivolous and willful woman came from the fact, that, until now, they seemed to have nothing in common. Yet now that she had met the tenants, there were common grounds for them to discuss.

From speaking of the tenants, they had digressed to the crops he and his tenants lived on and their planting cycles. He had waited steadily for Sarah to tease him and bring up the subject of plows and whatnot. She never did. She appeared truly interested in what he had to say. The meal had become a long one. Yet at the end, Geoffrey found he was not ready for the evening to end and had asked Sarah if she remembered the game of chess. Thus they sat, playing comfortably.

Sarah finally moved a pawn and said, "I have been thinking."

"Not with that move, you haven't," Geoffrey said, smiling. He immediately took a piece from her.

She frowned at the board and then looked at him, laughter in those brilliant eyes. "I thought I remembered this game, but apparently I do not."

Geoffrey studied the board a moment and moved his chess piece easily. "I have discovered, Amy, that every time you fail at something or draw censure, you immediately claim it is from lack of memory." He grinned at her. "Whatever did you do for an excuse when you did have your full memory?"

Sarah's eyes twinkled. "I wouldn't know now, would I?"

He laughed. "Indeed, but I would lay odds on the fact you had some other equally clever or useful reason at hand." Sarah's eyes widened, and then she looked down at the board. Her face was slightly flushed and she studied the pieces as if in deep concentration. He had apparently upset her in some manner and had not meant to do so. "What were you thinking?"

"I was thinking," Sarah said and moved another piece, "that perhaps I should see Mrs. Wraxton and cancel some of my purchases. I am sure she could not have sewn them all up yet."

Surprise coursed through Geoffrey. "What has made you decide that?"

She shrugged. "I fear I did not consider the expense." She looked up and gave him a winsome smile. "I'm sure I would have known better if I were in possession of my full memory."

"No doubt," Geoffrey said, chuckling. "However, since they are ordered we cannot disappoint Mrs. Wraxton."

"But it will be a drain on your resources," Sarah said. "I did not think, I'm afraid. I must confess I had this notion that in some way I would be able to repay you . . . when I remember who I am, and surely I must sooner or later."

"What if you are a pauper?" Geoffrey asked. "And your family as well?"

Sarah's eyes widened and then she smiled. "Why, then . . . then I shall marry a rich man post haste and repay you."

"What if you are already married?" Geoffrey asked.

"I couldn't be," Sarah said, shaking her head.

"Why not?" Geoffrey asked.

"Why because . . . because . . ." Sarah stopped, frowning. "I did not have a wedding ring upon my finger, did I?"

"No," Geoffrey said. "But you could have been robbed of it. Perhaps that is what happened."

"I am not married," Sarah said, her voice firm. "I refuse to believe I would forget a husband. Let us not talk about it anymore. It gives me a headache."

"Of course," Geoffrey said, discovering he was all too relieved to end the conversation as well. There were far too many confusing questions to ask when thinking about Sarah's past. In truth, Sarah, just as she was now, presented enough of a challenge without delving into a history she could not remember. The time would surely come for that, but not tonight, not during the first time they had managed to remain in a room together without coming to loggerheads.

"Do not cancel your orders," Geoffrey said. "I must own your dress is looking uglier every day." Sarah gasped and he picked up his knight with a smile. "Checkmate!"

"Why . . . why, you beast!" Sarah said, laughing.

Her laughter was drowned out by an ear-splitting screech from outside the doors.

Geoffrey jumped, as did Sarah. They both looked at each other.

"That is Mrs. Biddington," Sarah said.

"Clearly," Geoffrey said, rising. "What the devil is her problem now?"

"I don't know," Sarah said, standing. "But I am sure we'll not escape finding out."

Geoffrey stifled a laugh as Mrs. Biddington dashed into the room, her eyes wild, her skin ashen.

"Oh, my lo-o-ord!" she wailed.

"What is it, Mrs. Biddington?" Geoffrey asked.

The little woman quivered and shook. "There is . . . there is . . ." Her mouth worked and she broke into indistinguishable gurgles.

"Yes," Geoffrey said. "Get it out, Mrs. Biddington."

"There . . . there is a n-naked man!" Mrs. Biddington gabbled. "A naked man . . . in the hall!"

"Not exactly naked," Amy said sotto voce as a scrawny man stumbled into the room. Bare-chested and barefooted, the man's lower half was fortunately covered—in what appeared to be female pantaloons with pink rosettes and ribbons lacing the legs!

"My lord," the man cried, his bloodshot eyes bulging with rage. "I've come to have a w-word with you. D-damn, I've come to have a w-word with you!"

Mrs. Biddington spun around. Screeching, she flapped her hands wildly at the intruder. "Begone, with you. Begone!"

"Not t-till I talks to Lord Grey!"the man shouted, waving clenched fists, his face purpling. "I will talks to him!"

"That will be all Mrs. Biddington!" Geoffrey said quickly.

"Begone you . . . you scandalous heathen," Mrs. Biddington cried, heedless of his order. "You . . . you will not appear before my lord undressed!"

"Too late for that," Sarah murmured, her voice definitely amused.

"I's got to!" the man shouted. "I ain't got any clothes!"

"Mrs. Biddington," Geoffrey said, raising his voice to a roar himself. "You are dismissed. Leave us."

Mrs. Biddington froze. She looked at Geoffrey with stricken eyes. Her face crumbled. She emitted a wailing sob and ran from the room.

"Bleedin b-belldame, "the little man muttered, squaring his bony shoulders and puffing out his thin chest, a rather ridiculous gesture since he stood in pantaloons.

Geoffrey turned a dark frown upon him. "Now, what the devil is the meaning of this, Simpson?"

"Simpson?" Sarah gasped. "Bob Simpson?"

Geoffrey glanced quickly at her. A flush covered her face and her eyes showed alarm. "Yes, Amy . . ."

"Amy?" Simpson cried, his eyes goggling "She's Amy?"

"I—I believe I shall leave you two," Gaze lowered, Sarah moved speedily toward the door.

"You bloody bitch!" Simpson shouted. "I'm going to kill you!" He charged at Sarah, his hands outstretched. Startled, Geoffrey cursed, and sprung after him.

"No!" Sarah said, rearing back. Before the short Simpson's hands could reach her throat, she boxed his ears resoundingly.

Simpson's hands fell to his side and he howled, shaking his head madly. Geoffrey rammed into him at that moment and the little man flew, crashing to the floor. He sat up slowly, his knobby legs and arms akimbo as he blinked and bobbed his head back and forth.

"Now what in blazes is this about?" Geoffrey said, breathing heavily. He strode over to stand over Simpson. "Speak and speak fast!"

"That . . . that bitch," Simpson wheezed, extending a shaking finger to point in a completely different direction from whence Sarah stood. "Sh-she had m-my Joy throw me out."

"What?" Geoffrey asked.

"She t-told my Joy to-to throw me out of the house," Simpson said, "and she did!"

Geoffrey turned to glare at Sarah. "Is this true?"

Sarah lifted her chin. "I simply told Joy she should not tolerate his behavior!"

"See!" Simpson cried. "Joy listened to that witch. T-turned a damn pistol on me when I—I was undressin'. Said Miss Amy was right and I 'twernt gettin' into bed with her until I stopped me drinkin' and phil-plilanderin'. Sh-she d-drove me out of the house, she did. Me without a stitch on!"

"Then where did you get those lovely pantaloons?" Sarah asked.

Simpson's face reddened. "Sh-she tossed them out ter me. Said s-since I liked gettin' into ladies' drawers so much I could have them." Sarah laughed and Simpson turned an outraged look to Geoffrey. "Sh-she ain't never talked that way afore! It's all that bitch's fault. She talked m-my Joy into it."

Geoffrey stared at Simpson. Then he turned to glare at Sarah. "Is this true?"

"I don't remember telling her to use a pistol."

"Your convenient lack of memory again," Geoffrey said.

"No," Sarah said, shaking her head. "Merely an oversight, which Joy evidently took care of. I cannot help but applaud her."

"Why you . . ." Simpson shouted, starting up.

"Stop it!" Geoffrey said. Exasperated, he bent over and slammed the little man back down. Simpson howled as his backside skittered across the floor. "You'll not go near Amy again, do you understand?"

" 'Taint fair," Simpson cried out, clenching his fist but wisely not rising. "She's come betwixt me and my Joy."

"No, a pistol did that, I believe," Sarah said.

"You goin' to let her say that?" Simpson asked. "You going ter let her get away with this?"

"I shall deal with Amy afterwards," Geoffrey said. "Now, why did you come here?"

" 'Cause you gots to stop her!" Simpson shouted. "I don't got anywhere to sleep, I don't got any clothes. Joy locked the door and said she wouldn't open it till I became right and proper. Said she didn't need a drinkin', cheatin' husband and she'd take care of herself and the children 'cause she has a job sewing fer you."

"Sewing?" Geoffrey's brows snapped down. He turned an accusing gaze upon Sarah.

She shrugged. "You do not like my sewing and I noticed

Joy is a fine seamstress. Only look at those lovely rosettes on Simpson's pantaloons."

"Whot?" Simpson asked, staring down at his legs as if they betrayed him.

"I have no doubt she sewed them," Sarah said. "And they show expert needlework."

"Here now!" Simpson gabbled, drawing up his legs and trying to cover the rosettes with his hands. "Don't you listen to her. You can't give Joy that job! Sh-she don't need it. Sh-she needs ter take care of me! She's my wife!"

"You didn't take care of her," Sarah said. "And you're her husband!"

"Amy!" roared Geoffrey. "Be quiet." He turned a frown upon Simpson. "You and I are going to leave here and discuss this in another room." He spun and glared at Sarah. "And you, madame, are going to remain here. If you so much as move I will turn a pistol upon you myself, since you think it such a fine notion."

"That's the right of it, my lord!" Simpson nodded, crawling to a stand. "Put her in her place fast like. We men can't be allowin' this."

Geoffrey looked at Simpson's pantaloons and shook his head. "Simpson, just be quiet and come with me."

Sarah stood, marshaling all her energy and waiting. Moments dragged by slowly. She heard the slamming of the outer door and tensed. The parlor door opened, admitting Geoffrey.

Sarah smiled quickly "See, I have not moved one jot as you ordered."

He halted and his face darkened. "Don't think to appease me. What you did was unforgivable!"

"Was it?" Sarah asked. "And what that man was doing to Joy was not?"

He stalked up to her. "Coming between man and wife is not your place."

"I know!" Sarah said angrily. "Or I thought I knew." His eyes were piercing. Sarah made an exasperated sound and spun away from him, distancing herself from his anger, from her own. Drawing in a breath, she said, "The truth is, I don't know. Not anymore. But I—I could not see the way Joy was and not speak to her. She is a proud woman, but he humiliates her. They have so little money, and he spends it on drink. At least he is not violent." Sarah laughed. "Or that's what Joy told me."

"And what if he was violent with her?" Geoffrey said, his voice soft. "What then?"

Sarah's gaze flew to his. His tension showed in every line of his body. His eyes asked the question she dared not answer. She looked down. "I do not know." Silence filled the room. Sarah would not raise her eyes to him; she could not.

"Very well," Geoffrey finally said. She heard him move and she looked up. He walked over to the table.

"What are you doing?" she asked.

He picked up the chess pieces and began returning them to their rightful place. "I believe we've had enough chess for one night." He looked up at her, his hand upon the queen. "No wonder 'tis not your game. A mere board is not broad enough, life must be your scope." He shook his head. "I really had thought you were being kind when you offered to send your clothes back. Now I see you had this planned all the time."

"I did not intend to order as many from Joy," Sarah said.

"I see," Geoffrey said. "Very magnanimous."

She drew in her breath. "What are you going to do?"

He glared at her. "If I followed Simpson's advice, I'd horsewhip you."

Sarah tensed. "You wouldn't."

"No," he said. "I do not believe in violence."

She nodded her head. "And Joy?"

"Unlike some," he said levelly, "I refuse to come between man and wife, and so I told Simpson. Despite your interference, he must come to terms with Joy on his own. I warned him, however, that since he is the stronger of the sex, and Joy the weaker, if I heard he had settled his marital difficulties with force, I would take steps."

The sweetest tingle coursed through Sarah. She feigned a nonchalance. "And what of employing Joy?"

Geoffrey paused a moment and then said, "She will have her work cut out undoing the damage you've done to my clothes."

Sarah stood, amazed. She wanted to thank him, but knew better. Without a word, she slowly walked up to Geoffrey. He stiffened, a wary look in his eyes. She reached out her hand and rested it upon his arm one slight moment before drawing it back.

He remained silent and she just as quietly left the room.

Geoffrey stalked to the parlor and went directly to the cabinet which held the brandy. He was not a drinking man, but he decided today he might as well become one. News had traveled fast. Everyone knew that Joy Simpson had tossed Bob out of the house at pistol point, and all due to the counsel of Amy. Bob Simpson had seen to that. The little man had gone post haste to the tavern to becry his story and drink out his sorrows. The men in the village had joined him, both in drink and outraged agreement. Geoffrey was surprised they had not returned to him, demanding the right to burn Amy at the stake. He pulled out the brandy decanter and poured himself a bumper. Mayhap he could supply the flint and tinder.

Snatching up his drink, he stalked to the bell rope and jerked it viciously. Then he went to his chair, threw himself into it, and took a strong draw of brandy. As if Bob Simpson was not enough, Jacob Waltham had come to him as well, smelling far better but complaining that Millicent had forced him to take a bath in lye and he damn near caught his death of cold. Once again, his little amnesiac had been at work. Telling Millicent the fairies would leave at the scent of lye! He tossed back another swallow of brandy.

Just then, Mrs. Biddington entered the room. Geoffrey glared at her. "I am ready for tea. Please inform Amy I wish to see her."

Mrs. Biddington turned pale. Geoffrey wondered if the poor housekeeper would have one drop of blood left before Amy was finished with her. "She . . . she is very occupied, my lord, and said . . . said she would not take tea today."

"Did she?" Geoffrey asked. "How wise of her."

Mrs. Biddington dipped a curtsey. "I will bring your tea directly."

"No, hurry," Geoffrey said. "But inform Amy I intend to see her at dinner."

"Yes, my lord," Mrs. Biddington said quickly.

Geoffrey took another sip of his brandy and sighed, leaning his head back against the chair cushion and closing his eyes. Squire Donovan had also run him to ground, blustering over his wife's purchases—purchases prompted and designed by Amy. Squire apparently did not care to know his wife would soon be parading about in dresses sans sleeves or decent necklines. Geoffrey never doubted he would soon be hearing from more of the men as Mrs. Wraxton filled their wives' orders.

"My lord!" Mrs. Biddington's voice shrilled. Geoffrey opened his eyes. Now what? Mrs. Biddington followed her voice into the room. She halted and said, all but swaying, "There's been an accident. It's Miss Amy."

"What?" Geoffrey asked, clanking his glass to the side table and standing.

"She . . . she . . ." Mrs. Biddington broke down into the gibberish Geoffrey was growing to know.

"Show me," he said curtly, his heart pounding.

Mrs. Biddington nodded, and, still gurgling, turned to dash from the room. Geoffrey followed, fear thrumming through him. Uncontrollable, heart-wrenching fear. He barely missed treading on his housekeeper's skirts, so close did he follow her through the house and into the kitchen.

He came to an abrupt halt. Sarah sat sprawled upon the floor. Brilliant red dripped down her cheeks and smeared her dress. Geoffrey suddenly choked. It was not blood. It was jam. A myriad of surrounding jars, all draining their fresh contents onto the floor, testified the fact. The look on Sarah's face was not one of pain and death, but that of sheer anger and outrage.

Geoffrey, unable to stop himself, broke into outright laughter.

Sarah looked up, her eyes a spitting green. "Don't you laugh. Don't you dare!"

He laughed all the more. "In a jam, Amy?"

"Beast!" Sarah cried. "I've worked so hard . . . and . . . and you laugh!" So Geoffrey did, clutching his sides it hurt so much. "Stop it, I say!"

She scooped up a mass of jam and sent it flying. It never reached him, hitting poor Mrs. Biddington instead. The little housekeeper squealed as it splatted upon her skirts.

Geoffrey's laughter died. His eyes narrowed upon Sarah as she scraped up yet another handful. "Out of the way, Mrs. Biddington."

Mrs. Biddington jumped to his bidding and ducked quickly behind him. Geoffrey received Sarah's sticky missile upon his coat, even as Mrs. Biddington took his command one step further and fled the room completely.

"That you'll regret, Amy," Geoffrey said. Closing in swiftly, he bent and snatched up a half full jar of jam. In a broad reach, he extended it over Sarah's head.

"No!" Sarah cried, her eyes widening. "You wouldn't!" She started to scramble up, but her hands slid in the preserves and she plunked down again.

"I wouldn't?" Swiftly, Geoffrey upended the jar. A sucking noise sounded, and the jam plopped from its container directly onto Sarah's hair.

"Fiend!" Sarah sputtered, shaking her head. Jam flew and Geoffrey, chuckling, stepped back out of range.

Sarah, blinking and gasping, crawled to a stand. She looked at Geoffrey, murder in her eyes. She charged at him, clearly with ill intent. She hit a patch of jam, however, and skidded directly into him. She hit with full impact. The jar flew from Geoffrey's hand and he clutched Sarah as both rocked, skated backwards, and toppled.

Geoffrey cursed as they hit the ground. He rolled quickly from Sarah and sat up. "Are you all right?" Sarah sat up, a dazed look upon her face. She looked so bewildered that Geoffrey shifted close to her and wrapped his arm about her. "Are you all right?" he asked again.

Sarah swiftly turned her head from him. "Of course."

Geoffrey gently turned her head toward him. She looked at him defiantly, but a suggestion of tears lurked in the back of her eyes. "You are upset."

"Wouldn't you be?" she said, her body stiffening. "I've worked all day on this and then . . . I don't know how it happened, I knocked something and it all went down. I tried . . . tried to do something nice for you, to thank you and . . . this happens."

Geoffrey stared at her. Other than the one time on the first day, Geoffrey had never seen her lose her composure. Since then, no matter their battles, she had always maintained her dignity, her unshakable confidence. She had neither at this moment. Oddly enough, it did not please him as he thought it would. Regret knifed through him instead. Melanie had told him he was too demanding of her, and at this moment, he knew the truth of it.

Geoffrey forced a smile. He reached out, and with a gentle finger, brushed some jam from Sarah's cheek. Her eyes widened as he put his finger to his mouth and tasted it. " 'Tis the sweetest I've seen you."

Sarah blinked and then gave a watery chuckle. "And the stickiest."

"No," Geoffrey said, shaking his head. "You were far worse the first day." He ran his finger down her cheek again. "It tastes much better than mud."

"I'd be surprised," Sarah said with a grimace. "Since I made it."

"Try it," he said, and held his hand up to her mouth. Sarah, her eyes cautious, hesitated. Then she leaned forward and tasted it. A tension corded through Geoffrey as her lips touched his finger.

"It-it isn't that bad," Sarah said, her voice low. "It's a shame it is all on the floor."

"Not all of it," Geoffrey said softly.

Unable to stop himself, he leaned over and kissed her cheek where a bright smear of jam lay. Sarah gasped. Then, all too easily, their lips found each other's. Whether his lips sought hers first, or hers his, Geoffrey did not know. Nor could he care as passion flared within him. The sweet taste of the jam could not match the sweeter taste of Sarah's lips and Geoffrey, with a groan, deepened the kiss with a driving hunger.

Geoffrey had placed his arms around Sarah to comfort her, but now he drew her close in heated need. Her arms slid to his shoulders and pulled him to her, her supple body straining against his. He growled deep within his throat and pushed her back, needing to feel the full length of her stretched beneath him. Their bodies twined and melded, coming to lie in perfect alignment.

"M-my lord?" Mrs. Biddington's voice quivered. "Wh-what are you doing?"

Geoffrey's head snapped up. Blinking, he stared down into Sarah's intriguing eyes, aquamarine with passion. They widened, appearing as stunned as he felt. He stifled a curse and rolled from Sarah, springing up. Sarah was swift to follow, and he automatically held out his hand to steady her as she nearly slipped again.

Mrs. Biddington stood within the kitchen entrance, watching them with wide, aghast eyes.

"I . . ." Geoffrey stopped. There wasn't one decent thing he could say, not with such raw desire still coursing through him.

"He—he wasn't doing anything," Sarah said quickly. Geoffrey looked at her, his brows shooting up. She flushed. "What I meant is that he was just tasting me . . ." Her eyes widened and she groaned. "I . . . I mean, the jam."

"Disgraceful," Mrs. Biddington gasped, her entire body shaking. "I came back to . . . to see if . . . if . . ."

"We had killed each other?" Geoffrey asked.

"Yes," Mrs. Biddington said, her hands fluttering. "I thought that . . . But you two were . . . oh, 'tis utterly disgraceful!"

"Er, yes, Mrs. Biddington," Sarah said, looking down. Her face showed extreme embarrassment. She was indeed a sight, her blush close to matching the red of the jam covering her.

Geoffrey suddenly could not hide his smile, nor his singularly male pleasure. "Why is it disgraceful? After all, the jam was meant for me." Recklessly, he let his gaze fall to the blotch upon Sarah's chest.

Mrs. Biddington gasped.

Amy gasped and appeared stricken. Slowly, though, amusement seeped into her eyes and across her face. The poise, which Geoffrey had missed, returned. "Indeed, my lord."

Geoffrey lost himself for a moment in her mirthful gaze. Then he straightened and coughed. "I believe, Mrs. Biddington, we'll need a bath."

"A bath?" the woman squeaked.

"Yes," Geoffrey said, frowning, "of course."

"He means separate baths," Sarah said, chuckling as the little housekeeper swayed.

Geoffrey shook his head. "Of course I do, and you should know that by now, Mrs. Biddington. Do attend to it." Mrs. Biddington stood, her mouth working. "And double your salary again."

Mrs. Biddington clamped her mouth shut. "Y-yes, my l-lord." She turned and tottered from the room.

"What do you mean *again?*" Sarah asked him.

"Never mind," Geoffrey said with a grimace. He looked at her then and said, "Forgive me, Amy, that was unpardonable."

"Yes, it was, wasn't it?" The slightest smile upon her lips, she held out her hand. "May I have your handkerchief?"

"Of course," Geoffrey said, frowning. He reached into his vest and withdrew the handkerchief, offering it to her.

She did not employ it as he expected, but merely glanced at him with teasing eyes. "Should it be a pansy or a different flower, my lord?"

Geoffrey stared, and then laughed. "Make it a strawberry."

She frowned. "I most certainly shall not. I don't want to see another strawberry in my life."

"I don't know, I'm fond of them," Geoffrey said. He realized he was definitely taking the wrong course. He breathed in deeply. "We best go get that bath."

"Our separate baths," Sarah said, flushing.

"Of course," Geoffrey said. He looked at her and frowned. "That dress will be unsalvageable. Will you need . . ." He halted quickly.

Sarah cocked her head to one side, eyes quizzing. "Are you offering me the use of your clothes, sir?"

Geoffrey smiled " 'Tis the least I can do."

"There is no need for the sacrifice," Sarah laughed. "My new clothes arrived this afternoon."

"Did they?" Geoffrey asked. Knowing full well he still tread the wrong path but unable to restrain himself, he said, "There will be a dance tomorrow, would you like to attend it with me? And Melanie, that is."

Pleasure leapt into Sarah's eyes. "That I would, my lord."

"Very well," Geoffrey nodded. He turned and walked toward the door, but halted of a sudden. He turned with a frown. "Amy, don't . . ."

"Don't what?" she asked.

"Don't strive so hard to learn all the accomplishments I told you to learn. There is not that much need."

Sarah's gaze skimmed the room and then returned back to him. "Coward. You simply are afraid of what I will do next."

Geoffrey laughed. "I should be gallant and say no. But in truth, I am, Amy, I am."

Six

Sarah left the dance floor, flushed with heat and invigorated. It felt good to be dancing again, to be wearing a decent dress again, and to be flirting again. She owned she needed to flirt to the best of her ability, for coming to the Squire's dance had shown her there were undercurrents she needed to stave off.

This dance apparently was to have been a barn dance. It was the traditional celebration before the hay mowing began, and, as such, everyone was invited. Squire had roared when his wife told him it would be held formally in the ballroom because she had a new dress to sport, as indeed did most of the other ladies, and she was not going to waste it on a barn dance.

Sarah controlled a chuckle as she made her way toward Geoffrey and Melanie, who sat on silk chairs. The room was full of bare-armed women with dashing décolletage. Oddly enough, the male contingency did not respond in pleasure but in disgruntlement. No doubt when they gazed at their beloved's charms, they were counting the cost and not their enhanced beauty.

"You two have not danced as yet," Sarah observed as she settled down in the chair next to them.

"No," Melanie said with a smile. "Geoffrey does not care for dancing."

"Indeed?" Sarah said, laughing to hide her disappointment. "Then I suppose I need not leave a place for him upon my dance card. Figuratively speaking, of course, since nothing as formal as dance cards are used here."

"You wouldn't have a place for me if you had," Geoffrey said, frowning.

"Sir," Sarah said, "you flatter me."

"I do not mean to." Geoffrey's tone was cool. "You have the most normally sane of men acting like fools tonight."

"Do I?" Sarah asked, casting him a wicked glance.

Geoffrey visibly stiffened. "I warn you. These are not the men to play off your airs upon. They do not take lightly to flirting."

"Really? I thought they were going on famously. Why, that Mr. Nash told me my hair reminded him of his finest demn mares. Now if that isn't flirting, I don't know what is."

"He did?" Melanie asked. "Gracious."

"And Jacob Waltham told me he guessed he didn't mind smelling like lye if that is what it took to be able to dance with me," Sarah said. She looked coyly down. "The rogue asked if I didn't want to lean closer so I could really smell the lye."

"Oh, dear," Melanie said, laughing.

"It is not a laughing matter." Geoffrey's face darkened. "If you continue to flirt as you are, there will be trouble before the night is through."

"Trouble?" Sarah asked, unconcerned. She never doubted she knew how to handle men, and if Geoffrey was growling at her, all the better. Jealousy was ofttimes good for a man. Especially a man who had far too many times informed her she would not be able to attract the males in the vicinity. "No. In fact, I am trying my poor best to lift everyone's spirits." She leaned toward Geoffrey, her eyes wide. "Imagine, some of the men arrived here tonight in ill tempers. And merely because their ladies are properly dressed in the height of fashion."

"Indeed," Geoffrey said, with an ill-tempered look himself.

"But gratefully," Sarah continued with a sweet smile, "most of them are coming out of their sullens and enjoying themselves. It has taken some coaxing, I own—"

"Which you are freely supplying," Geoffrey interrupted.

Sarah smiled. "But they are seeing it in a much better light."

"You mean they are seeing you," Geoffrey's eyes were trained upon Sarah's low décolletage. "And it doesn't require a light."

"Faith," Sarah said. "Another compliment."

" 'Tis not a compliment," Geoffrey sounded as if he were gritting his teeth. "You are . . ." He halted with a frown as Jeremy Tolbot, still upon crutches, came before them. "What do you want, Tolbot?"

"I—I came for my dance w-with Miss Amy," Jeremy stammered.

"Why, Jeremy," Sarah smiled at the flushing boy. "How kind of you."

"Dance?" Geoffrey said. "You are on crutches, Jeremy. Just how do you think you are going to be able to dance?"

"I—I will set them aside," Jeremy said. "If I can dance with Miss Amy. She . . . she promised me a waltz if I got better."

"She did?" Geoffrey asked, his tone stern.

"I most certainly did," Sarah said, rising. "But surely you haven't learned the waltz yet, Jeremy?"

His face turned deep red. "That I have, Miss Amy. I—I asked Squire's wife if she would play one for us."

"The waltz?" Melanie's eyes widened. "Surely she isn't going to do so. Squire Donovan considers it far too fast."

"Jeremy!" Rachel Donovan's voice called and she came striding up, the skirt of her midnight-blue dress swishing. The dress, needless to say, was similar in design to Sarah's. In London, being caught at a dance in a dress similar to another's would have been a scandal and killing affair, but Rachel Donovan only cast a proud smile upon Sarah. "So, me gal. What do you think?"

"It is very fetching," Sarah said, schooling her face.

She nodded briskly. "Yer mighty fine too. It's the right thing for us tall ladies. And I have asked the musicians to play a waltz. Said they didn't think they knew it, but I told them they'd best if they ever wanted to play in my house again. I'm not going to let this dress go to waste. It's high time we become modern, and so I told the Squire."

"Mrs. Donovan," Melanie said, frowning. "Never say he will dance the waltz with you!"

"No, Bert said he wouldn't!" Rachel Donovan's eyes shot fire. "I told him he was acting like a country hayseed, but he still refuses. However, Mr. Waltham said he'd stand up with me. The man's changed for the better. He don't smell one whit. So come along!" Turning, she sailed forth into the center of the room and clapped her hands loudly. "Ladies and gentlemen, we are going to play the waltz now." The room immediately responded with gasps, whispers, and exclamations. Rachel seemed not to notice as she waved broadly at Sarah and Jeremy. "Amy and Jeremy! Come here."

Jeremy, blushing, asked Geoffrey if he would be so kind as to hold his crutches, and after divesting himself of them, offered Sarah an awkward bow.

Sarah rose and curtsied. When she took Jeremy's hand, she noticed he was forced to lean heavily upon her. They made it to the dance floor in what suddenly appeared complete silence. Sarah noticed Mr. Waltham came to stand beside Rachel. Since he nodded and winked at her, it was impossible not to do so.

Her eyes widened as another couple took the dance floor. It was none other than Joy with an unknown man. Joy looked shyly at her and nodded. Sarah smiled back as encouragingly as she could.

"Are these the only ones who wish to learn the waltz?" Rachel boomed.

"Wait! I do," a dark-haired girl said. Melanie's sister, whom Sarah had just met, came dashing up to the floor, dragging a young man with her.

"Musicians," Rachel said. "Please begin. Miss Amy, we will watch you."

The musicians struck up a very, very odd strain. Sarah listened to it a moment, and after catching just a hint of what could be considered a waltz, put one hand to Jeremy's shoulder and the other in his. He flushed, and after a second, placed his hand upon her waist.

"Excuse me, Miss Amy," he muttered as if he were taking the greatest liberty.

"Most certainly, it is the dance," Sarah said. Jeremy, his face set in severe determination, proceeded to push her about in an awkward shuffle. Sarah attempted to follow his lead and bit her lip as she noticed that the others were miming them, all with the awkward, limping steps. However, the couples smiled and appeared so very proud of themselves Sarah refrained from attempting to change their progress.

"Joy! Stop that!" a male voice shouted loudly. Bob Simpson suddenly burst through the onlookers, not in formal attire but at least fully clothed. He pedaled onto the dance floor, a definite weave to his motion. "Stop that I say!"

The musicians obeyed his command and screeched to a halt.

Joy was not so obliging. She remained in her partner's arms, refusing to look at her erstwhile spouse. "Excuse me, Bob, I am waltzing."

"You shall not waltz!" Bob cried. "I'll not have it. 'Tis indecent!"

"And your behavior all these years has not been?" Joy said, her face pale.

"You will not waltz!" Bob shouted. "Yer me w-wife and yer going ter listen!"

"Sir, until you act as a proper husband should, I will not consider myself your wife," Joy said. Small titters and laughs echoed through the room.

Bob growled, clenching and unclenching his hands. Then he spun and his bleary eyes focused upon Sarah. " 'Tis your fault, 'tis all your fault," he cried, charging toward Sarah. "Look whot ye've done!"

Jeremy, with a noble chivalry, hobbled to stand in front of Sarah. "Step back, Miss Amy, I'll take care of this."

"Bob Simpson," Rachel bellowed, stomping over and dragging Mr. Waltham in tow. "You weren't invited here and you are disrupting our dance. Now get off the dance floor!"

"I shall not! That woman's a witch," Bob cried, shaking his finger at Sarah.

"She is not," Rachel said, stiffening. "She is fashionable, 'tis all."

"Rachel!" the Squire's voice barked, and he too strode up to the group. He stood a full foot shorter than his wife, but his frame was bullish and strong. "I've had enough of this fashionable nonsense. Look what it has caused."

Rachel turned on him. "Caused! Bert Donovan, don't you dare side with that drunken, no good Bob Simpson. He is disrupting our dance and I want him thrown out."

"Ain't going to throw him out," Bert said, his face reddening. "The man, drunk or ney, makes sense. It's the gal you need to toss out. Look what she's got you doing! Tricked out like a hussy and dancing that heathen dance. Next you'll be pointing pistols at me, damn it!"

"I might just," Rachel said, glaring down at her husband. "Unless you throw Simpson out!"

"See, Squire!" Simpson cried. "She's got yer wife doing it too!"

"Perhaps I should go," Sarah said quickly. Not only was the crowd starting to press in upon them, but Geoffrey, grim faced, was approaching them, Jeremy's crutches still in hand. "Really, I do not mind."

"No!" Rachel said.

"No, Amy," Joy cried. "It's Bob who should leave."

"Bl-loody right," Jeremy said, glaring at Bob.

"Oh, will I?" Bob Simpson cried, purple faced. He reached out and shoved Jeremy. Jeremy, his leg already overtaxed, toppled over.

"Sir," Sarah said, bending swiftly down to the fallen Jeremy. "That was uncalled for!"

"You bitch!" Bob shouted, balling up his fist.

"Simpson!" Geoffrey's voice cracked as he closed the distance, tossing down Jeremy's crutches.

Simpson spun. "Whot?"

"I said *no* violence." In one swift move, Geoffrey's fist shot out and planted Simpson a facer. Simpson cried out, careening backwards. He tripped over the fallen Jeremy and toppled over.

"Here now!" Squire shouted, rushing forward. Geoffrey spun with lightning speed and Squire received a handy fist to the bread basket.

Sarah merely gaped at Geoffrey in amazement. Amazement ascended into shock as, with that, everyone followed his suit and began swinging.

"Gracious! What an entertaining evening it was," Sarah said, pretending to straighten her hair as she sat on the carriage seat across from Geoffrey. "Your local entertainments are quite rambunctious, are they not?" She received only a grunt from the man across from her. "Rachel certainly has a powerful arm upon her. Though I cannot feel it was exactly sporting of her to have 'floored' the Squire. I do believe that is the term you gentlemen use, after you had already 'floored' him. And Jeremy, faith, he was positively lethal with those crutches! He cannot waltz well, but give that boy a pair of crutches and he is a genius." Once again, Sarah received a grunt. "What is the matter, is your jaw hurting you? I do hope you didn't lose any teeth."

"I did not," Geoffrey finally said. His tone was low and unfriendly.

"Ah, then you can speak," Sarah said. "I was worried for a moment." She reached into her reticule and withdrew a handkerchief. "Here, you are bleeding over your one eye." She leaned over with the handkerchief.

Geoffrey gripped her wrist, holding it from him. "Madame, I need no assistance from you. You have already done enough. You are a menace to society."

Sarah froze. "No, I'd say society did very well as a menace all by itself. I am sure you were too busy to take note, but I did not once throw a punch. I was tempted, I own, since all the other ladies were swinging, but I refrained."

"It never would have happened," Geoffrey said, "if you hadn't set Joy against her husband."

"No, it never would have happened," Sarah said, "if you hadn't punched both Bob and the Squire. Whatever possessed you? I thought you were the man who did not believe in violence."

"I don't!" Geoffrey said, withdrawing his hand quickly. "But you drive a man to it."

"I drive a man to it?" Sarah asked. "Surely it was Bob and the Squire who drove you to it."

"No," Geoffrey said. "It was you."

Sarah sat stunned. Disgracefully, she felt a moment's pleasure, totally feminine and illogical. Yet contrition followed swiftly on its heels and she said softly, "I am sorry, Geoffrey."

"Not as sorry as you are going to be," Geoffrey said.

Sarah tensed. Surely he would not send her away. "What do you mean?"

"I mean, madame," Geoffrey said, his eyes glittering, even in the darkened carriage, "that you are not going to leave my sight again."

Sarah blinked. "What?"

"I will not have you turning the village on its ear as you have," Geoffrey said. He paused. "Therefore, you will stay with me, where I can be ascertained you will not cause trouble."

Sarah bit her lip. In truth, the punishment did not seem that dreadful to her. Not anymore. She culled a free look of indignation, however, and said, "You mean I shall be your prisoner?"

"You can either remain in my company—and I warn you, I intend to go about my business as always," Geoffrey said. "Or else you can remain within the house where only I must suffer your havoc."

"Those are very hard choices," Sarah said, biting back a smile.

"Those are the only two you have," Geoffrey said. "You may accept, or you may leave."

"No," Sarah said. "I—I don't think I should. You yourself said I am dangerous in society."

"Don't I know it," Geoffrey grumbled. "I rue the day I pulled you from the pond. But I did, and I shall not shirk the responsibility."

"No," Sarah said in meek tones. "You have too much honor for that, I hope."

"Damn my honor," Geoffrey muttered.

At that moment the carriage came to a halt. Sarah wisely remained silent as the door opened. She alighted first, and then Geoffrey stepped down, far more slowly and stiffly. He was a sight, with his jacket rent and his face sporting bruises. He winced visibly. "Confound it."

Sarah could not help herself. "Perhaps I could kiss it and make it feel better?"

Geoffrey stiffened and his gaze shot daggers. "We, madame, shall never kiss again." Without another word he stalked past Sarah.

Sarah watched him as he strode toward the steps with the

slightest of limps. "A shame," she murmured. She hid her smile. Geoffrey thought to punish her. He might find his sentence more punishing to himself than to her.

Geoffrey spotted the rabbit in the dim morning light. Slowly, he raised the gun.

"Are you going to shoot that darling rabbit?" Sarah's voice echoed through the woods. The rabbit started up and streaked away.

"Damn it, Amy," Geoffrey said, turning to glare at her.

She stood not a foot behind him, with the most innocent expression upon her face. "Well, are you going to shoot it?"

"Not anymore," Geoffrey said, eyes narrowed. "You frightened it off."

"I am sorry," Sarah said.

"You always are," Geoffrey said.

Geoffrey had discovered in the past few days that the woman decidedly got her own way far too often. Not once had she argued over anything Geoffrey said they would do, but Geoffrey had found that doing things with her, the things he intended, always turned into something with totally her stamp upon it. He took her fishing only to find their expedition changed into an al fresco picnic, complete with napkins and wine. When he had objected, Sarah said she saw no reason if they were going to feed the fish worms, why they themselves should not eat as well. When he rode out to inspect the fields, he wound up more often than not racing with her, for she proved to be an excellent horse-woman who challenged not only her horse but him. And when he drove to town for an auction, he discovered she would barter far more quickly than he and then remain fully determined that her price was the correct one.

Geoffrey looked at her sternly. "You did that on purpose."

"Indeed no," Sarah said. "To prove it, I'll go find that rabbit again." She flashed a smile and, waltzing past him, proceeded through the woods, calling out, "Oh, rabbit, please come back. We wish to put a ball through you."

"Stop it," Geoffrey said. "You are scaring off all the animals."

"What?" Sarah turned around and cast him a laughing look. "I'm only trying to help."

"No, you are not," Geoffrey said. "And if you persist, it will be you who I will shoot."

"Oh, dear," Sarah said. She quickly rushed to hide behind a tree. "Oh, rabbit, wait up! I'm hightailing it with you."

Geoffrey laughed and stalked toward her. He saw Sarah flit away to another tree. "I refuse to go home empty-handed again. There's been no fish on the table, and now you are ruining the game."

"No, I'm not," Sarah called, her voice sounding farther away. " 'Tis the game of hide-and-seek."

Geoffrey, realizing there wouldn't be an animal within miles which hadn't fled, cast in his chips. "You better hide," he called out, and chased after her, crashing through the woods. Amy laughed and ran before him. Knowing the land better, Geoffrey ducked off the path and circled around very silently. He heard Sarah's laughter subside and soon heard her calling out to him. He hid in the bushes, waiting. He could hear her coming directly into his path. When he gauged she was close to him, Geoffrey jumped out of the bushes. "Found you!"

She screamed and quickly struck out at him, hitting him hard against the chest. Geoffrey wheezed at the blow but grabbed her quickly. "Amy, it's me!"

She went still within his arms. Her eyes were wide and frightened. He saw recognition flit through them and then relief. "Geoffrey! You frightened me for a moment."

"Are you all right?" Geoffrey asked.

"Yes, yes, I am." She pushed away from him and turned her back upon him.

Geoffrey, frowning, took hold of her shoulders and spun

her back to face him. Sarah would not meet his gaze. "You remember something, don't you?"

"No," she said, her voice low. "No, I do not."

"Yes, you do," Geoffrey said softly, his hands tightening upon her. "What is it? Who did you think I was?"

Sarah looked up at him and said angrily, "I don't know, I tell you! I don't remember."

"You don't remember?" Geoffrey asked. "Or you don't want to remember?"

"Both," Sarah whispered, pain flashing across her face, hollowing out her eyes.

That pain knifed through Geoffrey, as if it were his very own. He slowly released her and stepped back. God help him, but he didn't want her to remember either. He didn't want her to remember whatever caused that look upon her face. He didn't want her to remember her other life, that life which would have nothing to do with playing hide-and-go seek in the woods with him.

"Come. We might as well return," Geoffrey said. He forced a smile. "Mrs. Biddington will not be pleased the only thing I caught was you."

"She's been regretting that from the very first day," Sarah said, her face relaxing.

Geoffrey laughed. "She might feel better if I told her you were to be our next meal."

"No," Sarah said, shaking her head. "She wouldn't know how to dress me, would she? She has no turn for fashion, after all."

"Are you already finished, Geoffrey?" Sarah asked, sitting on a blanket upon the ground, holding her parasol up to shield herself from the sun. She nodded toward the field before them and the men in it. "There is still much to be done, is there not?"

"Yes," Geoffrey said. "I intend to return, but first I wish to take you home."

"Why?" Sarah asked, surprised. "I am enjoying myself, I assure you."

Geoffrey's brow lifted. "Watching men work pleases you?"

Sarah ran a quick eye over Geoffrey. His shirt lay open at the throat and sweat matted the cloth to his chest. A tingle coursed through her. It should have been one of ladylike disgust, but in truth it was one of pleasure. She had never seen a man thus, for no man of her acquaintance would have ever appeared before her in anything but his finest clothes. Yet oddly enough, Geoffrey in his work clothes looked as appealing to her as any man dressed to the nines, and Geoffrey in his sweat and dirt did not revolt her but only drew her attention to his muscles and strength.

"Of course," Sarah said, laughing. "Since I am the one watching, and you are the one working."

"I had thought that," Geoffrey said, though a slight smile tugged at his lips. "But the men are unhappy with it."

"Why?"

"Because you are watching them, looking as cool and grand as you please while they are toiling."

"Grand?" Sarah asked. "Thank you very much, but this skirt and blouse I have on are anything but grand. I look the veritable peasant."

"These men are attracted to peasants," Geoffrey said.

"And are you?" Sarah asked, batting her lashes. Geoffrey only frowned at her. She knew she shouldn't flirt so with him, but she could not resist. It simply was too tempting of a challenge, since he never responded in kind. "For if you are . . . ?" Sarah reached up and pulled the ribbon from her hair, shaking her head.

Geoffrey merely frowned. "Come."

"Very well," Sarah said. Snapping down her parasol, she rose. Geoffrey bent to pick up the blanket. They proceeded to walk through the field in a companionable silence. Yet when they passed a freshly made haystack Sarah stopped and said in the most innocent of tones, "Geoffrey, you may have not noticed, but I vow I saw a man and girl disappear into one of these the other day."

Geoffrey cast her a wary look. "Yes?"

"Whatever were they doing?" Sarah asked.

"They were . . ." Geoffrey halted and frowned at her. "They were going there for rest."

"Rest?" Sarah asked. She promptly threw down her parasol. "Faith, that is what I need. Watching men toil is so enervating." Laughing, she ran to the haystack, and quickly began digging a hole within it. She made sure to swing the handfuls of hay toward Geoffrey.

"Stop that!" Geoffrey ordered.

"Am I not doing it correctly?" Sarah asked, turning to look at him in devilment.

A challenging light entered Geoffrey's eyes. "No," he said, stalking over. "This is how you do it." Geoffrey moved the hay far faster than she, and when there was quite a hole, he put his hands to her waist. "And this." He lifted her and all but tossed her into the hay.

"Geoffrey," Sarah sputtered only once, for then she felt him crawling in, his large body sliding up alongside of hers. His arms went about her, and the scent of hay and warm male invaded her senses.

"I warned you about flirting with country men," Geoffrey said. His lips were descending very quickly to hers.

"But we aren't going to kiss ever again," Sarah said, her heart suddenly pounding. "Remember?"

"And you've teased the very devil out of me for that," Geoffrey said. "It's going to stop right now." His lips covered hers, strongly and in full demand. His hands, with no hesitancy, but rather a surety, pulled her body to his, molding it. Sarah moaned slightly, feeling a shivering heat course through her. Surrendering, she kissed him back, delighting in the friction of his lips upon hers, the hardness of his muscles beneath her fingers, the strength of his body driving hers into the fragrant hay.

Yet those sensations changed and Sarah became truly lost. It seemed that no longer were the sensations themselves engulfing her, but the very essence of the man himself. His spirit drew and held her more tightly than ever his arms could. Sarah, deep inside, felt her heart opening with each touch, each kiss, and she offered everything of herself back with each touch, each kiss.

Geoffrey suddenly jerked back. His eyes were dark with passion, and something else. His gaze seemed to recognize her in a completely different way. "Damn you, Amy," he said, his voice low and hoarse.

His words struck to the very core of Sarah's newly opened and vulnerable heart. "Damn me?" Pain choking her, Sarah shoved at Geoffrey, becoming a fighting fury. She ignored his exclamation and scrambled out of the haystack. Picking up her skirts, she took off running, fleeing her newfound feelings, escaping his wounding words.

Sarah heard Geoffrey shouting from behind her. She glanced hastily back to see him far in the distance. Suddenly, she heard a horse neigh and a man curse. Looking back around, she came to a gasping halt. Two horsemen were directly in her path.

"Whoa!" the one cried as his horse reared up. The other man beside him cursed as his own animal caracoled about.

Sarah stood frozen in fear as the two men brought their animals under control. She recognized them. One was Sir Harry Monteath and the other the right honorable George Stanton. Sir Harry was a drinking partner of Ravenwich.

"Gads!" Sir Harry sniffed, as he looked down from his now-quivering, subdued animal. "Watch what you are about, wench. You damn near unseated me."

"S'truth," George Stanton said. "Ought to know better, chit." Then his eyes widened upon Sarah, who found she could not move. "Odd's blood! Harry, don't she look like Lady Sarah?"

Sir Harry grabbed at the string of his looking glass and raised it to his eye. "Damn, but she does at that!"

Sarah's own eyes widened, yet a small hope entered her. Shaking herself into action, she dipped an awkward curtsey and said in a country twang, "I be frightful sorry, me lords, I twern't watching where I was going."

George Stanton shook his head, his expression dumbfounded. "She could be the perfect spit for the Incomparable."

Sir Harry brayed a laugh. "Wait until I tell Ravenwich I saw a peasant girl who looks just like her."

"Tell Ravenwich?" Sarah gasped, shocked. Neither man appeared to notice her stunned reaction, so busy were they amusing themselves with their joke. Sarah forced a smirk. "Who's this here R-ravenwich you be talkin' about?"

"He is a fine duke," Sir Harry said. "And far above your touch, you impertinent baggage."

Sarah swayed her hips. "Ye said I looked like this here Im-compar—arable? Is she as perty as me?"

"Far more so!" George said. He snickered. "But then again, she wouldn't have straw in her hair. Faith, it's too, too good. Should tell old Ravenwich we've found Lady Sarah's replacement for him. Might cheer him up while the Incomparable is away visiting those relatives of his."

Sir Harry hooted a laugh and then shook his head. "Too bad old Ravenwich is in such bad skin of late."

"Ain't it?" George said, sighing. "Should take it as a jest, but wouldn't be surprised if he called us out instead. He's been riding damn rusty."

Geoffrey called her from behind. Sarah turned quickly. He was walking toward them.

She spun back. "Excuse me, gents, but here comes me man. He . . . he won't be loikin' me talkin to yers. He's the jealous sorts."

"Gads," Sir Harry said, his eyes popping. "He's a bleedin' giant. Best be off, George, no time to brangle with a Johnny raw, not if we're going to make it to old Blackwell's auction. Don't want to miss the chance of buying that bay."

"S'truth," George said. Both men kicked their horses and took off without another word.

Sarah turned quickly and stood as calmly as she could as Geoffrey approached. He stopped and looked at her, waiting.

She forced a smile. "They needed directions."

"I see," he said solemnly.

"They are going to a horse auction," Sarah said, beginning to walk.

"It would be Blackwell's," Geoffrey informed her, as he fell into step beside her. "He's one of the finest horse breeders in the area, in the country, in fact."

"I did not know," Sarah said. Emotions roiled and careened within her. She had been both cursed and blessed. Cursed in accidentally meeting two men, simply on their way to an auction. Blessed in that they were fools and had not recognized her. Blessed in that Ravenwich still lived. Cursed in that Ravenwich still lived.

Shaking, Sarah reached out to clasp Geoffrey's hand. Gratefully, he took hold of it without speaking a word.

Seven

Sarah stood, looking out at the dark night from her bedroom window. She hugged herself close, wrapped in Geoffrey's nightshirt. It was beyond foolish, she knew, but she had kept it and wore it tonight rather than the ones she had commissioned from Mrs. Wraxton. She wore it for comfort, as a reminder that she should be safe within Geoffrey's household.

She chuckled dryly, so dryly it hurt her throat. She should be happy. She was not a murderess. Ravenwich still lived. Yet if he lived, he would be waiting to exact revenge upon her. Now, knowing and understanding the man as she did, she never doubted it. If he was acting the lovelorn fiancé still, and had told his friends she was out of town visiting relatives, he had a purpose to it.

A chill chased down Sarah's spine. Was he looking for her in earnest? Or was he simply waiting for her to come out of hiding? Most likely he waited, like a cat with a mouse. Sarah turned from the window, her face set. She must stay very close in her hole and make her plans.

Geoffrey awoke to screams, piercing screams. He started up, his heart pounding. He knew whose screams they were. Rolling swiftly from the bed, he snatched up his smoking jacket, rammed his arms into its sleeves, and tore from the room.

As he approached Sarah's door, the screams ceased. It only drove the fear deeper into him. He slammed open the door and burst into the room. He halted, adjusting his eyes to the moon-shadowed room. He finally saw her, sitting up in her bed. She screamed again.

"Amy, it's me," Geoffrey said, quickly crossing to the bed.

"Geoffrey?" she said. "Faith, you frightened me."

"I frightened you?" Geoffrey said, peering closely at the woman. Moonlight bathed her skin to alabaster marble. Her eyes were the opposite, dark, haunted pools. "You were screaming."

Sarah looked down. "Yes. I had a nightmare I'm afraid."

"Clearly," Geoffrey said. "What were you dreaming?"

"I . . ." Sarah halted. Then her voice came out more calmly. "I dreamed I was a mouse."

Geoffrey stared. "A mouse?"

"Yes," Sarah said with dignity. Her chin tilted. "I was being chased by a cat."

"And who was the cat?" Geoffrey asked, watching her closely.

"I do not know." She shrugged. "I did not stop to ask its name. No doubt it was Tom, or something like that."

"It wasn't Tom," Geoffrey said, very positive.

"Oh, do you know his name, this cat in my dream?" Sarah asked.

"No," Geoffrey said. "But you do, or you will. Once you regain your memory."

"Indeed?" she asked.

"I have been reading up on the matter," Geoffrey said. "It can be difficult when one begins to have memories come back."

"I see," Sarah said in a low voice. She shifted in her bed. "Perhaps that is what is happening, or perhaps it was merely indigestion. Either way, forgive me for waking you. I am fine now. You may return to your room."

Her tone clearly dismissed him. Geoffrey nodded curtly. "Very well."

He turned and walked to the door, grabbing hold of the doorknob. Something stopped him, however, and made him turn back to look at Sarah once more. She sat in her bed, straight and stiff, watching him. No matter her rumpled nightshirt, her disheveled hair, she appeared completely possessed and controlled. Her appearance told him he should leave. Yet past the appearance, past her words, he could read fear within her, and feel it as if it were his own. It was like this afternoon in the hay mow. He had kissed her because she had flirted with him until he could stand it no more. But when he had tasted the passion which had driven him, it had suddenly faded and he had felt as if he had held a different woman in his arms, a woman whose very essence captured him more dangerously than did her passion. He had damned that moment. As he damned this moment, knowing he would not leave her, could not leave her knowing the fear she hid. Growling, he closed the door rather than walking out of it. Then he stalked back to the bed, looking at Sarah with level eyes.

Her eyes widened. "Wh-what is the matter?"

"Move over," Geoffrey said rather roughly. He did not wait, but promptly sat down upon the bed.

"Why?" Sarah asked, though she scrambled quickly to the middle of the bed.

He paused. "Because you will have another nightmare, and I prefer to remain here, rather than hurry back and forth between the rooms."

Her chin lifted. "You do not need to return if I have another nightmare."

"No, I don't," Geoffrey said, settling himself back against the pillow.

"Geoffrey, you cannot . . . cannot remain here."

"Can I not?" he said, shifting to a more comfortable position. "You always seem to do whatever you want. Now I believe I shall." He suddenly noticed something. "You are still wearing my nightshirt."

He saw Sarah stiffen. "I told you, I have discovered your clothes are far more serviceable than those for women. I suppose you want it back?"

"Not at this moment," Geoffrey said with a smile. Sarah's gaze flew to his and then she looked down. He heard just the slightest laugh from her. "Now, you may do what you wish, but I am going to remain here."

Sarah sat staring at him, the moment drawing out. Then without a word, she moved over and lay close to him, putting her head upon his shoulder. With far less hesitation, Geoffrey put his arms about her, enfolding her. "Go to sleep, Amy, there is nothing to fear."

"I'm not afraid," she murmured.

"No, of course not," Geoffrey said.

"Not now," she said in a soft tone and he felt her body slowly relax.

Geoffrey did not answer, but his arms tightened around her. The woman could suddenly give; and in a way which always knocked the wind from him. Sarah's breathing slowed and steadied into the gentle one of sleep and still Geoffrey lay, staring into the dark, holding her close.

"Geoffrey, what is the matter?" Melanie said as she picked up a teacup.

"What?" Geoffrey looked up from frowning over his own cup of tea. He had almost forgotten Melanie's presence.

"What is the matter?" Melanie asked again. "Have you and Amy had an argument again?"

"No," Geoffrey said. "No, we haven't." He set his cup down quickly.

In truth, he wished they had had an argument, or a row,

or even a full-scale battle, anything but the silent, reserved distance they shared now. She was driving him insane, and in the devil's own handcart at that. Ever since three nights ago, when he had held the sleeping Sarah until dawn, and left her before she woke to erase any confusion or embarrassment there might be, she had avoided his company.

It could very well be he had overstepped the bounds that night and Sarah indeed was embarrassed about it and reluctant to be in his company, but he didn't believe so. She was treating everyone else in the same fashion. She refused to leave the house, saying merely she was not feeling the thing. Even worse, though she refused to talk to him, Geoffrey knew she still harbored fear . . . and something else. It was as if there was a tension in her, a waiting. What she feared, what she waited for he did not know, but it distracted him from his own work, robbed him of his own sleep.

"She has not come to tea for two days," Melanie said quietly.

"I know," Geoffrey said. He hesitated. "She says she is simply not feeling well. I asked if she would like me to call Doctor Hobbs, but she told me not to do so." He ran his hand through his hair. "I cannot be certain, but I've been reading about her condition, and I believe Amy is close to remembering her past and it frightens her."

Melanie's brown eyes darkened in concern. "Is there anything we can do for her? Anything I can do?"

"Yes," Geoffrey said, expelling a tired breath. "She clearly does not wish my company nor will she confide in me. Perhaps if you were able to spend more time with her, she will confide in you. If not, at least she will have your company." He frowned. "I am not sure what will happen if she suddenly regains her memory and it is a cruel one. The books say each case is different and unpredictable. I asked Doctor Hobbs and he was of no help whatsoever. He said the only experience he had with this was when old Jamison's mule kicked him in the head."

"And what happened there?" Melanie asked.

Geoffrey laughed dryly. "He said Jamison didn't know his own name for a month, nor could he put two words together. Certainly not Sarah's failing."

"No," Melanie laughed. "Indeed no."

"Then one day old Jamison suddenly remembered his name and everything else. Apparently the first words out of old Jamison's mouth was 'Get my gun, I'm shooting that cursed mule.' " Melanie laughed, but Geoffrey did not. "I think Amy's case is different. She doesn't want to remember, and when she does it may very well be traumatic. I do not wish for her to be alone if that happens."

"No, of course not," Melanie said, turning serious. "That would be dreadful. I will make certain I spend more time with her."

"Thank you," Geoffrey said. He frowned. "I know it will be difficult for you with all your family duties. I notice Joy is coming to sew often. Perhaps we could ask her to help as well."

"Certainly," Melanie said. "I am sure she would be pleased to do so. She holds Amy in high esteem."

"As we all know far too well," Geoffrey said. He fell silent a moment and then said, "It is important Amy does not know we are watching her. We do not want to make her uncomfortable. 'Tis why I know I cannot be too much about her." He saw a look of surprise enter Melanie's eyes. "What?"

"Nothing," Melanie said, looking down. " 'Tis merely that it is not normal for you to behave with such . . . such circumspection."

Geoffrey started. He could not tell Melanie that his behavior was anything but circumspect. He said, rather stiffly, "I merely am doing everything the book suggests in order for Amy to regain her memory."

He also refrained from confessing that if she did not soon regain her memory, or at least stop behaving in the manner she was, he'd gladly go and hunt out old Jamison's mule and prompt it to kick him in the head in hopes that he would forget everything himself.

Sarah paced her bedroom. She was past tired, but she could not sleep. Nor had she been able to in the past four nights. It was a very lowering thing, but she, the Incomparable Lady Sarah, had come to point nonplus. She could not, to save her life, seem to make any decisions, and certainly not any definitive ones. And if she were to save her life, she simply must make them.

Simple intelligence told her she must take action. Ravenwich was out there, and as the days passed, new worries had crept into her consciousness. What if Monteath and Stanton did end up being the idiots they were and told Ravenwich about their jolly meeting with her after all? Ravenwich, unfortunately, was not as much of a fool as they were.

Therefore, it would behoove her to leave here. The wisest and simplest course would be for her to regain her memory, confess it to Geoffrey, and ask him to assist her in a safe return to London. Yet Sarah found herself cringing from the prospect. Why, she could not say. Perhaps it was because she was losing her confidence in her acting ability when it came to Geoffrey. Which was ridiculous, since their whole relationship was based upon her acting ability. Or it had been. Lately it seemed Geoffrey saw through her more and more, divined the truths all too easily.

If she tried this new lie upon him, he might finally see through her completely. And then, as sure as the day dawned, Geoffrey would also see past her. He was not a man who would be impressed with Lady Sarah, London debutante and toast of the ton. Nor was he a man who would appreciate that such a one as she had duped him as well.

Sarah paced across the room once more. It was ridiculous, so totally ridiculous. She actually feared receiving the cut direct from a rough, ungallant country lord. She endangered herself merely because she could not muster the courage to tell him one more little lie. No, she could not muster the courage to tell him the larger truth, the truth of who she was.

Sarah halted and stiffened. She was not ashamed of herself. Everyone adored her, and if one man, one man who had no part in her real world, did not feel the same, it mattered not. Certainly she wasn't so proud and vain she could not accept that one sole man did not fall at her feet. That was all it was. Vanity! She simply must forget it. She must stop fretting over Geoffrey's reaction and have done with it.

But first, she must gain some sleep. A woman could not attack the ticklish situation of recapturing her memory and cozening a man into taking her to London if she was not at her fittest. Faith, she must look a positive hag, and being in good looks was another thing of paramount importance when a lady entered into battle with a man. She hadn't had one night's sleep since the evening when Geoffrey had remained to chase away her nightmares.

She started back as a thought passed through her mind. Then she relaxed and she came to the most decisive decision she had made in days. It clearly was not the wisest, nor the fairest. In fact, it was unconscionable, but Sarah refused to waste a moment to debate the issue or permit sanity to take control.

She moved quickly to the door and cracked it open. Then she rushed to her bed, crawled into it and blew out her candle. She did not lay down but sat straight up, drew in a deep breath and let out a piercing scream. She paused and emitted another shriek. She was on her third scream when the ajar door slammed open. She quickly halted as Geoffrey charged into the room.

He stopped only when he stood by the side of her bed. His silk dressing jacket was barely on, and a nightshirt very much like the one she wore showed beneath it.

Sarah looked down quickly and said, "I am sorry. I must have had another nightmare."

She peeked up. Geoffrey stared at her, his face showing signs of weariness and stress. He expelled a breath and asked, "What was it this time? Was it the cat?"

"No," Sarah said, and shook her head. "It was . . . was a lion this time."

He frowned. "A lion?"

"And I was a deer," Sarah said.

"I see," Geoffrey said, and ran his hand through his already rumpled hair. Something flitted in his eyes and he said in a rather stiff tone, "Will you be all right?"

Sarah bit her lip. "I—I'm not sure."

"I see," Geoffrey said, refusing to look at her. Sarah held her breath, waiting. He seemed to shake himself and straighten his shoulders. "Well, I am sure you will be fine. Y-you have nothing to fear." He spun swiftly and walked toward the door. "Good night, Amy."

"Good night?" she asked, stunned. His hand was upon the doorknob, and Sarah all but shouted, "Geoffrey!"

He jumped and turned. "What?"

"I'm . . . I'm afraid," Sarah said in a rush, "that I'm going to have another nightmare!"

A silence fell. "Are you sure?"

Sarah nodded, her body tense. "Yes, I'm sure of it. I—I can't sleep because of them."

"Good," Geoffrey said. Sarah's eyes widened. "What I mean is that I am glad you warned me." He shut the door and Sarah breathed a sigh of relief. He moved quickly to the bed and Sarah just as quickly handed him her pillow. She barely waited for him to settle before she shifted close. She sighed in contentment as his arms went about her. She was surprised to hear Geoffrey echo her sigh.

"I am sorry about this," she murmured, trying to sound regretful as she nestled her head upon his shoulder.

"Don't be," Geoffrey said. "This way we both can rest."

"You haven't been able to sleep?"

"Hmm," Geoffrey murmured.

"Haven't you been able to sleep?" Sarah asked again.

"No," Geoffrey said, his voice sleepy. "I've been . . . waiting for you . . . to have nightmares."

"I won't now," Sarah said, smiling as she shut her eyes. "I promise."

Geoffrey's arm tightened slightly. "Don't worry about the lion . . . deer."

"What?" Sarah asked, her eyes snapping open. She twisted her head to discover Geoffrey's eyes closed. He was clearly asleep. Sarah blinked. It was exactly what she had intended to do, but that he had fallen asleep on her so swiftly only showed her once more how very little sway she held over the man.

Sighing, she laid her head back down. She'd refuse to think upon it anymore, not when she was feeling more secure and comfortable than she had in days. She could sleep well now. The slightest frown marred her brow as she drifted off. It was not a good thing when a woman needed a man beside her to help her sleep. That was not how it was supposed to be. Not if the world was to be believed.

Sarah woke to hear what sounded like knocking. She cracked her eyes open. Bright sunlight assaulted them, so she closed them tightly and moved closer into Geoffrey's warm embrace.

"Miss Amy," Mrs. Biddington's voice drifted through her fogged mind. "Miss Amy, are you awake?"

"Yes, Mrs. Biddington," Sarah sighed, opening her eyes in aggravation. "What do you want."

"May I come in?" Mrs. Biddington's voice quivered.

Sleep fell swiftly from Sarah and she scrambled up. Geoffrey, clearly still asleep, grunted a complaint. Sarah slapped her hand over his mouth and shouted, "No! I mean, no, I . . . I am dressing."

She felt Geoffrey stir and she glanced at him. His eyes

were open now, and despite the sleepy look in them, he lifted a brow. Sarah pulled her hand back swiftly.

"I am sorry, Miss Amy," Mrs. Biddington's voice came again. "But Lord Grey did not come to breakfast this morning, nor can I find him anywhere."

"What does that have to do with me?" Sarah asked, flushing a deep red, as Geoffrey slowly sat up in the bed.

"I—I just wondered if you knew his plans," Mrs. Biddington said. "Mr. Nash is downstairs and . . . and wishing to speak to him. He said he . . . he had an appointment with my lord."

"I am sorry," Sarah said. "But I do not know where Lord Grey is."

"Very well, Miss Amy," Mrs. Biddington said.

They remained quiet, waiting to ensure that Mrs. Biddington was truly gone. As Sarah sat there beside Geoffrey, the oddest feelings rose within her. What she could define was healthy embarrassment and unhealthy passion. Somehow, almost being caught drove home the total impropriety of the situation, and the dangers of it. She had been insane last night, and now, with a good dose of sleep, she realized it.

Geoffrey merely sat there, quietly studying her. As the moment elongated, amusement entered his slumberous gaze. Finally, he laughed. "I never thought to see you blushing, Amy. But you are, and a very bright red."

"You need not tell me," she said. She lifted her chin and said in her most imperious tone, "I think you best leave."

Geoffrey shook his head. "It's not working this time, Amy. Perhaps the pose is ruined by your nightshirt and rumpled state." He leaned forward. "Would you like to give me a good-morning kiss?"

"No!" Sarah said, leaning back.

"Strange," Geoffrey said. " 'Tis what I thought I saw in your eyes."

Sarah looked at him, and realized it would not help to lie. "It does not matter. We certainly cannot kiss here."

Geoffrey's brow shot up. "You can lure me into the haystack for a kiss, but you cannot kiss me in bed? A very odd consideration. I was under the impression that bed was one of the most common places for kissing."

"That is why we cannot," Sarah said, and for self-preservation scrambled far too indecorously from the bed. She regained her stature and said as calmly as she could, "And I did not lure you into the haystack for a kiss."

"You didn't?" Geoffrey asked.

"No, I didn't think you would kiss me," Sarah confessed.

"You thought only to flirt and tease me," Geoffrey said, nodding. Then he smiled and patted the bed. "Come, Amy, flirt with me now."

"No."

"But you do it so well," Geoffrey said, grinning. "And didn't you say I needed to learn how to flirt to please a lady."

Sarah's eyes widened. "You are flirting now!"

"Anything to please a lady," Geoffrey laughed. He slowly rose from the bed and stood. "Aren't you going to reward me?" He moved stealthily around the bed toward her.

Sarah, deciding her pose was failing anyway, dashed for the safety of the ugly rose chair. "You may stop flirting with me now, Geoffrey."

"Why?" Geoffrey asked, still walking toward her. *"You* never desist."

"Just why are you acting like this?" Sarah asked.

Geoffrey laughed. " 'Tis morning. I've finally gotten a good night's sleep and I am feeling very . . . flirtatious, should we say?"

"Well, go and be flirtatious somewhere else!"

"Come, Amy," Geoffrey said, the chair gratefully halting him. "Give me a kiss. We are not in bed after all."

"We are in the bedroom," Sarah said. "That is close enough."

"Yes, it is," Geoffrey said, grinning. Before Sarah could react, he leaned over the chair and gave her a swift kiss upon the lips. She blinked as he pulled back, his eyes alight with laughter. "There's nothing like a morning kiss." He sighed and strolled toward the door. She could swear there was smugness in his every move. He turned and bowed. "Good morning to you, Amy. I've enjoyed flirting with you very much."

Geoffrey cracked open the door, peered out, and then stepped out, closing the door behind him. Sarah, frowning in bemusement, lifted her hands to her lips. This country gentleman's brand of flirting was far more virulent than she could have ever imagined.

"You put this many eggs in it?" Sarah asked, peering into the bowl.

"Yes, you do," Melanie said. "This is how you crack them." She tapped an egg with one hand upon the side of the bowl and somehow dropped the egg and not the shell into the flour.

"I see," Sarah said, quite impressed.

"Try it," Melanie said, handing her an egg. Sarah looked at the egg dubiously.

Joy walked over from the fireplace at that moment and said, "You can use both hands, Amy, if you want."

"Yes, yes," Mrs. Biddington said, dashing over as well. "Using one hand is not easy."

Sarah gazed at the three ladies now surrounding her. Her hand shook with the egg and her heart failed a second. Gracious! Hosting a diplomatic ball, or circumventing Prinny's roving hands at a state dinner appeared far easier than this business with an egg.

"All right." Sarah cupped both hands over the egg and cracked it smartly on the bowl. It squashed precipitously into her hands, the greater share oozing down the sides of the bowl with very little reaching the insides. "Heavens!"

The ladies started laughing as Sarah dropped the glutinous mess immediately upon the table.

"It does take practice," Melanie said as she picked up another egg.

"Well, she ain't going ter get it!" a booming, rough voice said from the corner of the kitchen. Mrs. Biddington squeaked and Sarah jumped. She turned toward the voice. A tall, burly man, flanked by a smaller, gangly man, stood within the entrance of the kitchen's outer door. Both men leveled large, dark pistols upon them.

"Lord! Lord!" Mrs. Biddington cried, twitching.

"Shut up," the larger man roared.

"Oh, oh!" Mrs. Biddington squeaked to mute.

"What do you want?" Sarah asked, a tremor coursing through her. She knew very well what they wanted.

"You, missy," the man said with an ugly grin.

"You can't have her," Joy said, her voice amazingly calm. She stepped directly in front of Sarah.

"Indeed," Melanie said and followed suit.

"Gawd," the shorter man said, his pistol flicking back and forth as he clearly attempted to cover all of them. "Gets out of the way, loidies."

The large man's pistol didn't waver. "Don't matter, Lenny. If they's want to be shot, we'll shoot them and still get the meg."

"Gore, Tom," the man Lenny gurgled. "D-don't want to have to pop them all orf."

"What's it to be?" Tom asked, ignoring his partner and glaring at Sarah from over the heads of Melanie and Joy. "You want these here women shot 'cause of you?"

"No," Sarah said. She gently placed a hand upon Joy and Melanie's shoulders.

Melanie turned, her eyes amazingly steady. "Amy, you cannot leave with them."

"I fear I must. Please, I do not want you hurt." She forced a smile. "Do not worry over me . . . and th-thank you."

"Come on, come on," Tom said. "You can save yer tender good-byes."

"Good-bye, Joy," Sarah said, coolly ignoring Tom. "Keep your course. I'm proud of you."

"I . . . I will," Joy said, and tears glistening at the corners of her eyes.

"Gawd," Lenny said. "She's going to bawl."

"No," Sarah said, walking calmly and slowly toward the two waiting men. "She is not. Now let us leave."

Tom grinned. "Smart mort, ain't ye? Lenny, ye keep these here ladies covered till's me and Her Highness are clear."

"What?" Lenny's voice squeaked. "Yer leaving me with them heres?"

"Ye got the bloody popper, don't ye? And they're just women fer God's sake!" Tom said, grabbing Sarah's shoulder roughly when she stood close enough and ramming the pistol into her ribs. She gritted her teeth and permitted him to shove her out the door. She said not another word as he dragged her toward an awaiting carriage, its coachman as large and burly as the man beside her.

"N-nows, don't any orv you move," Lenny stammered, waving his pistol menacingly at the three remaining ladies, though his face showed signs of nervous sweat.

"Oh, dear," Mrs. Biddington moaned, her hands fluttering.

"I said don't move!" Lenny shouted.

Mrs. Biddington started, her faded blue eyes rolled back until only the whites showed, and she swayed alarmingly. Lenny's pistol weaved like a drunken snake as it followed her.

"Damn it, stop that!"

Mrs. Biddington wheezed and toppled forward. Lenny shouted and fired. The shot hit high, very high indeed, since

Mrs. Biddington had already crumpled to the floor. The errant ball plowed into a hanging pot and rang loudly.

"Bejesus! Bejesus!" Lenny cried, standing transfixed and dazed.

Melanie saw her chance.

"Lenny! Look!" she cried. Lenny did look, and Melanie lifted the egg still in her hand and pegged it at him. It cracked against his chest and Lenny jerked, dropped the pistol, and clapped his hands to his chest as if he himself had been shot. Melanie dashed at him, knowing she must offset him before he could react. She cannoned into him and they fell over in a tangle.

"Move away, Melanie," Joy cried. Melanie rolled as swiftly as she could from the cursing Lenny and stood. Lenny, not so quickly, sat up. Joy brandished in her hands a particularly large kitchen knife. Melanie gasped and Lenny gurgled as Joy lowered it toward him.

"God, don't cut me!" Lenny begged.

"I will if you so much as move," Joy said. "I hope you know I've held a pistol to my husband, and taking this knife to you is far easier."

"Yer own husband?" Lenny asked, gaping.

"She did," Melanie said. Seeing that Joy held Lenny's attention riveted, Melanie glanced hurriedly about for the pistol. It lay a few feet from Lenny and she ran to catch it up. She went to stand over Lenny on the side across from Joy. She lifted the pistol up like a hatchet. "And I'll hit you with this as well."

"Gore," Lenny breathed. All three stared at each other a frozen, tense moment.

"Er," Lenny said, hesitancy in his voice. "Whots yer going ter do with me?"

"We are going to . . ." Melanie stopped and looked hopelessly at Joy.

"We are going to . . ." Joy stopped as well.

Melanie looked desperately about. "I know what we are

going to do! Watch him, Joy," she said, and ran over to the still body of Mrs. Biddington. She snatched the keys from the housekeeper's pocket and came back, holding them up in triumph. "We are going to lock you in the pantry!"

"G-good idea," Lenny stammered, casting a nervous look at Joy's knife.

"Get up and don't make any fast moves," Joy said.

"I—I won't, ifn' you don't," Lenny said. He rose slowly, cautiously, his eyes wide upon Joy's knife. "Wh-where's the p-antry?"

"Over here," Melanie directed, and went to open the door to the small room. Lenny scurried over, Joy chasing behind with the knife. His sweating face actually appeared relieved as Melanie closed the door upon him. She turned the key in the lock, and then, sighing, leaned against the door. "Joy, you must go and get Geoffrey."

"Yes, of course," Joy said, dropping her knife to the floor with a clatter. "Wh-where would he be?"

"It's almost tea time," Melanie said. "H-he should be coming home by the left lane."

Joy dashed out the door, and Melanie, unable to help herself, slid down the pantry door and sat, clasping the key and pistol to her chest.

A low moan arose from Mrs. Biddington and soon she staggered up from the floor. She blinked hazily. "What happened?"

"You fainted," Melanie said. "We've got Lenny locked in the pantry and Joy has gone to get Geoffrey."

"What?" Mrs. Biddington exclaimed, her hands flying to her mouth. "My lord is coming here? It is tea time and nothing is prepared. Tsk. Tsk."

Melanie watched, stunned, as the little housekeeper moved to the table and began arranging it. "Mrs. Biddington?"

"Yes, yes," Mrs. Biddington said. "We must hurry. There is no time, no time at all."

"I—I don't think Geoffrey will want tea, Mrs. Biddington," Melanie said rather weakly.

"He will . . . he will. I must prepare," Mrs. Biddington said, her movements slow and mechanical. She picked up an egg and cracked it into the bowl. "It is my duty. M-my lord must have his tea."

Melanie shook her head in resignation, and permitted the dazed little housekeeper to continue upon her disconcerting path. The minutes ticked by interminably and Melanie felt her own sanity sliding away as Mrs. Biddington cooked and fussed and arranged the tea set.

The scones were cooling upon the rack when finally the outer door burst open. Geoffrey stood within its portal, eyes flashing and looking very much like an enraged Viking.

"Geoffrey!" Melanie cried in a flood of relief.

"Where is this man?" Geoffrey said, his voice low and lethal.

"In here!" Melanie said.

"My lord," Mrs. Biddington called, her face beaming. "The tea is ready! I had to rush . . ."

"Give me the key," Geoffrey commanded, stalking across the kitchen. Melanie scrabbled up and handed it to him. She stepped aside as Geoffrey unlocked the door and tore it open. A growl came from him, more animal than human, and he dove into the pantry. A high howl arose. Then crashes and thumps.

"Oh, dear," Mrs. Biddington said, her hands fluttering over the tea set and shifting the cups.

At that moment, Joy dashed into the kitchen, panting as she ran up to Melanie. "I—I'm sorry, I—I . . . c-couldn't keep up. Where is . . ."

A shriek rose from the pantry.

"In there," Melanie said, quite unnecessarily.

Two roiling bodies suddenly crashed out of the pantry and Melanie and Joy jumped back, barely avoiding being milled over by them. Melanie's eyes widened as Geoffrey grabbed Lenny by the shirt and plowed a fist into his face.

"You damn bastard!" Geoffrey said.

Melanie's mouth fell open. Never in all her life had she seen Geoffrey like this. His rage was frightful and the blow he delivered Lenny caused the little man to sag.

"Geoffrey, no!" Melanie cried. Spurring into action, she ran over to grab his arm. "You'll kill him!"

"Please, my lord," Joy said, running to clutch onto Geoffrey's other arm, the one which held the dangling Lenny.

"It is tea time!" Mrs. Biddington cried out.

"Geoffrey!" Melanie gasped. "You mustn't kill him. He . . . he might be able to tell us where they took Amy!" Geoffrey's arm arched back for another swing, but Melanie clung determinedly to it. "Geoffrey, stop!"

Geoffrey froze a moment. His muscles quivered beneath Melanie's fingers. He narrowed a fierce gaze upon Lenny. "Can you tell us where they are taking Amy?"

"Y-yes," Lenny stammered. "Tom's takin' her to Lonnon."

"Why?" Geoffrey asked, not only shaking Lenny but the women hanging upon both sides of him.

"I—I's don't know," Lenny gasped. "Tom gots the order. H-he don't tell me nothing."

"Who gave the order?" Geoffrey growled, rattling him again.

"I—I said I don't know," Lenny gasped. "Some flash cull. A high and mighty one. Got's even Tom f-frightened of him, he does."

"My God," Geoffrey muttered, and slowly, very slowly eased his grip upon Lenny. "It's her cat."

"Ain't a c-cat, gov," Lenny said, shaking his head. "Tom ain't afraid of no cat. And a cat don't pay what this swell does."

Geoffrey's eyes narrowed. "Where in London is Tom taking Amy?"

Lenny coughed, and his skin turned ashen. "Th-that I ain't going ter tell you."

"You will," Geoffrey said, tightening his grip and shaking him. "You will or I'll kill you!"

"Y-you'll kill me if I do!" Lenny wailed.

"Lenny," Melanie said, trying for a reasonable tone. "If he promises not to kill you, will you tell us?"

Lenny looked at her with frightened, dogged eyes. "Won't!"

Melanie moved fast, for Geoffrey's muscles were bunching again beneath her hands. "Will you take Geoffrey there if he promises not to kill you?"

"I'll take ye both there," Lenny said. "Don't hold with what was going on, anyways. But ain't going to tells you now. He'll kill me. W-on't go alone with him, he'll kill me."

"I won't kill you," Geoffrey said, and unfortunately shook the little man again.

"Geoffrey!" Melanie cried, exasperation for her longtime friend spilling out. "Let him loose! We are wasting time. We must prepare to leave for London."

"Indeed," said Joy, her tone breathless but soothing. "You are wasting valuable time."

"We?" Geoffrey said, swinging his thunderous gaze to Melanie.

Melanie had never seen this side of Geoffrey, but in this instant she could not help but take up Lenny's defense. "I am going with you. If you kill Lenny before he takes us there, we will never find Amy."

"My lord, the scones are g-growing cold," Mrs. Biddington's quivering voice interrupted. Everyone, including Geoffrey, turned to stare at her. The poor housekeeper was jerking uncontrollably and tears streamed down her face. "Is it not tea time?"

"Blimy, she's crying," Lenny said. "Gov, have her tea, for the love of God. I—I promise to take ye to where Tom's suppose ter drop the mort." He looked appealingly to Melanie. "Ye promise ter keep him from killing me?"

Melanie smiled. "If you promise not to lie or deceive us but take us directly to Amy."

"You have my word," Lenny said. His gaze skittered to Geoffrey whose head had snapped back around and who was looking at him with murderous intent. "Gov, it ain't me you wants ter kill. I swear it!"

"No, it isn't," Geoffrey said curtly. Melanie sighed in relief as Geoffrey released Lenny. "But I will kill you if you don't take me to Amy. Or if I find her harmed. And that I swear."

"I'll take you," Lenny said, straightening and rubbing his throat. His battered face lightened and he asked, "Now ain't it tea time? Scones is me favorite!"

Eight

Sarah sat in the one lone chair, looking about the gaudy red room. Its red velvet-covered bed was pillared with woefully tasteless gold posts, with equally tasteless unclad nymphs and cherubs dancing up them. She had been blindfolded when Tom finally brought her to this room after a long day and night journey. She wondered why the blindfold was necessary, for it took little imagination to determine just exactly what kind of room she was in. The laughter and shrieks outside the door, and certain other noises best not defined, would have warned her if the atrocious room had failed to do so.

Mumbles sounded outside the door, and Sarah stiffened as the door opened. The Duke of Ravenwich strolled in and closed the door. Sarah heard the grate of the key in the door and knew they were locked in. Ravenwich nodded with a smile. "Hello, darling."

Sarah studied Ravenwich. He was indeed a handsome man, tall, slim, and dark, with glittering dark eyes. She had often laughed and said he looked the perfect villain. Now she *knew* he was the perfect villain.

"Hello, Ravenwich," she said coolly.

He raised a brow. "What, you are not surprised to see me?"

"Not at all," Sarah said. "Though I own to a distaste at seeing you."

He merely laughed. "Ah, Sarah, you truly are the Incomparable. If only I had gained your measure before, none of this would have happened." He slowly walked over and gazed down at her. "But, alas, I didn't. I thought you but the beautiful ornament you appeared, the society darling whom we all love so dearly."

"I assure you, if I had known it would have helped to allow you to see my measure," Sarah said, "I would have."

He sighed and walked over to the bed and sat down, crossing his knees and swinging a shining Hessian. "I suppose if I told you I have your measure now and promised never to mistake it again, in fact promised to respect it fully, you would not let bygones be bygones?"

Sarah smiled and nodded. "You are correct, Ravenwich. For, unfortunately, I have your measure now as well and am not as forgiving."

"I thought as much," he said with a sigh. He studied her. "You really should have pity. It was very cruel of you to hit me over the head with my ornamental statue."

Sarah laughed. "I knew that would be the most wounding blow to you."

"You quite ruined the statue."

"Only because your head was so hard," Sarah said. "In fact, it was far harder than I thought."

He stiffened and then his eyes lighted. "Faith, you thought you had killed me. So that is why you disappeared so swiftly."

"I must admit," Sarah said, "I thought I had accomplished the task. But I see I failed."

"Cruel, cruel indeed," Ravenwich said, shaking his head.

"I thought you cruel to try to strangle and rape me," Sarah countered.

"Hmm, yes." Ravenwich frowned. "You must forgive me. You angered me and I reacted without thought."

"It must be society's wish that you remain a thinking man," Sarah said.

He laughed. "Yes, I am now a thinking man."

Sarah leaned back, forcing a calm. "And as a thinking man, are you going to tell me what you have thought?"

"Indeed," Ravenwich said. He sprung up and walked over to one of the golden bed posts. He ran his hand along the gilded wood. "Tell me, dearest, can you guess where you are?"

Sarah batted her lashes. "I don't have the faintest notion."

He laughed. "Come, Sarah. We've already admitted to understanding each other."

"Very well," Sarah said, shrugging. "I would gather this is a house of ill repute. Since the furnishings are quite intact and considerably plush, I would consider it one of the better brothels."

"Indeed," Ravenwich said. "I am pleased to see you value the nicety of my choice." His eyes darkened. "I assure you, there are far less well-appointed whorehouses."

"So I have heard," Sarah said.

He sighed and walked over to her. He reached to pick up her hand. Sarah, though her skin crawled, permitted him to do so, surveying him with cool eyes. "Now, if we come to an agreement, sweet Sarah, it will remain only that you have heard of such places. But if not, you shall come to know them quite well, and on your back at that."

"Good God," Sarah said, stunned. "Never say you think to sell me to one of these!"

His grip tightened. "Yes, I shall. I was marrying you for your money, and if I cannot make it by bedding you, I shall make it by other men bedding you."

Sarah smiled wryly. "And here I thought you wanted to marry me for love."

Ravenwich dropped her hand quickly and spun away from her. "I did think I loved you." He turned, a twisted smile upon his face. "And I wanted you. But I shall always want women. And with money, I shall always have them." He paced back to her. "But if you marry me, none of this need be discussed. I own I will never be faithful, but with your money, I assure you, I will be able to pay to be discreet. I shall even be able to pay for any byblows, which appears to be an objection of yours."

Sarah stiffened, holding tight reign upon her temper. "It was not my only objection, but as you said, none of that need be discussed. You said you were a thinking man, but you are not thinking if you believe you can succeed in selling me into the trade."

Ravenwich shook his head. "No, Sarah, 'tis you who are not thinking. You must see the errors of your ways, as I have seen the errors of mine. I was an angry fool when I thought to force you into marriage by rape. I realized, upon consideration, that your father, when he returned, might very well not support me in my efforts. Your father, unfortunately, can be a very unpredictable man, with some very reactionary whims when it comes to women. You are very much like him."

"Thank you," Sarah said, nodding graciously.

Ravenwich walked over and sat upon the bed again. He ran his hand over the coverlet. "However, he is out of the country for the moment." He looked at Sarah closely. "I suspected that was why you disappeared. You were waiting for his return, were you not?"

"Yes," Sarah said, "I was."

He laughed and shook his head. "If only I had known you thought you killed me. It would have been of such great use to me. However, I would have preferred you not to have escaped me at all."

"Then I do not regret my mistake," Sarah said, smiling. "Though it did cause me considerable effort and time."

Ravenwich laughed. "As it did me, I assure you. Making discreet investigations, since I had not thought to set up a hue and cry after you, was no easy task. You did far too well, my dear. I truly could not find a trace. Not until Monteath told me the amusing story of meeting a peasant wench who looked exactly like you."

"I hoped he had forgotten it," Sarah said. "Else been wise enough not to relate it."

Ravenwich smiled. "When a man is in his cups it is amazing what little details he will remember, and Monteath even sober is never wise. Besides, why should he not relate it? He saw no connection since the Lady Sarah was out of the country."

"Where did I go, by the way?" Sarah asked.

"To a small villa in Spain," Ravenwich said.

"Spain?" Sarah asked. "I wish you had made it Paris."

"No," Ravenwich said. "Everyone knows you in Paris. No, you went to Spain only to visit a distant relation of mine, on my behalf. Therefore, if it becomes necessary to report your final disappearance, it will be quite plausible to relate that you were set upon by bandits and killed. I shall know no end of grief, of course. It was in consideration of me that you went, after all."

Sarah shook her head. "Fantastical."

"Yes," Ravenwich said. "Society has always been a fool for such romantic tripe. The story will hold, however, and by the time your father returns, even he will have difficulty unraveling it." His dark eyes taunted her. "And also, by the time he arrives, if you do not consent to marry me, you will have become such that you will not wish to contact him, nor will you be able to do so from the flop house to which I will have consigned you."

Sarah stiffened. "Why all this excessive work? Let us simply cancel our engagement and you may go on to greener pastures."

Ravenwich shook his head. "There are no greener pastures than you, my dear. If I am jilted by the Incomparable, no other man of fortune will permit me near his daughter. And I doubt, now that I understand you, that you will readily permit me to marry one of our rank." He sighed. " 'Tis the other important issue in my plan. I can see you are well on your way to becoming as powerful as your father. Unusual, but then your father has been such and raised you incorrectly. If you will not marry me and be my wife, and what a glorious couple we could be, then I will have to assure you are broken and broken swiftly."

"But you are in need of money," Sarah said. "This surely cannot gain you much."

Ravenwich smiled. "Alas, it is not just money, darling, but revenge. You did spurn me, and did ruin my best bronze statue . . . upon my skull at that. Also, you do not know how much a man will pay for a virgin, nor how much more a man will pay to bed The Incomparable Lady Sarah."

"Impossible!" Sarah said.

"No," Ravenwich said, shaking his head. "You hold yourself too cheaply, my dear. I promise you, I know many men, men of my ilk, who will gladly pay to deflower you and do it secretly. It adds unutterable spice to it, and none of the consequences. Some of the very men you have denied, or your father has, will be glad to pay . . . even after the first bloom of the rose is gone, shall we say?"

"Definitely men of your ilk," Sarah murmured.

Ravenwich frowned, appearing to study his Hessian. "You are still a virgin, are you not?"

"I beg your pardon?" Sarah asked sharply before she thought.

Ravenwich looked at her quickly and smiled. "Ah, I can see by your outrage that you are still untouched. You must forgive me, but Monteath rambled on about the country bumpkin you were frolicking with in the field. I only wondered if you exchanged favors with your Lord Grey in return for his protection."

"Perhaps I did," Sarah said coolly.

Ravenwich's eyes flashed, and then he laughed. "An excellent effort, my dear. But it would make no difference." He rose. "Now, I will give you a day to think matters over."

"Only a day?" Sarah asked. "Surely you can give me more time to decide upon two such infelicitous choices."

"No," Ravenwich said, his eyes narrowing. "We have wasted enough time. I do not intend to leave anything to chance. Either you will marry me shortly, so that we are quite happily wed before your father's return, or you will soon dream of the plushness of this room rather than the crib of which you will be queen." He strolled to the door and bowed. "I have you heavily guarded, and, as you notice, there are no windows for escape."

Ravenwich rapped on the door and called for Tom to open it. It opened, and after bidding Sarah adieu, he departed. Sarah heard the grate of the key in the door once more.

"What is this place?" Melanie asked, wide-eyed, as she peered out the carriage window at a large, opulent white house, with what appeared only men entering it. She thought her eyes would pop out at the sights and sounds of London as they drove through it in the evening, but this house stunned her more. It seemed quite ominous.

"Ain't going ter say," Lenny muttered from the one seat of the carriage. "He'll kill me."

Melanie glanced hastily at Geoffrey. His face was unspeakably grim as he looked out. "Geoffrey, what is it?"

Geoffrey turned his head sharply, his eyes a glittering, hard silver. "I won't tell you. But if Amy is here, I will kill whoever brought her here."

"I didn't, gov," Lenny said, raising his hands up. "Was with you the whole time. 'Fact, brought you here, didn't I?"

"Don't worry, Lenny," Melanie said quickly. "Geoffrey won't kill you. We've promised you that."

Geoffrey growled, but said, "All right, Lenny, you are going to lead me to Amy."

"But I don't know exactly where she is," Lenny said.

"All's I know was Tom and me were suppose ter bring her ter . . . well, ter here."

Geoffrey looked at Melanie. "You will remain in the carriage."

Melanie shook her head. "No, Geoffrey, whatever this place is, if Amy is in there, I am going with you. You might need me."

"Gov, I agrees with her," Lenny said. "I ain't going nowhere without Miss Melanie. Don't want you killing me when she ain't around."

"Very well," Geoffrey said, sounding as if he could crunch bones. "We will go through the back. I don't frequent these places, so you better assist me or . . ."

"I know, you'll kill me," Lenny said, nodding. Then he grinned. "But you ain't going ter, 'cause I know these kinder places. Not this here fancy, mind you, but I know them."

"Melanie, you and Lenny are to stay here," Geoffrey said, his voice stern. "I should never have brought you in the first place, and I'll take you no further."

Melanie glanced around the virulent purple-and-gold room they stood within. She had never seen such a room in her life and wondered who could have possibly decorated it. However, she also wondered what kind of residence it was, where each servant they met, once handed a few coins, told them where they should go and when. They met scandalously dressed women with men holding them close within the halls, and Melanie, despite her best efforts, could not refrain from gasping in shock. That was when Geoffrey had mumbled a curse, and after looking into the room in which they now stood, ordered them to enter.

Melanie realized Geoffrey was now glaring at her, awaiting her agreement. She flushed and nodded. "Yes, Geoffrey. D-do go and find Amy. This . . . this does not seem the proper place for a lady."

"Damn right," Geoffrey muttered. He glared at Lenny. "You watch over Miss Melanie, or else . . ."

"I know," Lenny sighed. "You'll kill me."

Geoffrey nodded. "Once I have found Amy I shall return."

"Yes, do," Melanie said. "And do not worry. We will be safe, I am sure."

Geoffrey's frown only deepened, but he did not say another word as he left them. Once the door was closed, Melanie could not resist whispering, "Lenny, what place is this?"

Lenny looked nervously about. "It's a bawdy house, Miss Melanie."

"Oh!" Melanie said, her eyes widening. "You mean like the tavern at home, where . . . well, where married men like Papa daren't go, and where ladies who are what they oughtn't be do go?"

Lenny scratched his head. "Guess that's what I mean, Miss Melanie."

"I see," Melanie said, frowning.

Lenny rushed up quickly to her and Melanie, startled, stepped back. "You've got ter excuse me, Miss Melanie, but I have ter leave now."

"Leave?" Melanie asked.

"I don't mean to be leavin' you in a scrape, but I gots to be gone before yer gent comes back. If he finds that Amy, he'll want ter kill me, and even if he don't find her, he'll want ter kill me. 'Fraid you wouldn't be able to stop him then, miss."

Melanie frowned at the nervous little man. Thinking deeply, she realized he was most likely correct. "Yes, I see what you mean."

Lenny dashed to the door. "You're a right one, Miss Melanie. Can't say I wants ter cross yer path again, but you're a right one. Now you stay right here and don't let no one in, do you hear? No one! Except yer gent of course."

"Of course," Melanie said well nigh to empty air. Lenny was gone so fast and the door slammed upon her. She gazed

about the odd room and then studied the door. She frowned.
Just how was she supposed to keep someone out when she
had no key? She scanned the room once more and her gaze
settled upon the single chair in the room. It was large and
of a loud purple-and-green stripe. She walked over, and stepping behind it, gave it a healthy shove. The chair resisted her
efforts, so she moved to its front. Bending down, she grabbed
hold of the armrests and tugged hard.

"Yes, yes," a voice suddenly said. "A very fetching per-
spective."

Melanie, who had been intent upon pulling the chair,
straightened and spun. "Oh, dear, hello," she breathed. A tall
man, indeed as tall as Geoffrey, if not an inch more, stood
upon the threshold. His hair was the glossiest black, yet
wings of silver distinguished it and showed his age to be that
of the well seasoned.

"Yes, hello," he said in a rich voice, bright green eyes
twinkling. "I assure you, the view was far better than any
I've seen in the jungles."

"Ahm, yes," Melanie said, flushing. "You must forgive
me . . ." She discovered she was losing herself in the green
of the man's eyes. "I . . . I was trying to move the chair."

"Move the chair?" he asked, strolling up to her.

"Y-yes," Melanie stammered. "Lenny said t-to let no one
in. I—I was going to put it against the door."

"I can see why," the man said, laughing. "Lenny must be
a sage if not territorial man." He stepped past her and
grabbed hold of the chair. "Let us take care of that right
now." With an ease which amazed Melanie he pulled the
chair across the room and shoved its sturdy back against the
door.

He turned, a heart-catching smile upon his lips. "Now,
since that is accomplished, let us get down to business, far
more pleasurable business." He walked directly over to
Melanie, and without a word, wrapped strong arms about
her, bending his head down to hers.

"What . . . ?" Melanie began, but never finished. His lips covered hers and muffled any question. Melanie stood stunned and amazed. Yet the warmest tingle went down her, and she found herself leaning into the gentleman and permitting him to kiss her.

The man drew his head back. His green eyes studied her with a frown. "That is a kiss of an innocent. Are you acting, sweetings, or are you truly untried?"

"No," Melanie said quickly, embarrassed and uncertain as to why she was. It was terribly wicked of her, but his kiss had been quite stunning, and to have him recognize hers as lacking disappointed her. Geoffrey was not a demonstrative man, and his kisses had been swift and detached. She had no other experience than that. She looked down. "I am sorry, I—I guess I am."

He laughed. "One does not guess, sweetings, or else you *are* an innocent. One knows when one has been loved. That is, if it is done correctly." He gently tapped her chin up. Melanie gazed at him in anguish. "My dear, it is not an insult. In truth, innocence is held in great esteem by society."

"But you do not like it," Melanie said, instinctively knowing it was so.

The man frowned. "I must own, I do not seek it out. I am quite past those years and so I told Madame Lucille. I fear I may be in the wrong room. Permit me to return to her and we shall straighten out this confusion." His arms began to loosen from around her.

"No, no," Melanie said, grasping his jacket. "Please, you do not need to go to her. You . . . you are not in the wrong room, I assure you."

He studied her and said in a very serious tone, "Are you here upon your own free will, child?"

"I am not a child!" Melanie said, stiffening.

He laughed. "I am sorry, but I doubt you are much older than my daughter." His eyes darkened. "Are you here on your own free will . . . mademoiselle?"

"Well, yes," Melanie said, blushing. "I guess I am."

"You guess? Again?" The gentleman laughed and Melanie heard it rumble through his chest into her very being. "Let us take some of this 'guessing' out of the situation." He withdrew his arms and stepped back. Melanie felt a stab of disappointment, until he clasped up her hand in his large one. He looked toward the large bed with the purple coverlet and shook his head. "No, not yet, to be sure." He turned and, smiling, led Melanie over to the chair. He sat promptly. "Come, sit on my lap."

Melanie looked down at the large man. "Sit on your lap?"

"Indeed," the man laughed. "Come and talk to Papa."

"Very well," Melanie said. Flushing, she sat down upon his lap. His arms wrapped about her once more, and she found she enjoyed being envcloped so warmly and comfortably. "I must admit," she said, glancing down, "I—I don't see you as my papa."

"And I must confess," the gentleman said, a frown upon his face, "I don't see you as my daughter. However, since you are in a state of guessing about whether you mean to be here or not, we will have the understanding that if you become certain at any time you do not wish to be here, then you have but to say the word and I shall try my level best to abide by your decision."

"Very well," Melanie said, as she unconsciously snuggled closer. She realized her brazenness and said, "I am sorry."

"Don't be, sweetheart," the man said, smiling that stunning smile. He leaned over and kissed Melanie gently but firmly. Her eyes fluttered shut with the breathlessness of it.

She opened them, though, when he drew back once more. She looked at him worriedly. "Was that better?"

"Yes," he said, his voice deepening, even as he laughed. "Practice makes perfect." He leaned forward, his lips very close to hers. "And I've had practice."

Melanie looked at him and smiled. Feeling daring, she

wrapped her arms about his shoulders. "And I haven't." She put her lips to his and kissed him as firmly as she could.

Sarah lay upon the red velvet coverlet. She wasn't sleeping, but she deemed she'd need her rest. Her mind whirled with schemes. None of them included her saying she would marry Ravenwich, unless it would help stave off the fell event. Nor did they include her becoming a victim to the white slave market. She would finish her handiwork upon Ravenwich's skull before she would ever permit that to happen.

Suddenly, a loud commotion sounded outside the door. The sounds were neither of laughter or rowdiness, but of grunts, curses, and thuds. She sat up, her fingers gripping the velvet spread beneath her. Clearly a fight was ensuing. A fight within this habitat was not abnormal, but that it progressed directly outside her door could not bode well.

Silence soon fell. Then she heard the grate of a key in the door. Sarah steeled herself, unsure she wished to meet whoever sought entry. The door burst open and Sarah squelched the shriek upon her lips.

Then her mouth fell open. "Geoffrey!"

"Good God," Geoffrey said, halting.

Sarah laughed as Geoffrey's gaze widened at the sight of the bed she sat upon. She tumbled from the velvet monstrosity and flew to throw herself upon him. "I am so glad to see you!" She kissed him fervently. "You cannot know how much."

Geoffrey drew her into a close embrace, and his eyes, the one bruised upon its ridge, gleamed. "Amy, if you thought it unwise to kiss me in a bedroom before, this is most definitely not the right place to kiss me."

"No, indeed not."

"Come," he said. "Before that lout wakes up."

Sarah stepped quickly from Geoffrey's arms, wishing she

could stay there, but knowing she could not. She peered past him to view a large, misshapen form on the floor in the hallway. She smiled with pleasure. "You took care of Tom, I see."

"Yes," Geoffrey said. "We'd best move him in here."

"Yes," Sarah said, and they both went to the fallen Tom, grabbing up his arms. "However did you find me?"

"Lenny brought us here," Geoffrey said, as they dragged Tom from the hall into the bedroom.

"What?" Sarah asked, dropping Tom's arm in surprise. It thumped to the carpet loudly.

"Melanie and Joy caught him after you left," Geoffrey said, dropping Tom's arm with equal carelessness. "And I persuaded him to bring me here."

"Persuaded him?" Sarah asked, brows raised.

"Yes," Geoffrey said, his tone curt. The look upon his face decided Sarah not to pursue the issue for the nonce.

"We must hurry," Geoffrey said. "Melanie and Lenny are waiting in another room."

"What?" Sarah exclaimed. "Melanie is here as well?"

Geoffrey ran a swift hand through his hair. "Yes, she is."

"Heavens," Sarah said. "We certainly must hurry."

They left the body of Tom sprawled upon the red-carpeted floor, locking him in securely. Geoffrey turned and strode down the hall, setting a pace Sarah was hard pressed to maintain. She drew in a relieved breath when Geoffrey finally halted before a door.

"She's in here," Geoffrey said, grabbing hold of the doorknob and turning it. The door did not budge. "What the devil!"

"This is the correct room?" Sarah asked.

"Yes," Geoffrey said. He pounded heavily upon the door. "Melanie! Open up!"

A muffled shriek arose from the other side of the door. Alarm washed through Sarah, even as Geoffrey cursed and rammed his shoulder hard against the door. Another cry drifted to them, but the door held firm. Swearing more flagrantly, Geoffrey backed up and charged at the door, slamming his entire weight upon it. The wood buckled and splintered, a heavy thud sounded, and then the door gaped open.

Geoffrey burst into the room and Sarah chased behind him. She skidded to a halt, stifling her gasp. A tall man held Melanie in a close embrace, a huge green striped chair tumbled in front of them. His air was protective and Sarah recognized the stance all too well.

Clearly, Geoffrey did not. "Take your hands from her, damn it."

He dove at the man, all but vaulting over the chair.

"Sorry, my dear," the man muttered, swinging Melanie swiftly behind him. He met Geoffrey head on. The two men collided, their arms locking in fierce struggle.

"Geoffrey, no!" Melanie cried, scuttling from behind and throwing herself at Geoffrey.

"Father, no!" Sarah shouted. She bolted toward the men whose hands had found each other's throats.

Her command froze all three participants, their gazes turning to Sarah.

"Father?" Melanie asked, her eyes widening.

"Sarah?" Kendall Bevington asked, his brows arching up.

"Sarah?" Geoffrey asked, his brows slashing down.

"What are you doing here?" Kendall asked.

"Never mind what I am doing here," Sarah said, flushing. "Only please release Geoffrey."

"I don't think I shall," Kendall said, his gaze narrowing. "Not if he is the man who has brought you here."

"He didn't," Sarah said, tugging at his arm. "Ravenwich did. Geoffrey came to rescue me."

"Ravenwich?" Kendall exclaimed. His hands dropped swiftly from Geoffrey's throat and he frowned at Sarah. "The man may be your fiancé, Sarah, but I cannot approve him bringing you to a brothel."

"Fiancé!" Geoffrey's arms promptly fell from Kendall and he stared at Sarah. "What is he talking about?"

Sarah's heart plummeted to her toes. Drawing in a deep breath, she tried to look innocent. "Geoffrey, I . . . forgot to tell you, b-but I've regained my memory."

"You forgot to tell me," Geoffrey said, his eyes narrowing.

"Regained your memory?" Kendall asked.

"You have? How wonderful!" Melanie cried, clasping her hands together. Then her gaze skittered to Geoffrey, whose face was thunderous. "Isn't it?"

"Yes, y-yes it is, Melanie," Sarah said, attempting a brave smile.

"Melanie?" Kendall asked, turning to study Melanie. "Is that your name, sweetheart?"

"Sweetheart?" Geoffrey growled.

Sarah quickly grabbed hold of Geoffrey's clenching fist. "Father, Melanie is Geoffrey's fiancée."

"Fiancée!" Kendall exclaimed. He drew in a breath. "Hmm, I see." He turned a stern frown upon Geoffrey. "As I said, I highly disapprove of men bringing their fiancées to a brothel."

"I did not bring her," Geoffrey said. He frowned and waved impatiently. "Very well, I did, but only because I was under the mistaken impression I was rescuing your daughter."

"You *were* rescuing me!" Sarah said hotly.

"From your fiancé?" Geoffrey snorted his disdain.

"I told Ravenwich I would not be his fiancée," Sarah said, beginning to shake with rage.

"Excellent," Kendall said, smiling. "I knew you would come to your senses, my dear."

"Come to her senses?" Geoffrey said. "She never lost them. She is merely playing a game with us all. Just like when she had us believing for weeks she had amnesia."

"Amnesia?" Kendall looked at Sarah. His green eyes lightened and he said in extremely solicitous tones, "I am sorry, dear, to hear of your lapse of memory."

Geoffrey barked a laugh. "There's no need for your concern, sir, your daughter never lost her memory. Did you. . . . *Sarah?*"

"I—I . . ." Sarah began. She choked. "I . . ."

"Don't!" Geoffrey said. "You know I can tell when you are lying."

"Hmm," Kendall said. "A very dangerous situation, to be sure. However, if my daughter says she lost her memory, then she lost her memory. It would not be gallant to say otherwise."

"Gallant?" Geoffrey asked, his gaze shooting toward Kendall. "Sir, I need no further instruction upon gallantry. Your daughter has already taken it upon herself to instruct me on the matter."

"As she should," Kendall said, his green eyes sparkling. "However, if that does not serve, permit me to suggest you not insult her so when in my company. I fear I would feel it necessary to call you out."

Sarah looked at her father, and stifled a laugh. Kendall Bevington never called anyone out.

Melanie, however, gasped and said, "You could not call Geoffrey out, sir."

Kendall looked steadily at Melanie. "Could I not?"

"Indeed no," Melanie said, shaking her head.

"Indeed no," Sarah said, frowning. There was an odd air between the two, an air she misliked heartily. "Father, what are *you* doing here?"

Kendall straightened and gave her a quelling look. "If you do not know, Sarah, I certainly shall not tell you. This is all rather improper as it is."

Sarah waved a quick, impatient hand. "No, what I meant, is I thought you were still in Africa."

"Oh, that," Kendall said, and shrugged. "I grew bored and decided to return home. Which, despite the . . . confusion of the moment, shall we say, I am very glad I did. It appears matters have grown sadly tangled in my absence. To discover you suffered amnesia and I was not here to support you in your time of . . . forgetfulness, pains me. Pains me deeply."

"She did not suffer amnesia," Geoffrey said. "And the 'tangle' was of your daughter's own making, I assure you."

"Hmm, yes," Kendall said. "Well, where as you are quite certain of the facts, I am not. Indeed, I find myself with a host of questions." He glanced quickly about the room. "But first, do let us adjourn from this . . . establishment. I see no reason to keep your fiancée and my daughter kicking their heels here." He cast a quick look at Melanie. "Someone might come into this room and possibly tumble to all the wrong assumptions. Let us rather adjourn to our town house."

"No," Geoffrey said.

Kendall's brow rose. "You may not care if your fiancée remains here, but I do object to my daughter doing so."

"I meant," Geoffrey said, his voice dark, "that Melanie and I will return home directly."

"But it is late," Sarah exclaimed. "Surely you cannot mean to return to Grey Manor tonight. It will take a night and day's journey."

"Indeed no," Kendall said, frowning. "Miss Melanie should not suffer such rigors. There is no need."

"We shall stay at a hotel then," Geoffrey said, his tone implacable.

Kendall's brows rose. "Never say you have Miss Melanie's maid and chaperone here in one of these rooms as well. When you enter a brothel, you do bring a large contingency, do you not?"

"She does not have a maid or chaperone," Geoffrey said.

"Then you may not go to a hotel," Kendall said, his tone firm. "It will present Miss Melanie to all forms of low gossip." He looked to Sarah. "And where is your chaperone, for that matter?"

Sarah blinked. "Miss Kensington? You know, I really

hadn't thought of her. I fear I have lost her somewhere along the way, Father."

He frowned. "You lost your chaperone?"

Sarah sighed. "Yes, Father, I did."

Kendall Bevington shook his head. "You lost your memory and your chaperone? This will clearly be a tale worth the hearing."

Sarah peeked a glance at the silent, ominous Geoffrey. She shivered. Her father might think her tale worth the hearing, but Geoffrey surely would not. Nor did she look forward to being the misfortunate one who told it.

Nine

"Good evening, Meekum," Kendall said in a pleasant tone as a notably silent group entered into the marble foyer of the large, palatial Bevington town house. It was considered one of the most beautiful in London. Melanie's gasp of surprise and look of wonderment showed she was suitably impressed. Geoffrey's narrowed gaze and frowning look showed he was not.

"My lord," Meekum said with his customary dignity. " 'Tis a pleasure to see you again. Did you have a pleasant journey?"

"My lord?" Melanie whispered.

"Yes," Kendall said, smiling. "I fear in the confusion we were not properly, or shall we say, formally introduced. I am Lord Bevington and this is my daughter, Lady Sarah." Geoffrey's face only darkened, while Melanie's mouth fell open. Kendall waved a hand. "But let us not go into all the titles. It is quite dull."

"Yes, yes, it is," Sarah said quickly, feeling she would sink if her father were to annotate the string of titles attached to their names. She looked hastily to their butler. "Meekum, Father and I both intend to remain in London for the nonce. And would you please prepare two rooms for our visitors as well. They shall be staying with us for the night."

"Indeed, my lady," Meekum said, nodding.

"I believe it should be the gold room and the green room, Meekum," Kendall said. He looked at Melanie. "If your room does not suit you, my dear, only tell me, and we shall find you another. We have plenty of them, I assure you."

"And Miss Melanie will require the service of our maids, Meekum," Sarah said quickly. "She did not arrive with her own."

"N-no, I didn't," Melanie said.

Kendall smiled. "Please do not hesitate to make use of our servants. And Geoffrey, isn't it?"

"Lord Grey, Father," Sarah said quietly.

Kendall's brow rose. "Faith, we did forgo our formal introductions, did we not? Lord Grey, my valet will be at your disposal."

"I will not require him," Geoffrey said. He looked directly at Sarah. "I know how to dress by myself."

Sarah flushed and Kendall's eyes widened. "Indeed. I did not mean to suggest otherwise. Now, since we have finally, at last, settled the formal introductions, perhaps we should attempt to settle other matters as well." Kendall looked at Sarah with raised brow. "Am I correct, Daughter, in assuming your tale is not exactly a pleasant one?"

"No," Sarah said, "it is not."

"Then I do not believe it is a proper one for mixed company," Kendall said, nodding. "Therefore, permit me to show Miss Melanie about while you and Lord Grey hold your discussion."

"We need no discussion," Geoffrey said, his voice low.

"Ah, but I think you do," Kendall said in a kind but firm tone. " 'Tis clear you think my daughter has in some way misled you. I own to my own curiosity, but since I shall believe my daughter in whatever she says, 'tis your discussion which should hold precedence." He turned. "Meekum, Lady Sarah will require tea in the parlor, and a brandy for Lord Grey, please."

"Certainly, my lord," Meekum said. He bowed and departed.

"Come, Miss Melanie," Kendall said, very lightly taking hold of Melanie's arm. "Permit me to show you my home."

"It is . . . is beautiful," Melanie said as Kendall led her away from Sarah and Geoffrey.

"Thank you," Kendall said. "Though I have a few others I believe to be just as lovely."

"A few others?" Melanie's voice drifted back as the two disappeared.

Sarah glanced at Geoffrey, noting the way his jaw clenched. She lifted her head proudly and said, "If you will please follow me, my lord."

"Indeed, *my lady*," Geoffrey said.

Sarah lifted her skirts and walked toward the parlor, not waiting to see if Geoffrey followed. She entered the large, spacious room and sat down upon the silk settee. Geoffrey entered behind. He took up a chair across from Sarah.

His gaze flicked to the plush curtains, the gold ornaments, and costly artwork upon the walls. Bitterness entered his eyes. " 'Tis clear why you never knew how to do anything for yourself. It is not that you forgot, it is that you never knew."

"I own you are correct," Sarah said in a cool tone. "There are only some, like you, who hold having a convenient living as a fault."

"I do not hold you having a 'convenient living,' if this is what you call it, a fault. I hold it against you that you lied to me. You played quite a game with me, did you not?"

"It wasn't a game," Sarah said. "Far from it."

"It wasn't?" Geoffrey asked, his tone sharp. "I know how it is with women of your sort. With the money and position you have, everything is a game, and one you can well afford."

"No," Sarah said. She rose swiftly and walked to the fireplace. Drawing in a deep breath, she turned to him. "This was not a lark or a whim. Can you actually believe that, considering the condition you found me in? Mud is not a chosen fashion of mine."

"No," Geoffrey said, with a short laugh. "I can very well believe that. At that particular moment I don't doubt you were being honest. Of course, you were unconscious at the time. But when you told me you had lost your memory, that was when the game began, didn't it? When you flirted with me and kissed me, that was a game."

"It wasn't," Sarah said weakly.

"You had a fiancé, and you can tell me it wasn't a game?" Geoffrey asked, his eyes flashing.

"I didn't think I had a fiancé," Sarah said, in as calm as voice as she could. "I thought he was dead."

"What?"

Sarah cringed inside. "I thought he was dead, because I thought I had killed him."

Geoffrey stared at her. "You thought you had killed him?"

Sarah tried for a laugh, but failed miserably. It came out like a strangled choke. "Yes, I thought I had killed him. Ravenwich and I'd had an argument, an argument where I told him I would not marry him. He did not take kindly to the rejection and tried to rape me. Those marks on my throat were from him."

"I see," Geoffrey said. His eyes had gone suddenly cold, enigmatic.

"I—I hit him over the head with . . . with a statue and he fell." Sarah shook her head. "I checked to see if he was alive, but . . . but I thought he was not. And no matter my wealth or position, I did not think it would help me in the particular circumstances. I was at his family's estate, you see, with none but his relatives present. So I fled. I rode through the night, met with an accident, and that is when you found me."

"I see," Geoffrey said. His tone was not encouraging.

"What would you have had me do?" Sarah asked. "Tell you the truth? Or the truth as I knew it? That I had killed a man, a duke at that, and expect you would take me in with open arms and offer me sanctuary?"

"No!" Geoffrey said, rising and walking a distance from

her. He turned, and the anger in his eyes assaulted Sarah. "But you did not settle for just sanctuary, did you, my lady?"

"I—I do not know what you mean," Sarah said, her nerves jangling in warning.

"You were determined I *would* accept you with open arms," he said, walking slowly toward her. "You had to flirt with me, tease me . . . kiss me."

"You kissed *me!"* Sarah said, lifting her chin.

"Yes, I did," Geoffrey admitted. "But it was by your design. What was it, my lady? Captivate the country bumpkin to doubly ensure your safety?"

Sarah drew in a stunned breath. God help her, she had foolishly thought that at one time. She lowered her gaze, unable to meet Geoffrey's eyes. "N-no. It wasn't like that at all."

"Yes, it was," Geoffrey said, his voice implacable. "And when you found you had not killed Ravenwich, what of that?"

"What do you mean?" Sarah stiffened.

"You discovered you hadn't killed him, didn't you?" Geoffrey asked, his tone low. "I am not sure, but it must have been when you spoke to those two men. It was the time when you started having the nightmares, wasn't it?"

"Yes," Sarah said. "I—I intended to tell you the truth, but I was frightened."

"You were frightened?" Geoffrey said, and barked a sharp laugh. "No, I was the one who was frightened. You had me so wrapped up in your stories, drawn into your web of lies, that I actually feared for you." He shook his head. "I worried about when you would regain your memory and all the time you were in complete control of your faculties, and of me."

"No, I was not in control," Sarah said, springing up. "And I was frightened. I had a right to be. Only look what happened. Ravenwich did find me!" A shiver ran through her. "Do you know why Ravenwich took me to that brothel?"

Geoffrey stared down at her. "No, I don't. But I certainly played the idiot rushing in to save you."

"He took me to that brothel," Sarah continued, determined to ignore his cutting words, "because he intended to force me to marry him. Otherwise he said he would sell me into the trade, and into a lower brothel than even that one."

Geoffrey's eyes blazed, hot and fierce. Then he seemed to shake himself and he said in a bitter voice, "The man missed his opportunity. With your wiles and ploys, he would have fared better in setting you up as an expensive courtesan."

Rage, driven by raw pain, overwhelmed Sarah. Her hand flashed out and she slapped Geoffrey resoundingly.

Geoffrey's head snapped back. When he looked at her once more, his eyes were dead, void of all emotion. "Are you through with me now, my lady? I believe I have served my purpose just as you wished."

"Yes," Sarah said, shaking. "I am through with you. I need no crude, country bumpkin like you, sirrah!"

"And I need no supposed 'lady' like you," Geoffrey said. He turned and stalked from the room.

Sarah moved slowly and sat down upon the silk settee. Her hand still stung and she looked at it in a daze. She had actually slapped a man. Never in her life had she slapped anyone. Never in her life had she ever felt such rage either. Or pain and hurt. Or regret.

"I suppose you are extremely shocked by my behavior," Melanie said, as Kendall showed her the picture gallery, rattling off names of ancestors and pointing at the paintings in the most urbane of manner.

Kendall turned and surveyed her. He smiled. "You will find that I am rarely shocked. I may once in a while be surprised, but never shocked." He turned his gaze back to a picture and said, "Though I must admit to surprise. Sarah said you are engaged to this Lord Grey."

"Yes, yes, I am," Melanie said.

"I see," Kendall said. "I presume you are just lately engaged to him."

"Oh, no. It has been an engagement of long standing. Why?"

Kendall appeared stunned and then he shook his head. "Perhaps I am close to shock after all."

"Y-you mean because I kissed you?" Melanie asked, flushing.

"There is that," Kendall said, frowning. "But in truth, it is because you do not kiss as if you have been engaged to a man for very long."

Melanie blinked at him, feeling a heat rise from her toes to the very top of her head. "How . . . how does a woman kiss when she's been engaged to man a long time?"

"Forgive me, but you kissed as if it were your very first time," Kendall said. "Surely Lord Grey has kissed you many times."

Melanie shook her head. "No, indeed not. I—I do not know how it is in London, but in the country we do not believe that merely because a couple is engaged that . . . that they may behave improperly."

Kendall laughed and turned his gaze to the painting before them. "Then I am glad I am in London, for if I were engaged to you, I fear I would kiss you very often."

"W-would you?" Melanie stammered, her heart pounding.

Kendall shook his head. "Your Geoffrey appears a far stronger man than I."

"Perhaps," Melanie said weakly. She swallowed. "But . . . but Geoffrey is also n-not demonstrative by nature either."

"Is he not?" Kendall asked, turning to study her. "In truth, he appeared quite a young fire-eater to me."

"Oh, no," Melanie said, shaking her head. "Geoffrey is normally very self-possessed and controlled. 'Tis only of late that he . . . that he . . ."

"That he what?" Kendall asked.

"Well," Melanie sighed. "That he seems to wish to . . .

to kill everybody. Not that it isn't understandable, the men who took Amy, I mean Sarah, were dreadful. But until now, I thought Geoffrey was a man of peace."

"As well as an undemonstrative man," Kendall said, frowning. He sighed. "I fear my little girl seems to have caused some turmoil."

"Your little girl?" Melanie asked, her eyes widening.

His eyes lit. "She is little to me."

"Yes," Melanie said, laughing. "That makes sense. But she truly is an amazing woman."

"And so are you," Kendall said, his tone soft.

"Oh, no," Melanie said, turning quickly and strolling down the gallery. "I am nothing out of the common."

"I would not be so certain," Kendall said.

Melanie looked at him, her heart skipping a beat. She looked swiftly back to the paintings. "I had not c-considered, but . . . but do you have a wife?"

"No," Kendall said. "Maria died many years ago when Sarah was young."

"I am sorry," Melanie said. Unable to stop herself, she asked, "Wh-which is her picture?"

Kendall was silent a moment. "Her picture is not here."

"Oh, of course," Melanie said. "Her picture would . . . would be somewhere else."

Kendall shook his head. "No. I refuse to have her picture within the house."

"You do?" Melanie asked.

He walked up to her, his gaze calm. "I am not a man who believes in living in the past. And to have Maria's picture here, or anywhere, would only take me back to that past. Remind me of the love that is lost." He smiled. "She may remain in my heart, but I refuse to have her upon the wall as well."

"I see," Melanie said. Not knowing what else to say, she quickly pointed to a picture. "Who is that gentleman?"

Kendall laughed and proceeded to regale her with the story

of that particular, infamous ancestor. Then they meandered down the row, he relating amusing facts about the person in each painting. Melanie nodded her head and murmured comments, but in her mind's eye she could only see the picture that was missing, and not the ones that were there and in the open.

Kendall sat reading his paper in the parlor after breaking his morning fast. A knock sounded upon the door and Geoffrey entered the room.

"Good morning, my lord," Kendall said, his tone convivial, quite at counterpoint to Geoffrey's stern and controlled demeanor.

"Good morning," Geoffrey said, and went to take up a chair. "Melanie and I will be leaving this morning."

"I am sorry to see you go," Kendall said. "After all, now that you are in town, you really should stay and perhaps show your fiancée London."

"I have never liked London," Geoffrey said. "And Melanie, I am sure, will wish to return. She is missed at home."

"Yes," Kendall said. "She mentioned as much. Then I shall wish you a pleasant journey. 'Tis unfortunate Sarah will not be able to make her good-byes, but I believe she is still abed. Even for her, I would imagine the past days have taken their toll."

"She told you her stories then?" Geoffrey asked, frowning.

Kendall laughed. "I do not consider them her 'stories,' Grey." He frowned. "Sarah says you do not move in our circles, so you do not know Ravenwich. It is no loss to you, I assure you, but what Sarah has related to me is not difficult to believe if you know the man. I was not pleased in the beginning when Sarah said she would marry him."

"Why did you not stop her then?" Geoffrey asked, eyes narrowed.

Kendall laughed. " 'Tis clear you do not know Sarah."

"No, I do not," Geoffrey said. "I knew her as 'Amy,' and even then she did not take to orders, no matter how reasonable."

"Then you know Sarah as well," Kendall said simply. He raised his brow. "I have no doubt you do not care for Sarah, or so she has told me." Geoffrey remained silent, only looking levelly at Kendall, his expression solid. Kendall looked away and said mildly, "I loved Sarah's mother very much. I loved her strong spirit and quick, independent mind. I would not raise her child in any other manner. It would have been a betrayal to Maria, since she was not here to raise her herself." He turned his gaze back to Geoffrey and laughed. "You may censure me in how I reared Sarah. Many have been before you in that condemnation, I assure you. Yet for all that, those same men ask for her hand in marriage, fawn over her and make much of her. They have no notion what truly attracts them to Sarah, nor do they have any notion upon how to make her happy." He frowned. "Ravenwich was such a man, only he was the worst of the lot. Sarah made a mistake there, a very grievous mistake."

"Yet you let her?" Geoffrey asked, his voice low, angry.

"Let her?" Kendall asked, eyes sparkling. "No, I only waited and permitted her to discover the truth for herself. I did not journey to Africa to hunt. I went to Africa so that Sarah would promise to hold the wedding until I returned." He frowned. "She is a competent woman, and I felt no concern over the outcome. I fully expected she would throw Ravenwich over before I returned home. I must own, I had no expectations that there would be such contretemps. I knew Ravenwich was a cad, but I did not know he was a true villain."

"I see," Geoffrey said. "What do you intend to do with Ravenwich now? Now that you know he is a villain."

Kendall frowned, his gaze steady upon Geoffrey. "What do you think I should do with him? Sarah intends to send the announcement to the paper severing the engagement. That surely should be enough."

"You intend nothing else?" Geoffrey asked, his gray eyes flaring.

"But what else is there for me to do?" Kendall asked, brows raised.

"What else?" Geoffrey asked. "You can call Ravenwich out, that is what else you can do."

"Me? Call Ravenwich out?" Kendall shook his head. "No, I am a man of peace. I do not engage in duels."

"You said you would call me out," Geoffrey said.

"Yes," Kendall said, nodding. "But I did not intend for you to take up the challenge."

"I see," Geoffrey said, his tone stiff. "Then you do not intend to call Ravenwich out?"

"No, of course not. A man of my age would look a fool to call out a man of Ravenwich's. Besides, Ravenwich is a crack shot. He has gone out many times and has never been the loser."

"You will let what he did to Sarah go unavenged?" Geoffrey asked, standing and striding to the fireplace.

"Unavenged?" Kendall asked. "If you mean will I refuse to meet Ravenwich upon the dueling field, then yes, you can say I intend to permit Sarah to go unavenged."

Geoffrey turned, glaring down at Kendall. "You will do nothing to protect your daughter's honor?"

"Hmm," Kendall said. "From your behavior last night you led me to believe my little girl had no honor. Indeed, from what Sarah told me, you thought she might have been just as well left to become a member of the muslin trade."

A dull flush crossed Geoffrey's face. "That is beside the point. I am not her father."

"So you have noticed," Kendall said, smiling.

Geoffrey's gaze narrowed. "As her father you should take the proper steps to ensure Ravenwich never dares to come near her again."

"So I should call him out in a duel?" Kendall asked. He shook his head. "If I wish to protect Sarah's honor, I will not duel with Ravenwich. The whole world would speculate upon it and I would make Sarah the object of every form of salacious gossip imaginable. No, I will not call Ravenwich out." Kendall returned his attention to his paper and murmured, "Besides, I do not exaggerate. Ravenwich is a fine shot."

"You will not call him out?" Geoffrey's voice cracked like a whip.

Kendall glanced up. "I said I would not."

"Very well," Geoffrey said. He stalked toward the door.

"My lord, where are you going?" Kendall asked.

Geoffrey turned and glared at him. "If you shall not tend to Ravenwich, then I shall."

Kendall paused. "I assure you, there is no need for you to do so."

"I believe there is," Geoffrey said. "Ravenwich will not go unchecked. I will make certain of it."

Kendall shook his head. "I have told you, Ravenwich is an excellent shot."

Geoffrey waved his hand. "So am I."

"Ah," Kendall said, nodding. "Then I should not worry over your death if you follow this course?"

"No, my lord," Geoffrey said. "I do not."

Kendall pursed his lips. "You would fight for my daughter's honor, even though you say she has none?"

Geoffrey stiffened. "Despite her lack of honor, I will not lower mine."

"I see," Kendall said slowly. "There is nothing I can say to sway you from your decision?"

"No, there isn't," Geoffrey said. "I shall deal with Ravenwich and then I shall return to the country."

"Hmm, yes. Very reasonable," The slightest smile hovered upon Kendall's lips. He let out a sigh. "If you feel you must call Ravenwich out, then you must. But I beg of you, no matter the lack of esteem you hold Sarah in, please do not let her name be attached to this duel. It would do neither she nor you any good."

Geoffrey stiffened and bowed slightly. "Since I do not fight for her, I will make certain of it." He turned to go, but then stopped, a frown upon his face. "Where may I find Ravenwich?"

"He is usually at Brooks," Kendall said. "Do you know where that is?"

"I will find it," Geoffrey said, his gaze dangerous.

"I am sure you will," Kendall said. "But Ravenwich is rarely there anytime before the late noon."

"Very well," Geoffrey said. Without another word, he turned and walked from the room.

Kendall picked up the paper again, shaking his head. "Young fire-eater."

"Forsooth, cuz," Terrel said, lifting his glass of brandy as he eased back into his chair. "Never thought to see you in town. But jolly good to see you. Pleased you remembered me. How long do you intend to stay?"

"Only briefly," Geoffrey said, searching the interior of Brooks. Elegantly dressed men sat comfortably about, sharing a drink, or reading journals, or playing cards. It was already well past one o'clock with the better part of the day gone, but these men seemed to just now be waking up.

"Indeed?" Terrel said. "A pity. Should enjoy the pleasures of town, what?"

"I shall enjoy myself for the time I am here," Geoffrey said, his gaze still raking the crowd. "I heard Ravenwich attends this club."

"Ravenwich?" Terrel asked. " 'Course, 'course. He is right over there." Terrel nodded to a dark-haired man who sat playing cards with two others. "But what do you want with Ravenwich?"

"I have a slight acquaintance with him," Geoffrey said, studying the movements of the dandy. He was indeed a handsome man, with a negligent, rakish air. Anger rose within him. That Sarah had been attracted to such a man sickened him.

"You know the duke?" Terrel asked. "E-gads, didn't know you swam in such elevated company. Would he beholden to you if you would introduce me to him."

Geoffrey looked at his flushed cousin. He smiled grimly and rose. "Certainly."

Terrel jumped up. "Really? Gads. Awfully good of you, cuz. Awfully good of you."

Geoffrey walked directly over to the duke's table, Terrel bounding after him like an excited rat terrier. Placing himself firmly in front of the dandy, Geoffrey said, "Ravenwich."

The man looked up, frowning. "Yes?"

"Terrel, meet Ravenwich," Geoffrey said, and leaning over, drove a clenched fist into Ravenwich's nose.

"Great Zeus!" Terrel squeaked, and the room broke into sudden exclamations and roars of shock.

"You said you wanted to meet him, Terrel," Geoffrey said, flexing his hand. "And so do I, but upon the field."

Ravenwich shook his head and swiped the trickle of blood from his nose. A feral smile crossed his lips as he surveyed Geoffrey. "You must be the country yokel."

Geoffrey nodded, smiling back. "So I am."

"Richard," the man sitting beside Ravenwich said. "Who the devil is this man?"

Ravenwich's dark eyes glittered and his lip curled. "A mere nobody, Winston. Just a Johnny raw up from the country."

"True," Geoffrey said, smiling. "Certain 'business' brought me to town. But since I'm here, and have heard that Ravenwich has never been bested in a duel before, I thought I'd try my hand at it. If he accepts, that is."

"Oh, I accept," Ravenwich said, eyes narrowed. "With pleasure."

"Richard," Winston said as the onlookers muttered. "You can't be serious. Why go out with this man? 'Tis clear he's a jumped-up mushroom, wishing to make a name for himself."

"My name is honorable at least," Geoffrey said.

A hush invaded the room. An unknown had dared to cast aspersion upon a duke of the realm's honor. Ravenwich stood slowly, his eyes cold. "We shall put that upon your epitaph to be sure. It shall be pistols. Name your seconds."

Geoffrey turned to look at Terrel, whose face had turned as white as his high cravat. "Cousin, will you second me?"

Terrel's eyes widened. "Y-yes. If I must."

"James and Danton," Ravenwich said. "You'll stand for me?"

"If you are determined," Danton said, throwing down his cards. "Think it beneath you to fight this fellow, but will do so."

"So will I," Danton said, nodding.

Ravenwich smiled at Geoffrey. "And who will be your other second?"

Geoffrey looked around the room and shrugged. "Anyone who would be kind enough to do so." He scanned the room. Not a man stepped forward. Some lowered their gazes, while others stared openly at him, their expressions varying shades of disapproval and disrespect. A slow smile crossed Geoffrey's lips. "My name is Geoffrey Vincent, the Earl of Grey, and I shall lay odds with whoever so wishes that it will be I to shoot Ravenwich first."

"You can't be serious," Ravenwich said, stiffening.

"I am," Geoffrey said. "If you are desirous of making a few pounds, as I know you are, you'd best lay your money upon me."

"Blast and damn," an old man in a wig cried. "Boy's got

more brass than brains, but I'll wager on him! And second him, damn if I won't!"

"So will I!" a callow youth dressed in a wasp-waisted, canary-yellow jacket called, his face flushed and eager.

"I'm for Ravenwich!" another man shouted. "I'll bet a pony!"

"Y-you will?" Terrel said. "W-well, I bet on me cousin, by Jupiter."

The finest of England forged forward, the fever of a good wager burning in their eyes.

"Terrel," Geoffrey said, over the shouts and calls. "Take down the bets for me, please."

"Yes, yes," Terrel nodded. "W-waiter, paper! I need paper!"

Geoffrey looked at Ravenwich, and nodded his head shortly. Turning, he strolled toward the door.

"My lord," Geoffrey's youngest, and third second cried out. "Where shall we come round to make the arrangements?"

Geoffrey turned. "I am residing with Lord Bevington."

"A nobody did you say, Ravenwich?" hooted the old man in the wig. "Double my wager. The boy's a damn dark horse fer God's sake and I'm bettin' on him!"

Sarah sat in the parlor and sipped her tea, listening with only half an ear as Melanie chatted to her father, relating to him the stories of her family. Her father laughed often and seemed as amused by Melanie's revelations as Sarah had been the first time Melanie had told her.

Neither seemed to notice that Geoffrey was absent from the tea, nor did either remark upon the fact that he had been absent the entire day. Since both had shown complete unconcern, Sarah refused to ask exactly where Geoffrey was, or why he and Melanie had not departed for Grey Manor that morning.

Whatever the delay, she was sure she did not care. Geoffrey would leave tomorrow and she had determined she would be a sublimely happy woman once he had departed and was out of her life forever. She had just that morning sent notice to the paper canceling her betrothal with Ravenwich. It was the first step toward making herself free. When Geoffrey left, it would be the second step. Once he was gone, she promised herself she would forget the whole frightful episode and take up her life once more.

Meekum entered the room at that moment and requested Kendall's attendance. Kendall nodded, and after excusing himself, withdrew.

A twinge of unease entered Sarah as she noted Melanie's gaze and how it followed her father's exit. Melanie finally looked at Sarah, a flush upon her face. "Your father . . . is an unusual man, is he not?"

Sarah smiled, despite herself. "Many think so."

Melanie looked down. "He must have been very much in love with your mother."

Sarah frowned slightly. "I believe he was. But she died many years ago. Now I fear Father enjoys his bachelor state far too much. I own I was not pleased to discover him at that house last night."

"No," Melanie said, her voice quiet. "It must have been a shock to you, but he is unmarried and men do go to such places when they are unattached."

"Yes, I know," Sarah said, laughing. "And though I am grateful Father is home at last, I do wish our reunion had not been in that particular place."

"Indeed," Melanie said. "It . . . it was rather strange, was it not?"

Sarah shook her head in amusement. "Ravenwich had threatened me with the fact that no one would ever be able to find me in such a place, and most certainly not my father. Faith, he clearly misjudged the matter . . . and my father. I fear, if he didn't want Father to find me, he should have taken me to a convent."

Melanie giggled. "Yes, that would have been the safest place from your father."

At that moment Kendall strolled back into the room, and Sarah and Melanie quickly grew silent, peeking at each other in silent amusement. Sarah's lips twitched as she said, "Is everything all right, Father?"

"Indeed," Kendall said, taking up his chair again, his green eyes showing their own secret amusement. "I must own, Lord Grey is a far more inventive man than I had at first thought."

"What do you mean?" Sarah asked, frowning.

"He's managed to call Ravenwich out," Kendall said, picking up his tea cup.

"What!" Sarah's heart stopped. "He couldn't have!"

"But he did," Kendall said, his tone rueful. He shook his head and laughed. "And he did it in such a way that no one knows his purpose. He placed a bet with any man who wished that it would be he to shoot Ravenwich first. He's turned it into a regular sporting event. Everyone is so taken with that, no one cares exactly why he called Ravenwich out. I must hand it to the boy. It was well done."

"Well done?" Sarah asked, aghast. "Well done that he has called Ravenwich out?"

"Oh, dear," Melanie said. "I was afraid something like this would happen."

"But why?" Sarah asked, a cold numbness entering her. "Why?"

"Geoffrey has always possessed a deep sense of responsibility," Melanie said helplessly. "Ravenwich took you from his home by force, and Geoffrey will not accept that lightly."

"He has no responsibility to me," Sarah said. "He let me know that in no uncertain terms last night."

"Yes," Kendall said. "He did give me a chance to call Ravenwich out first, but I declined. He was distinctly displeased with me, and said since I would not tend to the matter, he would."

"Will it be pistols?" Melanie asked, her eyes dark and concerned.

"Yes," Kendall nodded.

"Thank heaven," Melanie said, sighing.

"Thank heaven!" Sarah exclaimed, shocked. "How can you say that?"

"Geoffrey is an excellent marksmen," Melanie said, her tone soothing. "Indeed, there is no better hunter in the shire."

"Ravenwich has always shot his man," Sarah said. "He might kill Geoffrey."

"He doesn't dare, even if he says he will," Kendall said, shaking his head. "He'll have the whole world watching."

"And do you think Geoffrey will care about that?" Sarah asked. "Do you think he'll not kill Ravenwich if he can?"

Melanie blanched. "Oh, dear. I had not considered. H-he has been in such a mood of late."

"Geoffrey must not duel with Ravenwich," Sarah said with vehemence.

"But I fear he will," Melanie said quietly. "He will not be satisfied otherwise."

"I have no care of whether he is satisfied or not," Sarah said. "He must not go out with Ravenwich. I refuse to allow him to do so." With that decree, Sarah stood up smartly and stalked from the room.

Kendall sighed and stood, walking over to sit beside Melanie. "Do you think she will be able to sway him from his course?"

Melanie shook her head, a frown marring her brow. "I'm afraid not."

Kendall sighed. "My poor Sarah, she is not accustomed to meeting with such resistance." He studied Melanie a moment. "Are you frightened?"

Melanie drew in her breath. "I—I don't believe so. Geoffrey truly is one of the finest marksmen. I cannot believe Ravenwich to be better."

"I applaud your loyalty and common sense," Kendall said. " 'Tis a shame Sarah cannot do the same. She does not understand your young fire-eater must do what he must."

Melanie's laugh was shaky. "Indeed. I never thought I'd say it, but Geoffrey is becoming hotheaded."

Kendall smiled. "Yes, I fear he is. I wish he had not called Ravenwich out, but I believe it shall all work out for the best. Your Geoffrey must be allowed to relieve his spleen . . . or uphold his honor as it were." He frowned. "As long as he does not kill Ravenwich, all will be fine."

"Yes," Melanie said, paling. "As long as he does not kill Ravenwich."

Ten

Sarah sat quietly in the chair of the gold room, Geoffrey's room. The hour had grown late and still she waited. Finally, she heard a sound at the door and Geoffrey entered. He turned to see her sitting there. His face showed no surprise, his eyes no warmth. "I should have known you would be here," he said, and walked to sit in another chair.

"Yes," Sarah said. "Remaining away from the dinner table and sending no word to us, were not the actions of a gentleman."

Geoffrey laughed. "As you know, I am not gallant at the best of times, and I assure you, tonight I would have been even less so. If you wish for pretty manners, I suggest you leave now."

Sarah refused to move, refused to turn her gaze from Geoffrey. "Why have you called Ravenwich out?"

"I have my own reasons," Geoffrey said, his face stiff. "None of them pertain to you."

"No, of course not," Sarah said, laughing shortly. She rose and walked to the fireplace, keeping her back to Geoffrey. "What if I told you I lied about Ravenwich, that he did not do all I said?"

"It would not matter," Geoffrey said after a moment.

Sarah turned swiftly. "Would it not?"

Geoffrey's smile was not kind. "I told you I do not fight

Ravenwich because of you. What you say or what you do not say, no longer matters to me."

Sarah's eyes narrowed. "But you would not go out with Ravenwich if it were not honorable. If I tell you that you have called him out based on facts which are not true, it would not be honorable."

Geoffrey stood. "But they are true. You lie to me now, to serve your purpose. You do not want me to duel with Ravenwich. Why?" he asked, stalking toward her. "Do you still care for him that much?"

"No," Sarah said, shaking with rage. "I hate him. But he may very well kill you."

"What? Would you suffer a twinge of conscience if I were to die?" Geoffrey asked, his voice stern, cutting. "Or would it be that you would miss one of the pawns you've employed." He shook his head. "No, my lady. You will not stop me from dueling with Ravenwich. If anything, I would kill him because it was his actions which brought you into my world. I would never have known you if not for him."

Pain knifed through Sarah. She lifted her chin, blinking back foolish tears. She had come to plead with Geoffrey. But to tell him the truth now, to tell him she shivered at the thought of him facing danger or death, would be useless. She drew in a breath and said, "Indeed, that is sufficient reason to call Ravenwich out. I would that I had never met you either. But if you kill him, it will be messy, my lord. It will interrupt my life and make it extremely uncomfortable. I do not wish to be a nine-day wonder."

Geoffrey cracked a laugh. "So, the real reason comes out. It will be inconvenient for you. Rest your mind, Sarah, the world will not connect your name with the duel. No, I duel with Ravenwich to satisfy my own conscience, in order that I may return home without another thought of you. You shall be out of my life, and I most certainly shall be out of yours." He snorted. "You may then return to your grand social life, and its balls and fêtes and *gallant,* fawning men."

Sarah stiffened, for he had described her life, the very life which had made her foolishly accept Ravenwich. Geoffrey must have read something in her eyes, for he laughed and said, "Yes, I've learned much about The Incomparable today. It appears every man is ready to laud and acclaim the great Lady Sarah. What a heartbreaker you are, my lady. I don't know why you seem concerned over this duel. From what I've heard, you are accustomed to duels being fought in your honor."

Sarah's eyes narrowed. "You talk about Tommy Jamison and Lord Nevington, no doubt. They fought over me, or so it was said. In truth, they were both drunk and managed to call each other so many names they were forced to call each other out to uphold their honor. Saying it was over me was merely more convenient and fashionable than admitting they were fools whose tempers and tongues had led them into a duel."

"And what of the men who you've left heartbroken?" Geoffrey asked, turning and walking swiftly away from her. "What of all the proposals you've turned down? You've gathered hearts right and left and then spurned them all." He turned and glared at her. "What of Lord Haden who tried to commit suicide over you?"

Sarah swallowed hard. "You *have* been listening to all the gossips today, haven't you? Lord Haden was all to pieces. He had gamed everything away at the tables. I did not know him well, I only stood up with him at a dance or two. When he tried to commit suicide and failed, he needed a better story and he found it in me."

"There is always a plausible reason with you, isn't there?" Geoffrey said, his tone bitter.

"I don't know if it is plausible," Sarah said. "But it is true. I am 'The Incomparable' of the season, my lord. 'Tis fashion to fall in love with me. It matters not if they even know me, or truly care. 'Tis the fashion."

"I thank God I've never held with fashion," Geoffrey said, his eyes cold, insulting.

Sudden rage flared through Sarah, covering the pain, hiding her ragged emotions. "No, you've never held with fashion and you are proud of it, are you not? I may be The Incomparable, but you, you are the great Lord Grey, so far above the rest of us. You are pleased to lift an eye at men's foibles, pleased to be rude and ungallant. Say what you will of polite society, but their cruelty comes from their frailties, their lack of understanding. But yours comes from self-importance." Sarah walked up to Geoffrey, looking levelly at him. "Have your duel, and then return to your mighty manor, where you are always right and your world is always ordered. You are correct; you have no place in fashionable society. You have no place in my society."

Geoffrey's eyes darkened, but Sarah did not wait for another cutting word from him. She spun and walked hastily toward the door. She held her head high as she departed, even though it felt as if her heart were bleeding anguish into her very soul.

Morning mist swirled about the men. Geoffrey stood in his shirtsleeves, feeling the weight of Kendall Bevington's Manton. It was a fine piece, with perfect balance. He held it, feeling not fear but rage. It had cooled and crystalized into a diamond hardness, but it was rage nonetheless, rage at the man who had dared to mar Sarah, dared attempt to rape her, and dared to steal her from his home and think to make her a whore.

Terrel ran up to Geoffrey, sheets of papers clutched in his hands. "Cousin, only imagine, the Duke of Avon has placed his bet. He sends his regrets that he could not attend, but he has sent his marker."

Geoffrey cast a quick glance about. His lip curled. The mist could not hide all the different gentlemen who stood around, waiting for what to them was now a sporting event. "I believe we can survive without him."

"Without him?" Terrel gasped. "You do not understand. He is one of the leaders of the ton. That he took note is an honor indeed."

Geoffrey gritted his teeth. "Terrel, if you could let off the tallying, we need to proceed."

"Oh, yes," Terrel said. "Yes."

"Go inspect Ravenwich's piece," Geoffrey said. "And take mine as well." He handed the Manton to Terrel.

"Hmm, yes," Terrel said, and took the pistol by two fingers as if it were a dead fish. He turned and stumbled off, holding the fine Manton out and away from him, while the sheets of bets he nurtured close to his chest.

Geoffrey waited, watching with narrowed eyes as the group of seconds inspected the pieces. The other onlookers crowded close, offering comments. Geoffrey shook his head sharply. They were all mad, ridiculously mad. He turned his gaze to Ravenwich, the man he would kill within the hour. Ravenwich stood in the middle of the group, clearly taking last-minute bets himself.

Finally, the seconds nodded, and Terrel hurried back to offer Geoffrey the Manton. He sighed deeply as Geoffrey took it. "Gads, I hate those things."

"So I noticed," Geoffrey said.

"Are you ready, Grey?" Ravenwich called to Geoffrey, he and his contingent approaching.

"I am," Geoffrey said.

"I hope your estate can bear your losses," Ravenwich said.

"It won't have to do so," Geoffrey said. "And the world will most readily bear the loss of you."

Ravenwich's eyes narrowed. "I doubt it."

"All right, gentlemen," Terrel cried. "The duel is about to begin. Please step away, step away."

The group fell silent and the onlookers moved back to a proper distance. Geoffrey felt his anger surging within him as they performed the formalities of the duel, as they turned their backs to each other, as Terrel called out the paces, his voice squeaking with excitement. With each pace Geoffrey's anger mounted. He would kill Ravenwich. Never would he touch Sarah again. At the call of five Terrel suddenly stopped. Geoffrey halted, awaiting the call. It never came.

Murmurs and mutters sounded from behind. Geoffrey, cursing, spun. "Terrel, what the devil is going on?"

"I'm sorry, cuz," Terrel said. "But Lord Stanton wished to change his bet."

"What?" Geoffrey asked, stunned.

Ravenwich had turned as well. Shaking his head, he strode back. "Then change it quickly and be done with it. Stanton, just what were you betting?"

Geoffrey stood frozen a moment. The men were not mad, they were complete fools. He started as the absurdity of the situation cracked through the ice of his rage. Those men were no more ridiculous than he, for he intended to kill a man for a woman who did not care. Indeed, Sarah's only request had been for him not to make things "messy." If he killed Ravenwich now, it would not only be messy, but beneath him. There would be no honor in it. A dry chuckle escaped Geoffrey and he walked back toward the intent, wager-taking group. His mind was cleared and he knew a different purpose.

"Has everyone placed their bets now?" he asked.

Terrel's thin face flushed. "Yes. Sorry, cuz, I forgot to tell them the betting was closed. It was my fault."

Geoffrey scanned the crowd with a cool look. "Gentlemen, I have decided I will not kill Ravenwich."

Ravenwich stiffened. "You wouldn't be able to."

"For the sake of the betting," Geoffrey said. "I thought it only fair to warn you I'll not kill him. He's not worth it."

Ravenwich's eyes flared. "Damn you, Grey."

Geoffrey laughed and said to the men, "I will shoot him

in the right shoulder." He reached out and pointed. "There, to be exact."

"Like hell you will," Ravenwich said, rearing back.

"You wish the other shoulder?" Geoffrey asked.

The men laughed, and Ravenwich's face turned a dull red. "No, blast it. And I will kill you, no matter this turn of yours to save yourself."

Geoffrey smiled slowly. "Men, please place your bets quickly this time."

A babble arose, the men shouting out their new wagers. Terrel's hand scribbled wildly upon his sheets, crossing and recrossing the lines. Geoffrey shook his head and strolled away from the group. He settled himself against a tree and waited.

Within ten minutes, Terrel rushed up to him. "I have all the bets now, cuz. Though I worry about those who are not here, they do not have a chance to change their wager now."

" 'Tis their own loss," Geoffrey said, pushing himself away from the tree. "If they did not choose to attend this fine affair."

"Yes," Terrel nodded, scurrying after Geoffrey as he strode back toward the waiting men. "But Avon wagered you would kill Ravenwich."

"Terrel," Geoffrey said crisply. "If I have decided not to kill Ravenwich, then I have decided. I'll not kill him for the sake of the Duke of Avon."

"Er, no, of course not," Terrel said. "I—I guess it is understandable. Avon's a sporting man, he shouldn't take snuff." His voice brightened. "He did place a wager on Ravenwich killing you as well."

Geoffrey started a moment and then laughed. "Hedged his bets, did he? Well, he'll be out on both counts then."

"Yes," Terrel said with a sigh.

Geoffrey shook his head and proceeded toward the group. He looked quickly at the group of waiting men. "Are we ready? The betting is definitely closed now."

The consents were firm and quick, the crowd taking up their watch from the distance. This time when the men stepped back and they performed the formality of the duel, Geoffrey smiled. Terrel counted off the paces, steadily, with no halting. Geoffrey just as steadily walked it, turned on the call, and shot Ravenwich directly in the right shoulder.

Ravenwich's arm jerked from the impact and his Manton fell from his grasp. "Damn it!"

The men applauded and shouted. One rushed up to Ravenwich, who clutched his hand to his shoulder. Peering close, the man shouted, "Bedamn, right on the mark, gentlemen, right on the mark!"

Sarah sat in the drawing room with Melanie and Kendall. She attempted to focus on her sewing, but her gaze strayed every few minutes to the gilt clock upon the curio table. The minutes ticked by, and with each movement of the hand, she envisioned in her mind's eye Geoffrey taking a bullet from Ravenwich and dying. It should not matter to her, she told herself fiercely. Geoffrey had made it plain the duel had nothing to do with her. He did not care for her one whit, and she should not care for him either.

"Sarah," Melanie's voice said gently. "He really is an excellent shot, you know."

Sarah tore her gaze from the clock to discover Melanie watching her with sympathetic eyes. She lifted her chin and said, "I was not thinking about Geoffrey. I am sure it is no business of mine. I—I was thinking that now we are in town once more, we should hold a ball."

Melanie's eyes widened, and then she looked back down to her sewing. "I—I see."

Kendall, who sat across from the ladies, lowered the paper he was reading, his green eyes showing amusement. "Were you?"

At that moment, the door opened and Geoffrey, quite un-harmed, entered.

"Geoffrey!" Melanie cried. Throwing down her sewing and standing, she rushed over to him. "Thank heaven you are not hurt."

"Of course not," Geoffrey said, taking the hands Melanie offered him.

Sarah sat staring at him. Her heart somersaulted and then beat madly. Geoffrey was safe. Every fiber in her being clamored with the need to rush to him as Melanie had, to hold him close and feel for herself that he was warm and living. Rather, she forced a cool smile and said, " 'Tis pleasant to see you alive, my lord. It would have been no end of bother if Ravenwich had killed you." Melanie gasped and Kendall coughed. It sounded suspiciously like a laugh.

Geoffrey's gaze met hers over Melanie's head, and his eyes narrowed. "Indeed."

"May I ask how Ravenwich fared?" Sarah asked, lifting a brow. "Or do we need to pack your bag in order for you to flee to the Continent."

"Oh, dear!" Melanie gasped. "Geoffrey, you . . . you didn't kill Ravenwich, did you?"

"No," Geoffrey said, smiling down at her. "I merely winged him." He then looked to Sarah. "It was a very neat and clean shot to the shoulder."

"Fine work, Grey," Kendall said, nodding.

Geoffrey's gaze did not leave Sarah's. "I was instructed not to make things messy."

"What?" Melanie asked with a gasp.

Kendall started and then laughed outright. Rising, he walked over to Melanie and Geoffrey. "Miss Devon, now that we know Geoffrey is safe, do let us prepare for that carriage ride I promised you. You have not seen the sights of London sufficiently and it is a beautiful day." His green eyes alight, he glanced at Geoffrey and Sarah. "Would you two care to join us?"

"No, no, thank you," Sarah said, tearing her gaze from Geoffrey's, an embarrassed heat flushing her.

"No," Geoffrey said, and shook his head. "I intended for us to leave shortly."

"Must we?" Melanie asked, her face falling.

"Then we shall have your bags packed," Sarah said. "I shall order the maids to do so directly."

"I shall pack them myself," Geoffrey said, his tone curt.

"Grey, you cannot leave today," Kendall said with a firmness. " 'Twill surely take a day or two to collect the bets. Indeed, I myself am a richer man today. I placed my own bet you would wing Ravenwich."

Geoffrey looked at Kendall, his gaze level. "That was a risky bet, my lord. I had not decided to allow Ravenwich to live until a few minutes before the duel."

The slightest smile hovered upon Kendall's lips. "I had complete faith you would come to your senses and do the right thing."

The two men's eyes held for a moment. Then Geoffrey laughed, his tone rueful. "It had turned into such a farce, I could not do otherwise, my lord."

"Then it was providence," Kendall said. He chuckled. "I have no doubt Ravenwich was sadly put out."

Geoffrey smiled a slow smile. "You could say that. Since everyone was betting so seriously, I made certain to tell them exactly where I meant to mark Ravenwich."

"Did you?" Kendall asked, his eyes widening.

"And you hit him there!" Melanie said. "Didn't you?"

"Yes," Geoffrey said, "I did."

Kendall chuckled. "I have no doubt Ravenwich is packing his bags this very instant, or he will after the surgeon is finished with him. He'll be the laughingstock of town. The pain to his shoulder will never match the pain of his disgrace. Especially since he has cost those who bet on him a tidy sum of money."

Sarah's eyes narrowed. "Yes, my lord. I am so glad to know you have been paid well for your honorable deed."

Geoffrey's gaze locked with hers. "I have no care for the money. My satisfaction will be in returning to Grey Manor."

"Indeed," Kendall said softly. "But surely you could remain one more day. If only to permit Miss Melanie a chance to see London. It would be a shame for her to miss the opportunity since she is here now."

"Please, Geoffrey," Melanie said. "London is so very interesting."

Geoffrey glanced down at Melanie. He sighed. "Very well. I am sure there are certain things I may do today. We'll leave early tomorrow morning instead."

"Oh, thank you," Melanie said, her eyes shining.

"Come. I shall order the carriage," Kendall said, walking toward the door. Melanie was swift to follow him. Kendall turned at the door and glanced at Sarah and Geoffrey. "Are you certain neither of you wish to join us?"

"No!" Sarah said quickly at the same time as Geoffrey did.

"Very well," Kendall said, and led Melanie from the room.

Sarah glanced hastily at Geoffrey. "That was kind of you to permit Melanie this day, considering how anxious I know you are to depart here."

"She deserves the pleasure," Geoffrey said, his tone stiff. "In light of her trials these past few days, it is only fair she has some enjoyment."

"Indeed," Sarah said, setting her sewing aside. "Of course, she would have been spared the trial altogether if you had not gone out with Ravenwich."

"No," Geoffrey said. "She would have been spared the trial altogether if she had never met you."

"Very well, I do not intend to argue with you upon that head," Sarah said, rising. She walked toward Geoffrey, pinning a smile upon her face. "I doubt I shall see you before you go, my lord. I go to see my modiste now and will attend a musical this evening. No doubt you shall leave tomorrow before I rise." Geoffrey's gray eyes watched her steadily, narrowly. She shrugged. "Perhaps while you are in town you can look at some new plows and whatnot. That should delight you." Still Geoffrey did not speak. Sarah drew in a breath and held out her hand. "Good-bye, Geoffrey."

It was a mistake, for when Geoffrey clasped her proffered hand, an electricity coursed through Sarah. Her gaze flew to his, unguarded and unprotected. They stared at each other a moment, and then without thought, even without conscience, Sarah leaned into him. Geoffrey's free hand rose and curved around Sarah's neck, drawing her slowly closer and closer until their lips met. Sarah, the slightest sound escaping her, surrendered to his kiss, her eyes closed, sudden tears stinging them. How she needed to draw in his breath, smell his scent, and feel the warmth of his body. Only this could ease the fear burrowed within her, only this could heal the hurt.

Geoffrey broke the kiss, as Sarah knew he would. She neither moved nor opened her eyes as he broke their clasp, as he stepped away.

"Good-bye, Sarah," Geoffrey's voice said, low and rasping.

Sarah merely lowered her head and said, "Good-bye."

She waited until she heard the sound of Geoffrey leaving the room. Only then did she open her eyes and let the tears fall.

Geoffrey strode down the streets of London, taking no particular path and no particular direction. He had sworn he would be glad to leave, glad to have Sarah out of his life. Yet then he had kissed her. The simple touch of her hand had swept all his good intentions away, and the look in her eyes had compelled him to kiss her one more time before he left.

Society called Sarah The Incomparable. They should call

her the devil instead. She made him do things he never imagined he would. This morning he had almost killed a man
because of her. No matter his denials and lies, the simple
truth was, he had been walking, breathing rage ever since
Sarah was stolen from his home. Yet he had regained a small
portion of his sanity this morning, and before he lost it again,
before he ever kissed Lady Sarah Bevington again, he would
leave. He would break the hold she had over him if it were
the last thing he did.

"Hello, milord," a rough voice suddenly said from behind.
Before Geoffrey could turn, his left arm was grabbed
roughly, and a large man fell into step with him.

"Easy does it, milord," another man said, snatching up his
right arm in a brutal grip. He jabbed a pistol into Geoffrey's
side. "Ye'll be coming with us."

Geoffrey tensed, but permitted the two men to propel him
into a nearby alley.

The man with the pistol stepped away, while the other held
Geoffrey's arm.

"We've got a message for ye, milord," the man said, cock-
ing the hammer.

Geoffrey didn't wait for the message. He shifted his weight
and spun the man holding him to the forefront as the gun
exploded.

Sarah paced the parlor. Her father and Melanie had not
returned yet. Neither had Geoffrey. She had not gone out to
her modiste, nor to any other place. She was in too much
turmoil, and all because of a country gentleman who said
he wished to leave her and never see her again. Faith, she
had actually cried over the man. She shook her head angrily.
She had not even cried when she thought she had killed Ravenwich, but she had cried over Geoffrey Vincent.

'Twas ridiculous, she told herself firmly. She could have
almost any man she wished, and instead, she was acting like

a lovesick fool over the one man she could not have. She halted sharply and drew in a ragged breath. Lovesick? Impossible! The word love and Geoffrey Vincent did not belong in the same sentence, not for her. Nor would they ever. They were worlds apart and that was how it would remain.

"My lady!" Meekum's voice suddenly called.

Sarah looked up, never even realizing he had entered. His normally calm face showed perturbation. "What is it, Meekum?"

"There is a driver of a hack who wishes to see you," he said, his fine nose twitching.

"A driver of a hack?" Sarah asked, frowning. "Whatever would he want with me?"

"I do not know, my lady. He said he would not 'deal' with me," Meekum said. "He seems to be afraid he will not be paid."

"Paid for what?" Sarah asked.

"That, my lady," Meekum said, "is what he will not discuss with me."

"Very well," Sarah said, sighing. "I will see him."

Meekum followed her as she went into the hall and to the door to discover a small, wiry man standing upon the stoop.

"Meekum says you wish to talk to me?" Sarah asked.

"Ye be the lady Sarah?" the man asked, his eyes suspicious.

"Yes, I am," Sarah said, nodding.

"I's got a gent in the hack that gave me this here address, said I's was to bring him to yer and you'd pay me well."

"He did?" Sarah asked. "Who is this gentleman?"

"Don't know," the driver said. "He 'twern't in no shape to tells me. Looked like bloody hell when he came to me. I's didn't want ter give him a ride, but he wasn't takin' no for an answer, and since he's a big bloke, I wasn't planning to argue."

"A big bloke?" Sarah asked "My God! Geoffrey." She picked up her skirts and ran toward the hack.

The little driver scurried behind. "He's gone orf and I's wants ye to know, it ain't my fault. Not my's responsibility. I's just wants me money."

"You'll have it," Sarah said, snatching open the hack's door. She froze. Geoffrey sat hunched in the corner, bloodied and appearing unconscious. "Geoffrey!" Sarah cried, her heart racing as she climbed into the hack. "Geoffrey!"

Thankfully, his eyes opened. "Hello."

"What happened?" Sarah asked, trying to control her wrenching fear at the sight of blood seeping across his chest.

"Two men," he said. "Alley. S-sent by . . ."

"Ravenwich," Sarah said, drawing in a breath. "You should have killed him this morning."

"No," Geoffrey said, the slightest smile upon his lips. "Too messy."

" 'Tis you who are messy now," Sarah said, striving for a calm.

"Y-yes," Geoffrey said, his head falling back. "S-sorry. Not used to knives."

"Knives?" Sarah asked, and then shook herself. "Never mind. I don't want to know." She crawled closer to him. "C-can you move?"

Geoffrey groaned and placed a heavy arm about her shoulder. "Think so."

"Good," Sarah said, and wrapped strong arms about him. She heard him draw in a rasping breath. "Did I hurt you?"

"N-no," Geoffrey said, groaning.

"Liar," Sarah said softly.

Geoffrey's chuckle was faint. "Yes."

"Come," Sarah said. Adding her strength, and all her prayers, Sarah helped Geoffrey from the hack, his shallow breathing shortening her own breath in fear. They stumbled toward the house, Meekum and the driver both gaping at them. Suddenly, Geoffrey groaned and his weight pressed heavily upon Sarah. She could not hold him, and they swayed. Refusing to release him, Sarah clung to him desperately, even as they slowly sunk to the ground. Huddled together, Geoffrey lowered his head to her shoulder and whispered, "N-not going to make it."

Sarah's arms convulsed about him. "You cannot die on me, Geoffrey, do you hear? You cannot!"

"I w-on't," Geoffrey said, his breath wheezing. "Unless you squeeze the life f-from me."

"Oh," Sarah said, quickly relaxing her hold. "I'm sorry."

"Meant," Geoffrey gasped. "W-we w-won't make it to the house. T-too weak."

"Do not cast aspersions on my powers, my lord," Sarah said, laughing to hide her ridiculous tears. She was becoming an absolute watering pot.

"Never," Geoffrey murmured. "Y-you have t-too damn m-many . . . over me."

"What?" Sarah asked. She received no answer. Shaking herself, she looked up, blinking back the dratted tears. Meekum and the driver still remained standing, watching her with bemused, slack expressions. "Meekum, do not just stand there. Get the footmen to carry Geoffrey up the stairs. Also send one to bring Doctor Kingsley to us. No, send two. Have them find him wherever he is and tell them not to return without him. Also have the maids bring hot water and bandages." Cradling Geoffrey close, she looked at the driver and tears escaped down her cheeks. "I'll pay you, sir. I'll pay you whatever you want for bringing him back to me."

Geoffrey opened his eyes slowly. It was dark, the dim flicker of a candle the only light. He blinked as his bleared vision cleared. He blinked once more as he discovered Sarah sitting upright in a chair drawn close to his bed. Her eyes were closed in sleep, her hair disheveled and awry. Dark shadows hollowed out her eyes, and one hand was stretched out on the arm of the chair as if reaching for him.

Geoffrey studied her, wondering if it was truly her or if

she was merely part of a laudanum-induced dream. In the pained haze of memory, he remembered fighting. One man had taken the bullet meant for him, but Geoffrey had been unprepared for the knife the other had pulled upon him. That man had slashed Geoffrey well before Geoffrey had finally overpowered him. Messy, Geoffrey thought, terribly messy. The only compulsion which had dragged him from the alley was the need to see Sarah, to bring his wounded body and spirit back to her.

Now she sat sleeping in the chair beside him. He shut his eyes. He could be dreaming. Was she truly sitting in that chair, watching over him like a guardian angel? He closed his eyes. She had said so many cruel words to him. She did not care for him. He was beneath her society. Yet here she was. Who was she really? Liar, flirt, and tease or guardian angel. Or was she simply Sarah, the Sarah who called to his heart and made him foolish and mad?

He opened his eyes and gazed at Sarah. Slowly, fighting the pain, he stretched out his hand to hers and clasped it. Warmth flooded him. She was real.

Sarah's eyes flickered open. She stared at him one moment, sleepiness softening her eyes to a dark aquamarine. A gentle smile curved her lips. "Hello."

Angel or not? Geoffrey swallowed hard. "Who are you?"

"Who am I?" Sarah asked. She sat up quickly. "What do you mean, who am I?"

Geoffrey held tightly to her hand, despite the pain. He swore he would leave her, yet he could not even release her hand. "And who am I?"

"Don't you know?" Sarah asked, her eyes darkening. There was fear there. Why?

Then Geoffrey realized what she thought. He smiled. "No, I do not."

Sarah's eyes narrowed. "Geoffrey, please tell me you know who I am. Please say you remember me."

"I remember you," he said softly, sighing. The flash of a

memory of a kiss in a haystack drifted through his mind. "Your name is Amy, isn't it?"

Sarah's face darkened. "No, no, it isn't."

Geoffrey smiled. That kiss in the haystack. "But I remember you as Amy. If you are not Amy, who are you?"

Sarah shook her head. "Don't tease me."

Geoffrey closed his eyes. "I do not believe I am the one who teases."

He felt her hand start in his and then he heard her say, "You are teasing me now. Do not!"

"Yes," Geoffrey said, opening his eyes, "my lady."

Sarah's eyes widened and she shook her head. "Go back to sleep, my lord."

"Are you going to leave?" Geoffrey asked directly.

Expressions flitted across her face, expressions that Geoffrey in his drugged state could not fathom. "No, I'm not going to leave." She smiled. "You might . . . have a nightmare. You might need me."

Geoffrey studied her a moment and then closed his eyes with a sigh. There was no "might" about it. He did need her. Whoever she was, and whoever he was, he needed her. What he was going to do about it he didn't know, but tonight it didn't matter. She was here with him. He fell asleep holding her hand.

Eleven

Kendall studied the two ladies seated at the table with him over a late breakfast. Sarah was sleepy-eyed, in fact almost glassy-eyed. As for Melanie, she remained quiet, her expression one of deep worry.

"Sarah," Kendall said, "you are not eating much, my dear."

Sarah blinked and looked up. She glanced at her unattended plate with a rather surprised expression, as if she hadn't even noticed its presence. "I am sorry, Father. I fear I am not hungry."

Kendall cast a discerning glance toward Melanie. "Are you not hungry either, Miss Devon?"

Melanie looked down, shaking her head. "No, I fear not."

"I do believe it is our patient who is on a restricted diet and not us," Kendall said. "It will be a shame if Geoffrey recovers only to have both of you fall ill."

"We will be fine," Sarah said, picking up her fork.

"Indeed," Kendall said, noting she did employ the tine upon her eggs. She pushed them about into quadrants. "As will Geoffrey. He is a very strong man. Doctor Kingsley said the knife wounds in his chest are not as deep as he first expected. In truth, I suspect the most difficult part of Geoffrey's recuperation will be remaining confined to his sick room."

"He most definitely will remain there until the doctor says

so," Sarah said, the first spark of life entering her dulled eyes.

Melanie glanced at Sarah, her look clearly dubious. "Surely he will."

Kendall chuckled. "I believe I will be going out for a while. I have some small matters to attend. I have no doubt Geoffrey is in capable hands between you two charming ladies. However, I would suggest you both take turns in sitting with him. Melanie, I hope you will take the next few hours. 'Tis clear Sarah is lacking her sleep."

Sarah's gaze met Kendall's. "I am perfectly all right."

"I am sure, but I believe Miss Devon, as Geoffrey's promised, should be permitted a few hours of time with him as well," Kendall said. Both ladies flushed deeply. Kendall hid his smile and rose. "Now I fear I must leave you. Sarah. Do try to get some sleep. You are looking slightly ragged." He ignored his daughter's outraged expression and strolled from the parlor.

Ravenwich sat propped up in bed. His shoulder hurt like the devil and his mood was black. He watched his valet with a sullen gaze as the man moved silently about the room. "Do not forget everything I've told you to pack, Hillard. And remember to pack my jewels separately this time, you dolt."

"Yes, Your Grace," Hillard said in a quiet voice.

Ravenwich shifted in discomfort and winced. "Leave out the buff jacket and unmentionables. I shall wear them today. Do not worry over a cravat. I will do without one."

"A wise idea," a new voice suddenly said from the bedroom doorway. "It might remind you of a hangman's noose."

Ravenwich stiffened, and his gaze flew to the door. His eyes widened. "Bevington, what are you doing here?"

"You act surprised," Kendall said, strolling across the room and sitting in the one chair without articles upon it.

"Surely you expected me. I've never considered you a dull-ard. Many other things, but not a dullard."

Ravenwich stared at him and then shouted, "Beakner, where the devil are you?"

"No need to call your butler," Kendall said, smiling. "A very good man of sorts. He is in my employ now."

"Is he?" Ravenwich asked, his eyes narrowing.

Kendall nodded. "I knew you wouldn't mind since you are leaving town."

"Yes," Ravenwich said, leaning back against the pillows. "Since your daughter has seen fit to jilt me, I will not remain to wear my heart upon the sleeve, no matter my injury."

"Very good," Kendall said, his tone commendatory. "An excellent story. It may be slightly difficult to pull off, since your duel with Grey yesterday, but I have no doubt if given the chance you might be able to succeed."

Ravenwich smiled. "Everyone knows of my devotion to Lady Sarah. That she should cast me off so quickly when I am wounded is cruel, cruel."

"I don't know," Kendall said. He picked a speck of lint from his superfine jacket. "Everyone should empathize with Sarah's loss of respect for you and her unwillingness to unite with a man who was not only bested by a country yokel but caused many of the ton to lose their wagers upon him." Ravenwich started up in anger, and then fell back, cursing from the pain.

Kendall looked at him and asked in a tone of concern, "Does it hurt you much?"

"No," Ravenwich said, gritting his teeth. "The shot was clean. I'll mend shortly."

Kendall nodded. "You'll be glad to know that Grey's wounds are lighter than expected as well. He too shall mend shortly."

Ravenwich tensed and looked warily at him. "Grey's wounds? Whatever are you talking about?"

"Ah, then you did not receive the report of Lord Grey's

attack by Mohawks yesterday?" Kendall shook his head. "Of course not. What am I thinking? One man was shot through and the other, despite his skill with the blade, evidently fared no better. I did wonder if the man lived to tell or not."

Ravenwich forced a shrug, unable to meet Kendall's gaze. "What would I know of all this? I've been confined to my sickbed. 'Tis clear Grey is new to town and did not know enough to beware of its dangers."

"Yes," Kendall said, smiling. "However, I am not new to town and fully understand the dangers." He turned his gaze to the valet, who quietly continued his packing. "My good man, if you do not wish to accompany your master to the Americas I shall find you employment elsewhere."

Hillard froze. The Hessian he held in his hands thunked to the floor. "T-the Americas, m-my lord?"

"What the devil?" Ravenwich exclaimed.

"Yes," Kendall said, still looking at the stunned valet. "I have heard it is rather savage over there and they actually curl their lips at men with valets. Quite plebeian but understandable, since they have no society or fashion to speak of." He frowned. "And then there is the niggling issue of whether your master will be able to pay you or not."

"Nonsense," Ravenwich said through slitted eyes. "I am not going to the Americas, I am going to France."

"I am sorry for the confusion, Ravenwich," Kendall said, and leaned back in his chair, his manner relaxed. "You would have known of your traveling plans before this, but young Grey seemed quite determined to duel with you. Since I am never one to thwart a man when his intentions are honorable, I let him have his way. I own, I am very pleased he decided not to kill you." Kendall smiled. "You see, Grey is the direct sort of man. He has no understanding of a man like you. He doesn't realize that killing you would not have been the best manner in which to deal with you."

Ravenwich clenched his fist, though his heart failed him

at the cool, confident look in Kendall's eyes. "I am not going to America."

"Oh, but you are," Kendall said, his tone soft. "I have bought up all your mortgages, your vowels, and your debts. A quite hefty sum. You amaze me."

"What?" Ravenwich asked, stunned.

"As does your departed father," Kendall said. He shook his head. "His legal papers were in quite a disorder, and the entail so easily broken." Kendall rose and walked over to pick up one of the valises. He carried it to the bed and set it down. "How fortuitous this is already packed. I am sure in your condition, you will wish to travel light. Dealing with luggage when one has no servants can be so tedious. However, in consideration of your infirmed state, I have two strong men awaiting you downstairs, They shall see you safely to your ship. It is certainly not first class, and I am not sure if the cargo of pigs won't set up an offensive odor upon the high seas, but I thought it wise for you to accustom yourself to such conditions before you arrive at your new home. Indeed, I have no doubt you will find friends amongst the pigs, since they are of your nature."

"Damn you, Bevington!" Ravenwich exclaimed, choking. "Damn you to hell. I am not going."

Kendall smiled. "If you do not go, I will send you to debtors' prison. It would be a joy for me to permit you to languish there, I assure you. Of course, your family will be left to survive the scandal. The ton should be pleased to see your estate employed in the noble purpose of housing unwed mothers and reformed prostitutes."

"You can't do that, damn it!" Ravenwich exclaimed.

"But I can," Kendall said, his gaze steady. "And I shall. You see, it struck to my very heart when I discovered my daughter in a house of ill repute."

Dread coursed through Ravenwich. "You were there?"

"Yes," Kendall said. "It was one of those fateful coincidences. And quite embarrassing, I must own. Imagine, I had gone to Madame Lucille's with the same purpose any red-blooded Englishman does, but upon discovering my daughter there, my view changed dramatically. One could say I had an absolute epiphany, in fact. It made me start wondering when I go to a such a house if I may not be accidentally defaming another man's daughter or ruining a possible innocent." He frowned and shook his head. "I believe it only proper that one of the first unwed mothers to take haven in your estate should be that little maid whom you and Sarah had such an unfortunate tiff over. Don't you agree?"

"No, I don't," Ravenwich said, shaking with impotent rage.

"I really do wish I could throw you into debtors' prison," Kendall said. "Perhaps it would help you see the light. However, there is no sense in repining over what cannot be. Since you set your men on Grey, I doubt he will be satisfied now with anything less than killing you. We cannot have you tempt his goodness twice." He shook his head. "And even if he failed, I really fear my own sweet daughter would kill you. I do not wish her to soil her hands for the likes of you. So you shall be leaving at this moment, no matter your condition." Kendall withdrew a card from his vest pocket and walked over to the valet, holding it out to him. "My good man, do come and see me. I hear Lord Fawnsworth is looking for a man. He is a veritable tulip and a valet's delight, I assure you."

Without another word, or glance at Ravenwich, Kendall strode from the room. Ravenwich sat staring after him, shocked and sickened. Hillard, his gaze upon the card in his hand, walked toward the door. Ravenwich frowned. "Hillard, where are you going? I must dress." Hillard neither answered nor stopped. "Hillard!"

Sarah, feeling no better for her sleep, walked down the hall toward Geoffrey's door. Her dreams had been fitful and frightening. She dreamed she was back in the brothel, and instead of Geoffrey coming to save her, he had wagered with Ravenwich that she would be the Incomparable Courtesan within a year. She had begged Geoffrey not to wager with Ravenwich, but he had looked at her and said he didn't know her, nor did he care to know her, for he needed to return to Grey Manor and could not be deterred.

Sarah shook her head, pushing the dream to the back of her mind. Looking up, she saw Melanie advancing down the hall, carrying a covered tray. Sarah forced a smile. "Melanie, how is the patient?"

Melanie stopped quickly, a startled look upon her face. "Oh, hello, Sarah. I—I thought you would still be sleeping."

"No, I couldn't." She frowned at the tray. "Geoffrey has not eaten yet?"

"No," Melanie said, a flush painting her cheeks. "Geoffrey would not eat the broth and I had your chef prepare something different."

"Something different?" Sarah asked. She walked swiftly over and lifted the cover. A full course of beefsteak, eggs, and toast met her gaze. She slammed the cover back down. "The doctor said he is to have only broth and tisanes. He cannot eat this."

"He says he'll not accept the broth and tisane," Melanie said. "He is in a rather contrary mood."

"Is he?" Sarah said. "Well, no matter his mood, he is now in my house and will follow the doctor's orders. I shall see to that. Allow me to return this to the cook."

"Sarah," Melanie said. "Geoffrey is set upon having more than broth."

"Is he?" Sarah said, taking the tray from her. "Well, it is not healthy for him and I will not permit it."

It appeared Melanie would object, but then she looked down and said, "Very well. If you wish it."

"I do," Sarah said, and walked in a militant stride toward the stairs. Autocratic Geoffrey was, but for him to endanger his health was beyond enough. She swished down the stairs, her irritation high. As she entered the foyer on her trek to the kitchen, she noted Meekum, who started and rushed toward her. His face was harried and he carried a large silver bowl.

"I must inform you," Meekum said, "we have had many calls."

"Not now, Meekum," Sarah said, refusing to slow her pace. "You told them we are not receiving, I hope?"

"Yes, my lady," Meekum said, chasing behind her. "But . . ."

"That is fine then," Sarah said. "You will excuse me, but I must exchange Lord Grey's trays."

"But . . ." Meekum's voice trailed off and Sarah was glad to see he followed her no more.

She entered the kitchen and swiftly informed the chef of her wishes. She waited impatiently as he went once more to ladle a bowl of broth from the fire. Thanking him, she turned and retraced her course. She was still fuming over Geoffrey's obstinacy as she entered the foyer.

"Oh, Sarah dearest," a female voice called. " 'Tis so good to see you."

Sarah stopped dead in her tracks and looked up from the tray she was frowning upon with severity. Lady Elizabeth Driscoll, dressed in a stunning blue dress in the highest kick of fashion, fluttered her hand at her from the front entrance. Meekum stood respectfully with the door open.

The honorable Miss Stanton stood beside the lady Elizabeth. The girl giggled and waved at her. "Oh, yes indeed. Meekum just said you were not receiving." Her cornflower-blue eyes widened as she surveyed Sarah's rumpled dress and falling hair. " 'Tis clear you are not . . . not feeling well, most certainly." Her tone also implied not appearing well.

"I am feeling fine," Sarah said. She harbored a dislike for both ladies, and held but the merest acquaintance with them.

"But you must excuse me, a guest of ours has been injured and requires attendance."

"Oh, yes, the divine Lord Grey," Lady Elizabeth said, sighing and fluttering her hand to her bountiful chest. "The town is positively agog with his feats. That he bested the duke in such a manner! Why, it simply takes my breath away."

Sarah wished heartily that it *would* take her breath away, every last gasp of it, in fact.

"Yes, indeed," Miss Stanton said, performing a pretty pout. "Elizabeth and I came to lend our support, dear, dear Sarah. I declare you must be positively overset by your broken engagement to Ravenwich. But we understand. We truly do. You, as the Incomparable, could not wed the duke after he appeared in such a foolish light. It must be so mortifying for you."

"Indeed," Lady Elizabeth said, nodding her head, though her eyes were those of a feline finding a mouse in a corner. "But with the devastating Lord Grey staying here, I am sure your spirits cannot help but be lifted. Rumor has it that he is as attractive as he is brave. You sly, sly thing. Wherever did you meet him?"

"I met him in the country. He has an acquaintance with my father," Sarah said without compunction. "Now, if you will excuse me, I must take this broth to Geof—Lord Grey before it cools overly much."

Miss Stanton's eyes widened and she giggled. "Cannot your maid do that?"

Lady Elizabeth laughed. "Do not be a goose, Melissa, would *you* let your maid attend Lord Grey when you could . . . nurture him instead?"

Both ladies laughed in trills and titters. Sarah discovered she was clenching her jaw. She unlocked it, and said as sweetly as she could, "If you will excuse me now, ladies. Do have a pleasant afternoon. I have no doubt I shall see you some other time . . . when I am receiving."

"Oh, of course," Lady Elizabeth said, showing not one

whit of discomfort. "We did come before the proper hour, but since we are such friends we knew you would forgive our little indiscretion. We simply knew we must hasten to your side to offer our support." She smiled and her eyes lit. "And in proof of it, we wish to invite you to our social on Thursday next, and please do not hesitate to bring Lord Grey with you."

"Please do," Miss Stanton said, her blue eyes aglow. "We so look forward to welcoming him to town."

"Of course. Leave your card and invitation with Meekum then," Sarah said, offering a wide smile. Geoffrey would be long gone by then, she knew.

Meekum bowed and walked to pick up the silver bowl he had carried before. The two ladies all but ripped their reticules to shreds in their haste to draw out their cards. Lady Elizabeth was the winner of the contest, and waving her card in triumph, dropped it into the silver bowl. Then her eyes widened and she bent over the bowl. "My goodness, so many already?" She promptly put her hand back into the bowl, causing Meekum to jump and Sarah's eyes to widen. Her face was as intent as if she were searching for a diamond instead of her card.

"Yes!" she cried, in anything but a delicate tone, and plucked out her card. Smiling, she sashayed past Meekum and approached Sarah, laying the card upon the tray she held. "Since you said you are going up directly to Lord Grey, I am sure you would not mind presenting our cards to him. Please, do tell him how eager we are for him to attend our social. We intend to make it one of the finest!"

"Oh, and do take mine!" Miss Stanton said, skittering over to place her card on top of Lady Elizabeth's.

Sarah stared down at the cards and then looked back at the ladies with the haughtiest of her expressions. She was pleased to see she had not lost her knack and that her gaze had finally pierced the thick hides of Lady Elizabeth and Miss Stanton. Both ladies flushed and backed away hastily, all the while chattering on about their sincere friendship. They were both gabbing and cooing as Meekum, wise butler that he was, shut the door upon them with alacrity.

Sarah gazed at Meekum through slit eyes. She asked in a low, dangerous tone, "You mentioned other visitors, Meekum?"

"Yes, my lady," Meekum said, coughing. "That is what I wished to tell you. There has been a . . . er, steady stream of them, I fear. Some of the gentlemen have come to pay their vowels, you see. However, most have been . . . er, social calls. There are quite a few invitations."

Sarah's gaze focused upon the silver bowl. "Exactly how full is it?"

Meekum drew in a deep breath. "Very full, my lady. I attempted to inform them Lord Grey was infirmed, but the ladies . . ." His eyes widened and showed no small amount of shock. He continued, "The ladies did not wish to . . . to listen."

"The ladies, is it?" Sarah asked, through clenched teeth. "Very well! Put the bowl upon the tray. Since I am to be lackey to Lady Elizabeth and Miss Stanton, I might as well take the rest of them up to Geoffrey." Suddenly she laughed, her good humor returning. "Faith, I cannot wait to see Geoffrey's face. He'll bolt for Grey Manor for certain once he knows he has all of London society chasing him. If he thinks me frivolous, Lady Elizabeth and Miss Stanton should surely give him a bad turn."

"Yes, my lady," Meekum said, and placed the bowl upon the tray.

Sarah trod up the stairs to Geoffrey's room, a satisfied smile upon her lips. She looked forward to presenting the ladies' cards to Geoffrey and watching as he tossed them away. Faith, for once she could sympathize with Geoffrey's contempt for society women. They acted like veritable widgeons, flocking to the door of a man they didn't even know, merely because he was the new man of the hour. They would soon find out their "new" man was not the type to be dallied with, nor easily added to their string of admirers. She chuckled. It was not kind, but it assuaged her tattered pride to know that shortly all those other frivolous debutantes would join her in the ranks of the spurned.

She forced a sober expression, however, as she entered the room, to discover Melanie sitting beside the bed, and Geoffrey sitting up in it, looking much better. "Your meal, my lord," she said, and walked over to set the tray upon the bedside table.

Geoffrey frowned at her. "You did not bring me broth, I hope."

"I most certainly did," Sarah said with a smile.

His face darkened. "Melanie told me as much. I will not have it."

"Indeed, you will," Sarah said, laughing. "It is what the doctor ordered for you."

"I shall not," Geoffrey said with a growl. "I need some true sustenance if I am to heal."

Sarah smiled sweetly at him. "For shame, Geoffrey. I very well remember a time when I wished for substantial food and you would only feed me broth. You would not defy the doctor's orders then, how can you ask me to defy them now?"

Geoffrey's gaze narrowed. "If I remember correctly, my lady, I finally gave you your request."

"You remember incorrectly," Sarah said, fluttering her lashes. "You did not *give* me my request. I was forced to come down to the dinner table for a decent meal."

"If that is what is necessary," Geoffrey said. He sat up quickly, clearly intent upon leaving his bed.

"Geoffrey no!" Melanie exclaimed.

"Don't!" Sarah cried, rushing over to him and placing a staying hand upon his shoulder. Geoffrey paled of a sudden, and, grunting, fell back against the pillow. He closed his eyes and drew in his breath.

Shaking, Sarah pulled her hand back quickly, lest he feel

her tremble. Striving for a calmness she did not feel, she said, "Geoffrey, please don't be difficult."

Geoffrey opened his eyes. They were dark against the paleness of his skin. "I am not being difficult. I request food, real food. I gave you such when you were under my roof, and I request you give me as much under your roof." His eyes narrowed. "I even served it to you."

Sarah drew in her breath. "Indeed you did, as I will do now." She promptly sat down upon the bed. "But it will only be broth . . . for the moment." She ignored Geoffrey's fulminating glare and picked up the bowl and spoon.

"I can feed myself," Geoffrey said.

"No, I shall do so," Sarah said in determination. The stubborn man had already taxed his energy far enough. "I'll not have you throw it in my teeth that I was less of a hostess than you were host, my lord."

"Do not my lord me," Geoffrey said, his words clipped, "if you intend to feed me like an infant."

Sarah laughed as she raised up a spoonful of broth. "God forbid I ever have a baby like you." She froze as Geoffrey stiffened. Realizing what she had said, she flushed. "I—I mean, a child straight from the cradle and demanding meat would be . . . quite disconcerting."

"You would rather have them crawl from the cradle already fashionably dressed, no doubt," Geoffrey murmured, eyeing the spoon with a wariness. "And reaching for a bell-pull."

"Of course," Sarah chuckled, and shoved the spoon directly into Geoffrey's mouth. He choked, but swallowed it. Broth trickled down the side of his mouth. Sarah dropped the spoon into the bowl and reached to pick up the napkin. "While a son of yours would crawl directly toward the fields. That or demand bedtime stories of plows and sheep."

Geoffrey's eyes lit in amusement as Sarah wiped his mouth. "A daughter of yours would flirt immediately with the doctor who delivered her until he forgot to swat her upon the . . . posterior to make her cry."

"Indeed," Sarah nodded with a smile, placing the napkin in her lap and taking up another spoonful of broth. "Heaven forefend any of our children, for I am already of such a height and you . . . well, they may very well be giants."

"A race of Amazons," Geoffrey said, nodding.

"Surely not a race," Sarah exclaimed as she extended the spoon to Geoffrey's lips. "Perhaps one or two."

"No," Geoffrey said, his eyes teasing. "Five."

"Five!" Sarah dropped the spoon, and it bounced down Geoffrey's chest, splattering broth. "I am sorry," Sarah said, gasping. Disconcerted, she set the bowl and spoon aside and grabbed up the napkin. "How utterly clumsy of me."

" 'Tis all right, I'll take care of it, Sarah," Geoffrey said, reaching to hold her hand and the napkin. Sarah started as a jolt of electricity shot through her. She glanced breathlessly at Geoffrey. He smiled. "And it would have to be five. Two to be farmers, two to be debutantes, and the last one to break the tie."

Sarah gazed at him a stunned moment. Then, shaking her head swiftly, she jerked her hands from Geoffrey's grasp and stood. She turned quickly from him, only to discover Melanie sitting there, watching her with the oddest expression in her eyes. Embarrassment coursed through Sarah. She had forgotten Melanie's presence entirely. "Melanie," she said, "perhaps you should feed Geoffrey instead. You surely should be better at it than I."

"No," Melanie said, shaking her head slowly. "I think you are doing very well."

"No," Sarah said with a shaky laugh. "I have exhausted all my serving abilities." She looked hopelessly about as silence filled the room. Her gaze lighted upon the silver bowl with the invitations. In dire need of a diversion, Sarah reached over and picked it up. Determined to be light and airy, she turned with it in her hand and looked at Geoffrey with feigned amusement. "I forgot to give you these."

Geoffrey's brow rose. "What are they?"

"They are invitations," Sarah said, reaching in to pull out a handful of cards and flourish them. "You best listen to the doctor and do all you should, if you intend to effect a safe escape to Grey Manor."

"Escape?" Geoffrey asked, his gaze wary.

"Escape," Sarah nodded. "These, I'll have you know, are invitations and calling cards. From well nigh half of the ton."

"What?" Geoffrey asked, his brow shooting up.

"Yes." Sarah smiled wickedly. "You succeeded in making a name for yourself, Geoffrey. Society is breathless to meet you." Geoffrey's shocked look sent Sarah into peals of laughter. "Eat the broth, Geoffrey. Build your strength. You'll need every bit of it to make it safely back to the country."

An odd, considering look entered Geoffrey's eyes. "I'm not sure I can recuperate so swiftly after all."

It was Sarah's turn to be astonished. She shook her head. "Geoffrey, I'm not sure you understand. Most of these invitations are from ladies, the very kind you will heartily dislike."

"Will I?" Geoffrey asked.

"Yes, you will," Sarah said, her humor fading fast. "They are the very sort you hold in low esteem. They are frivolous, and . . . and light minded . . . and vain. They merely look to add another man to their list of admirers. You will be a prize for them, nothing more."

Geoffrey barked a laugh. "I see."

Sarah forced a laugh herself. "Yes, it is humorous. I can just see you squiring them about, fawning and kissing their hands. You'd have so many handkerchiefs tossed in your direction you'd be in a permanent crouch. That is, until they get a taste of your manners. You'll disappoint them mightily."

"Will I?" Geoffrey asked, his eyes suddenly sparkling with challenge.

"Yes, you will," Sarah said, the unworthy emotion of jealousy tightening her chest. "I cannot wait to see their looks when you state in your forbidding tones that you do not dance. They are looking for another gallant in you, and will be sadly surprised when they discover they are mistaken." Sarah heard Melanie gasp. Rattled, Sarah looked hastily to Geoffrey.

Rather than the dark frown she expected, he smiled. "Perhaps not."

Sarah's eyes narrowed. "These women are every one of them the social debutante and lady. If you do not like me, you will most assuredly not like them."

"We shall see," Geoffrey said, that irritating smile still upon his lips.

"Ridiculous," Sarah snapped. "Why, you will no more fit into London society than . . . than I fit into country life."

"I said," Geoffrey said, his tone firm, "that we shall see."

Sarah laughed. " 'Twill be hard to see, my lord, since you are returning to Grey manor shortly."

"Oh, no, not shortly," Geoffrey said, smiling. "I've changed my mind. I'd like to see those invitations now."

Sarah hugged the bowl to her. "You cannot be serious."

"Oh, but I am," Geoffrey said. "To not even look at them would be rude, would it not?" His eyes glinted. "And you, of all people, have taught me not to be rude."

"I have not taught you anything," Sarah said angrily. He merely gazed at the bowl. "Very well, if you wish." She strolled over and, with ruthless disregard for his condition, dropped the silver bowl onto his lap.

"Thank you," Geoffrey said with a wheeze.

"My pleasure," Sarah said sweetly, seeing red. Or perhaps green. She spun sharply to leave, but remembering of a sudden, she marched over and scooped up Lady Elizabeth's and Miss Stanton's card from the tray. She turned back and stuck them out. "Do not forget these two, they were particularly intent in making sure they were not lost in the shuffle. Two finer ladies you could not wish to meet."

"Are they beautiful?" Geoffrey asked, reaching to take the cards.

"Some would consider them so," Sarah said with a non-chalant shrug. "I personally do not."

"Not up to the Incomparable's standards?" Geoffrey asked, laughing. "I shall certainly wish to meet them. After all, I am just up from the country and know better than to set my sights too high. Most certainly not as high as the Incomparable."

Sarah felt as if he had dashed a bucket of cold water upon her. She lifted her head and said with as much dignity as possible, "Indeed." She turned and fled the room, unwilling to stay while Geoffrey studied the invitations.

Melanie strolled down the picture gallery, studying the paintings in distraction.

"Miss Melanie," Kendall Bevington said. "Meekum told me I could find you here."

Melanie started and turned to discover Kendall standing close to her.

"Oh, I am sorry," she said. "I did not hear you."

"No. You seem enthralled with the paintings," Kendall said. His brow lifted. "Odd. I fear you like my ancestors far more than I do."

"I enjoy history," Melanie said, turning quickly away, hoping he did not read her face.

Apparently he had, for he said, "What is it, my dear? Something has overset you."

Melanie looked at him and then flushed. "Sarah and Geoffrey have had another fight."

"I have heard," Kendall said, nodding. In a gentle movement, he took up her hand, gazing down at her with a kindness. "You must not let it concern you, it is their way."

"Yes, it is their way," Melanie said, and quickly withdrew her hand. It tingled and she clenched it as she turned away from him. "Their natures are rather strong." Her laugh was small. "Almost with . . . with a passion in them I'd say."

Kendall was silent a moment. Melanie looked at him quickly. He gazed at her with far too much understanding. She flushed and walked down to look at another picture. "How . . . how was it with you . . . you and your wife?"

"Maria?" Kendall asked. He laughed. "She was very much like Sarah."

"I wish there was a picture of her," Melanie murmured before she thought.

"Does it bother you so much?" Kendall asked.

Melanie glanced up. His green eyes were intent upon her. She shrugged. "I can understand why you do not have a picture of her, but I do wonder."

Kendall laughed. "You have only to look at Sarah and you will see Maria. Indeed, perhaps, for all my talk, the simple truth is that I need no picture. When I look at Sarah, I see Maria. They are very much alike. Though I believe Sarah has some of me in her as well to temper . . . her temper, as it were."

"Then your wife was very strong and . . . and passionate as well," Melanie said, sighing.

Kendall walked up to her and studied her. "There are many forms of strengths, my dear. He paused, then continued, "And many forms of passion."

Melanie laughed shakily and looked away. "Do you know, I've known Geoffrey all my life? We . . . we are promised to each other. He has always been a . . . a steady man. Perhaps autocratic and rather negligent in his manners, but always steady, dependable. But since Sarah came, he . . . he is another man, a different man."

"And which man do you think he truly is?" Kendall asked softly.

Melanie flushed. "The one he is when he is with Sarah."

"I see," Kendall said, his tone soft. "It takes a strong woman to not only see that but to admit it. Does it pain you greatly?"

"No," Melanie said, looking up at him in confusion. "And that is what surprises me, and embarrasses me. I watched them today. Sarah was serving Geoffrey his broth . . ."

"What?" Kendall asked, his brows rising.

Melanie laughed. "Indeed she was. And they were arguing . . . but then, then they began to talk and . . . and I could see their . . ." She drew in a deep breath and continued, "Their love for each other." She shook her head. "And I could not be upset. In fact, all I saw was that my dear friend, whom I have known for so long, has found love."

"What do you intend to do?" Kendall asked.

Melanie shook her head. "I do not know."

Kendall sighed. "Neither do they. And they must work that out in their own fashion and time. But if you believe Sarah is right for Geoffrey, then it means he is not right for you. If he is not, have you thought which kind of man would be right for you?"

Melanie held tight to Kendall's large, comforting hand but would not meet his gaze. She knew she was not a strong woman and she dared not say what she felt. "N-no, no, I have not."

Kendall was silent a moment. Then he said in a calm voice, "I have heard Geoffrey intends to stay in London. Please accept my hospitality as well. This would be an excellent time for you to be able to meet other men. You can then perhaps discover what type of man you do want."

Melanie refused to release Kendall Bevington's hand. She only nodded, and blinked back a tear.

Twelve

"Good afternoon, Meekum," Sarah said as he opened the entrance door for her. Her arms were laden with packages, and the maid behind her hugged band boxes and parcels. "Please have the footmen bring in the other purchases from the coach." She forced a smile and said as merrily as possible, "I have been on a shopping expedition."

She was not about to admit she had indeed almost bought the shop up, sending Madame Celeste into transports. Sarah herself had not found as much pleasure in the morning. Perhaps it was because she knew she had done it as an escape. Worse, her mind continually betrayed her and wandered back to fret and stew over the invalid in her house.

She silently pledged to herself she would steer clear of Geoffrey, no matter what transpired. Whatever the man did, she was determined it would not overset her. He could order up an entire rhinoceros to devour and she'd not care. He could do handstands down the stairs and she'd not notice. He could . . . he could . . . well, he could do anything and she'd not bat an eyelash. From here on out she would be totally detached. She'd reclaim her sanity and composure if it were the last thing she did.

A sudden burst of female laughter wafted across the foyer, interrupting Sarah's train of thought. She frowned. "Whoever is that, Meekum?"

"My lord has company," Meekum said, his face paling.

"Father is entertaining?" Sarah asked. Another orchestra of laughter arose and Sarah's gaze roved to the parlor door from whence it derived. "It sounds like an absolute party."

"So it is," Meekum said. "But it is Lord Grey who entertains."

"What?" Sarah exclaimed, stunned. "Impossible."

"I fear not," Meekum said.

"He should be resting," Sarah said in sudden anger. Then she drew in a deep breath. " 'Tis of no moment, I am sure."

Another gale of laughter came, taunting and teasing to her ears.

"Yes, madame," Meekum said, nodding, though he watched her with a cautious eye.

A loud female titter titillated from the closed parlor.

"That is enough," Sarah muttered. She promptly shoved her packages at the surprised Meekum. She did not wait to see if he caught them, but sped toward the parlor. She pushed the door open and entered. She came to an abrupt halt and clenched her jaw before it fell open.

Geoffrey rested upon the length of the sofa, propped by a multitude of pillows. Surrounding him was an absolute harem of ladies, the ladies in turn surrounded by their chaperones. The parlor was a mass of beautiful dresses and color. At that moment, Lady Elizabeth was offering the designated sultan a chocolate.

"Geof—my lord, just what are you doing?" Sarah asked, her eyes narrowed.

Geoffrey glanced up, his gray eyes glinting in amusement. "These ladies have taken pity upon me and have been kind enough to entertain me."

"Fie, my lord," Elizabeth Driscoll giggled. " 'Tis you who entertain us." She turned triumphant eyes to Sarah. "We never dreamed my lord would be able to receive us. We had merely stopped by to inquire after his health, I assure you."

"Did you?" Sarah asked in a dry tone.

"Imagine our surprise . . . and delight," Lucy Tillington

said, turning a limpid gaze to Geoffrey. "When my lord condescended to see us."

"So kind of him," Sarah said.

"Yes," Elizabeth said, batting her lashes. "Poor Lord Grey said he has been absolutely bored to flinders until we came ... with no decent company."

"And we couldn't have that," chimed in Lady Amelia Chandler. "Why, he is a hero, after all."

Sarah choked. "A hero?"

"Indeed," Lady Elizabeth said. She pursed her lips and widened her eyes in feigned surprise. "Never say you haven't heard."

"Heard what?" Sarah asked, frowning.

"Why, about Ravenwich," Elizabeth said. "My lord has completely bested him. The duke has left town."

"I do not find that amazing," Sarah said coolly. "Ravenwich is not the type of man who would stay once he's been made a laughingstock."

"And you should know," cooed Elizabeth. "Since you were engaged to him."

"But, Lady Sarah," Amelia said, her eyes wide, "you do not understand the full import of it. Ravenwich has not just quit town. He has disappeared. His home has been closed and his servants turned out."

Lucy Tillington giggled. "It's whispered he has gone to the Americas."

"He has?" Sarah asked. A flood of relief washed through her.

"Indeed," Elizabeth said. She turned her gaze to Geoffrey, her lashes fluttering. "No doubt he knew he could not even share this continent with Lord Grey."

Geoffrey shook his head. "You make too much of it, Lady Elizabeth. I am sure I had nothing to do with Ravenwich's decision."

"You are too, too modest," Elizabeth said with a sigh and adoring look. She turned her gaze back to Sarah and said in a sickeningly sympathetic voice, "But I am sure we should not discuss it anymore. It cannot help but give poor Lady Sarah pain. After all, she was to wed Ravenwich."

"It does not give me pain," Sarah said, lifting her chin. "I believe you saw my notice in the paper. 'Twas I who canceled the engagement."

"Of course," Lucy Tillington said. "And we all understand, I assure you. What else could you do after Lord Grey disgraced Ravenwich so in the duel."

"I did not throw Ravenwich over because of what Geoffrey did!" Sarah said hotly.

"Geoffrey?" Lucy murmured and then tittered. The young ladies all giggled then, while their chaperones frowned upon Sarah.

"Of course not," Lady Elizabeth said. "However, we all shall strive to turn your mind from such 'unfortunate' events. To that purpose, I intend to give a ball." She turned her gaze to Geoffrey. "I do hope you will attend, my lord. It is to be in your honor, and will help introduce you to our society."

Geoffrey hesitated and Sarah smiled. "I am sorry, Elizabeth, but Lord Grey does not care for such social functions. He considers them frivolous."

Geoffrey cast her a narrowed glance and then turned his attention to Elizabeth, smiling. "I would be delighted to attend your ball."

"You have made me so happy," Lady Elizabeth cried, clapping her hands together. "I thought to hold it within three weeks time. I want you to . . . to be totally fit."

"Three weeks?" Sarah asked. She looked at Geoffrey with a stern look. "Surely *my lord* does not intend to remain in town that long?"

Geoffrey's eyes lit and he offered her a bland smile. "For dear Lady Elizabeth's ball I shall. It would be very . . . ungallant not to attend, since she holds it in my honor." A challenge entered his eyes. "That is, if you and your father do not mind extending your hospitality to me for that amount of time. I would not care to trespass upon your good graces overly much."

"Oh, surely you do not mind, Lady Sarah," Elizabeth said. All the ladies added their pleas.

Sarah looked hastily about at their expectant faces. Geoffrey smiled at her from amongst his eager court. A bitter taste rose in Sarah's throat, but she smiled and said, "Of course I do not mind. You may stay as long as you wish. I assure you it matters not one whit to me."

Geoffrey's gaze narrowed. "You are all graciousness."

"Thank you," Sarah said in dulcet tones, her mind working furiously. "But I fear you did not come prepared for an extended stay, my lord. Do you wish for me to send a servant to the country to bring you the necessary wardrobe for a stay in town?"

"No," Geoffrey said. "Do not tax yourself, my lady. My wardrobe was in quite disrepair when I left the country." Sarah flushed and he nodded. "I shall take the time to acquire another one while I am in town."

"Famous," Lady Elizabeth said, leaning toward Geoffrey. "I cannot tell you how excited I am about the ball. Do say you will dance with me."

Sarah laughed. "Lord Grey does not dance, Elizabeth."

"What?" Lady Elizabeth asked, her face falling.

"But that can be remedied," Geoffrey said, smiling to Elizabeth. "Just as my wardrobe can be. I would not wish to disappoint you."

"And you'll dance with me?" Lucy Tillington cried.

"And me too?" Amelia added.

"I will," Geoffrey said, laughing.

Sarah bit her lips as he turned his amused gaze upon her. "And you, Lady Sarah?"

She swallowed hard. "If you choose to learn to dance, I shall, my lord."

"Afraid I shall step on your toes, Sarah?" Geoffrey asked

softly. The ladies giggled and tittered. They sounded like a positive hen house.

"My lord," Lady Elizabeth said, "I would be pleased to teach you how to dance."

"We all will," Lucy cried. "What fun it shall be."

"Oh, yes!" Amelia said, clasping her hands together.

"When shall we do so?" Lady Elizabeth said.

"If you will excuse me," Sarah said, having had more than enough. "I'll leave you to your arrangements."

"But do you not wish to join the party, Lady Sarah?" Lady Elizabeth asked, her eyes wide.

"No," Sarah said with feigned nonchalance. "I fear I have already accepted too many engagements. When one returns to town, there are just so many friends one must see again."

"I see," Lady Elizabeth said, and looked to Geoffrey with a coy smile. "I fear you are left in our hands, my lord."

Geoffrey smiled back. "I am sure I shall fare well."

"If you will excuse me," Sarah said. She turned sharply on her heel and walked from the parlor. "Fare well, will he?" Sarah murmured to herself. *Not in my house,* she thought angrily. She'd promised herself she'd not let Geoffrey overset her, but that was before she knew he intended to follow through upon his threat to remain in town. And under her roof at that! It would be intolerable.

She halted a moment. What was she thinking? Geoffrey could not just arbitrarily decide to remain in London. He had Melanie to consider, after all. Melanie had obligations at home. For that matter, so did Geoffrey. He merely needed to have them brought to his attention. Sarah smiled in satisfaction and went in search of Meekum. She found the butler and asked him where Melanie could be found. He informed her Miss Devon was in the library, and Sarah made her way there directly. Once again Sarah discovered herself coming to a standstill upon entering a room.

Melanie sat in a large winged-back chair, her father upon the arm of it. Books surrounded them, and one rested upon

Melanie's lap. She and her father were laughing at the moment as he leaned over to point at the pages.

"Hello," Sarah said after a frozen moment, a moment in which neither party even noticed her.

Melanie glanced up. Her brown eyes sparkled in a fashion Sarah had never seen before. It suddenly struck Sarah how beautiful Melanie actually was. Hers was a quiet beauty, but with that glow in her eyes and flush upon her cheeks it could not be denied.

"Sarah, do come and look at this," Melanie said, smiling. "Your father has been telling me of his travels. I could not believe him when he talked about the savages in Africa. But, indeed, here is a picture and they look exactly as he described."

"Yes," Sarah said. "I have seen them."

"Have you?" Melanie asked. She shook her head. "I find it hard to imagine. And I thought London was strange compared to home."

"Yes, home," Sarah said with an eagerness. "I wish to talk to you about that. I just came from talking with Geoffrey . . ."

"Did you?" Kendall asked, his tone amused. "Amazing you could even get near him, let alone speak to him, what with all the ladies attending him."

Sarah frowned. "Indeed. He should not be up, let alone entertaining."

"I thought so myself," Melanie said with a sigh. "But you know Geoffrey. He is not one to listen, and he had been in such a . . . a dark mood, that when he said he would receive company, I could not help but think it might be beneficial for him."

Kendall laughed. "The pleasure of a lady's company, or should we say *ladies* in Geoffrey's case, can be far more healing than any draught Doctor Kingsley could devise. Besides, you cannot expect an active man like Geoffrey to remained confined too long."

"He is most certainly active," Sarah said, irritation rifling her. "Do you know he has promised to attend Lady Elizabeth's ball?"

"Has he?" Melanie asked, her eyes widening. "I cannot credit it. He does not like such affairs. Why, even the country assemblies bore him."

"He says he will attend," Sarah said. She looked pointedly at Melanie. "And it will not be for another three weeks."

"Ah," Melanie said, smiling when by rights she should be frowning. "Then he should be in better health."

"Melanie," Sarah said, doing the frowning. "He could not be thinking when he promised it. Surely neither of you can remain away from home so long. He still has hay to bring in . . ."

"What?" Kendall exclaimed, brow raised.

"The hay must be brought in," Sarah said impatiently.

Kendall stared at her and then broke into laughter. "Forsooth."

"What do you find so amusing?" Sarah asked with arched brow.

"Nothing, dear," Kendall said, "Other than hearing a daughter of mine talking about hay with such evident concern."

Sarah flushed and turned her attention to Melanie, ignoring Kendall's chuckles. "What of you, Melanie? Your mother must be frantic without your company. Surely you cannot remain away for three weeks."

Melanie's eyes darkened and the glow left her face. "Oh, dear. You are quite right. I—I had not thought."

"Nonsense," Kendall said, casting Sarah a severe look. "You should not cause Miss Devon such worry, Sarah. I've already taken that into consideration and it is attended to."

"What?" Melanie said, looking up at him in surprise.

"Is it?" Sarah asked, not surprised but very suspicious.

Kendall turned to smile at Melanie. "I hope you do not mind, but I realized you could not help but be missed at home, for who would not miss you? Therefore, I took it upon myself to send a governess and nursemaid to assist your mother."

"You have?" Melanie asked, gasping.

"It is the least I could do," Kendall said. "After all, you are here due to my daughter's contretemps."

"Thank you, my lord," Melanie said, her smile brilliant.

"I have no doubt we shall be receiving word soon," Kendall said, his tone gentle. "I gave orders for them to send information on how your family is faring."

"Good gracious," Sarah said, finally stunned.

Kendall looked at her, brow raised. "Yes?"

"Nothing," Sarah said, shrugging. "Other than I never thought to hear my father concerning himself with governess and nursemaids."

Kendall's eyes lit, but he said, "You were once a child yourself, my dear. I do have a memory of such."

"You are too, too kind," Melanie said, her eyes brightening.

"Nonsense," Kendall said, waving his hand. "That reminds me, dearest. I forgot to tell you, Cousin Esmerelda will arrive later tomorrow."

"Cousin Esmerelda?" Sarah asked, her eyes widening.

"She has promised to be your new chaperone," Kendall said.

"My chaperone?" Sarah asked, blinking. "Esmerelda?"

"Yes," Kendall said. "Things transpired so quickly, it was difficult for me to make arrangements. Esmeralda was kind enough to come to our aid. I do hope you do not object."

"No, of course not," Sarah said, still blinking.

Cousin Esmeralda was a reclusive widow with no other care in the world but for reading and devising epic stories and odes, none of which had ever made their way to print. Even her connection with the great house of Bevington had not swayed a publisher to such folly. Esmeralda was a quiet woman who generally lived in her own world. Whereas her body might be present upon this earth, her spirit rarely ever made an appearance. The thought of Esmeralda as a chaperone was befuddling. One might as well not have a chaperone as to have Esmeralda.

Sarah frowned at her father. "You truly intend to have her as my chaperone?"

"Yes, and she may also act as Miss Devon's chaperone while she is here," Kendall said. He smiled at Melanie. "I do not believe you shall find Esmeralda overly offensive or imposing."

"Indeed not," Sarah said, laughing. The problem would be in finding Esmerelda at all.

"Thank you," Melanie said. "I—I have never had a chaperone before. Except my mother, I guess."

"You must have one in London," Kendall said, smiling. "Only remember that if anyone asks, Esmerelda has been your chaperone since the day you arrived here." He looked to Sarah. "Esmerelda understands she must do the same."

"Of course," Sarah said, now realizing her father's logic. When one had a secret, it was best kept within the family. Esmeralda was a far better choice than she had at first thought. She smiled. "It seems you have arranged things very satisfactorily."

"I strive," Kendall said, returning that smile. He looked at Melanie, "So you see, there is no reason you cannot attend the ball."

"Thank you, I—" Melanie suddenly halted and she flushed. "I am not certain I will attend."

"Why not?" Kendall asked.

Melanie shrugged. "I simply do not think I shall."

"You will enjoy it, I assure you," Kendall said, frowning. "There is no reason you should not attend."

Sarah studied Melanie's downcast gaze. She looked to her father, who was clearly displeased. She stifled a laugh. Her mastermind of a father was evidently not as clever as he thought. Only for a moment did Sarah toy with the notion of allowing the situation to continue. Knowing it was beneath her, she said, "It would be a shame, Melanie, if you didn't attend. For where else do you plan to wear the ball gown I am going to buy you?"

Melanie looked up, her eyes wide. "What?"

Sarah laughed. "I could not help myself, but I was shopping this morning and I saw the most beautiful dress, just perfect for you. And like Father, I wish in some manner to show you my gratitude."

Kendall's eyes widened and he nodded at Sarah, his smile wry. "I am proud of you, daughter."

"Oh, but I could not . . . not accept," Melanie said.

"I believe you shall," Sarah said, laughing. "Especially if you realize how selfish I am being. I enjoy buying clothes above everything else, and showing my gratitude in this fashion. It will be a pleasure to me. Now, if you wish me to post the gown to your home I shall, but either way, I intend to purchase it for you."

"I am sure you can wear the dress anywhere," Kendall said, his tone solemn.

Melanie stared at father and daughter, and then she laughed. "No, I shall wear it for the ball."

"Good," Sarah said. "Let us go shopping tomorrow. I would like your opinion upon it. Madame Celeste will also need your order as swiftly as possible, if she is to have it prepared for the ball."

"Yes," Melanie said, smiling. But then she frowned. "Perhaps we should not leave Geoffrey so unattended tomorrow."

"I believe he will do just fine," Sarah said. She looked at her father. "I intend to attend the Jacksons' musical this evening in the company of Miss Jackson and her mother. Would either of you care to attend as well?"

"No," Kendall said. "I am prepared for a quiet evening at home."

"No," Melanie said just as swiftly. "I—I will be glad to

stay here." She flushed. "Just in case Geoffrey needs company later."

"Have a good time," Kendall said.

"I will," Sarah said, forcing a smile. She turned and left, wondering exactly how everything could possibly have gone so awry. Geoffrey and Melanie would certainly be encamped here for the next three weeks. She shook her head. It should be surprising to her that Ravenwich had left for the Americas, but she wasn't sure he didn't have the right of it. She was tempted to pack herself.

"Oh, yes," the tailor Giovanni breathed, clapping his hands together and all but jumping up and down before Geoffrey as they stood within his room. "Those shoulders, my lord. They are marvelous, simply marvelous!"

Geoffrey started, and then frowned down at the small man. "Indeed?"

"We'll need no padding there," the tailor said, tittering like a schoolgirl. "You cannot know, my lord, but I positively run out of buckram in some of the jackets I sew. Like Lord Pendleton's. La!" he cried, shaking his head. "The man should take stock in the manufacturing of buckram, indeed he should."

"S'truth," Terrel said, nodding from where he sat upon the bed. "Old Pendleton's spavine, he is."

"I'll take your word for it," Geoffrey said, waving his hand impatiently.

"Oh, my!" Giovanni cried out, and grabbed up Geoffrey's hand. "Tsk, tsk. This will never do. Your hands, my lord," Giovanni said, shaking his head. "So well shaped, so manly, but those calluses. A gentleman never has such rough hands."

"This gentleman does," Geoffrey said in a dangerous tone.

"Er, yes," Giovanni said, stepping back. He frowned but

a second and then said, "Oh, toll loll. You shall wear gloves until we can rid ourselves of those ungenteel calluses."

"I shall not," Geoffrey said sharply.

"Can wear them at night," Terrel said, nodding. "With ointment. Makes the hands soft in no time. Be glad to lend you my ointment."

"You actually do that?" Geoffrey asked, stunned.

"Most of us men do," Terrel said, smiling.

"Yes, yes," Giovanni said, and once again circled around Geoffrey, running an intent eye over him as if he were a horse for auction. "My lord, are your calves real?"

Geoffrey blinked. "I beg your pardon?"

"You do not use sawdust?" Giovanni asked, his gaze now trained upon Geoffrey's legs.

"Sawdust?" Geoffrey asked. He glared at Terrel. "What in blazes is he talking about?"

Terrel flushed. "Got to present a good leg to the ladies, cuz. If you don't got one, you make one with sawdust. Do it myself."

"Good God!" Geoffrey exclaimed. "All I want are some clothes suitable for London. Not to be stuffed and padded and gloved."

"So you shall be, my lord," Giovanni said in soothing tones, "So you shall be."

"Let Giovanni take care of you," Terrel said, his face beaming. "As good as any tailor there is. And ain't as expensive. Ain't everyone in the know like me." He smiled to the little tailor. "Glad you could come by this morning. When old Geoffrey sent message to me, knew you could help us."

"It's my pleasure," Giovanni said, and cast Geoffrey the strangest, almost adoring gaze. "All my pleasure."

Geoffrey found himself clenching his teeth. "Well, get on with it then."

"Yes, yes," Giovanni said. He drew out a length of measuring tape from his vest and snapped it. Geoffrey thought the tape looked more like a hangman's noose than anything else. The little man bent down and wrapped the tape around Geoffrey's calf muscle. "Oh, 'deed! The size!"

Suddenly Geoffrey felt the tailor's hand wrap around his calf, squeezing it. He jumped. "What in God's name are you doing?"

"It's definitely real," Giovanni said in a loud whisper toward Terrel.

"Would be," Terrel said, nodding his head to and fro.

Before Geoffrey could say ought, Giovanni shifted his tape higher, strapping it around Geoffrey's thigh. "Forsooth, the muscle," Giovanni breathed, and, reaching his hand out, clamped it upon Geoffrey's thigh. "All real, too." The little man laughed and his hand moved insidiously higher.

"Enough!" roared Geoffrey. "You will not see if that is real!" He reached down and hauled the stunned tailor up by his shirtfront. Giovanni shrieked as he dangled in Geoffrey's grasp.

"Cuz, cuz," Terrel shouted, jumping up from the bed. "D-don't take offense. He's just measuring you!"

"And I've measured him," Geoffrey gritted out, shaking the tailor. "He's leaving."

"But don't you want new clothes?" Terrel asked over Giovanni's choking.

"Not that badly," Geoffrey said, pushing the tailor from him.

The tailor lurched and stumbled, crying in a high, enraged voice, "I protest! I protest!"

"Do it on your way out," Geoffrey growled. Grabbing hold of the tailor's shoulder, he propelled him ruthlessly toward the door.

"Unhand me, you beast," Giovanni said, slapping ineffectually at Geoffrey.

"Geoffrey!" Terrel cried, chasing after them. "Ain't no cause for violence, forsooth."

"There won't be now," Geoffrey said, shoving Giovanni

out the door. Terrel shouted out his objections, but Geoffrey did not heed him as he pushed the gabbling, screeching Giovanni through the hall and down thc stairs.

Geoffrey noticed Meekum standing at the bottom of the stairs, looking up with a flabbergasted expression upon his face. "Open the door, Meekum!"

"Yes, my lord," Meekum said. He turned and ran full tilt to the door.

"I'll sue!" Giovanni cried. "You are mad! A beast! A fiend!"

"Can't do this, Geoffrey," Terrel cried. "Can't toss him out like this."

At that moment Kendall stepped out from the library, frowning. "What is going on here?"

Geoffrey didn't even break to answer, but drove the shouting tailor toward the open door and pushed him out of it.

"Cuz . . ." Terrel panted from behind.

"Good-bye," Geoffrey said. Turning, he grabbed Terrel by the collar and tossed him out after the tailor. Breathing hard, he stepped back and said, "Close the door, Meekum."

"Yes, my lord," Meekum said, and slammed the door shut with alacrity.

Geoffrey, drawing in a painful breath and wincing, turned. He discovered Kendall watching him, his green eyes twinkling.

Kendall raised a brow. "Care for a brandy, Geoffrey?" He smiled, and without another word walked back into the library.

Geoffrey followed more slowly, his wound making its objections known loudly. He found a chair and lowered himself into it with a groan.

"I recognized Terrel," Kendall said quietly as he went to the bar and poured two snifters of brandy. "But whomever was the other man you ejected so efficiently from my house?"

"A tailor," Geoffrey said, shifting uncomfortably. "Or so he claims."

"Really?" Kendall asked, picking up the glasses and turning to look at Geoffrey. "Terrel's man, I presume?"

"Yes," Geoffrey said.

"That explains it," Kendall said, walking over and handing Geoffrey the brandy. "May I ask what you wanted with Terrel's tailor?"

"Not what he wanted," Geoffrey said. He lifted the brandy and quaffed it. The liquid burned down his throat but in no way quenched his anger. An anger, he realized now, which had very little to do with the tailor and everything to do with himself. He sighed. "In truth, I don't know what I wanted with him. I was an idiot. Why in God's name I thought to try and outfit myself . . ." He cut his sentence short and laughed in disgust. "Your daughter is right. I am not cut out to be a London dandy. I need to return to Grey Manor."

Kendall studied him a moment and reached out to take Geoffrey's empty glass. He walked to the bar again. "Do you know why Sarah became engaged to Ravenwich?" he asked as he poured another draught.

"No," Geoffrey said, sighing. "And I do not care."

Kendall turned with glass in hand. "She became engaged to him, I believe, out of boredom, and because he was different." He walked over and offered Geoffrey the glass. "It was a lethal combination, and very dangerous as she discovered."

"And foolish," Geoffrey muttered, taking the glass.

"Yes," Kendall said, going to his chair and sitting. "But Sarah is not normally foolish, you see. She lives in a world of foolish people, however. People who fawn over her and flatter her, impressed with her wealth and beauty. I am sorry to say that she has learned from very young how to manipulate them very well."

"She could flirt with the grim reaper himself," Geoffrey said, shaking his head.

"Yes," Kendall said. He frowned. "It is all too easy for her. She has no challenges, and that is her problem. She knows her world and no one ever surprises her." Geoffrey stared steadily at Kendall. Kendall smiled. "You most certainly have the right to return to your home . . . and prove Sarah correct once more. After all, it is not as if you need the challenge yourself. You do not need to prove her wrong. But Sarah very nearly lost a great deal when she took on the challenge Ravenwich presented. I cannot deny that I would prefer a far better man to challenge her this time."

Geoffrey's gaze locked with Kendall's for a moment. He nodded slightly and set his glass down. "I'll not tolerate that damn tailor again."

Kendall laughed. "I am glad to hear it. I would prefer you to go to Weston, who is my tailor. In fact, I thought to see him later this afternoon, if you would like to accompany me there?"

Geoffrey stood, and drew in a breath. "Very well."

Kendall rose. "Remind me to also introduce you to Gentleman Jackson. I believe you'll have a need to visit him often." He smiled. "You won't always have a tailor to box about, you know?"

Sarah sat next to Melanie in the carriage as John Coachman drove it slowly through the throng in the park. Esmerelda, who had finally arrived two days before, sat across from them. She was a small, white-haired woman, and her faded gray eyes gazed out upon the scene with a rather distracted, far-off gaze. Her face wore a pleasant expression, and Sarah smiled. She knew better than to ask her relative anything, for if she did, she would no doubt disturb Esmerelda's creation of a sonnet, or ode, or whatnot.

She turned her attention, therefore, to Melanie. Melanie's

face was far different, her expressions mobile and attentive as she watched the pageantry in press. She wore a soft pink gown, which brought out the golden glints in her brown hair and the sparkle in her brown eyes.

"You look lovely," Sarah said to Melanie. "I am so glad Madame Celeste was able to have that dress ready for you so swiftly."

"So am I," Melanie said. "I really must thank you again."

"No, please do not," Sarah said, laughing. She nodded to an acquaintance.

"Do they do this every day?" Melanie asked.

"Yes," Sarah said, smiling. "I knew you would enjoy seeing it."

"I do," Melanie said. She shook her head. "But I wouldn't have wanted to come before this. Everyone is so very well dressed."

"The ton on parade," Sarah said in a dry tone. "It is very import—" She halted suddenly.

"What is it?" Melanie asked.

"Father is here," Sarah said. She swallowed hard "And Geoffrey."

"Are they?" Melanie asked, her tone eager. "I am so pleased. I told your father we would be here."

"Did you?" Sarah asked in a weak voice, unable to tear her gaze away from her father and Geoffrey. No, in truth, she could not tear her gaze away from the latter. The man she knew as Geoffrey Vincent, Lord Grey, appeared completely different. Astride a gleaming black stallion, he wore a jacket of blue superfine, superbly cut and molded to his broad shoulders in such a fashion as to make a woman's heart fail. His gleaming blond hair was cropped just as expertly, the cut showing in relief the masculine angles and planes of his face. The combination of sartorial elegance and the actual strength of the man was overpowering.

Sarah saw her father wave, and then he and Geoffrey rode toward them. She could not move or seem to speak. When the two men were finally before their carriage, Sarah found she could not even meet Geoffrey's gaze, not until she could gain control of her ridiculous, rampant emotions. She schooled her gaze upon her father instead.

"Good afternoon, ladies," Kendall said, a smile hovering upon his lips. "Esmerelda, have you met Lord Grey?"

Esmerelda awoke from her thoughts and said, " 'Tis a pleasure to meet you." Surprised, Sarah glanced at the tiny woman. Her faded gray eyes were focused for once, and brilliantly so, upon Geoffrey.

"Esmerelda," Sarah said gently. "You have already met Lord Grey."

"No," Esmerelda said, shaking her head. "I am sure I have not."

"He—he resides with us," Sarah said lowly.

Esmerelda's gaze widened and she peered at Geoffrey once more. "Y-you are *that Lord Grey?*"

"I am, Mrs. Carstair," Geoffrey said, nodding.

"Oh, my," Esmerelda said, blinking.

"Indeed, Geoffrey," Melanie said with a laugh. "I feel just like Mrs. Carstair. I almost did not recognize you myself."

"Or I you," Geoffrey said. "That is a beautiful dress, Melanie."

"Yes," Melanie said. "Sarah bought it for me."

Geoffrey laughed. "Ah, you are in the hands of an expert."

Sarah's gaze flew to Geoffrey. His gray eyes were void of sarcasm, light and quizzing as he studied her. She summoned up a bright smile. "As it appears are you, my lord."

He nodded his head. "Do you approve, my lady?"

In truth, with her heart fluttering and behaving so oddly, Sarah did not approve. "Of course," she murmured.

"I do not know about you, Geoffrey," Kendall said, smiling, "but I believe our ladies are looking far too enchanting, and I for one do not intend to waste a moment in ensuring I have a dance with them at Lady Elizabeth's ball." He smiled at Melanie. "Miss Devon, may I have the honor of the first waltz with you?"

Melanie blushed. "I—I would like that, my lord. But I fear I have never waltzed before. I have seen Lady Sarah perform the dance, but . . ."

"No, Melanie," Sarah said with an embarrassed laugh. "What you saw performed could not be called waltzing."

Kendall frowned. "Were you not at your best, my dear?"

Sarah shook her head ruefully. "No, Father. My partner was just off crutches." She cast a glance to Geoffrey. "And the dance was interrupted."

Geoffrey nodded. "My fault, I must own, Lady Sarah." Sarah blinked. Not only did Geoffrey appear a different man, but he acted like one, too. "Permit me to make it up to you and request a waltz at Lady Elizabeth's ball."

Sarah hesitated. "Then your dancing lessons are going well?"

"They are," Geoffrey said, nodding. This time he looked at her with full challenge. "Do permit me to show you the improvement, my lady."

"Of course she will," Kendall said, smiling. "Sarah would never be so ungracious as not to permit you to rectify matters."

Sarah looked at her father, her gaze narrowed. She distinctly felt as if she were being maneuvered in some way or another, expertly maneuvered. She lifted her chin. "Of course I shall."

Geoffrey laughed. "Let us make it the second waltz then. To ensure I have enough practice before I stand up with you."

"Very well," Sarah said, nodding.

"And Miss Devon," Kendall said. "I still request a waltz with you."

"I do not know," Melanie said, her voice hesitant.

Sarah smiled. "Perhaps you can join Lord Grey in his lessons."

"No," Kendall said. "I believe all Geoffrey's teachers are ladies, are they not?"

Geoffrey smiled. "That I cannot deny, Kendall."

"Ladies do not teach ladies well," Kendall said, and then laughed. "Only look at Sarah. She has a tendency to try and lead rather than follow." Sarah glared at her father. Kendall merely smiled and said, "If she taught you, Miss Devon, you would fall into the same problems, I fear. Permit me to teach you the correct way. I am a fairly good teacher. After all, I broke Sarah of the habit of leading, and that was indeed a task."

Geoffrey laughed. "I grow to respect you more and more, my lord."

"If you mean," Sarah said, her ire fanned. "That—"

"I only meant," Geoffrey said, his eyes twinkling, "that your father must be an excellent teacher."

"And I shall gladly accept the offer," Melanie said quickly.

"Excellent," Kendall said. "We should be on our way. As much as we would delight in keeping your company all to ourselves, it would not be fair." He nodded his head to the left. " 'Tis clear another gentleman wishes to approach, if but given the sign."

Sarah quickly looked over to where her father indicated. The young Earl of Torrington was watching them, a clearly hopeful look upon his face. Glancing from beneath her lashes at Geoffrey in triumph, Sarah said, "Indeed, Torrington is such a droll man. Melanie, you simply must meet him." She smiled her most charming smile and waved at Torrington. The young man jerked up as if he were shot. Sarah, stifling a chuckle, motioned for him to approach them. Torrington goaded his horse forward so abruptly that the beast snorted and reared.

"Hmm, we best leave, Geoffrey," Kendall said, laughing. "Before we are trampled down. Ah, I see Deirdre Wolverington waving to us. Permit me to introduce you to her. She is a widow. Very wealthy . . . and very friendly."

"It will be my pleasure," Geoffrey said with what appeared to Sarah a smirk upon his fine lips.

Sarah sniffed and turned her head away in feigned indifference, refusing to watch as Geoffrey and Kendall directed their mounts toward the powder-blue carriage of the voluptuous and voracious widow Wolverington.

"Mrs. Wolverington . . . is extremely attractive," Melanie said, her voice small as she gazed after the two men.

"Yes," Esmerelda said, her eyes wide as she too gaped after them. "She—she appears very sophisticated."

"She is," Sarah said rather tartly. Refusing to join the two ladies in their moonling behavior, Sarah directed her own gaze toward the young earl. Torrington had finally gained control of his objecting beast, and was at that moment attempting to circumvent another carriage. Smiling and waving at him, Sarah said through gritted teeth, "Though why Father wishes to introduce Geoffrey to Deirdre, I cannot fathom. 'Tis not a connection which should be fostered. Deirdre is the greatest flirt, and her morals do not bear close scrutiny. If Geoffrey thinks me bold, he will find Deirdre far more so."

"Perhaps your father enjoys her company," Melanie said.

"Not he," Sarah said. "She's been after him for years and he'll have none of it. He may be polite, but he knows better than to fall into her clutches."

"He does?" Melanie asked, her voice sounding much lighter.

" 'Tis Geoffrey you should be concerned about," Sarah said. "He is not accustomed to women such as Deirdre."

"Oh, my," Esmerelda sighed. "Such a charming knight to be so encaptured by the beautiful, wicked sorceress. I must write the story." Sarah frowned at Esmerelda, stunned and rather indignant. The chaperone's eyes were bright and teary. "What a poignant tale it shall make."

Melanie giggled. Sarah met her mirthful eyes, and shaking a rueful head, she too began to laugh. She stifled her chuckles as young Torrington finally drew his horse up beside their carriage. "Lord Torrington, 'tis such a pleasure to see you again."

The slim, pleasant-looking man blushed a bright red. "And . . . and I you, my lady. And I you."

Thirteen

Melanie's heart fluttered as Kendall led her out to the crowded, heated dance floor. Chandeliers glistened and shone down upon them. Laughter and conversation encompassed them. Elegantly dressed and bejeweled women, partnered by men in stunning formal attire, took their places around them.

The sounds and the people disappeared from Melanie's consciousness as Kendall put his arm about her and took up her hand. Only his touch and his gaze mattered.

Kendall smiled down upon her. "Thank you for saving this first waltz for me."

Melanie flushed. "How could I not? After all, you are my teacher."

"And you have been the best of pupils," he said. The music began and he swung her into it. Melanie laughed lightly, an exhilaration shooting through her. Swirling amongst such glittering company was even more exciting than learning to dance in a silent room.

"You surpass every lady here," Kendall said, his smile soft.

Melanie smiled up at him. Their gazes met and held, the emotion between them more fluid and beautiful than the music and dance itself. She found no need to speak, but only silently, willingly bent to the touch of Kendall's hand upon her waist, moved to the rhythm he led her through. Yet suddenly Kendall broke their gaze, looking swiftly away. Melanie felt as if he had taken the very life from her, and she looked down. A new silence held them as they danced and twirled, a silence which hurt.

"Thank you, Miss Devon," Kendall said quietly as the waltz finally ended and he escorted her from the dance floor. He said with a lightness, "You will be the belle of the ball tonight, my dear."

Melanie once again followed his lead, determined not to show her confusion. She shook her head, forcing a laugh. "No, I believe Sarah is that."

Kendall looked over to where Sarah now sat, encircled by a large group of gentlemen, the smaller Esmerelda barely noticeable beside her. "Indeed." A slight smile touched his lips. "I believe all of our party is popular tonight."

Melanie glanced across the ballroom to where Geoffrey stood, reigning over a court of ladies. "Yes. I wonder if Geoffrey will even remember his dance with me."

"He will not forget," Kendall said. "But if he does, I am sure you will readily have another partner. Is not your dance card already full?"

Melanie looked at him hesitantly. "It is, but . . . but for the second waltz."

Kendall frowned. "Impossible!"

"I thought you . . . you might like to dance it with me," Melanie said, her voice breathless.

He shook his head and his eyes grew solemn. "I cannot."

"Oh," Melanie said, looking away. "You have already asked another lady." She could not help but notice how the women gravitated to Kendall, all of them far more beautiful and sophisticated than she was.

"I have not yet," Kendall said, a guarded look entering his eyes. "But I shall."

"Of course," Melanie said, flushing. "Forgive me."

He shook his head. "You do not understand, my dear. A lady should not stand up for two waltzes with a man unless she is engaged to him."

Melanie looked up at him, stunned. "Truly? I—I did not know."

He smiled. "I did not think you did. And though the rule may not be so strict considering our positions, I will not take advantage of it."

"Our positions?" Melanie asked, frowning. "What do you mean?"

"I am not only much older than you, but I am your host," Kendall said.

Melanie's eyes lighted. "Then . . ."

He shook his head. "No. It may still give rise to gossip, and that I will not permit."

"I see." Melanie said. It was shocking, but Melanie realized she'd not care what type of gossip arose, not if she could dance with Kendall again.

Kendall smiled gently. "This is your night, Miss Devon. You will have far too many men vying for your hand to save the waltz for me." He looked away. "Indeed, it is the perfect time for you to study which kind of man interests you." His smile grew tight. "In fact, if I am not mistaken, here comes your next partner."

Melanie glanced up. Indeed, a young man to whom she had been introduced before, but whose name she could not remember, approached them. She forced a smile and greeted the gentleman as he stepped before her. Kendall murmured a polite good-bye and drifted away. She covertly watched Kendall's every move, even as she chatted with the young man who led her out to the dance floor. Kendall soon joined the dancers with an older, clearly alluring woman.

Melanie, despite what Kendall had said, did not feel as if it were her night.

* * *

Sarah laughed and waved away the group of men who surrounded her, telling them they must find their partners, for she intended to sit this dance out. The men, many of them longtime admirers, bantered and offered their devotion as they left her side. Only Lord Torrington declared he did not care to dance and would gladly keep her company. Sarah realized if she were not cautious, she would soon receive a proposal from the young, adoring earl.

Torrington had not missed a single function which Sarah had attended within the last few weeks. Indeed, she had graced an inordinate number of social affairs, and the earl had not lagged either in his attendance or his seeming devotion of her. Unfortunately, another man who appeared regularly at these affairs was Lord Grey. Not that Geoffrey danced attendance upon her, far from it. Rather, he danced attendance upon the ton and the ton danced attendance upon him.

Sarah herself only saw him in passing, both at home or out upon the town. That, or when some foolish woman wished an introduction to him. Sarah thought if one more simpering, foolish debutante approached her to ask her coy questions about Geoffrey, or plead for an introduction to him, she would scream. At first it had been amusing. She had blithely introduced the ladies to Geoffrey, gleefully awaiting the time when he would lose his patience and exercise the sharp side of his tongue upon the widgeons.

Yet, he never did. He greeted those same ladies with a grace and charm Sarah had never thought to see in a man of his stamp. Worse, the silly ninnies fell for his false gallantry. Witness this evening. A veritable throng of women surrounded Geoffrey. A sharp twinge of emotion piqued Sarah. It was not an emotion she cared to define, but one she had unfortunately experienced far too often of late. No doubt Geoffrey would be too involved with the flibbertigibbets around him, to remember he had requested a waltz from her. She tossed her head. She was sure she didn't care if he forgot, for she did not desire to dance with him, not one whit.

"My lady?" Lord Torrington's voice said.

Sarah looked up quickly, shocked she had entered such a brown study that she had not even noticed the earl was speaking to her. She was becoming as lost to reality as poor Esmerelda, who sat beside, mumchance and staring out at the dancers with a bemused smile upon her lips. Sarah shook herself sternly and smiled. "Forgive me, my lord, I fear I was woolgathering."

"I . . . I said I enjoyed our dance tremendously," he said.

"Indeed, so did I," Sarah said, laughing. She was not about to confess she could not remember their dance together.

"The Suffolks are . . . are holding a soirée two days hence," Torrington said, his fair skin flushing to a muted red. "M-may I escort you, my lady?"

"I am sorry, my lord," Sarah said, remembering her new resolve. "But I am promised to attend with Lord Darymple." Or she would be once she informed Lord Darymple of the fact.

"Lady Sarah," a deep, all-too-familiar voice said. Sarah glanced up swiftly. Geoffrey stood before them. He offered her a graceful leg. "I came to ensure you remember your promised waltz with me."

Sarah's heart fluttered, and because it did, she lifted her chin and said in a light tone, "La, my lord, I am amazed you remembered."

Geoffrey bowed, his eyes teasing. " 'Tis not my memory that has ever been found wanting."

Sarah stiffened, drawing in a deep breath. "How should I have known that? 'Tis the first I have seen of you this evening."

Geoffrey smiled. "I am here now."

"True," Sarah said tartly. He came to her only after he had attended all the other ladies. "But I fear it is too late. With my sad lack of memory, I quite forgot."

"But, Sarah," Esmerelda gasped, suddenly turning her gaze from the dancers and looking at Sarah. "Surely you remember, Lord Grey asked you that day in the park, just before he rode over to talk to the sorceress in the powder-blue carriage . . ."

"No," Sarah said quickly, heat rising to her face. She fought the urge to shake the tiny woman beside her. She hadn't spoken all evening, but *now* she spoke. "I'm sorry, Esmerelda, I forgot. In truth, it did not even enter my mind. I—I have given . . . given Lord Torrington the next waltz."

"You did?" Esmerelda asked, looking all at sea.

"You have?" Lord Torrington exclaimed. His brown eyes flared. "My lady. I am honored. To be able to waltz with you again tonight. You have made me the happiest of men."

Sarah stared at Torrington, her heart sinking. She had not only forgotten she had danced with Torrington but that she had danced the waltz with him. It would not do. Geoffrey's low chuckle fueled her irritation and she swung an angry gaze upon him.

He smiled and clapped his hand to his chest. "And you have made me the unhappiest, my lady. I do hope you will be so kind as to offer me another dance, in consolation as it were."

"I am sorry," Sarah said. "But I fear those are all taken as well, by men who requested them from me earlier this evening."

"Tsk, tsk," Esmerelda said, sighing.

Sarah thought she saw a flare of anger in Geoffrey's eyes, but it swiftly disappeared. He said quite softly, "You promised me a dance, Sarah. I should not have had to ask again."

"I am sorry," Sarah said, shrugging. She smiled sweetly. "However, I am sure the other ladies will be glad to dance with you."

Geoffrey gazed at her one hard moment. Sarah met that gaze, though her heart quelled. Then he bowed and walked away without another word.

"I cannot like that fellow," Lord Torrington said, frowning. "He presumes too much."

"Indeed, he does," Sarah said calmly, even as her conscience castigated her for being a petty, malicious woman.

"The poor knight," Esmerelda said, blinking and shaking her head. "Cast aside for dandies, varlets, popinjays, and men of lesser valor."

"What!" Torrington gurgled, staring at her.

"Oh, dear," Esmerelda said, jumping. She flushed. "I . . . I meant to write it, not say it."

"Then write it," Sarah said, her teeth on edge. She refused to even mention Esmerelda's incongruous mix of words. 'Twas no wonder she had never been published.

Esmerelda fluttered her hands and looked dejected. "I—I cannot. I—I have no paper and pen. I—I often carry it in my reticule, but did not."

"Perhaps you could ask Lady Driscole for those articles," Sarah said.

"But dearest, dare I leave you for a moment?" Esmerelda asked.

"Certainly," Sarah answered promptly and without conscience.

"Very well," Esmerelda said, standing and meandering away, a small sparrow circumventing the birds of brighter plumage.

"She's r-rather odd," Lord Torrington said, staring after her.

"I believe writers often are," Sarah said, laughing. "Their flights of fancy lead them astray, I fear."

Torrington shook his head. "Seems like a bedlamite to me."

Sarah laughed in honest delight for the first time that evening.

"Please, Miss Devon, I would like thish waltz with you," Marcus Driscoll, Lady Elizabeth's brother, said. He bowed close over Melanie and puffed a reeking breath of brandy upon her. He righted himself with an unsteady jerk and peered down at her, his eyes bloodshot and hazy. They gleamed with a familiarity which unsettled Melanie.

"I am sorry, sir," Melanie said, clutching her dance card in tense fingers. "I am already promised to another for this dance."

"Who'sh the man?" Marcus asked, his face darkening. He reached down and snatched the dance card from her hands before Melanie even realized his intent. He swayed precariously as he brought the card close to his nose. "Ah, ha! Don't shee a name here!"

Melanie flushed. She had left it open, still hoping Kendall Bevington would dance with her. "His n-name is not there, but I—I have already promised it to the gentleman."

"Ain't written down," Marcus said, shaking his head. "So's it don't matter if you dansh it with me in-shtead."

"Sir, I have given my word," Melanie said, drawing in a deep breath along with her courage. "And a lady does not break her word." She stood swiftly. "Now, if you will excuse me, I must find my partner." She did not wait, but sped away from Marcus. She searched quickly for Geoffrey or Kendall, wishing for an ally. Geoffrey was nowhere to be seen, and Kendall stood far across the room, appearing deep in conversation with the lady whom he had just led from the dance floor. Melanie, her heart sinking, looked for Sarah, or even Esmerelda. Neither were visible.

Melanie glanced nervously over her shoulder. Marcus Driscoll stood, arms crossed and face sullen, watching her. Melanie tore her gaze away in alarm. Lifting her head high, she hastened to the nearest exit and left the ballroom. Marcus would surely know she had lied to him, but at least it would not be so obvious as it would if she were to remain when the orchestra struck up the waltz and she was still unpartnered.

She entered into a hall and walked down it, discovering a door to the right. She cautiously opened it and peeked in. A book-lined room, with a warm fire crackling in the grate, presented itself to her. Not only was it inviting, but it was also mercifully vacant. Melanie entered quietly and closed the door. Sighing with relief, she trod over to a chair and lowered herself into it.

Her nerves were just losing their tension when the door opened. Melanie gasped and her eyes widened. Marcus Driscoll, a definite weave to his steps, entered the room and closed the door. He grinned at her, his lips forming a wide smirk.

"Knew I l-liked you," he slurred and stumbled toward her. "L-little minx. This ish much better than any ole dansh."

Melanie spun up. "What are you doing here?"

"Always heard y-ou country g-irls were fash," he said. Reaching out, he hauled her up hard against his chest.

"Unhand me!" Melanie gasped. She attempted to struggle, but Marcus held her tightly. He lowered his lips, and though Melanie twisted and turned her head, his lips captured hers, wet and smothering. Revulsion shot through Melanie and she choked, closing her eyes in sheer loathing.

"Excuse, me, Driscoll," a calm voice said. "I wish to have a word with you."

Melanie's scrunched eyes snapped open and relief swept through her at the sound of that well-known voice. Driscoll lifted his head and growled when he saw Kendall standing within the doorway.

"What do you want, Bevington?" he said. "Can't you shee I'm busy?"

"Indeed," Kendall said, strolling into the room. "I can also see you are far in your cups. Release Miss Devon."

Driscoll's arms tensed about Melanie. "Why? Sh-she in-nvited me here."

"I did not!" Melanie exclaimed. She shoved at Driscoll with all her might. His arms slipped away and he stumbled back.

"It really does not matter," Kendall said. "You will not take advantage of her."

"Why?" Driscoll asked with a snicker. "If the lady ish w-willing . . ."

"I'm not willing!" Melanie gasped.

"Driscoll," Bevington said, his tone low. "A gentleman does not argue with a lady. Now, do attempt to hold this within your sodden brain. You will not come near Miss Devon ever again. Is that clear?"

Driscoll puffed out his chest. "I'll come n-near her anytime I wish. Whosh you to tell me not to? Y-you ain't got no right."

"She is a guest of mine," Kendall said. "And as such is under my protection."

"Guest, you say?" Driscoll asked. A sneer twisted his face. "You're actin' more like her bloody father."

Kendall's gaze narrowed, but he smiled. "Since he is not here to protect her, I will stand in his stead."

"Ish that what you're doing?" Driscoll lurched toward Kendall. "Or do you want her for yourself, you randy old—"

In the strangest, easiest manner, Kendall's arm shot out and delivered a blow to Driscoll's jaw. Driscoll stiffened, swayed, and toppled back. He lay sprawled. Not a muscle twitched. Kendall, shaking his fist, glanced down, a look of surprise upon his face. "The boy has a glass jaw, it appears."

"My lord," Melanie said, rushing to him. "Are you all right?"

"Yes, of course I am," Kendall said. He frowned. "I am sorry. I did not intend to brawl in front of you."

Melanie, country girl that she was, did not regard one swift blow as a brawl. She bit back a smile and lowered her gaze. "I did not mind. I—I thank you for arriving when you did."

"Young Driscoll did not hurt you?" Kendall asked, stepping closer.

"No," Melanie said. "H-he only kissed me. It was dreadful."

"The lad did lack finesse," Kendall said, shaking his head. "Youth and wine are not the best of combinations. But do not dwell on it, I beg of you, for you'll not have to suffer such an unpleasant experience again. Put the memory from your mind."

Melanie looked down. In truth, the memory was fading fast with Kendall standing so very close. A far sweeter memory of a far different kiss supplanted it. She realized 'twas an experience she desperately wanted repeated, and she suddenly knew she would do anything to ensure that it did. She glanced up at Kendall and drew in a quick breath of resolve. "I—I do not know if I can put it from my mind."

"Surely you can," Kendall said, concern in his eyes. "He only kissed you, did he not?"

"Yes, but . . . but it was terrible." Melanie shook her head and forced a sigh. "I fear, I may never wish to be kissed again."

"Do not say so," Kendall said, stepping even closer. "You cannot permit one bad experience to affect you. The boy was drunk and clearly inept."

Melanie, her heart pounding, peeked up at him. "You are not drunk, are you?"

"No, I am not," Kendall said, seeming to stiffen. "Why?"

"I—I thought if you w-were to kiss me," Melanie said softly. "Then . . . then I might forget his kiss."

Kendall's eyes widened and he appeared stunned. He shook his head. "I could be your father."

"But I do not think of you as my father," Melanie said with a trembling smile. "And . . . and if you were my father, you . . . you wouldn't want me to dislike kissing, would you?"

"If I were your father," Kendall said, placing his large hands on her shoulders, "that is exactly what I would want."

"Truly?" Melanie whispered, brazenly extinguishing the last space between them.

"Should want . . ." Kendall murmured, bending his head down to hers. Their lips met and clung. Melanie closed her eyes with a soft sigh, and Kendall's hands slid from her shoulders to draw her into a powerful embrace, one which felt safe and dangerous to Melanie all at the same time. Emotions swirled through her, a whirlwind of sensations that seemed to tear her very soul from its moorings. Kendall groaned, and the sound sent the sweetest shiver through Melanie, warming her heart as surely as did his kiss and touch heat her body. He was not in control either. He did not look at her in the light of a father.

Kendall finally pulled back, but Melanie held tightly to him. She burrowed her head upon his chest, the rapid beat of his heart beneath her ear encouraging her. "I—I am glad you are not my father."

She felt him breathe in deeply and glanced up. Kendall's eyes were dark. "I believe we should return to the ballroom, Miss Devon."

"But I like it here," Melanie said, smiling.

"My dear, I am sorry, but I am not old enough as yet to remain here without . . . without taking further advantage." He placed firm hands upon her shoulders and gently pushed her away. "I realize you are too young to understand . . ."

"Am I, my lord?" Melanie asked. "Most women my age are already married."

Kendall fell silent a moment. "Yes, they are. As you shall be one day too, I am sure. That is, once you find the right man. 'Tis the purpose of your stay here in London, is it not?"

"Perhaps that is more your purpose than mine," Melanie said, looking down. Then she looked up and smiled. "But you are right. I need only to find the right man. Until then, if a man kisses me and I find it unpleasant . . . w-would you be so kind as to kiss me afterwards? It would be of great assistance to me."

Kendall stared at her a moment. Drawing in a breath, he said, "We are going to return to the ballroom this instant, Miss Devon."

"May I at least have the next dance with you?" Melanie asked.

"Yes," Kendall said. "That you may."

Melanie laughed and sped toward the door. "If we hurry, it will be the waltz."

Kendall stiffened and then he laughed as well. "You are not so very young after all, are you?"

"No, my lord," Melanie said. "I am not."

Kendall chuckled. Then he glanced back at the fallen Driscoll. "What should we do with him?"

Melanie blinked and giggled. "I'm sorry, I had quite forgotten him, I fear."

"Had you?" Kendall asked, a smile twitching at his lips. He bowed. "Then by all means, let us continue to do so."

Together they left the room and returned to the ballroom to dance their second waltz.

"I thank you, Lord Torrington, for escorting me out here. I am sorry we have missed our dance together, but I truly needed some fresh air," Sarah said as they stood upon the balcony, and the beginning strains of the waltz began. "The heat and . . . and crowds, I fear, overwhelmed me."

"I . . . I deem it a far greater honor," Lord Torrington said, his gaze bright and eager. "T-to be here with you my lady, rather than dancing."

Sarah realized that her maneuver to make certain she did not dance a second waltz with Torrington had now placed her in an even more ticklish situation. Clearly, the young lord thought she had invited him to the balcony for romance. "Could you humor me even more and go and command a glass of punch for me?"

Torrington's face fell. "Of course, my lady."

He bowed and disappeared through the French doors. Sarah turned back to enjoy the evening air and the beauty of the star-cut night.

"An excellent move," Geoffrey's voice came from behind her. "I wondered how you should escape the waltz with Torrington."

Sarah spun. "Geoffrey, what are you doing here?"

"I've come for my dance," Geoffrey said, smiling. "I didn't think you would actually stand up one more time with Torrington. It would not be proper. And though you never showed such considerations in the country, 'tis clear you know London's ways to a nicety."

"It appears so do you, my lord," Sarah said.

"With such an excellent example as you to study, how could I not?" he said, strolling up to her. His gaze was steady as he held out his hands. "Dance with me."

Sarah stiffened. "I told you, my lord, I will not."

"You've forgotten how, perhaps?" Geoffrey asked. " 'Tis simple, really." He slowly put his hand to the curve of her waist. Sarah started slightly at his touch but refused to move. He reached out and clasped her hand. "Very simple."

She stared up at him one moment, her heart pounding. To be close again to him and feel his touch felt wonderful, and far too right.

Geoffrey's eyes darkened. "And now we dance." He drew her close and swung her swiftly about. Sarah instantly put her hand to his shoulder, automatically began to move with him. Sudden elation leapt within her as he twirled her. Geoffrey's size and strength made them the perfect match, and they swayed and turned in smooth, easy accord.

"You are a fine dancer, my lord," Sarah said, laughing. "Indeed, as fine as my father."

"A true compliment, my lady," Geoffrey said. He smiled. "But then 'tis easy . . . when you permit me to lead."

" 'Tis the requirements of the dance, my lord," Sarah said, casting him a teasing look.

Grinning, he pulled her even closer. "I should have learned the waltz sooner, I see."

Sarah chuckled, but said rather breathlessly as a heat flashed through her, "I must inform you, though, that you are holding me far too close for proper decorum."

"Am I?" Geoffrey asked, his smile bland. "It must have been a lesson I overlooked." He shook his head, though he did not relax his hold one whit. " 'Tis so very hard to learn all the small, particular details of society's ways."

"I believe you have learned them, my lord," Sarah said, "far too well."

"Have I?" he asked, slowing their movements. " 'Tis a high compliment, my lady."

Sarah flushed and suddenly looked away. "I—I suppose 'tis what you have been waiting to hear, is it not? That you have proved to me I am wrong and that you can fit into this society quite well."

"I would not say that was the purpose," Geoffrey said, his tone strange.

Sarah glanced quickly at him. His eyes were unfathomable. She forced a lightness to her voice. "Admit it! 'Tis the truth." Sarah laughed. "And now you are ever so gallant."

"Is that not what you wished, my lady?" Geoffrey asked, his gaze intent.

Sarah stared at him. He was stunning in his formal attire, but suddenly she missed him as he was in his work clothes, honestly sweaty, and tired from a day's labor. She missed hunting with him, fishing with him, even missed arguing with him. He was the fête of London now with no time for such anymore. He said the correct words, did the correct things, but no longer could she know for certain if he told the truth. She smiled and forced the lie to her lips, "Of course, my lord."

She thought she saw disappointment trace through his eyes, but it disappeared. He nodded his head and said, "Then surely that should be sufficient reason enough for you to stop avoiding me."

"I am not avoiding you," Sarah said quickly.

He gazed down at her a considering moment. The slightest smile touched his lips. "My mistake, I am sure. But if you were avoiding me, can we not cry pax?"

"Since I am not avoiding you," Sarah said, lifting her chin, "there is no need to cry pax."

He laughed and twirled her around. "Then we shall let bygones be bygones."

Sarah's heart jumped and winced all at the same time. She forced a smile. "Of course, my lord."

"We may become friends then?" Geoffrey asked.

Sarah's smile froze. "If that is what you wish."

"I do," he said, nodding, his voice quiet. Then he smiled and raised a quizzing brow. "Does this mean I dare to ask for the Incomparable Lady Sarah's hand in a dance without suffering rejection?"

A laugh escaped Sarah. " 'Tis I who dare not turn you down, my lord. You are quite the man of the hour, are you not? I declare, I should be swooning that you tore yourself away from your court to dance with me."

" 'Tis not as great of court as yours," Geoffrey said. He shook his head. "How you ever survived in the country away from your entourage, I do not know."

Sarah found she could not answer him directly. "Do you not miss . . . the country, my lord?"

He paused a moment and then said, "I am enjoying myself."

Sarah looked up at him, disappointment coursing through her. "Are you?"

"Of course," he said, watching her. "How could I not?"

"Indeed, my lord," Sarah said, laughing lightly.

"But there's one thing I miss," he said, and slowed her to a halt.

"What is that?" Sarah asked, her heart suddenly racing.

"If we are to be friends," he said, "could you please call me Geoffrey once more?"

"Yes . . . Geoffrey," Sarah said, her heart slowing. "If you will call me Sarah."

"I will . . . Sarah," he said, smiling.

They both laughed a moment. Then they fell silent. The music still drifted out to them, but Geoffrey did not move to resume their dance. His arms shifted more securely about her and Sarah unconsciously pressed close to him. Her gaze focused upon his lips. She wanted him to kiss her. Geoffrey slowly bent his head toward her and Sarah closed her eyes in anticipation.

"My lady!" Torrington's voice said, almost in a shout. Sarah jumped and snapped her eyes opened. Geoffrey lifted his head. They both looked toward the interruption. Torrington stood, two crystal punch cups in his hand, a look of wounded surprise on his face.

"Lord Torrington," Sarah murmured.

"Hello, Torrington," Geoffrey said. He withdrew his arms from Sarah and stepped back.

"Wh-what were you doing?" Torrington asked, his voice sounding young and reedy.

"Lady Sarah deigned to have mercy and dance with me after all," Geoffrey said, smiling. He picked up Sarah's hand and, bending, placed the politest of kisses upon the knuckles. Sarah watched him in frustration. It was a small consolation when she desired his kiss upon her lips instead.

Geoffrey glanced up, his eyes laughing. "Thank you, Sarah, for the dance lesson."

"Sarah!" Torrington exclaimed, the punch sloshing from the crystal cups as he charged toward them, his expression outraged.

"Y-you're welcome, Geoffrey," Sarah said.

Geoffrey straightened and looked at the now quivering earl. "I'll leave you two to your punch." Nodding with a smile, he strolled from the balcony.

"He called you Sarah, my lady," Torrington gulped.

"Yes, my lord," Sarah said, taking her drink absentmindedly from his grasp as she gazed after Geoffrey. She sipped a long, cooling draught. Confusion swirled within her. Just exactly who was Geoffrey? She walked without thought toward the French doors.

"And you called him Geoffrey!" Torrington cried, following Sarah.

Fourteen

"What is it, Kendall?" Geoffrey asked, studying the older man. Kendall had asked Geoffrey to join him in the library after breakfast.

He appeared tense and his movements were stilted. "I have something I must ask you," Kendall said, and walked over to the bar. Almost absently he poured a brandy. "Would you like a drink?"

Geoffrey's brows rose. "It is rather early in the morning for that, is it not?"

"I believe we should both have one," Kendall said, and poured out two brandies. He handed one to Geoffrey and then walked over to a chair and sat. He motioned for Geoffrey to sit also. He looked at Geoffrey and said, "I wish to tell you first that I will not duel with you. At least I do not wish to do so." He frowned. "I hope I am not that far gone, but perhaps I am."

Geoffrey frowned. "Why should you duel with me?"

Kendall looked at him a moment. He took a swift drink and then said, "Because I wish to ask for Melanie's hand in marriage."

"What!" Geoffrey almost dropped his glass. He stared at Kendall. Kendall looked back, his eyes almost as confused. Suddenly Geoffrey thought of the past weeks, and things began to click and fall in place. "Good Lord."

"Yes, good Lord," Kendall said, and drank quickly from

his glass. "You know, I did not plan this, I truly did not." He frowned. "No, I cannot say that. I must own I—I have been paying particular attention to Melanie. I do not wish to say I intended a dalliance, but then at my age, what else could it have been?" He shook his head, his expression rueful. "All I know is I desired her company and set out to have it, no matter the ramifications or . . . or the consequences."

Geoffrey nodded, the haze of confusion clearing. He could not castigate Kendall, for had he not done as much with Sarah? What he thought should happen to Melanie, the woman who had been a friend to him for so many years, he could not say. No, now he could say. She would marry this man across from him, who would treat her as an Incomparable. "You love her then?"

"Yes, I love her," Kendall said, sighing. "That is not the problem. The problem is, I would marry her."

"That should not be a problem," Geoffrey said, "if Melanie wishes to marry you."

"Yes, if . . ." Kendall stopped, rose abruptly, and paced across the room. "If she does not wish to marry me, I do not know what I will do. I simply cannot continue to kiss her after each and every time some young dolt disappoints her, no matter if she asks it of me."

"What?" Geoffrey exclaimed, and this time he did take a swift gulp of brandy.

Kendall turned and glared. "Now you see why I am drinking."

Geoffrey shook his head. "Melanie asked you to kiss her?"

Kendall waved a hand. "I should not have spoken of it, forgive me. But . . . but I am at points non plus."

"You certainly are." Geoffrey schooled his face to a frown. "For I do indeed intend to call you out."

"Very well," Kendall said, his gaze solemn. "If you feel you must."

"I feel I must," Geoffrey said, smiling slightly. "I'll not

permit you to kiss Melanie and not ask for her hand in marriage. You'll not play fast and loose with her, my lord." Kendall stiffened, his gaze turning frigid. Geoffrey merely cocked his brow. "Well?"

Kendall laughed abruptly. "No, Geoffrey, I do not wish to play fast and loose with her." Then he sighed. "But I am too old for her. Faith, I have already lived one more lifetime than she."

"She asked you to kiss her," Geoffrey said gently. "I don't remember her asking me to kiss her." Sarah had asked him, but not Melanie.

"Melanie said it was not in your nature to be demonstrative," Kendall said. He frowned. "You really should have kissed her more often."

Geoffrey choked back a laugh. "Do you wish me to rectify matters?"

Kendall frowned and then smiled. "No, I shall attend to that."

"Very well," Geoffrey said, grinning. "You have my permission to ask Melanie to marry you." He hesitated. "Are you going to ask Sarah?"

Kendall shook his head. "No. Asking one lady I love is enough, without asking the other." He frowned. "But I wanted your consent. Sarah may have difficulty with this."

"She may not," Geoffrey said.

"True, she may not," Kendall said, pursing his lips. "In truth, this is one time I cannot be certain how Sarah will react." He looked at Geoffrey, a considering look in his eyes. "You could help her in this regard. After all, you now have no entanglements."

Geoffrey looked at Kendall, knowing full well what he meant. He shook his head. "One marriage will have to do." He laughed. "A man does not marry a woman who will not even dance with him without a fight."

"Hmm, yes," Kendall said, frowning. "She has been avoiding you. I'd consider it a good sign."

Geoffrey's brow rose. "I consider it a good sign that the best we can do is to become friends, and nothing more."

Kendall's eyes sparkled. "That is now your intention?"

Geoffrey clenched his teeth. "Yes, that is my intention. What would have me do?"

"Nothing," Kendall said, widening his eyes and appearing innocent. "Friendship can be a fine thing."

"Yes," Geoffrey said, glaring at Kendall.

"And Sarah will need a friend at this time," Kendall said smoothly. "I am glad to know you will be there to stand by her and support her."

"Yes," Geoffrey said, though the prospect did not seem so pleasing as it should have. He forced a smile. "Well, I best leave you. You have a proposal to make, do you not?"

"Once I've gained my courage," Kendall said, smiling. He shook his head. "I am a fool. I should allow Melanie to find a younger man, but I cannot."

Geoffrey laughed. "It does not sound as if she wishes to find a younger man. And you are not so old that a second life is not possible."

Melanie sat in the parlor with Sarah and Geoffrey. She smiled slightly. It was a surprisingly pleasant time. It was rare these days for Sarah and Geoffrey to remain at home for dinner. Yet tonight they had both said they did not intend to go out until much later, and they both remained in the same room, carrying on convivial, easy conversation.

The door opened and Kendall entered. A warmth flooded Melanie and she looked down hastily. She had not seen Kendall the entire day, and she could not help but wonder if her behavior of the night before was the cause of it. She truly had been brazen and might very well have given Kendall a disgust of her.

"Good evening," Kendall said, bowing. He stood gazing at them, a rather odd expression upon his face. "I see we have everyone here. Sarah, I thought you were taking dinner with the Tindletons."

"I decided not to do so," Sarah said. She smiled, and her eyes showed amusement. "Esmerelda is presently deep at work on a 'poignant' story and I am loath to tear her away. I have discovered that when the muse is upon her, 'tis better to permit her to write. Else she makes a confusing dinner partner, to say the least. She promises to attend the Randalls' musical with me later this evening. I believe it shall be safe to take her there. Perhaps Madame Parvoir's singing will wing her spirits to greater heights."

Melanie giggled, despite herself. "That might be dangerous, Sarah."

Sarah grinned, and she cast Geoffrey a covert glance. "Heaven only knows what she'll have her gallant knight perform."

"I see," Kendall said, nodding, though it did not appear as I were listening.

"How was your day, my lord?" Geoffrey spoke up, his gaze intent upon Kendall.

"Busy, but I have still something to accomplish," Kendall said, frowning.

"There is no time like the present," Geoffrey said, his gray eyes alight. "Is there not?"

"True," Kendall said, nodding briskly. He looked at Melanie. "Miss Devon, may I be permitted to have a private word with you before dinner?"

Melanie's heart sank. His tone and manner were solemn. "Of course, my lord."

"We will be but a moment," Kendall said, looking at Geoffrey and Sarah. "If you will excuse us."

"Of course," Geoffrey said. "Take all the time you need."

Kendall unaccountably laughed. Melanie, confused, rose and followed Kendall out of the room. He was unusually silent as they walked along, and Melanie's concern grew.

She found it difficult to speak, but she forced herself to say, "Where are we going?"

"To the picture gallery, Miss Devon," Kendall said. "I have noticed of late that you do not go there as often as before."

Melanie flushed. "No. You yourself said it is not good to always study history."

"Yes," Kendall said, and ushered her into the room. "But I would show you something."

Melanie nodded, and they walked down the gallery, still in an odd silence. She halted suddenly as her gaze fell upon a new picture upon the wall. It was a picture of a woman, a beautiful woman, one who looked amazingly like Sarah. Melanie stared at it in awe a moment and then turned. "Th-that is your wife?"

"That was my wife," Kendall said softly.

Melanie returned her gaze, pain knifing through her as she finally looked upon the face of the woman Kendall loved. "Why . . . why now do you have her picture here?"

"I told you she lived in my heart and I needed no picture upon the wall to keep her memory," Kendall said, his tone gentle. "And I still do not, but it is time for her picture to take its rightful place . . . in the history of my life and family."

"I see," Melanie said, looking down.

"And also," Kendall said, picking up her hand. "To show you who she was. I do not want her to be a ghost to you, Melanie. She is no longer a ghost to me. She has my memories, but you have my heart."

Melanie gasped, looking up in astonishment. "Wh-what?"

Kendall smiled, but it was a sad smile. "I know I should not ask it of you, but will you marry me?"

"Marry you?" Melanie asked, her eyes wide.

"Yes, marry me." Kendall drew in a breath. "I love you very much, but I'll not kiss you again unless we are wed."

Melanie forced a pout, even as her heart sang. "Y-you will not?"

"I cannot," Kendall said, shaking his head and frowning. "It is not only improper, but when I kiss you . . ." He halted for a moment and then continued, "There will come a day when I no longer will be able to remain a gentleman."

Melanie's heart raced. Oh, how she hoped and waited for this day. Her lips twitched and she looked up with all the love she had showing in her eyes. "Then I shall have to marry you, shall I not?"

"Yes," Kendall said, his laugh for once sounding shaky. "You shall."

He stepped close and gently lowered his head to hers, kissing her tenderly. Melanie smiled slightly, and rose on tiptoe. Wrapping her arms strongly around his neck, she kissed him with all the new and growing passion she felt for him. No longer did she feel like a wicked hussy about it, only a woman desirous of showing her love.

Kendall groaned and drew back. His smile was wry, his green eyes glinting. "You, my dear, are becoming far too expert at this."

" 'Tis because I have an excellent teacher," Melanie said, smiling. She flushed. "And because I love you."

"I thank the Almighty for that," Kendall chuckled. "I fear I was not handling with equanimity your search to discover if any other man attracted your interests."

"They do not," Melanie said, looking down. "And do you . . . ?" She halted.

"Do I what?" Kendall asked.

"D-do you think that . . . that you will feel it necessary t-to visit the place where we first met again?"

Kendall cupped her chin and forced her to look at him. "When I entered that room, it was for the last time. I've found the only woman I'll ever want and need." Melanie blinked back sudden tears and he smiled. "So do not expect, my dear, a return visit there upon our wedding anniversary."

"No," Melanie chuckled. "I shall not."

His eyes twinkled. "Though I believe we had best devise a more proper story to tell our children as to how we met."

Melanie drew in her breath. "Y-you would not mind if . . . if we had children."

Kendall frowned down upon her, though his eyes glinted. "Madame, I am old, but certainly not *that* old. Maria and I were quite young when we married, and Sarah was born within a year of our union . . ."

Melanie did not wait for the continuing history. She grabbed hold of Kendall's face and drew it down to her for a fierce, happy kiss. Kendall drew back, blinking. "If you continue to kiss me in such a fashion, I fear there most definitely will be children."

Melanie flushed and laughed. "I—I shall remember that, my lord."

"Now," Kendall said, drawing her arms from about him and setting her at a distance. "I refuse for us to even talk about the subject of children until you have my ring safely upon your finger." He reached into his vest pocket and withdrew a box. He opened the lid and Melanie gasped. The largest, pear-shaped diamond rested in its silk interior.

"It is so beautiful," Melanie murmured. Kendall silently withdrew it and placed it upon her finger. Melanie held out her hand, gazing at the sparkling stone. "Truly beautiful. I had never thought to have a ring like this." A sudden thought jolted her. "Geoffrey. Oh, dear. I forgot Geoffrey!"

"Do not concern yourself," Kendall said, smiling. "I have his permission."

Melanie's eyes widened. "You have his permission?"

"I asked him this morning," Kendall said. "It would not have been proper to do otherwise."

Melanie stared at him and then giggled. "Y-you asked Geoffrey if you could marry me?"

Kendall chuckled. "Yes. I expected he might call me out, and he almost did."

"Oh, no," Melanie said, her heart sinking.

"After he had heard I'd dared to kiss you," Kendall said, smiling, "and not make an honest woman of you."

Melanie smiled. "He is . . . is a good friend." She paused. "And have you asked Sarah?"

Kendall shook his head, he expression rueful. "Now, *she* I have not told. I'd hoped to have you by my side for that feat."

Melanie laughed. "I will be pleased to be by your side. Always, my lord."

He took up her hand and said, "Then shall we go, my lady Bevington?"

"Indeed," Melanie said, flushing.

They turned to leave the gallery, and suddenly Melanie halted, to stare back at the picture of Maria Bevington just one more time.

"What is it, my dear?" Kendall asked.

"Nothing," Melanie said, smiling. "I was only promising her I would take as good of care of you as I could."

Kendall lifted her hand and kissed it. "And I of you, my dear. And I of you."

Sarah sat in the parlor, Geoffrey sitting across from her in another chair. At first she felt uncomfortable, but Geoffrey talked of inconsequential matters, of the next ball, the royal house, and whatnot. It struck Sarah then. He was carrying on the very social chitchat he had refused to enter into when in the country. A chuckle escaped her.

"What is amusing you?" Geoffrey asked, his brows raised.

"Nothing," Sarah said. "Except not one word of farming has entered your conversation."

He nodded his head, his eyes sardonic. "That would not interest a lady now, would it?"

Sarah bit her lip. In truth, somehow it had come to interest her. Whatever his conversation in the country, he was always totally involved with the subject, whereas now, he conversed smoothly, but his manner showed his mind was only half engaged.

"True," she murmured, and sipped quickly from her tea.

At that moment Melanie and Kendall entered the room. Sarah's eyes widened slightly, for they held hands. Melanie's face showed an excited flush, and her eyes a glowing radiance.

"Sarah and Geoffrey," Kendall said. "I would like to announce Melanie has consented to marry me."

"What!" Sarah exclaimed. Her teacup slipped through her nerveless fingers. She did not even notice the cup as it fell upon her lap, or the tea as it seeped across her silken skirts. She could only stare, her mind reeling. Her father was going to marry Melanie.

"Congratulations," Geoffrey said. He stood quickly, and, pulling out a handkerchief, he walked over to Sarah and held it out to her.

The light disappeared from Melanie's eyes and she said in a small voice, "Sarah, are you all right?"

"Of course she is," Geoffrey said, and knelt to take the cup from her lap and drop the handkerchief in its place. "Are you not, Sarah?"

Sarah, in a daze, looked at him. His gentle and firm gaze prompted her, offered her support. She swallowed hard. Flushing, she looked down and snatched up the handkerchief. She rapidly scrubbed at her skirts, striving desperately for control. "Of course I am. I . . . I was only surprised." Brutal, undefined emotions swirled within her. With a shaky voice she said, "My, what a clumsy I am." She rose swiftly. "I must go and tend to it. Faith, now I must find another dress. Do . . . do not wait dinner on me."

Kendall's eyes were solemn and Melanie's face turned deathly pale. Looking away, Sarah hastened from the silent room. She maintained her fragile composure until she reached the safety of her room. Only then did she cross over to the bed and sag down upon it. She stared into space, her world careening. Her father was to marry Melanie. Never once in her entire life had she thought of her father remarrying. Faith, it should not matter so very much, but it did. One of the strongest securities in her life had just been torn away from her.

She blinked, surprised she wished to cry. She had never felt the want of a large family, never missed not having a mother, never missed having siblings. Her father had always been more than enough for her. Many had commented upon their unusual relationship, for they had been friends as much as father and daughter. No doubt it stemmed from the fact they were the only two in their family. Now it would all change. Her father loved another woman as much as he loved her. Worse, she had never seen it coming, never even divined it. The ties between her and her father were already breaking.

A knock sounded upon the door and it opened before Sarah could call out and say she wished to be alone. Geoffrey entered. Sarah stiffened. "What are you doing here? Please leave."

His gaze scanned the room. "You have not called your dresser, I see."

Sarah looked away. "I shall in a moment."

"You must hurry," Geoffrey said. "Meekum says dinner is ready to be served." He strolled over to one of Sarah's armoires, and opened the door. "Yes, a fine selection." He reached in and withdrew a golden gown. "This should do, I believe."

Sarah stared at him a stunned moment. "What are you doing?"

Geoffrey turned, the gown in his hands. His gray eyes were steady. "I am helping you decide which dress you wish to wear, else you'll take an hour over it."

"And what if I do?" Sarah asked, springing up, anger shooting through her.

"You are not going to take an hour," Geoffrey said, his

tone firm. "Every moment you remain away will hurt both your father and Melanie. You left the parlor so fast, they are already hurt."

"*They* are hurt?" Sarah asked, laughing dryly. She turned swiftly away from him. "And what of me?"

"What of you?" Geoffrey asked. "You should be pleased your father has found a woman he loves . . . and who loves him."

Sarah spun, enraged. "You are mighty calm over all this, my lord. Does it not matter the woman he loves and who loves him, is the woman to whom you were promised?"

Geoffrey shook his head. "No, it does not. When your father asked me, I suddenly realized the truth of it. The very fact that I did not even know Melanie and he were falling in love proves I have no right to be angry."

"He asked you?" Sarah gasped, a pain knifing through her. "He asked you, and did not speak of it to me?"

"In light of your reaction, can you fault him for not telling you?"

Sarah looked down and said in a low tone, "Get out, Geoffrey."

"No," Geoffrey said. "I am here to help you dress. I'll not permit you to remain in your room sulking."

"I'm not sulking," Sarah said, lifting her head imperiously and leveling an icy stare upon him.

He raised a brow. "Are you not?"

"No, I am not," Sarah said. "I simply do not choose to return downstairs as of yet." Her throat tightened. "I—I cannot."

"Yes, you can," Geoffrey said.

"I tell you I cannot," Sarah snapped. She waved an impatient hand. "You do not understand. But then, I did not expect you to do so."

Geoffrey walked over to her to look down upon her with stern eyes. "I understand. You have teased me enough upon the fact that I do not take to change easily. Now, it is your turn to show me you can respond far better than I."

"That was in regards to arranging furniture," Sarah said with a short laugh. " 'Tis not the same. This is about my life."

"No," Geoffrey said. "This is about your father's life." Sarah glared at him. He held her gaze steadily. "You have always risen to the occasion, Sarah. I've seen you do it more times than I wish to recall and far too many times at my expense." He smiled slightly. "Surely this is an occasion which warrants your best."

Sarah smiled bitterly. "I have disappointed you before, have I not?"

"You shall not this time," Geoffrey said, shaking his head, his tone gentle. "Your father and Melanie are right for each other, Sarah."

Sarah gazed into Geoffrey's oddly tender, compelling eyes. Her anger melted, leaving only aching vulnerability within her. Unable to permit him to see it, she lowered her eyes and strode away. "Perhaps," she choked out.

"There is no perhaps about it," Geoffrey said. He laughed. "Faith, if I do not cavil at your father stealing my bride from me, I do not see why you should take exception to it. After all, Melanie is not stealing your father from you." Sarah turned with a gasp, staring wide-eyed at him. "They both love you, Sarah," he said, stepping toward her. And I . . ." He halted.

"Yes?" Sarah asked, her heart jumping, need and want coursing through her.

Something flickered and then died in his eyes. "I am your friend."

Sarah drew in a ragged breath. "I—I see."

"I shall stand by you in this," Geoffrey said, his tone low. "I promise you."

Sarah nodded, blinking away the sting of tears. Pride, perhaps her oldest friend, came to her rescue. She forced a smile, and then a laugh. "Very well. Though I must tell you, I believe you take this friendship a jot too far in offering to dress me."

Geoffrey's eyes lit. "Now that is the Lady Sarah I know."

Sarah smiled, even as she thought she heard a death knell ringing in her ears. "Yes, that is the Lady Sarah you know." She saw him frown, and said quickly, "Besides, the truth is, the dress you have chosen is meant for a ball, not for a dinner, no matter the h-happy occasion."

Geoffrey's eyes widened as he looked at the dress, and then he chuckled. "My mistake."

Sarah's smile quivered. "I'll accept your friendship, Geoffrey, but I fear I cannot accept your fashion advice." Their gazes met and held a second. Sarah looked away and moved quickly to the bell pull, giving it a swift jerk. "Now if you would please leave. I fear you are delaying me."

"Yes, I am," Geoffrey said, looking suddenly discomfited. He turned and strode toward the door.

"Geoffrey," Sarah called.

"Yes?" he said, turning to look at her in inquiry.

"Do you intend to borrow that dress?" Sarah asked.

Geoffrey looked down to the dress in his hands and grimaced. "No, I do not."

"I am pleased to know that," Sarah said, a chuckle escaping, despite herself. "You may very well outshine the ladies at the next ball, but I am loath to have you wear the dress before I do. 'Tis new."

"I thought I hadn't seen you wear it before," Geoffrey said, holding it out to study it. " 'Tis fetching."

Sarah's eyes widened in surprise. She'd never thought he noticed what she wore. "Yes, indeed."

He strolled over and handed the gown to her, smiling. "You'll look better in it than I would, I am sure."

Sarah chuckled, and took it from him. "You flatter me far too much, I fear."

"No," Geoffrey said softly. "I do not."

Sarah flushed. "Tell Father and Melanie I shall be down shortly."

"Yes, my lady," Geoffrey said, bowing once more. He turned and departed, closing the door behind him.

Sarah held the golden dress tightly to her for one moment, staring at the closed door. She drew in a deep breath. "Rise to the occasion, Sarah." Shaking herself quickly, she hastened to lay the gown upon the bed. Then she quickly reached to undo the tabs of her dress. She had it off even before her dresser entered. Her stay in the country had taught her at least that much.

It was less than fifteen minutes later when Sarah reached the entrance to the dining room. She straightened her curls with trembling fingers, drew in a deep breath, and entered the great hall, a bright smile pinned to her lips.

"I do hope I did not keep everyone waiting too long," she said, her tone light.

"Of course not, my dear," Kendall said, rising at her entrance, as did Geoffrey. He nodded, his gaze intent upon her. "Indeed, I'd not expected you to be able to change so fast."

" 'Tis amazing what one can accomplish," Sarah said, casting Geoffrey a look from beneath lowered lashes, "when one has the excellent services of . . ."

"The servants," Geoffrey said, smiling.

"Yes," Sarah said, smiling as she walked quickly to the table. "Nor did I wish to dally upon such an exciting occasion." She sat down in her chair, noting the awaiting glass of champagne before her, and the empty place setting. They had indeed delayed dinner until her arrival. She looked up, and forced a smile. "Now tell me, what plans have I missed?"

"You have not missed any," Kendall said, taking up his

own chair. His face was gentle. "We were waiting for you before we discussed them."

"I see," Sarah said, swallowing. "Do you intend to send the announcement to the paper tomorrow?"

"I do not know," Kendall said. "What do you think we should do, Sarah?"

"Yes," Melanie said, her brown eyes showing a concern and hesitancy. "If . . . if you think we sh-should wait, we shall."

"Gracious, no!" Sarah exclaimed. She looked directly at Kendall. "Neither Father nor I intend to permit you a chance to escape becoming a member of our family." He nodded, a deep gratitude within his eyes. Sarah looked to Melanie and said in a teasing tone, "You are truly caught, Melanie."

Melanie looked down, blinked rapidly, appearing close to tears. "I—I do not mind it at all."

"You shall," Sarah said, determined to keep the atmosphere light. "When I start calling you Mama."

Melanie started. "M-mama?"

"Or Stepmama," Sarah said.

Dismay washed over Melanie's face. "Oh, dear."

"Do not look that way," Sarah said, a true, unfeigned bubble of laughter rising within her. "It shall be great fun. We shall set the ton on its ears."

"I . . . I had not thought," Melanie said, flushing, "how it would appear."

"Do not worry, my love," Kendall's gaze met Sarah's in amusement and shared understanding. "Sarah and I are quite accustomed to upsetting society's expectations."

"And turning them around to seeing things our way," Sarah said, nodding. She looked to Melanie, the need to erase the hurt and worry she had caused strong within her. "Only have faith in us, Melanie. Society shall come to love you just as much as we do. I promise you, that."

"Thank you," Melanie whispered.

"I believe we should hold the engagement party within two weeks time," Sarah said, suddenly realizing the difficulties that lay ahead for Melanie and her father. Her eyes flickered to Geoffrey, who sat silently watching her. Faith, he had known. If she set herself against Melanie's and Kendall's marriage, so would the world.

"Two weeks?" Melanie asked, gasping.

"Certainly." Sarah smiled in as reassuringly manner as she could. "Yours is a whirlwind courtship, and it should be recognized as such."

"Yes," Kendall said, nodding. "An excellent plan."

"You mean an excellent strategy," Geoffrey said.

Sarah laughed. "You have already caused such a stir, Geoffrey, that it is only fitting we supply society with something new to astound them." She looked teasingly at her father. "And Lord Bevington's marriage cannot help but astound them."

"Keep them offset." Geoffrey's eyes twinkled. "They should not call you The Incomparable. They should call you The General instead."

"But . . . but I have not even told my parents," Melanie said, frowning.

"My dear," Kendall asked, his brow quirking up, "should I fear rejection in that quarter? Never say your father is so high-in-the-instep he'll not accept me as a son-in-law? My estates are equal to Geoffrey's and more."

Melanie giggled. "Since you put it that way, no. He is not *that* high-in-the-instep."

"Good," Kendall said. "You had me absolutely quaking at the prospect."

Everyone laughed and Geoffrey rose. He picked up his champagne glass, holding it aloft. "I wish to propose a toast. To the future Lady Bevington and her husband, Lord Bevington."

"Here, here!" Sarah toasted, raising her glass high. Geoffrey glanced at her as they sipped their champagne. Smiling, he then held the glass out to her in a silent salute. Sarah, nodding with a wry smile, lifted hers to him and returned the salute with one of her own.

Fifteen

Geoffrey eased back into his chair, willing himself to relax. Sarah sat at the large library desk, sheets of paper cluttering its surface and little Andrew Devon sitting upon her lap. With one hand she wrote upon the papers, and with the other she secured Andrew close to her. Upon the arrival of the entire Devon clan for the engagement ball, little Andrew had quickly detached himself from the litter and attached himself to Sarah. He sat perfectly still, gazing at Sarah in childish adoration. Geoffrey could not deny that he found himself gazing upon Sarah in the same hopeless manner, or either he felt an ignoble pang of envy for the boy who so easily gained Sarah's embrace.

Worse, he could not help but look at the boy and suddenly see a child with blond hair like his, and sea-foam eyes like Sarah's. Such would be a child of theirs. He gritted his teeth. It was an asinine train of thought for a friend to have toward another friend, and friends were what Sarah and he were. In the past two weeks, it could not be denied. Sarah no longer avoided him, but turned to him repeatedly in the preparations for the ball and in the ploys she orchestrated to coax society into accepting Kendall and Melanie's marriage. He could enjoy her society as much as he wanted, as long as he remained a friend. It was a bit of heaven and hell all wrapped up into one parcel. Very much like Sarah herself.

"I have seated Lady Driscoll upon your right, and Lady

Amelia Chandler upon your left for the dinner, Geoffrey," Sarah said, a frown of distraction upon her face. "Will that be to your liking?"

"What?" Geoffrey asked, starting from his unpleasant train of thought.

"You are seated next to Lady Driscoll and Lady Amelia." Sarah looked up. "Do you approve?"

"Yes," Geoffrey said, drawing in his breath. "That will be fine."

"I thought as much," Sarah said, and looked back to the paper. At that moment, young Andrew reached out a tiny hand and pulled upon Sarah's perfectly coiffed curls. Sarah laughed, and plucked his hand from her hair. "No, sir, you are far too young to be such a rogue already." She frowned, even as she held the child's hand. "I still am uncertain what is to be done with Lord Cothram. He is quite deaf, and anyone I seat him next to rapidly becomes the same. He does not converse, he roars."

"Excuse me, Lady Sarah and Lord Grey," Meekum said, entering the library. He carried a large bouquet of roses in one hand and a powder-blue embossed letter in the other. "These flowers have arrived for you, my lady. And this missive for you, my lord."

"Put the flowers with the rest of them," Sarah said, her tone sounding nonchalant.

"Yes, my lady," Meekum said, bowing. He moved to set the roses upon a large oval table, which was already overflowing with bouquets of every imaginable design, and surely consisting of every flower grown upon English soil. He then walked over to Geoffrey and proffered him the envelope.

"Thank you," Geoffrey said, taking it and quickly sliding it into his vest pocket.

"Yes, my lord," Meekum said, and departed the room.

Geoffrey looked at Sarah, whose head was bent once more

over her paper. His eyes narrowed. "Are not you going to see who sent you the roses?"

"No," she said, her voice muffled. "I am too busy. Are not you going to open up your letter?"

"There is no need," Geoffrey said, stiffening. He recognized the blue of the envelope, and the overpowering perfume wafting from the paper.

"Indeed not," Sarah said as she wrote. "Deirdre Wolverington's perfume is so very distinctive. Rather exotic, is it not?"

Geoffrey frowned. "I do not see how you could possibly have detected its scent, not with the smell of so many flowers in the air."

Sarah looked up, her brow raised. "As I said, it is very strong." She looked down again. "Besides, powder-blue *is* her color. She no doubt has missed you these past weeks. And I must thank you for all your help with the ball. Your ladies must be falling into declines without your presence in recent weeks."

"As must your men," Geoffrey said with a smile, though he wished to growl and glower. "And they are not my ladies."

"Ah," Sarah said. "Then you have singled one out in particular? Who is the fortunate woman?"

"The fortunate woman is . . ." Geoffrey said.

"Lady Sarah," young Beth Devon's voice called, and she dashed into the room, a stormy look upon her young face.

"Yes, what is it?" Sarah asked, looking at Beth.

"Melanie says I cannot attend the ball tonight!" Beth whined, and all but stamped her foot.

"That is correct," Sarah said, her tone gentle. "You are not yet out. In London that means you may not attend a formal ball. You must wait until you are properly introduced to society."

"But I want to be able to . . ." Beth objected.

Sarah raised a cool brow. "I said, you will not be able to attend the ball tonight."

Beth flushed a scarlet red. "Yes, my lady."

Sarah smiled. "I know it is difficult. But I assure you, 'tis better for you to wait for your proper introduction. You shall take the town by storm then, but you must be patient."

"Do you really think I shall?" Beth asked breathlessly.

"I most certainly do," Sarah said, smiling.

"Oh, thank you," Beth said. "You are the best of aunts . . . I mean sisters, I mean . . ." She flushed.

"I know," Sarah said, laughing. "It is confusing. But run along now. There will be a party for the children this evening as well. I know you are too old for that, but I hope you will help ensure the others enjoy it."

"A party for us?" Beth asked, her eyes lighting. Then she flushed. "I mean, for the children?"

"Indeed," Sarah said, nodding solemnly.

"Thank you!" Beth cried, and, face beaming, tore from the room.

"Now what were you saying?" Sarah asked, glancing back to Geoffrey.

"Nothing," Geoffrey said, shaking his head. He'd almost made a fool of himself. He forced a smile. "You handled Beth very well."

Sarah laughed and her fine lips twisted into a grimace. "I feel distinctly out of my domain, I vow."

"No," Geoffrey said, shaking his head. His gaze flickered to Andrew, who rested his head upon Sarah's chest, his eyes drooping. "You captivate children as surely as you do adults."

"Is that a compliment, Geoffrey?" Sarah asked, raising a brow in mock surprise. "Or are you—"

"Sarah!" Melanie's voice interrupted and she entered the room. "Have you seen little Andrew . . ." She stopped. "Oh, there he is. It is time for his nap."

A delicate flush rose to Sarah's cheeks. "Indeed, I am sure it is. I did not keep him here so overly long."

"I shall take him," Melanie laughed, and walked over.

Bending down, she reached to take Andrew. Andrew suddenly let out a wail, and wrapped his tiny arms around Sarah, clinging like a limpet.

"Hush, my dear," Sarah said, her tone gentle as she firmly untangled the small boy's arms from about her and handed him over to Melanie. "You must go with your sister. Be a good boy now, and I shall see you later."

Andrew sobbed, but far more quietly. With a wry smile, Melanie carried Andrew away. Sarah's face was warm and tender as she gazed after the two, her eyes the softest and sweetest Geoffrey had ever seen.

He suddenly could not tolerate any more. He rose swiftly and walked directly over to Kendall's bar. He grabbed up the brandy decanter and poured a stiff brandy.

"My," Sarah said, her tone mild. "Things do get tricky with children in the house."

"Yes," Geoffrey said shortly, and took a swift drink. He turned toward her, to discover her studying him.

"Do you dislike it so?" Sarah asked, her eyes quizzing. "All the children in the house?"

"Do you?" Geoffrey countered quickly.

Sarah looked away from him. "I . . ."

"Madame," Meekum said, entering the room once more.

"What is it now, Meekum?" Sarah asked, her tone sounding sharp.

"The flowers have arrived," he said, bowing.

"Then put them with the rest," Sarah said, waving an impatient hand.

"No, my lady," Meekum said, starting back a little. "I meant the flowers for the decorations of the ballroom."

"Oh," Sarah said, looking down. "Then inform Melanie they have arrived. She will be managing the decorations. I believe I have already told you that, repeatedly in fact."

"Yes, madame," Meekum said. "But . . . but I thought you might like to oversee their placement."

"No, I would not," Sarah said, her eyes cold, her words

clipped. "Miss Devon shall be your new mistress shortly, and you must learn to take your directions from her. Is that understood?"

"Yes, my lady," Meekum said, a red flushing his dignified features. He beat a hasty retreat.

Geoffrey frowned, studying Sarah. Rarely did Sarah speak so roughly with the servants.

Sarah glanced at him and then looked away. She stood abruptly and walked over to him. She smiled, rather ruefully. "I believe I would like to join you in that drink, Geoffrey."

Geoffrey started. "A brandy?"

"Yes," Sarah said. "Since it is the nearest at hand."

Her expression was so very comical that Geoffrey laughed. "Of course." He turned and poured out another brandy, offering it to her. "As long as this does not become a habit."

"No," Sarah said, sipping it and making the slightest face. "I assure you it won't."

"This week has been rather . . . taxing," Geoffrey said, and quickly swallowed his brandy.

"Yes," Sarah said, her gaze upon her glass. Her face held a strange sadness. She drew in a deep breath and looked at him, something hidden in her eyes. "But it soon will be all over."

"Thank God," Geoffrey said dryly.

"Yes, thank God." Sarah said, softly. Her smile twisted. "I—I wish to thank you for all your help this week. You have been a true friend, and I want you to know . . ." She halted, taking a sip of her brandy.

"Know what?" Geoffrey asked, frowning. She didn't say a word, and Geoffrey stepped closer. "Know what, Sarah?"

"Lady Sarah!" another voice called. Geoffrey expelled an angry breath and stifled a curse as Mrs. Devon entered the library. Her matronly body was drawn up, and 'twas clear she was in the boughs.

"What is it, Mrs. Devon?" Sarah's sigh was audible.

"I told your butler that we wished to serve the buffet at

eight, but he says it is not done," Mrs. Devon said. "He says it should be served at ten o'clock. I cannot accept that. Mr. Devon has a delicate system, and if he eats so late, he shall suffer an attack of indigestion. He does so often and it is very, very painful."

"We certainly cannot have that," Sarah said. "Only tell Meekum that you will have it served at eight o'clock and that he is to listen to you without question."

"As it should be," Mrs. Devon said, nodding her head vigorously, her air that of one rightly vindicated. She suddenly frowned. "Geoffrey, are you drinking this early?"

"Er, yes, Mrs. Devon," Geoffrey said, his tone muffled.

Her gaze widened as she then looked to Sarah. "And you, my lady. Is . . . is that a brandy in your hand?"

Sarah's lips quivered. "I—I fear it is."

"Well, I never," Mrs. Devon said, her plump chest puffing out. "Eating at such tardy hours, and drinking at such early ones. Tsk, these London ways." Turning, she strode from the room, shaking her head once more.

Sarah's gaze met Geoffrey's for a moment and they both laughed. She halted of a sudden. Her eyes widened. "Geoffrey, is this a London way, or is it a country way?"

Geoffrey shook his head. "I am not sure anymore."

She laughed, looking down. "You know, neither am I."

Silence fell a moment. Geoffrey drew in a breath and said, "Now, what is it you wanted me to know?"

Sarah's gaze widened. "It was nothing of import."

A loud crash sounded from outside the door. "Oh, dear," Sarah said. She took one more sip of her brandy and set it down. "I'd best see what that is all about."

Sarah did not look at him as she hastened from the room. Geoffrey stared after her, frowning deeply. His hand convulsed tightly around his brandy snifter. Why, he did not know.

* * *

"Rise to the occasion," Sarah murmured softly to herself as she studied herself in the glass of her dressing table. She knew she looked her best, the gold satin of her gown a perfect foil to her dark hair. The dress was the one Geoffrey had drawn out for her the night her father and Melanie had announced they would wed. It seemed appropriate.

For a week now she had known what she must do. Life had indeed changed and there was no use in regretting it. Nor could she do so. Melanie and her father were truly in love. Sarah felt a deep happiness for them, and a deep pain for herself.

Soon, if she did not take action, she would become a mar to their happiness. Melanie would never gain control of the servants and her household, as was her right, if Sarah remained under the same roof. Over the past few days it had been made all too clear. The servants were loath to change loyalties. Just as Sarah discovered she was loath to turn over control.

She laughed dryly. If she did not watch it, she would become a fractious, meddling spinster daughter, and in more ways than one. At present, the ton was far too busy gossiping over her father and Melanie's December and May romance, and the fact that Melanie, a chit with no background, had stolen one of the richest, most prominent men in London. That gossip would die shortly, however. None would be foolish enough to cut Melanie and chance being cut by Kendall Bevington in return.

The other gossip about herself would not die as easily. Sarah knew, in truth, that it would only increase. At present there were but whispers. The Incomparable had taken not one fall, but two. Her jilted fiancé had been so disgraced as to be forced to flee to America, and now she would be supplanted within her own house by a woman no older than she. Sarah's position was weakened substantially, and society would be a vulture hovering about her, waiting for her decline.

A martial light entered Sarah's eyes. They'd find her difficult meat for their talons. She'd not permit them to change the title of Incomparable to Spinster, and then Ape Leader. Nor would she permit Melanie to suffer torn loyalties and fractured control within her own house.

It was time for Sarah to marry as well, to find her own home and household to manage. She thought of young Andrew, and how she had delighted in him, and Beth who had come to Sarah over the past few days looking to her as the oracle of entry into womanhood. She sighed. She needed to find her own son to hold and love, her own daughter to raise and teach.

Sarah frowned. This time, however, she would not be so unwise in the choice of a mate. She had learned her lesson all too well with Ravenwich. This time she would make certain to find a comfortable, respectable man. She no longer needed adventure and danger. She needed safety and security. Young Torrington would fit her requirements nicely. He had no known vices and did not care for the jaded life. He also worshipped the ground she walked upon and would gainsay her nothing.

Sarah's gaze, despite her best efforts, turned to a white handkerchief which rested upon the table. She reached out and picked it up, smiling sadly. She had a few flowers embroidered upon it, but none of late. Geoffrey was now her friend. 'Twas strange, thinking over their times together. There was so much between them. She set the handkerchief down. There was also too little between them. At one time she had wanted Geoffrey's kisses only to tease him. Now she wanted his kisses for far different reasons. She laughed sharply. Faith, she could imagine herself asking him, that now they were friends, if he would be so kind as to marry her.

Sarah stood, drawing in a deep breath. That would certainly be asking too much of a friendship. No, young Torrington was her best choice. None of her other admirers were as malleable as he was. Wait, she meant as *amiable* as he was. Torrington worshipped her. No doubt it was her vanity, but she knew she wanted a husband who thought of her in that fashion. She did not want a husband who thought of her as frivolous and trite and too flirtatious, and too . . . well, too everything. Neither did she want a husband who received as many *billet doux* as she did flowers.

She glanced at the handkerchief one more time. A dry chuckle tore from her throat. What was she worried about? In truth, she had no right to the title of The Incomparable. She had slipped further than the world would ever know, and much further than she would ever permit Geoffrey to know.

"Are you . . . you feeling b-better, my lady?" Torrington asked as they stood upon the deserted balcony.

"Yes, of course," she said. "I do now. I fear I was overwhelmed for a moment." Her amazing eyes looked trustingly at him. "Thank you so very much for escorting me here."

"It was my pleasure," Torrington said. A hesitancy entered him. "D-do you wish for me to . . . to get you a glass of punch?"

"No."

Lady Sarah's laughter sounded like music to his ears. "You do not?" he asked, staring at her.

"No," she said, shaking her head. She looked down. "I—I enjoy your company."

Torrington sucked in his breath. "Y-you do?"

"Yes," she said, turning away.

For a moment, Torrington could only gaze at her. Moonlight bathed her hair in silver, and her gold dress shimmered in its rays. She was silver and gold, all silver and gold. He sucked in his breath. "You are . . . are very lovely tonight. The loveliest woman here."

"Upon this balcony?" Lady Sarah asked, turning to smile upon him.

He blinked. "N-no, I mean, here at the ball tonight."

Her brilliant eyes teased him. "No, my lord. The loveliest lady at the ball tonight, by rights, is Miss Devon."

Torrington flushed and swallowed. "Sh-she cannot c-compare with you."

"Fie, my lord," Lady Sarah said, drawing close to him. "You speak of the future Lady Bevington."

"She . . . she," Torrington choked, "she will never be L-lady Bevington to me. Y-you are."

"I would not be if I were to marry," Lady Sarah said softly.

"No, of course not," Torrington said, flushing. "Y-you w-would be someone different then."

"Yes, I would be," Lady Sarah said, her eyes soft limpid pools. "I think I would like that."

Torrington lost himself in those eyes. Then he started. She would care to be married. His heart pounded. 'Twas the moment he had been dreaming of every night. Quickly, he knelt upon one knee. Gazing up at the most beautiful woman in the world, he asked, "My Lady Sarah, would you marry me?"

She smiled. "Yes, my lord, I will."

"You will?" Torrington asked, his voice rising to a squeak. He lowered it. "I mean, you will?"

"Yes," she nodded. "I will."

"Oh, my lady," Torrington breathed. "Y-you have made me the happiest of men. The happiest of men." A sudden thrill shot through him, and with it a bold, bold thought. He stood quickly, shifting nervously upon his feet. "M-may I kiss you?"

"Yes," Lady Sarah said. "Y-you may."

Drawing in a deep breath, he leaned forward and kissed her quickly upon her upturned lips. He drew back, his heart pounding. His beloved looked down quickly. Surely he had stunned her. "I—I was not too forward?"

"No," Lady Sarah said, her voice sounding odd. He had been too forward. "But I—I do not think we should mention our engagement to anyone this evening."

"We shouldn't?" Torrington asked.

Lady Sarah smiled. "This is my father's engagement ball. It would not be right for you to ask him at this time. Perhaps tomorrow."

Torrington puffed out his chest. "Of course. I should have asked him before . . . before I proposed to you. Forgive me."

"No," Lady Sarah said. "There is nothing to forgive. Only you must ask him tomorrow, and we should wait a little before we make the . . . the formal announcement. It is not fair to steal the attention from Miss Devon's engagement."

"Yes, I see," Torrington said, masking his disappointments. "Y-you are right. It would be selfish." He gazed at her. "I should have known you would think of that. You are the sweetest, most wonderful woman in the world."

"Thank you," Lady Sarah said, smiling. "Now if you could give me a few minutes alone. I am overwhelmed. Perhaps you could command a glass of punch for me after all. No, make that champagne."

"Of course," Torrington nodded eagerly. "W-we must celebrate our engagement."

"Yes," Lady Sarah said. "We must. Do hurry with that champagne."

Torrington gazed at her one more moment and then turned to move in a daze toward the balcony doors. The Incomparable had promised to wed him. The most sought-after woman had deigned to give him her hand in marriage.

He entered the ballroom and gazed around. Pride and elation welled within him and he sucked in his breath. He must wait, but soon the world would know he had won the prize.

What every other man desired was his to have and to hold. Lady Sarah, his silver-and-gold lady.

Kendall and Geoffrey sat at the breakfast table. It was quite early and they alone were the hardy souls who had arisen upon their regular schedule. Neither man talked, but both sat companionably, reading the morning paper.

Meekum entered the room. "My Lord Bevington, I beg your pardon, but the Earl of Torrington wishes to have words with you."

"Does he?" Kendall asked. He sighed and put down his paper. "I suppose it has begun."

"What has?" Geoffrey asked, lowering his own paper and frowning.

"After such occasions as these," Kendall said "I generally receive at least one request for Sarah's hand."

"What?" Geoffrey asked, starting.

"I had expected young Torrington's address before this," Kendall said, his tone musing as he rose. "As no doubt sooner or later Hampton, Avery, and Templeton shall find their way to my side. She was rather stunning last night."

Heat flashed through Geoffrey. "Yes, she was," Sarah had been more than stunning last night. She had been vivacious, and witty, and altogether too enchanting. It had taken all his willpower to remain aloof as he watched man after man fall under her spell. Now that puppy Torrington dared to ask for her hand in marriage! "What will you do with Torrington?" he almost growled.

Kendall's gaze was amused. "Refuse him Sarah's hand, no doubt."

"Good," Geoffrey said curtly.

Kendall laughed. "If you will excuse me, it shall take me but a few minutes. I have this particular routine down to perfection."

He strolled from the room. Geoffrey picked up his paper once more and stared at the print. He waited impatiently. It seemed Kendall was gone for more than a few short minutes. When Kendall finally returned, Geoffrey feigned a nonchalance and asked in a cool tone, "You rejected him?"

"No," Kendall said, a mild look of surprise upon his face as he once again resumed his seat. "I did not."

"What?" Geoffrey asked, his brows snapping down, along with the paper.

Kendall sighed and shook his head. "It appears Sarah accepted his proposal of marriage last night."

"Impossible!" Geoffrey exclaimed. "She would never accept that young dolt's proposal."

"It seems she did," Kendall said. "Young Torrington appeared in earnest. I do not think he lies."

"What does it matter if he tells the truth or not?" Geoffrey asked. "Or whether Sarah says she will marry him or not? You should not permit it."

Kendall raised his brow. "What do you expect me to do? Tell her not to marry him?"

"Yes, damn it!" Geoffrey roared, rage engulfing him.

Kendall looked amused. "If you have not yet come to understand Sarah, I thought surely you would have come to know me. I shall not forbid Sarah to marry Torrington."

"Then *I* will," Geoffrey said, slapping down his paper directly upon his plate. He stood abruptly. "If you let her have her way, she may very well manage to marry the imbecile."

"Would that be so terrible?" Kendall asked. "Torrington seems a respectable sort of fellow. He's a far cry from Ravenwich. He'd make a convenient husband to Sarah, and if she truly wishes it, I see no reason to deny him. In truth, he is a better choice than many of her other admirers."

"She is not going to marry him," Geoffrey said through gritted teeth. "And she might as well know that right now, before she leads the poor devil a merry dance."

"You mean to tell her this very instant?" Kendall's eyes widened.

"Yes, I do," Geoffrey said, stalking away from the table.

"Sarah is never at her best in the morning!" Kendall called.

"I know bloody well how she is in the morning," Geoffrey threw over his shoulder. He ignored the sound of Kendall's laughter and stalked to the side stairs. He'd be damned if he'd let Sarah marry that young popinjay. The witch. She talked of friendship to him, but then went behind his back and accepted proposals from the likes of Torrington.

Geoffrey charged through the halls. So enraged was he, he didn't even notice Esmerelda until he slammed into her. She cried out and he grabbed her quickly before she fell. "Are you all right, Mrs. Carstairs?" Geoffrey asked.

"Oh, dear, yes," Esmerelda gasped, clutching to him. "I am sorry."

"It was my fault," Geoffrey said briskly. "Now, if you will excuse me, madame."

"Yes, yes." Esmerelda stared up at him, but not moving an inch. "But where are you going in such a hurry, Sir Geoffrey . . . I mean, My Lord Grey?"

"To speak to Sarah," Geoffrey growled.

"Ah, to the fairest damsel of all," Esmerelda said, nodding. She frowned. "Has she already arisen?"

"No, but she will," Geoffrey said. "Now if you will excuse me." Without further ado, he lifted the tiny woman and set her from his path, resuming his angry rampage down the hall.

"Sir Geoffrey!" Esmerelda's voice called.

"Do not think to stop me, Mrs. Carstairs," Geoffrey flung over his shoulder.

"Of course not," Esmerelda said. "I—I only wondered if you could help me. Do you perchance know another word for chivalrous?"

Geoffrey jerked to a stop. He swung around, glaring at her. "Yes, I do. It's stupidity."

"Stupidity?" Esmerelda asked, blinking like an owl.

"Stupidity, Mrs. Carstairs." Geoffrey clenched his fist. "Pure stupidity!"

"Sarah!" Geoffrey's voice bellowed through Sarah's fitful dream. "Wake up!" She was suddenly shaken violently. Sarah started awake, snapping her eyes open. In the fog of sleep, Geoffrey's face, looking angry and dark, floated above her. She groaned, and squeezed her eyes shut. It was surely a bad dream.

"Sarah!" Geoffrey's voice growled. "Wake up!"

She cracked her eyes open. Geoffrey was still there, still bending over her, a waking nightmare.

"Geoffrey, what are you doing here?" Sarah asked in a sleep-raspy voice, pulling herself up to stare at him. She could not successfully focus his image. She feared she'd imbibed more champagne last night than was perspicuous.

"What am I doing here?" Geoffrey's voice thundered through Sarah's misty mind like the sound of the Almighty. "I came to see if it is true. Did you accept a proposal from that fool Torrington last night?"

Sarah started, and Geoffrey's image came into focus all too swiftly and clearly. It was not a pleasing image. "How—who did you hear of that?"

"Torrington came this morning to talk to your father," Geoffrey said. "He said you accepted him. Did you?"

Sarah flushed, and gripped her sheets, dragging them up around her. As far as protection went, it was pitifully flimsy. " 'Tis none of your business, Geoffrey," she said in a sharp, irritated tone.

"Did you accept him?" Geoffrey persisted.

"I cannot believe," Sarah said, lifting her chin in a show

of defiance, and wincing from the incautious action, "that you have dared to wake me . . . and to ask me such a question."

"Did you?" Geoffrey asked, his voice a terribly loud rumble. "Tell me, damn it."

"Very well," Sarah said, clenching her teeth, anger sluicing through the champagne fumes. "I did. What of it?"

"The devil," Geoffrey said. "Why did you accept him? Were you drunk?"

"I was not drunk," Sarah said with frigid dignity. She had not started drinking until after she had accepted Torrington's proposal.

"You are not going to marry him," Geoffrey said, very lowly and evenly. "Do you hear me?"

Sarah's mouth fell open. "I beg your pardon?"

"I said, you are not going to marry him," Geoffrey snarled, and paced away from her. " 'Tis ridiculous, you wedding such a young cub. You know very well you don't want to marry him!"

Sarah flushed. Of course she didn't want to marry Torrington, but she'd never confess it. "You are wrong. I do want to marry him."

Geoffrey halted, spinning to rake her with an accusing eye. "I don't believe you."

"I do not care if you believe me or not," Sarah said, her teeth on edge and her head pounding. "I am going to marry Torrington and that is that."

"Why?" Geoffrey asked, stalking back to her. "Why would you want to marry him?"

Sarah glared at him. "I do not have to tell you why I wish to marry him."

"You do not have to tell me," Geoffrey said, leaning down and placing his two hands upon the bed. "But you will."

His face was but inches from Sarah's. Suddenly her heart

pounded even more raucously than her head did. "I—I shall not."

"You shall," Geoffrey insisted. He shifted adroitly and sat down, his weight impressing the mattress so deeply that Sarah slid closer to him. "I'm not leaving until you tell me."

Sarah scrambled back, choosing wisdom over dignity. "G-get off of my bed, Geoffrey."

"No," Geoffrey said, and leaned all the closer. "Now tell me."

Sarah's eyes widened, and alarms shrilled painfully through her beleaguered brain. The man had become a wicked devil somehow. He tempted her, indeed he did. All she wanted to do was to lay her aching head upon Geoffrey's shoulder and tell him anything and everything he wished to know, and even things he wouldn't wish to know. She choked at the dangerous thought.

Flinging back her covers, Sarah scrabbled from the bed. The minute she stood, dizziness overwhelmed her. She fought it. Turning, she trained her gaze upon Geoffrey in what she hoped appeared cool disdain. "Very well, I will tell you if it will make you leave. I am going to marry Torrington because . . . because I wish to be married."

"You wish to be married?" Geoffrey asked, staring at her. Sarah saw his eyes widen and then darken as his gaze perused her. A flush rose from her toes to her head. She was wearing one of her expensive but very revealing negligees.

"Yes, I wish to be married." Sarah lifted her chin in defiance. Now that she had regained her footing and her equilibrium, she refused to weaken or scurry for cover. "Isn't that the goal of every woman?"

Geoffrey barked a laugh. His voice was rough and odd when he said, "If that is all you want, then you might as well marry me rather than Torrington."

"What?" Sarah asked, astonished.

"Marry me." Geoffrey shrugged. "It would be better than marrying Torrington."

Sudden anger fired through Sarah. She had received proposals of every sort. Men had offered her their heart with poetry, and diamond rings, and pleas of undying devotion. Geoffrey offered it with a shrug and a "might as well." She shook with indignant fury. "You rude, obnoxious . . . lout! I would never marry you. Do you hear me? Never!"

Something flickered in his eyes, and Geoffrey leaned forward. "Sarah, I did not mean . . ."

"No," Sarah said, instinctively stepping back, even though Geoffrey was still far away from her. "You have not changed. You are still the country boor you have always been."

Geoffrey stiffened. "No, I am not." He rolled from the bed and stood to his full height. His gray eyes were molten, and his gaze burned into Sarah. "But you'll not accept that I've changed, will you? I can court and play the gallant well enough to please every other lady, but still it is not enough for The Incomparable, is it?"

"No, it isn't." Sarah lifted her chin. "I know you better than that."

"Yes," Geoffrey said, his tone suddenly very soft. "You know me better than that."

Sarah looked away. She not only knew him better than that, but she loved him better than that. She drew in a deep breath, and said in a rigid tone, "Please leave."

"Sarah . . ." Geoffrey said, walking toward her, stretching out a hand to her.

"I am going to marry Torrington," Sarah said quickly, for something in Geoffrey's eyes was turning her knees weak. "He—he is a far better choice than you. And—and I . . . I love him!"

Geoffrey halted abruptly. His gaze hardened. "Do you?" He closed the gap in an instant. He grabbed hold of Sarah's shoulders and, jerking her to him, kissed her ruthlessly. Sarah, befuddled and bemused, met his onslaught with a moan and melding body. Geoffrey tore his lips from her and glared down at her, his eyes dark and glittering. "Do you indeed?"

It was ice water dumped upon her head. Sarah, choking in mortification, shoved him away. "Yes! Now get out! And don't you ever dare to enter my bedroom again." She stormed over to the door and jerked it open. "Do you hear me?"

"I hear you," Geoffrey said, his voice low and rasping.

He stalked past her. Sarah slammed the door shut with a vengeance. Faith, she was glad she was going to marry Torrington, extremely glad! The earl had gone down on bent knee to propose to her. He hadn't tossed his proposal off in such a churlish manner. Neither would he ever be so rude as to enter her room uninvited as Geoffrey had, nor dare order her about and bully her as Geoffrey had . . . or kiss her as ruthlessly as Geoffrey had.

Yes, she was glad, truly glad, she was going to marry Torrington.

Geoffrey stormed back down the stairs. Sarah's kiss still burned upon his lips, and her rejection branded his heart. She would not listen to him, but Torrington bloody well would. He'd see to it.

Geoffrey halted at the foot of the stairs. Kendall leaned against the entrance door. Three footmen as well as Meekum were ranged on either side of him.

"How did your little chat go with my daughter?" Kendall asked, smiling.

"She says she'll marry the idiot," Geoffrey said, clenching his teeth.

Kendall nodded. "So now you wish to kill Torrington."

Geoffrey stiffened and glared. "I intend to speak to him."

Kendall chuckled. "If you proceed as you have this morning, I make no doubt you'll have called Torrington out within the hour."

"Perhaps," Geoffrey said, moving forward slowly. The

footmen, for some reason, stiffened, and one even dared to lift his fist as if ready for a fight.

"I'm not going to permit you to do so," Kendall said.

Geoffrey tensed. "I beg your pardon?"

"You were adroit in dealing with Ravenwich," Kendall said. "But if you call Torrington out as well, the world will finally see the truth of the matter. There will be far too much of a scandal."

"I'll not let Sarah marry that fool," Geoffrey said, eyes narrowed.

"Then let us discuss matters. Verbally, that is," Kendall said with a twinkling eye. Geoffrey glared at him and then scanned the faces of the footmen. Kendall laughed. "Very unsporting of me, isn't it? To employ my footmen as well?"

Geoffrey suddenly relaxed, his tension draining away. He smiled wryly. "Yes, it is."

Kendall nodded. "Come, let us adjourn." He shoved himself away from the door and strolled toward the library. Geoffrey gave the footmen one more considering glance, sighed, and turned to follow Kendall into the room.

"Have you ever thought," Kendall said, lowering himself into a chair, "that it might be better for you to simply marry Sarah, rather than to continue to call her admirers out? That could prove to become an extremely repetitious and exhausting process."

"She won't marry me," Geoffrey said, flinging himself into the chair across from Kendall. "I just asked her."

Kendall's brows rose. "You stormed into her room, woke her up, forbade her to marry Torrington, and then proposed to her? Forsooth, how could Sarah be so silly as to refuse you?"

Geoffrey flushed. "I was not thinking."

Kendall nodded, and continued for Geoffrey. "And bungled it."

"She says she loves Torrington," Geoffrey said.

Kendall's brows rose. "You riled her that much, did you?"

Geoffrey sighed and shook his head. "That would be the politest term."

Kendall pursed his lips. "If you have backed Sarah into such a corner as to make her declare she loves Torrington, you do realize, do you not, that if you exert any more pressure you will ensure that she walks down the aisle with Torrington, even if she has to drag him."

"Yes, I realize that . . . now," Geoffrey said. He grimaced. "Why in blazes didn't you stop me?"

Kendall smiled and shook his head. "I fear it was just too amusing."

"I am pleased to know I entertained you," Geoffrey said with narrowed eyes.

Kendall shrugged. "You were the one claiming you felt nothing but friendship for Sarah."

Geoffrey's eyes widened and then he nodded. "Very well, you thought I deserved it, and I did."

"I also try to remain out of yours and Sarah's affairs," Kendall said, with a rather self-righteous look.

Geoffrey laughed. "Do you?"

"Yes, "Kendall said, his eyes twinkling a moment. Then they grew serious and he said in an off-hand tone, "Did you know I had a long talk with Ravenwich before he departed for America? In fact, it was just minutes before he left, I recall."

Geoffrey blinked at the change of subject. Then he stilled. "I see. I had wondered about his departure."

"Yes," Kendall said. "Ravenwich had thought to leave for Paris, but I persuaded him otherwise. He did not wish to see reason, but since I had bought up all his vowels and debts, as well as his estates, he had very little choice."

Geoffrey stared at Kendall, stunned. He drew in a breath. "I see I was far kinder to him than you were."

"I am not a man who cares for public displays," Kendall said, his tone light.

Geoffrey nodded slowly. "Remind me never to get on the wrong side of you."

"Perhaps I am," Kendall said, the slightest smile hovering upon his lips. "But then, you wouldn't ever treat Sarah in such a manner, would you?"

Geoffrey smiled. "If I did, I'd be insulted if you treated me more lightly than you did Ravenwich."

Kendall nodded. "Very well. That said, I will also tell you that young Torrington is not as well heeled as he appears. His estate is not in such a state of shambles as was Raven-wich's, to be sure, but it is not so very hale either. He is young and not, I think, a very strong individual. Easily per-suaded, I would imagine. 'Tis the main reason Sarah should not marry him. He is no match for her."

"No, he isn't," Geoffrey said. He stood swiftly, and nod-ded his head. "I thank you for this enlightening discussion, my lord. Regardless of what transpires between Sarah and me, I hope you will permit me to be the one to visit Tor-rington."

Kendall smiled. "If you promise to be gentle with him. A light hand is all that will be required."

"An art I clearly need to practice," Geoffrey said wryly. "I promise, I shall not disappoint you this time." Bowing, he strolled from the library. He halted in the foyer and then returned. "Kendall, could you please call your footmen off? They are still standing sentry."

Kendall raised his brow. "I did forget them, did I not?"

Sarah sat, staring down at the missive in her hand. Im-possible. Torrington was jilting her. They had been engaged no more than a half a day, and he was jilting her! The coward had not even the courage to come to see her, but had written her this insulting letter. He begged her forgive-ness, but he feared he had asked for her hand in marriage when he truly had no right to do so. He did not deserve her, and never would. Since their engagement had not been announced, and none were privy to it other than her father and she, he wished to correct the mistake as swiftly as possible Though he found it necessary for him to quit town for an extended time, he would be eternally her faithful admirer and servant, etc.

Sarah crumpled the letter in a tight fist. Faith, if only it were true that she and her father alone knew of the engagement, it would not be so galling, so lowering. Yet Geoffrey knew as well. Sarah groaned. How he would laugh. She had been jilted by that young puppy Torrington. 'Twas fortunate the traitorous earl had departed, else Sarah would have killed him, she truly would have.

Sixteen

"I do not believe I can bear this anymore," Melanie said, laying her hand on Kendall's arm as they sat upon the gilt chairs at the Chandlers' ball. "Sarah is not even dancing. I never thought to see it happen."

Kendall glanced to where Melanie looked with frowning eyes. Sarah sat beside Esmerelda, laughing and talking to the chaperone as if she had not a care in the world. He smiled wryly. "Yes, Geoffrey has made a few more visits than I planned." He shook his head. "That boy learns far too fast, I fear. With a vengeance, s'truth."

"What do you mean?" Melanie asked.

"At least he has developed a light hand," Kendall said, and sighed. "Why he cannot employ it with Sarah is beyond me."

"Kendall," Melanie asked, gripping his arm. "What has Geoffrey done?"

Kendall chuckled. "He's basically warded off every other man from Sarah. I don't know how he has managed to succeed with those who do not have waning fortunes, but he's done it. I've not had a man ask for Sarah's hand in three weeks. A first, I assure you."

"What?" Melanie gasped. "That is terrible. You must do something about it."

"Why?" Kendall asked. "At least he is not calling them out. Besides, 'tis a holiday for me. He is doing all my work."

"But Sarah is miserable," Melanie said, her brown eyes darkening. "She will not speak to me of it, but I know she is."

"Geoffrey is as well, I assure you," Kendall said. "As cold as Sarah has been to him, the lad should be a veritable block of ice by now."

"It cannot go on this way," Melanie said, shaking her head. "What Geoffrey is doing is unconscionable. Sarah does not know why her admirers are deserting her."

"It would not be sporting to tell, my love," Kendall said. Then he laughed. "Besides, I still lay odds on Sarah. She'll give Geoffrey his comeuppance yet."

"I hope so," Melanie said, sighing.

Kendall laughed. "My dear, how cruel of you."

Melanie smiled. "No, 'tis only that I fear I am the weak-hearted one here. I simply cannot enjoy seeing the two at such loggerheads."

"Don't worry so, my dear," Kendall said, lifting her hand and placing a warm kiss upon it. "They are both leading each other a merry dance, but Sarah will have Geoffrey on his knees before long . . . and vice versa." Chuckling, he glanced once more over to Sarah. His eyes widened slightly. A slim, elegant man was just then bowing over her hand. He watched a moment and then broke into outright laughter. "Perhaps much sooner than we thought. Much sooner."

"Deirdre, who is that man leading Sarah out?" Geoffrey asked, frowning, as he stood upon the edge of the dance floor.

"Where?" Deirdre asked, scanning the room. She laughed. "Ah, de Torvel has returned to town. How delightful."

"Who is he?" Geoffrey asked, watching closely as the man took Sarah into his arms as the strains of a waltz began to play.

"Only one of the most charming rogues imaginable," Deirdre said, placing a light hand upon Geoffrey's arm, and stepping closer. "In fact, he's almost as charming as you."

"I should have known," Geoffrey said, eyes narrowed. "He is an admirer of Sarah's, no doubt."

"Yes," Deirdre said, sighing. "Once again like you."

"Fiend seize it," Geoffrey muttered, watching as Sarah threw her head back and laughed at something the man had said. "She'll have him propose to her before the night is out."

"Impossible," Deirdre said, shaking her head. "De Torvel has never been caught."

"You don't know my darling Sarah," Geoffrey said, smiling grimly. Sarah was employing her most flirtatious look at the moment.

"Your darling?" Deirdre asked. "If she is your darling, why do you not court her?"

"Because she'll not let me near her," Geoffrey said in exasperation.

"Now, that I find hard to believe," Deirdre said, chuckling. "With your address, surely you can change her mind."

Sarah waltzed by them, and Geoffrey's gaze met hers a moment. She looked away, her chin lifting. Geoffrey stiffened. "The little witch!"

"What?" Deirdre asked.

"She's going to make him propose to her right now," Geoffrey said, stifling the growl rising in his throat.

"I tell you, 'tis ridiculous," Deirdre said. "She'll never succeed, not with de Torvel."

Geoffrey's fists automatically clenched. "Would you like to make a wager?"

"Ah, a famous Grey wager," Deirdre trilled. "Of course, my lord. I'll wager . . . my carriage."

"Very well," Geoffrey said, his gaze still narrowed upon the couple.

"For one night with you," Deirdre said in a low voice.

Geoffrey glanced at her, stunned. Then he smiled. "I

would gladly wager it in all confidence I'd have your carriage, madame, but Sarah would have my head when she discovered my side of the bet."

"You are not even able to get near her," Deirdre said, her eyes teasing and seductive. "So what does it matter?"

"It matters," Geoffrey said softly. He turned his gaze back to the waltzing Sarah and de Torvel. "I'll wager money, but nothing else."

"Five thousand pounds, then?" Deirdre said, her tone mischievous.

"Fine," Geoffrey agreed, not even glancing at her, "my five thousand pounds for your carriage."

" 'Tis small compensation, but I'll accept," Deirdre said, sighing. Then she laughed huskily. "Of course, there is still the difficulty of getting near your lady."

"I'll get near her," Geoffrey said, gritting his teeth. "I've had more than enough of this." He stepped forward, but Deirdre clutched onto his arm.

"At least wait for the dance to end," Deirdre said, her voice breathless. " 'Tis part of the wager."

"Very well," Geoffrey said, every muscle in his body cording. "But that is all the time I'll give her."

"What are you going to do?" Deirdre asked, her gaze focused upon Geoffrey's clenched fist.

Geoffrey barked a laugh. "Merely employ my fine address with Sarah, what else?"

Sarah swayed in de Torvel's arms, smiling up at him in what she hoped was an enchanting smile. "I am so pleased to see you back in town, my lord. When did you arrive?"

"Only a few short hours ago," de Torvel said, grinning. "If you noticed, I hastened to your side immediately."

"I am honored," Sarah said, her mind racing. De Torvel could not have heard of the gossip then. No one could have told him yet of her descending star. She never thought things could have happened so swiftly, but her admirers were all but fleeing her side. In truth, the men could rarely even meet her gaze these days. She glanced at de Torvel. He was meeting her gaze, meeting it with a seductive zeal.

"Do you know, in all my travels, I have not once met a more beautiful woman than you?" de Torvel said, his voice low. His arms tightened about her. "In truth, I have dreamed of you every night."

"Palaverer," Sarah said, chuckling. She coyly looked away from him, and unfortunately caught Geoffrey's gaze as he stood at the side of the dance floor. His face was dark and stormy. Her chin lifted. How dare he glare at her so? She was heartily sick of his frowning looks. She was heartily sick of those men who no longer even looked her in the eye. She would show them all. She turned her gaze back to de Torvel. "I am sure you say that to all the ladies."

"No," de Torvel said. "You wound me. I am your devoted servant." His eyes flashed wickedly. "If you would but let me prove it to you, I would."

"Very well," Sarah said with a look to match the one he offered her. There was no time like the present. "Marry me, my lord."

De Torvel's arms tightened about her in a convulsive grip. His dark eyes widened. "M-marry you?"

"Yes, marry me," Sarah said. She cast him a brilliant, challenging look. "You said you wished to prove your devotion to me, did you not?"

"Yes," he said with a low laugh. "But marriage 'twas not what I had in mind, I must own."

"Then you wish to retreat," Sarah said, smiling sweetly. De Torvel was famous for his acceptance of any dare or challenge.

"No, minx," de Torvel said, his hand upon her waist pressing her closer to him. "I'll not draw back. I shall gladly marry you. I'd only thought you too far out of my reach."

Sarah smiled. "You've never thought anything out of your reach."

De Torvel threw his head back and laughed. "Forsooth, we shall deal well together. We shall deal well together."

"Yes, we shall," Sarah said, even as her heart plummeted. She had accomplished much, yet the taste of victory had more the flavor of ashes. She sighed in relief as the music ended.

De Torvel took her arm lightly to lead her from the dance floor. Both were forced to stop, however, when Geoffrey strode up to them, planting himself directly in their path. The breath wheezed from Sarah, for Geoffrey looked close to murderous.

"Well," Deirdre Wolverington's voice said merrily as she came to stand beside Geoffrey. "Tell us, de Torvel. Tell Lord Grey you did not propose to Lady Sarah."

De Torvel raised his brows. "News travels fast, I see."

Deirdre's mouth dropped open. "Never say that . . ."

"Lady Sarah has done me the honor of offering her hand to me in marriage," de Torvel said, his eyes teasing as he looked at Sarah. Sarah smiled at him in gratitude.

"She rescinds the offer," Geoffrey said. He stepped over and his fist arched up.

"Geoffrey, don't you . . ." Sarah began. Geoffrey's fist plowed into de Torvel's face. "Dare," she finished with a sigh. The confounded man was utterly too swift at times.

De Torvel, clearly unsuspecting and offset, reeled back from the blow, careening into the man behind him. It was Lord Hampton, an erstwhile suitor of Sarah's. Hampton caught de Torvel and bolstered him up.

"What the devil?" de Torvel cried, shaking his head and glaring at Geoffrey, blood trickling down the right side of his mouth.

"You are not going to marry Sarah," Geoffrey said, taking on an easy pugilist's stance. "She is going to marry me."

"What!" Sarah exclaimed, indeed, shouted. "I am not going to marry you, Geoffrey Vincent. I would rather . . ."

"Take him, de Torvel," Hampton growled, shoving de Torvel toward Geoffrey. "Even the bloody score for us all!"

"What?" Sarah asked. She received no answer, for de Torvel charged Geoffrey at that moment and Geoffrey met him with a blow which sent the man crashing to the marble dance floor. Sarah had not a moment to be concerned with her newly acquired and downed fiancé, however, because suddenly Hampton cursed, bolted over the sprawled de Torvel, and threw himself at Geoffrey.

"Hampton!" Sarah gasped, blinking. "Just what . . ." Her voice trailed away and her eyes widened in shock. Other men, men whom she knew well, were separating themselves from the surrounding crowd and converging upon Geoffrey, who was delivering fast and furious blows indiscriminately to whoever stepped before him.

"Move aside, Sarah," Kendall's voice said in her ear. Sarah glanced to find her father close. He was stripping his jacket off, his face a mixture of severity and humor. "This isn't going to be an even fight." Kendall flung his jacket down and stalked up to grab hold of a man's shoulder, spin him around, and drive his fist into the man's jaw.

"Come, Sarah!" Melanie commanded, appearing at her other side. She grabbed Sarah's arm and dragged her away just before the recipient of Kendall's blow toppled back and almost rammed into her. It was Lord Avery, one of her most ardent admirers until three weeks ago.

"Wh-what is going on?" Sarah asked, completely stunned. The nobles in the room were brawling as if they were in a low tavern. The ladies were shrieking and fainting, dropping to the floor in bright puddles of silk and lace. Few men attended them, however, for those not occupied in the row itself, ringed around those who were, shouting encouragement and advice. None appeared to be cheering for Geoffrey, though some shouted out wagers.

"It's Geoffrey," Melanie said. "He's been keeping all the men away from you. How, I don't now. Kendall wouldn't tell me."

"Oh, my Lord," Sarah breathed, comprehension striking swiftly. She saw Geoffrey's shining head pop up over the crowd of milling men, then disappear.

"I think they want to k-kill him," Melanie said, her voice breathless.

"They certainly do." Rage welled up within Sarah. No one was going to kill Geoffrey, but no one. That was her prerogative. She ripped at her satin cuff, dragging the material up to her elbow. "Come on."

"What are you doing?" Melanie asked.

Sarah lifted her chin. "Tonight, I believe I shall be a country lady."

With that, Sarah promptly strode toward the mass of brawling men, and, balling her fist, began swinging with abandon. Her uncommon height and weight stood her in good stead. It did not hurt one whit that as a woman, once she punched a man, he fell back and gallantly refused to return her attack. 'Twas not fair, but she'd never denied the use of the feminine advantage before and she didn't intend to do so now.

She lifted her skirts high and stepped over a fallen body. One man, Lord Templeton she believed, halted his attempt to charge into the melée and gaped down at Sarah's exposed legs. Frowning, she promptly kicked him in the shin. He yelped and hopped about on one foot. Sarah reached out and gave him a heartless shove which sent him sprawling to the floor.

She heard Melanie's laugh, even amidst the roars, curses, and grunts about her. She glanced back to discover Melanie following directly behind her, offering a very neat little fist to the stomachs and noses of the men Sarah had just attacked. Melanie made an extremely sufficient back guard, Sarah thought in amusement and she redoubled her own efforts. Brawling men jostled and buffeted her, but Sarah buffeted them back until she finally won her way to the central vortex of the fighting men. Geoffrey and Kendall were that central vortex. They stood back to back, greeting each newcomer with steady blows.

"Entertaining, again, Geoffrey?" Sarah called out, even as she came abreast of Lord Hampton, now her least favorite past suitor, and jabbed her elbow into his ribs.

Geoffrey ducked a blow and glanced her way. "Sarah, for the love of God, stay out of this."

"Don't give me orders, my lord!" Sarah shouted, once again lifting her skirts and kicking the man in front of her. He was a man she had never even recognized as a suitor of hers.

"Forgive me," Geoffrey said, flashing a smile as he gazed down at her lifted skirts. He received a fist in his face for that distracted moment and stumbled back.

"No!" Sarah cried, and bounded forward. Only one more man stood in her way, and she reached out and boxed his ears from behind.

Kendall had turned at that moment, his hand still clutching the cravat of a dangling Lord Stanton. His eyes widened. "Sarah, where did you learn that?"

"In the country, Father," Sarah said, pushing the dazed man of her way.

"I see," Kendall murmured, and returned to land a telling blow to Lord Stanton.

"From Mrs. Pendleton?" Melanie asked breathlessly as she came alongside Sarah.

"Yes," Sarah chuckled. "But what I wouldn't give for Jeremy's crutches right now." Suddenly a rocketing body slammed into her and knocked her off her feet. She cried out as she fell, stunned to discover her landing was quite soft.

"Sarah!" Melanie cried.

"Sarah, are you all right?" Geoffrey yelled.

"Yes," Sarah shouted, discovering she was sitting directly on top of an already downed man. Blinking, she shifted off the body and to the floor. Then she gasped. "De Torvel!"

De Torvel groaned and opened his eyes. He smiled through a blackened eye and said, "Devoted servant, my lady." Then he sighed and closed his eyes once more. Remorse knifed through Sarah, but it died quickly as Geoffrey charged up to her. She glanced up at him and for one mad moment she forgot her entire surroundings. His face was bruised and bloodied, but his gaze was strong and warm.

"Marry me, Sarah!" he panted. Another man jostled against Geoffrey and he stumbled, falling to his knees. "Marry me!"

"Marry him, Sarah!" Kendall roared, above the din. "He's finally on his knees to you!"

"Marry him, please, Sarah," Melanie said, her voice breathless as she trounced on the toes of another man.

Geoffrey leaned close, or was shoved close to her. "I worship the ground you walk on." Then he laughed. "I mean the ground you sit upon. You have my heart . . . you have my soul . . ."

"Do hurry, will you?" Kendall said, standing close and plowing his fist into an attacking noble man. "Work on the speech later."

"I'll try to be . . ." Geoffrey began again.

"Don't try," Sarah said quickly, noticing another man charging toward them. "I'll marry you, Geoffrey, I will. Only get us out of here."

"Your wish is my command," Geoffrey smiled, and crawled to a stand. He performed a courtly bow, one man's swing just missing his head as he bent.

"You interrupt, sir," Kendall said, and leveled the miscreant with a stunning blow to his stomach. Sarah, laughing, reached out her hand and Geoffrey dragged her up.

"Let's go," Geoffrey murmured, wrapping a strong arm around her and hauling her to his side, even as his free hand swung out to strike at an approaching man.

"Wise notion," Kendall said, nodding shortly.

The four, with their new strategy of run rather than stand

and fight, broke free from the roiling, confused mass and dashed toward the door. Sarah recognized one of the ladies on the floor, who was just now sitting up from her swoon, as her hostess. "Thank you for the lovely evening, Lady Chandler," she called out as they rushed by.

"Enchanting," Kendall nodded as he hastened past.

The four had made it to the room's entrance when Kendall suddenly stopped. "Sarah, your chaperone!"

Sarah skidded to a halt, panting. "Esmerelda! Where is she?"

"I don't know," Geoffrey said, tugging at her hand. "But you won't need her before long."

"There she is," Melanie said, and pointed.

Esmerelda still sat in the chair she had all evening. Her head was bent, and she madly scribbled upon a piece of paper.

"Perhaps this story she'll get published," Kendall laughed. "Let's leave her. We daren't disturb her muse."

Sarah laughed and the four bolted from the room, raced through the house, sped across the glistening foyer, and out into the streets. They dashed up to the first carriage they could discover.

"My good man," Kendall called to the driver upon the seat. "Who is your employer?"

"De Torvel, my lord," the coachman said, staring goggled eyed at the four.

"De Torvel?" Geoffrey laughed. "Excellent."

"I just spoke with de Torvel," Kendall said, delving into his pocket. "He wishes you to drive us." He drew out a pound note and held it up to the driver.

"He wants me ter drive you," the coachman said, snatching at the note and grinning broadly. "I'll drive you."

The four laughed and clambered into the carriage, Geoffrey shouting to de Torvel's loyal servant to spring them.

"Very kind of de Torvel," Geoffrey chuckled, placing his

arm around Sarah who sat beside him as the carriage jolted into motion. "To give me both his fiancée and carriage."

"Give?" Kendall asked from the other seat, his own arm about Melanie. He chuckled. "Sarah dear, I do believe that was the shortest engagement in history."

"She *is* The Incomparable," Geoffrey laughed.

Sarah flushed. "I should feel sorry for poor de Torvel." She gazed at Geoffrey, feeling an overwhelming surge of love. "But I fear I cannot."

"No," Geoffrey said, hugging her close. "Best feel sorry for me, instead."

Sarah smiled, and reached a tender finger out to touch the red swelling beneath Geoffrey's eye. "Shall I kiss it and make it better, my lord?"

Geoffrey's eyes glittered down at her. "It shall be one of your most important duties, my lady, as my wife."

Kendall chuckled. "I do hope you will not find brawling such a necessity after you two are married."

"No," Sarah said, shaking her head. She winced as her overtaxed muscles started to make themselves known rather painfully. "I believe we shall settle down and become quite dull."

"And raise Amazons," Geoffrey chuckled. "All little farmers and flirts."

Sarah laughed. "Yes, they'll know plows . . . and exactly where every bell pull within the house is."

Geoffrey nodded, and his eyes darkened in unhidden passion. "Perhaps our engagement will not be as short as yours and de Torvel's, but we can try, can we not?"

Kendall raised a brow. "I do hope you are not intending a large ton wedding?"

"No," Sarah laughed. "I believe such a wedding at this time would not be circumspect."

"Circumspect?" Melanie giggled. "No, I would say not."

"Thank God," Geoffrey laughed. "I do not intend to wait upon society ever again."

"Is that what you were doing?" Kendall asked in a dry tone.

Geoffrey laughed, and glanced at Kendall. "I do not know about you, but I'll feel far safer if there are only a chosen few present when the minister asks if there is anyone who believe there is just cause why Sarah and I should not marry."

"Faith," Kendall said, barking a laugh. "You have a point there."

Sarah narrowed her eyes in mock indignation. "I could say the same of you, my lord. You have a string of ladies who shall be just as disappointed at our marriage." She cast a teasing glance at Melanie. "I am glad none of them joined our little engagement party this evening."

Melanie giggled. "They lacked the proper training, I believe."

"Then it is settled," Kendall said. He glanced down at Melanie. "And you, my love. Do you wish for a large wedding?"

"No," Melanie said. Her brown hair was disheveled, but her eyes gleamed, even within the carriage's dark. "I do not."

"Then let us try to beat my daughter and Geoffrey," Kendall said. "And have our honeymoon in Paris. It should be lovely this time of year, and I believe, all things considered, it would be wise to leave town for the nonce."

A beaming smile crossed Melanie's lips. "Yes, I would love that, I truly would."

Geoffrey gazed down at Sarah. "Where would you wish to go, Sarah?"

Sarah laughed, and snuggled close to him. "I believe a repairing lease to the country is in order, Geoffrey."

A powder-blue carriage sat outside the large barn, quite unattended. The barn doors were shut, and barred from the inside. Laughter drifted down from the hayloft.

"Only read this, Geoffrey," Sarah said, sitting upon the

blanket spread out over the hay, an empty glass of champagne in one hand and a manuscript in the other. "The gallant Sir Geoffrey strove mightily against the dark knights, his fist a broad sword as he battled to save the fair damsel, Lady Sarah, from the knaves, varlets, and nincompoops." Sarah shook her head, chuckling. "Faith, Esmerelda's prose is so . . . so strong."

"Does she mention how the fair damsel Lady Sarah fought?" Geoffrey asked, shifting to sit behind her and look over her shoulder.

"No," Sarah said, scanning the lines quickly. "Though she does mention my sweet lady in waiting. That must be Melanie." She chuckled, thinking of the letter she had received from Melanie. 'Twas clear from the missive that Melanie was certainly no longer a lady in waiting, but a woman and wife complete.

"What are you laughing about?" Geoffrey asked, his breath soft upon her hair.

"Nothing," Sarah said, knowing she'd never recount the letter to Geoffrey. There were certain feminine confidences best kept secret from the men. She looked hastily back to the lines. "No, she does not mention it. Evidently she chose to overlook my unmaidenly behavior." She frowned as she read the last lines at the bottom of the page. "How odd. And Sir Geoffrey, carrying his lady off upon his steed, cried, let stupidity live!"

"I believe," Geoffrey said, kissing the tender spot below Sarah's ears and sending a shiver through her. "She meant chivalry."

"Chivalry?" Sarah asked, closing her eyes, as Geoffrey slid his arms about her waist. "H-how could she confuse the two words?"

"Some fool told her," Geoffrey murmured, his lips tracing a featherlight path along the column of her neck.

"Well," Sarah said, leaning back into his arms. "If they have promised to publish it this way, who are we to argue?"

"Indeed," Geoffrey murmured, sliding the peasant blouse she wore from her shoulder and warmly pressing his lips to curve of her neck. "Isn't that enough reading for now, wife?"

"Fie, my lord," Sarah said, shrugging her tingling shoulder. She pulled away and twisted around so that they faced each other. She cast him a teasing look. "This is art. You would not care to show yourself a country yokel with no respect to literature, would you?"

Geoffrey, his own gaze glinting, took the manuscript from her lap and glass from her hand and ruthlessly tossed them. "I am just a boor, I fear." Eyes full of devilment, he reached out for the laces of her blouse. "But you look to be a fine peasant wench."

"Tsk, I am a lady," Sarah said, raising a brow even as a heated flush covered her. "Just what do you think you are doing, sirrah?"

"I find," Geoffrey said, smiling as he loosened the laces, "that undressing you is far easier than dressing you." He leaned over and kissed her warmly upon the lips. "And far more pleasurable."

"Yes," Sarah smiled, leaning forward to wrap her arms around his neck. "With you, I have no need for a maid." Geoffrey's hand still tugged upon the laces, even as he gazed deeply into her eyes. Sarah drew in a breath. "Be careful not to rip it. Joy is no longer our seamstress, remember."

"She's only a proper wife," Geoffrey said, and grinned. "Since Bert has finally conceded to be a proper husband." He sighed. "How we men all do fall."

"Indeed," Sarah laughed, running her fingers through his hair.

Geoffrey gave a mock growl, and letting loose of her laces, grabbed her swiftly and shoved her back. Laughing, Sarah twisted and turned with him until they lay side by side. She gazed at him, her body already quivering with need and desire. "And how we ladies do fall."

"I do not care about ladies," Geoffrey said, rolling on top

of her and pressing her into the softness of the blanket and hay. "I care only about you."

"And I for you," Sarah said softly, her heart pounding in anticipation.

Geoffrey kissed her then, passionately, his hands roving over her with a surety that sent fire raging through Sarah. She moaned slightly. Geoffrey lifted his head. His eyes held a gentle, almost whimsical light. "Ever since we kissed in the haystack I've wanted this."

"This?" Sarah teased, wiggling wickedly beneath him.

"No, not just this," Geoffrey said, his voice low and husky. "But to know exactly who the woman was I kissed, to know her in every way."

Sarah's heart stopped. "And do you know me now?"

"Yes," Geoffrey said, tenderly brushing at her hair. "I love you, Sarah, always remember that."

"I will," Sarah said with a trembling smile. "I could lose my entire memory, but your love I shall never forget." Desire rose in her, still new and fresh, yet feeling as ancient as if Geoffrey had always been hers, and she his. She doubted it would ever change. Chuckling, she said, "Though I shall not care if you remind me of it often."

"Then I shall," Geoffrey said, grinning. His hands began to move gently over her. "A gallant gentleman should never deny a lady."

Sarah's breath caught as his touch became far more familiar. "I—I am glad to see you are not so completely gallant. You still have some rude country ways."

Geoffrey's eyes teased her. "You object?"

Sarah squirmed and laughed. "No, I find I like these country pleasures." She reached up and demandingly pulled his head down to hers. "Very much, indeed."

About the Author

Cindy Holbrook lives with her family in Fort Walton Beach, Florida. She is the author of eight Zebra regency romances, including THE COUNTRY GENTLEMAN, THE ACTRESS AND THE MARQUIS, LORD SAYER'S GHOST, A RAKE'S REFORM, COVINGTON'S FOLLY, A DARING DECEPTION, LADY MEGAN'S MASQUERADE, and A SUITABLE CONNECTION. Cindy's newest regency romance, MY LADY'S SERVANT, will be published in June 1998. Cindy loves hearing from her readers and you may write to her c/o Zebra Books. Please include a self-addressed stamped envelope if you wish a response.

WATCH FOR THESE ZEBRA REGENCIES

LADY STEPHANIE   (0-8217-5341-X, $4.50)
by Jeanne Savery
Lady Stephanie Morris has only one true love: the family estate she has managed ever since her mother died. But then Lord Anthony Rider arrives on her estate, claiming he has plans for both the land and the woman. Stephanie soon realizes she's fallen in love with a man whose sensual caresses will plunge her into a world of peril and intrigue . . . a man as dangerous as he is irresistible.

BRIGHTON BEAUTY   (0-8217-5340-1, $4.50)
by Marilyn Clay
Chelsea Grant, pretty and poor, naively takes school friend Alayna Marchmont's place and spends a month in the country. The devastating man had sailed from Honduras to claim his promised bride, Miss Marchmont. An affair of the heart may lead to disaster . . . unless a resourceful Brighton beauty finds a way to stop a masquerade and keep a lord's love.

LORD DIABLO'S DEMISE   (0-8217-5338-X, $4.50)
by Meg-Lynn Roberts
The sinfully handsome Lord Harry Glendower was a gambler and the black sheep of his family. About to be forced into a marriage of convenience, the devilish fellow engineered his own demise, never having dreamed that faking his death would lead him to the heavenly refuge of spirited heiress Gwyn Morgan, the daughter of a physician.

A PERILOUS ATTRACTION   (0-8217-5339-8, $4.50)
by Dawn Aldridge Poore
Alissa Morgan is stunned when a frantic passenger thrusts her baby into Alissa's arms and flees, having heard rumors that a notorious highwayman posed a threat to their coach. Handsome stranger Hugh Sebastian secretly possesses the treasured necklace the highwayman seeks and volunteers to pose as Alissa's husband to save her reputation. With a lost baby and missing necklace in their care, the couple embarks on a journey into peril—and passion.

Available wherever paperbacks are sold, or order direct from the Publisher. Send cover price plus 50¢ per copy for mailing and handling to Penguin USA, P.O. Box 999, c/o Dept. 17109, Bergenfield, NJ 07621. Residents of New York and Tennessee must include sales tax. DO NOT SEND CASH.